The Day Before Winter

The Day Before Winter

ELISABETH OGILVIE

DOWN EAST BOOKS
Camden, Maine

Text copyright © 1997 by Elisabeth Ogilvie
Jacket illustration © 1997 by Jim Sollers
ISBN 0-89272-411-0 (hardcover)
ISBN 0-89272-429-3 (paperback)

Printed and bound at Thomson-Shore, Inc.

2   4   6   8   9   7   5   3   1

DOWN EAST BOOKS
P.O. Box 679, Camden, Maine 04843
BOOK ORDERS: 1-800-766-1670

Library of Congress Cataloging-in-Publication Data

Ogilvie, Elisabeth, 1917-
    The day before winter / Elisabeth Ogilvie.
        p.   cm.
    ISBN 0-89272-411-0. — ISBN 0-89272-429-3 (pbk.)
    1. Islands—Maine—Fiction. 2. Women—Maine—Fiction. I. Title.
PS3529.G39D35   1997
813'.52—dc21

                                                        97-18302
                                                        CIP

With all my love to all the Bennett's Islanders,
including Pip, Dog Tray, Louis the store cat,
and—of course—Hank

BOOKS BY ELISABETH OGILVIE

Available from Down East Books

Bennett's Island Novels
*High Tide at Noon**
*Storm Tide**
*The Ebbing Tide**
The Dawning of the Day
The Seasons Hereafter
Strawberries in the Sea
*An Answer in the Tide**

Children's Books
The Pigeon Pair
Masquerade at Sea House
Ceiling of Amber
Turn Around Twice
Becky's Island
How Wide the Heart
Blueberry Summer
Whistle for a Wind
The Fabulous Year
The Young Islanders
Come Aboard and Bring
    Your Dory!

Other Titles
*My World is an Island**
The Dreaming Swimmer
Where the Lost Aprils Are
Image of a Lover
Weep and Know Why
A Theme for Reason
The Face of Innocence
Bellwood
Waters on a Starry Night
There May be Heaven
Call Home the Heart
The Witch Door
Rowan Head
No Evil Angel
A Dancer in Yellow
The Devil in Tartan
The Silent Ones
The Road to Nowhere
The Summer of the Osprey
When the Music Stopped

The Jennie Trilogy
*Jennie About to Be**
*The World of Jennie G.**
*Jennie Glenroy**

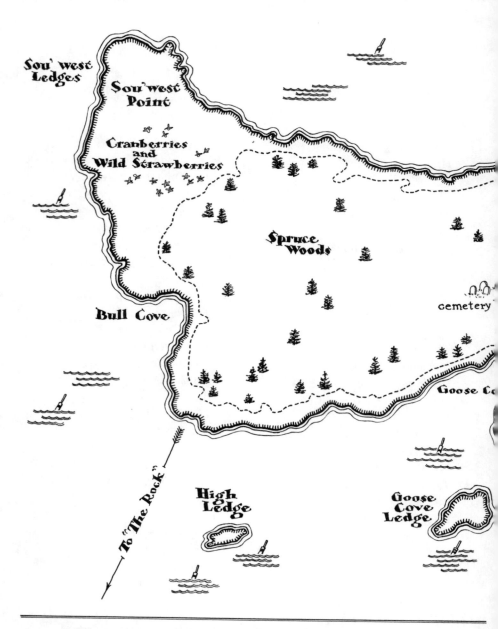

Sou'west
Ledges

Sou'west
Point

Cranberries
and
Wild Strawberries

Spruce
Woods

cemetery

Bull Cove

Goose C...

To "The Rock"

High
Ledge

Goose
Cove
Ledge

⊱ BENNETT'S · ISLAND ⊰

2½ miles from Sou'west Point to Eastern End Cove

Harbor Ledges

Western Harbor Point

To Brigport

arque Cove

Mark

Big Wharf

Eastern Harbor Point

Harbor Beach

Nils and Joanna

Harbor

Long Cove

Homestead

Schoolhouse

arles

School-house Cove

Ice pond

Barn

Owen's wharf

Owen

Woods

Windward Point

Pudding Island

Eastern End Cove

To Tenpound Island

Stephen

Shag Ledge

W N S E

OTHERS

① Fennell
② Clubhouse
③ Rosa & Jamie
④ Percy
⑤ The Well
⑥ Dinsmore [The Binnacle]
⑦ Philip
⑧ Harmon
⑨ Campion
⑩ Campion
⑪ Barton [Vanessa, etc...]

Paths ------

What isn't woods is ledge (all around shores) and field.

Map by A.B. Venti

Bennett's Islanders

Nathan and Stephen Bennett—These two brothers were great-grandsons of Charles James (Jamie I) and Pleasance Marriot. Charles James—known all his life as Jamie—took legal possession of Racketash in 1825. The island was officially named "Bennett's Island" when it achieved a post office.

Nathan m. Mary M. (from the mainland), their children:
    Jeffrey—now married, a father, living in Texas
    Rachel—m., children, living in Midwest
    Hugo—m., children, living in California (boatbuilder),
        father of Haliburton Bennett ("Hal")

Stephen m. Donna B. (came to teach school), their children:
    Charles—m. Mateel Trudeau, their children: Charles (drowned); Donna (m., living on mainland); Pierre (m., Merchant Marine); Hugo (island lobsterman, but now scalloping out of New Bedford—named for cousin Hugo, Nathan's son); Betsy (in college)
    Philip—m. Lisa Filippi, three adopted children: Sam (high school); Ross (island school); Amy (island school)
    Owen—m. Annie Laurie Gibson (came to teach), their children: Joss (through college, working away); Holly (in college); Richard (in high school)
    Joanna—m. first to Alec Douglas (drowned), one child: Ellen (m., children, living in Massachusetts); m. second to Nils Sorensen, their children: Jamie (been in navy, lobsterman and herring seiner, m. Rosa, one child: Sara Joanne); Linnea (through college, traveling in Sweden)
    Mark—m. Helmi, their child: Mark (Young Mark)
    Stephen—m. Philippa Marshall (came to teach), Philippa's son, Eric Marshall (teaching in Peace Corps); their child: Robin (high school)
    (All wives are from mainland, except Mateel Trudeau.)

Other early families:

The Sorensons: Gunnar and Anna, their sons: Karl and Eric

Karl's children (his wife died young): Sigurd (living on mainland); Nils (Bennett's Islander); Kristi (living on mainland); David (living on mainland)

Later families (since World War II):

Matt and Nora Fennell, Sr.: one son

Young Matt and Carol Fennell: one son

Barry and Vanessa Barton: one daughter

Ralph and Marjorie Percy: two sons

Rob and Maggie Dinsmore: two daughters

Myles and Nan Harmon: two daughters, one son

Sky and Binnie Campion: two sons, one daughter

Terence and Kate (Kathy) Campion: assorted Campion children

(Sky and Terence are first cousins, their children are second cousins.)

The Day Before Winter

1

Hurricane Eudora had merely kissed the coast of Maine on her way to Nova Scotia, but it had been a violent caress that had left rough seas and a continuous cannonade of surf from Sou'west Point to the Eastern End. Several days of tranquilizing light winds from the northwest had brought the island's lobstermen a chance to go haul and assess damage to their gear.

The sea was as blue as bachelor's buttons, and the billowing, drifting clouds graciously summery, but there was still that powerful surge; men searching for missing buoys would stay away from the boisterous confusion around the ledges. But there had always been those with an innocent or idiotic faith that they could get close enough to gaff up the errant buoy bobbing in the surf; that a following sea wouldn't deposit a boat on a spine of rock, or hurl her against it; that the engine wouldn't suddenly quit for the first time ever.

None of these adventures were likely today. Jamie Sorensen and young Matt Fennell had given up this form of Russian roulette when they became married men and fathers, and Richard and Sam Bennett, who were of an age to consider themselves invincible, were back in school. Neither of the two newcomers was a daredevil. Myles Harmon had been skipper of a deep-sea trawler and was bound to respect the sea wherever he found it. Sky Campion had grown into his teens on the island; he had been with his father when Foss Campion's engine had stopped, and the boat was carried into the surf off Goose Cove Ledge. They had something under a minute to get her started again and into reverse, and there was no one around to get a line to her if she wouldn't start. She did get them out, but Foss had never again asked it of her.

The rain had filled cisterns and rain barrels, and outside every house, washings flapped gently in the light wind. Here was economy as well as satisfaction; nobody used a dryer when free sunshine and perfect weather were just outside the door. The compulsion to get everything washed and out had been the same since washings had been soaked in tubs, and men's work clothes scrubbed on washboards with brushes and plenty of yellow soap. Dryers had put an end to the winter nightmare of clothes freezing on the line, taking forever to dry draped around the kitchen, or hung in the attic or spare bedroom, if you had either. But the gift of a good rain followed by fine weather had a deathless charm.

Joanna had washed some blankets, and they would be fluffy and good-smelling when she took them in. The next compulsion was to get herself out into this day for an hour or two. Crickets were loud in the grass, monarch butterflies hovered over the long drifts of goldenrod and puffs of purple asters, as if in no hurry to get to Mexico. Garrulous chickadees made up for the birds that had gone. All this could be had just outside the door, seasoned with the sad fragrance of the late petunias and the stocks that scented the nights until frost.

But it was the other world she wanted, off through the woods, and she wanted it *alone*. There was always someone to take a walk with, but she cherished the solitude. Most of the others felt the same way—it was a necessary obligation to preserve privacy in a small community. For Joanna, these times alone with the island, especially in late summer, had been her private treasure since the day when she had first claimed Bennett's as her own.

She had run away, when she was four and a half, to find the log cabin at Bull Cove that the boys talked about, as did her father and uncle sometimes. It had been gone for a long time, but brought up on stories of magic huts appearing in enchanted forests, she was at least three-quarters convinced that it could be there just for her. She knew that if she followed the shore away from Goose Cove and the windows of the Homestead, she would arrive at the miracle and only *she* would see it.

The boys were supposed to be watching her. She was down in Goose Cove with them while they considered the logistics of salvaging a battered old dory that had obviously been adrift for a long time. Dry planking saved from the boat could go toward the new camp they were building of used boards on a rise in the woods beyond the cemetery. Joanna wandered around on the popple rocks above the tide, collecting small, pretty ones.

Then she began watching the way a wave broke. No matter how far down the beach it came in, there was a monster out there that could suddenly launch itself after her. The boys had shown her its picture in a book called *Marvels of the Deep,* and so far the warning had worked. But this afternoon boredom overcame vigilance, and she easily persuaded herself it was a good time for the cabin to appear, either with a fairy godmother or a witch; she could tell when she got there. Pickie the dog went with her. Unobtrusively they moved away over the rocks while the boys were arguing noisily about what was worth lugging across the width of the meadow and up into the woods.

It was a long walk in her first long-legged rubber boots, but once she was out of sight of the boys and the house windows, exhilaration turned her boots into the Seven-League variety. The sun shone by fits and starts, silvering the restless water; the ocean scent of fresh rockweed and the rich tangles of kelp teased her nostrils. She went close to the woods, where she could throw her arms around a tree in case a giant wave (another Marvel of the Deep) suddenly rose up tall as a house, or a monster came for her. Holding tight to a spruce tree, she could kick hard. Besides, the tide was really low now, and the monster would have a scrapy path over the barnacled ledges. Joanna knew what barnacles could do to bare feet. What if you had to go all that distance on your bare stomach? Besides, Pickie was with her, and if he could handle the cows, even Contrary Mary, he could certainly drive off the monster if it did make that bloody trip.

Seals could flop up over the rocks, she'd heard, but seals were friendly. Out of sight of the house, she saw the island and the surrounding waters as hers, and she walked in triumph. Her whistle needed work, but neither she nor Pickie cared. Of course they might still meet a shipwrecked bear or a tiger, but Pickie would be a hero. He had never had to defend any of them against anything, but you knew he could do it if called upon. He was part collie and part Siberian husky, a blue-eyed pup bought from a transient fisherman and named Pickwick by Joanna's mother because he was so affable. He remained affable as well as blue-eyed.

Joanna and Pickie had a splendid afternoon, poking around the cabin site and the shingle beach that had been its dooryard. She found a patch of late cranberries in the cutting behind the lot and ate them all; Pickie preferred blueberries, which he could pick for himself. He traced every dog who had been there recently with other walkers; considering that there was no wildlife running over the ground but mice, he made the most of their tracks but was not set on making a kill. On the beach he found some dead crabs in the rockweed and ecstatically rolled on them, making overt sounds of pleasure. Joanna was happy for him even if she hadn't found a toy boat or a tennis ball or a whole oar. There were a couple of battered traps, and if she'd had the jackknife she coveted but was not allowed, she'd have cut the buoys free and carried them home, to collect the twenty-five cents each from the owners.

For herself, she stuffed her overall pockets with big blue mussel shells, and put two perfect bleached china-white sea urchin shells in a pocket by themselves. A whole whelk shell went into another pocket.

Pickie, thinking of supper, began urging her toward home, and she was willing. They walked briskly back along the rocks, and turned off into the woods at the point from which they'd departed earlier. Up in the sheltered orchard the cows were eating windfalls. Joanna and Pickie went home with them, out of the woods and down through the meadow. Joanna was eating two Yellow Transparents at once, one in each hand. Pickie had often tried these when the children did, but he couldn't cultivate a liking for them. He was looking forward to his own food and kept trying to hurry the cows, who were not impressed, being used to his impatient yips.

The three boys came rushing from the barn to meet the wanderers with flattering enthusiasm; they had been told to keep an eye on Joanna while the attention of the adults was concentrated on the birth of a new Bennett. The boys hadn't missed her until it felt like suppertime, and they believed she'd already gone back to the house. If she hadn't appeared just then, they'd have gone innocently into the kitchen to meet a dreadful question: *Where is your sister?*

Now they (even Owen) let her talk all the way home, and after a few concessions and offers on their part she agreed she wouldn't tell.

She hadn't meant to, anyway. Already her afternoon had become a personal treasure, more rare and wonderful than anything she could have found in the rockweed. She told the boys she'd been building a little house for fairies in the orchard, just out of their sight. Five years later, when she'd temporarily lost sight of a little brother, she'd realized how badly the others had been frightened that day, sick to their stomachs when they'd realized how long she'd been gone and what might have happened.

Finding a new baby at home couldn't touch the joy of her afternoon, but then everything seemed to have been touched with that joy: the scent of supper cooking (her father's haddock chowder) and the way he looked at her when he said, "Everything's fine, Joanna. But I'm afraid you didn't get what you wanted."

How long ago had she asked for a sister? It was all in the hazy past and didn't matter now. Her mother was sleeping, but Aunt Mary brought a placid black-haired baby to them; Pickie crowded among them, and she lowered the baby enough for him to see. He was as beautiful a boy, Aunt Mary said, as she'd ever seen, and she ought to know, she had two of them.

Mark sat in his high chair stolidly working his way through his supper of flaked haddock, mashed potato, and squash. He'd spent the afternoon with the Grants in Pete's store, where he'd been allowed to put things on the bottom shelves. He'd brought back animal crackers when he came home on Uncle Nate's shoulders. "That's when I made up my mind I'd be a storekeeper," he said once. "All those animal crackers."

Joanna was sleepy, hungry, and, it seemed, happier than she'd ever been in her life. She told her mother that, when she went in to kiss her good night, and everyone believed it was because of Stevie. In bed that night she lived it over, from the first step taken toward Bull Cove, and decided drowsily that she would tell Nils about finding his father's traps. Then she could have the money for the buoys.

If the cabin hadn't been there, the surprise of Stevie was a miracle in itself. By being born that afternoon, he'd shared part of its bloom forever afterward, but she never told him or anyone else. It was enough that she and Pickie knew.

2

With all the dogs she'd known and loved since Pickie, he was still with her, a companionable ghost who sometimes could be almost seen and heard, always at Bull Cove. He had been a pup when she was creeping, and he was the only dog with whom she had been on eye level. Even though she would grow taller, there had been those years in which they had looked intensely into each other's eyes as equals. I must tell Nils, she thought, that he is the first person since Pickie who can read my mind. At least I thought Pickie could, and that's what matters. . . . It must have been the blue eyes.

The beef stew was done, it needed only to be heated to boiling, and the dumplings mixed and dropped into it. She put on jeans and boots, a light jacket over a turtleneck jersey, and went to call Pip so he wouldn't follow her, in case she found anything useful or interesting to carry home. Pip thought every walk should end with his sitting on her arm, hanging onto her shoulder, and purring in her ear—when he wasn't browsing through her hair or leaning far out to take swipes at anything handy. Refused a lift, he could dangerously entangle himself with her ankles.

He didn't come to the back door when she whistled, so she went through the long sun parlor to the front door and saw him across the yard at Dave's house, wasting his charm on Nan Harmon as she draped her cleaning rags to dry on a barberry bush. Joanna could tell that the cat was talking; he was never discouraged by silence.

"I don't like cats," Nan had said bluntly when Pip first hurried to meet the new neighbors. Myles and the children had responded. Tracy Lynn picked him up, and he gave her cheek a rough lick, which enchanted the little girl. As for Nan not liking him, it was as if he couldn't believe his ears. Everybody else liked him, and she would too, given time.

"Pip, come," Joanna called him. "Don't be a nuisance. Hi, Nan!" Nan gave her a nod and a curt flip of the hand on the way to the back door.

"I don't think she likes Joanna either," she said to the cat as they went into the kitchen. Pip answered as usual with a question. "Yes, *her*," Joanna went on. "I'm not going to ask her again to go for a walk or to come to the Sewing Circle. She's finally got her message across." She opened a can of liver mix, and Pip landed on the counter beside his dish. She transferred both to the floor, left him eating noisily, and went out the back door.

What was I thinking of? she wondered. Keeping on after everybody else gave up? That as a Bennett I had an *obligation*? Good Lord, I hope not. Well, I'm emancipated now.

She was escorted across the yard by a little crowd of hens let out of their yard for the day. At the brook beyond the barn she shooed them back. The air had a spicy bouquet of spruce and ferny alder swamp, and the path was pleasantly squishy underfoot. Out in the big meadow a young poplar standing alone was a tree of trembling gold in the sun, shadowed as a cloud went over, and then glittering forth again. The whole meadow and the woods bordering it on two sides, and the Homestead on the rise between Goose Cove and Schoolhouse Cove, alternately gleamed and darkened. The tide was going and the surf had quieted down to the sound that made for good sleeping, and she wished she didn't have to hear it at night through trees. In the first hour of her life she had heard without knowing it the surf of a smoky sou'wester crashing on Homestead Point and breaking on granite all the way to both ends of the island. It would be with her in her last conscious hour, in her head if not in her ears. Her parents had both died away from the island, a monstrous injustice of Fate, but she was sure that the rough music had been there for her father even then.

There wasn't enough time for the Bull Cove walk and a good poke-around, so she went left along the foot of the meadow to the road that led from the harbor up to the Homestead, and crossed it to Schoolhouse Cove. Over the years a high, dense thicket of wild rugosa roses had grown on the top of the bank above the beach. There were still a few blossoms among the bright orange ripening hips, blooms so fragile that a puff of wind shook them apart, scattering fragrance as the red and white petals fluttered in the air. She went down to the beach. If any child in the schoolhouse glimpsed her before she disappeared below the sight level of those windows, she'd be suspected of poaching on what island children had considered their own preserve since the schoolhouse was built a century ago. She knew the suspicion and didn't intend to pick up so much as a net cork.

A narrow band of dry beach curved away in a broad gentle arc toward Windward Point at the far end. Below the rim of dry rubble marking earlier high tides was a broad expanse of wet shingle and sand, flung rockweed and kelp, broken by occasional boulders like miniature volcanic islands. The land sloped down to dying breakers; the dull, steady, distant roar in one's ears came from the still-violent assaults on the high outthrust points.

It was warm here in the lee of the land rising behind her. She left her jacket on the big rock halfway along the beach. Crows and gulls picked through the rockweed, looking for small crabs. Sparrows, starlings, and a couple of robins ate sand fleas. The next gleaners would be the children, finding stray buoys from other places; a whole rubber boot would be carried triumphantly home for a spare, with the hope that it hadn't come off a dead man who would come some night to claim it. (Someone could always swear this had happened once.) Work gloves weren't so romantic. If you could make up a pair, it was good luck for the day. No one on the island was that poor, but you had to take luck seriously. A whole lobster crate, good boards, an oar, a bait iron, a dented bucket with no holes—you never knew when things would come in handy. Of all the objects that the sea had brought in Joanna's lifetime, there was once a whole skiff that caused the long War of the First Sighting. Sigurd Sorensen had won it. There had never been a human body, but for all children there was a shivery anticipation about approaching a long thick roll of weed and kelp; half-hopeful, half-dreading. A dead seal was bad enough; a human body, long overboard, would give them a year of nightmares.

At the far end of the beach, Owen's wharf stood in the lee of Windward Point, with the bait shed and workshop tucked into the grassy inner slope. The dying surge still splashed around the wharf, and occasionally large seas exploded into showers and cascaded over the granite prow of the point, as if it were sailing into them.

Owen and Laurie had gone to Stonehaven for the day, fifteen miles across the bay toward the mainland hills, and Owen's sternman, bareheaded but wearing oilclothes, stood at the end of the wharf hauling

Richard's big gray dory in from her mooring. When she was bobbing at the foot of the ladder, he tethered her to a spiling and dropped something into her, then took the line, went down the ladder, and stepped aboard. Holding to the ladder with one hand, he looked across at Joanna on the beach and energetically swung his free arm. She waved back, smiling; he could have walked over to the harbor, but he'd rather take the dory and have a grand ride of it, with all the rough water between here and there. Well, who wouldn't? She wouldn't have minded going with him. She waited to see him go out around the point; the big outboard couldn't be heard, but almost instantly the dory was swinging away from the wharf, leaping into an incoming comber, throwing water back over the man's bare head. She slammed into the trough, rolled, and steadied herself; then she was gone beyond the point, until Joanna saw her heading out a little way for a slightly quieter passage. A sudden glint of sun turned the yellow oilclothes into a dazzling flash.

Joanna turned away so as not to watch man and dory out of sight. Some trip . . . she thought half-wistfully, and began to walk back along the beach. Emlyn had the use of the dory in his free time, and having done his day's work in the bait shed and workshop, he'd be on his way to the harbor for company, to yarn with anyone he found idle, drinking soda and watching the boats come in. If anybody needed an extra hand, he'd provide it. Like Pip, Emlyn wished the world well. And the world, especially on Bennett's Island, reciprocated.

It had gone hard with Owen when Tommy Wiley, Owen's former sternman, came home from a mainland visit to his parents and said he was going to be married. For Owen, Tommy wasn't grown up enough to be married, never mind his legal age. Laurie said he couldn't have carried on more if Richard had suddenly come home from school engaged at sixteen.

Tommy's mainland bride did not invite any Bennetts to the wedding, but she was given a good wedding present, chosen by the girls and Laurie; Richard and his father wanted nothing to do with it. "It's for Tommy," Laurie said. "We can't hurt him."

"Besides, he's a victim," Holly said. "He needs to know we still love him. It wasn't his fault we weren't invited. She's jealous of us."

"I trained the kid from a pup!" Owen said furiously.

"So at least he should have let you pick out his girl for him," said Laurie. Even Richard laughed at that. They received a thank-you for the double bridal-ring quilt; a very small card, with "Mr. and Mrs. Thomas Wiley" inscribed in very small writing.

"We ought to frame that," said Joss.

It had looked as if Richard would be going with his father that summer, tending his own gear on the side; the girls both had summer jobs on the mainland. Then Emlyn Jones arrived. It was one of those lucky accidents—he and Owen could so easily have missed each other. Emlyn had sailed a Parry-built sloop from the Down East Parry yard to Brigport, where the new owner would take over and sail her to Marblehead. Emlyn could have gone with him, and half-intended to, but he was in the Brigport store when Owen came in to put up an ad for a sternman, and Emlyn asked for the job. He said he knew all there was to know about his home waters, and he'd like to get acquainted with this particular group of islands.

He'd been lobstering full time since he left high school, except for a hitch in Vietnam. In thin times he worked at the Parry yard. His gear was all on the bank right now, and he had no responsibilities except himself.

He was, Owen said after that first meeting, as good a talker as any Bennett; some people might mistrust that. But he brought him home anyway for a week's trial, because he had new traps to set and some to be shifted. Emlyn hadn't been lying about his experience. He was quick, strong, and knowledgeable, and he didn't talk aboard the boat any more than was necessary.

Both the local lobster buyer at Parry's Landing and the local fisheries warden gave him good references as an honest man from an honest family, with no bad marks on his record as a lobsterman. He'd never been in trouble with the law, and he was not known to be a heavy drinker or a pot smoker—things pretty hard to hide in a small town.

Richard liked him, though not just because it set him free to concentrate on his own gear for the summer. Laurie liked him for his good manners. He was cheerful, a reader, and handy at fixing things Owen was likely to put off. The girls said he was easy to have around: he was good-looking, with wavy brown hair, almost chestnut, and interesting green eyes above high cheekbones, and a deep dimple in one cheek. But his eyes were merry rather than seductive, and if he secretly thought he was God's gift to women, he didn't show it. They half-regretted their summer jobs off the island.

"Good to have a grown man around for a change," Owen said.

"Combs his own hair, too," he added. The girls had been forever washing, combing, and trimming Tommy's hair; styling it, they said. They had taught him how to dance. They rehearsed him in the etiquette for such occasions, but he never would ask anyone to dance except Holly and Joss, and sometimes Laurie. In the square dances he would have to swing other women besides his partner, so the girls and Richard taught him how, and he swung with a strong arm and a kind of grim fervor.

"Taught him too well," Owen grumbled. "All this female fussing gave him a taste for it. That's how he got the guts to propose. *If* he did. She probably promised him he'd be the crown prince of the sand-and-gravel business, driving a big dump truck around as happy as if he had sense."

Emlyn had been here now since early summer, and so far his only known dissipation, besides playing cards, chess, and pool, was going to dances over on Stonehaven with a boatload of Brigporters. They always made a night of it, getting home just before daylight, but he was never slack in his work the next day.

Owen said with satisfaction, "At least I don't have to worry about this one getting snagged and carried off like a lamb to the slaughter by the first female to roll her eyes at him."

"But you don't know who he's meeting at Stonehaven," it was unkindly pointed out to him. "Lots of women over there. Summer kind looking for fun, and plenty of homegrown talent, too."

"He's a man, not a green kid, and he knows his way around," Owen said. "If he wants fun, he can have it with no strings. Yep, he likes it here, and he's looking forward to finding out what it's like in the winter. I figure I've got me just about what I want in a sternman."

"Owen," Terence Campion said, straight-faced, "you positive he came by water? You sure the stork didn't bring him?"

3

Walking back along the beach, she had gone by the schoolhouse and had almost reached the roses when the children burst out. Uproarious, they poured over the seawall. It was as if they had been penned up in solitary confinement in separate soundproof cells, not doing their lessons in the open informal atmosphere of a one-room school. But so it had ever been. Then she saw a familiar cap shoot into the air and heard an anguished yell from Stuart Campion, whose Red Sox cap it was. A small indignant girl shouted, "You're mean, Shannie Harmon!"

The tidal rush became a whirlpool, spinning around a center invisible to Joanna. "Stu, watch your glasses!" Johnny Campion commanded with eighth-grade authority. "Come on, Shannie, knock it off!"

"I already did, and now I'm going to kick the stupid thing overboard!" Shannie broke away from the whirling figures, holding the cap over his head as he ran down the beach, laughing raucously, the others close behind him like a comet's tail. Stuart was nearest, pounding on his back, and Dorrie Campion, younger but taller than her brother, nimbly skipped around them and was fast enough to kick Shannie at least once in the shins. He swore in a hoarse shout.

"Watch your mouth!" someone warned him. "Get him right in the kidneys, Stu!" Shannon was big for a sixth grader. Stuart was the same age, but short and slight; Shannie, exhilarated with triumph, would hardly notice him.

Philip's newly adopted son, Ross, was prancing around the fracas like a demented imp; he couldn't have seen such a good fight since he'd been taken from the city streets and deposited on the island. His younger sister, Amy, stood on the stone wall with little Tracy Lynn Harmon, holding hands and staring at the row as if in a fearful enchantment. Danny Campion, a notable bantam rooster, was mysteriously missing, but for action and noise they were doing well without him. In an accidental moment of breathless silence, Johnny Campion shouted, "Give him the damn cap before she comes out!" *She* being the teacher.

"The hell with her!" Shannie answered. Among cries of "You'll get it!" and other threats, one voice topped the others. "Give it back, you stuck-up mainland arsehole!" Joanna recognized the voice, but decided not to think about it. Anyway, it had produced a hush, a few swift glances back toward the schoolhouse, and it had even stunned Shannie, but not for long.

"Cry baby, cry!" he jeered at Stuart, who was scrubbing at his eyes, sobbing with rage and frustration. "Your father's a dirty drunk and always will be!" Dorrie sprang at him, clinging like a cat, and while he tried to sweep her away he was jumped by three other children. Somebody thrust a stick between his ankles and he went down in a heap, swearing. Stuart was instantly upon his chest, holding him by the ears and pounding his head into the sand. Cheers went up, Dorrie pounced on the cap and hugged it to her chest, and young Dennis Campion kicked at Shannie's legs, laughing in manic glee. A kind of victory dance began there on the sand, accompanied by pagan cries.

Johnny Campion and Tammie Dinsmore—both eighth graders—hadn't been active in the melee and stood apart from it. Joanna knew reluctantly that as the only adult present she'd have to appear, if Philippa didn't. Then Johnny took a few steps forward and hauled Stuart off Shannie and onto his feet. Still holding him, he ordered the rest away. "It's too many against one, even if he's owed it."

They fell back, not willingly, and Shannie bounded up as if on springs, and jabbed a finger at Stuart. "Your old man's still a dirty drunk!" Stuart sprang forward but was pulled back. Young Mark Bennett, of the seventh grade, silently handed him his glasses.

"Put a sock in it, Shannie," said Johnny, "or I'll stuff it full of rotten rockweed."

"That's right," Shannie taunted. "Jump a man when he's down. That's the way you bastards do it out here."

"That a fact?" Johnny drawled. "Then how come your father's out here and nobody's hauled his traps or sunk his boat?"

"My father wasn't run out of Limerock! He's not a crook!"

"That so, Chummie? I never said your father was a crook. But you better take back what you said about my uncle, or you'll swallow a few teeth along with that rockweed."

All at once Danny Campion was there, proudly important; Philippa was with him. Tracy Lynn left the seawall and ran to her, reaching for her hand. Joanna began walking toward them.

The silence was absolute except for some stifled snorts of laughter and the sound of Stuart blowing his nose. Shannie jammed his hands into his pockets and stared at Philippa with the boldness either of insolence or nervous bravado.

"I don't know what's been going on out here," she said without raising her voice. Some hands shot up, frantically signaling. She shook her head. "We'll go into that in the morning. You're all to go home now and get ready for practice. And remember this—no matter who started it—if I hear about any more fighting on the way home, your parents will hear about it too. So go your separate ways and stay out of trouble. Now *scoot!*"

She clapped her hands on the word, and there was a little ripple of relieved giggles. Except for Tracy Lynn, who still held Philippa's hand, and Shannie, who still held his ground, the children divided around Philippa as if she were a rock in the current, some heading across the marsh, the two Campion families and Anne Barton going past the schoolhouse for the path behind it that led to their side of the harbor. Stuart was trying to clean his smeared glasses with his shirttail. Philippa took them silently and polished them with a clean tissue. He gave her a quick upward glance of thanks and then went on behind his sister and small brother. Philippa looked after him, shook her head, and turned back to Shannie, who hadn't moved.

"Not gone yet, Shannon?" she asked politely.

He faced her like a belligerent young bullock. "You can't give orders to us outside the schoolyard!" he said loudly.

"Can't I?" Philippa was mild. "You'd be surprised how far the teacher's jurisdiction spreads around here, Shannon."

He reddened. "There's a law," he blustered, when an ear-shattering whistle transfixed them all. George Baxter appeared beside Philippa like a genie out of a bottle. His meager face was nearly obscured by the visor of his cap, but there was nothing meager about his voice. "None of that sass now, you just put for home and be back here in—" he looked at the large watch on his skinny wrist. "Twenty minutes. And don't cram your guts full like a shag in a school of herring." He watched sternly as Shannon stamped away toward the marsh. George was almost as thin as a stick figure in tight jeans and rugby shirt. He was nicknamed Jockey George; he was built like a jockey, he had wanted to be one, and he was still mad about horses. He was Sky Campion's brother-in-law.

"Hello, Punkin," he said to Tracy Lynn, who was still hanging on to Philippa's hand.

"You'd better go home, Tracy," Philippa said to her. "Aren't you going to play with Anne and Amy?"

"Oh, *yes!*" She wasn't a pretty child, but her gap-toothed smile was pure radiance. "We play *every* day," she told Joanna. "G'bye, Mrs. Bennett!" she said to Philippa, and scampered away past George. "See you tomorrow!"

"Sort of makes up for her brother and sister, don't she?" said George.

"Tracy's a darling," said Philippa. "George, you stole my thunder."

"Because you're too polite," said George, managing to sound respectful. "That kid would stand there sassing you till kingdom come."

"I'm not really that easy, George. You don't know me very well yet. But thank you anyway. That's a really powerful whistle when you hear it from a foot away."

"London bobby's whistle." George lifted it up and dangled it from the lanyard around his neck. "Says so right here. My sister gave it to me, but she won't let me use it near the house because it startles the sh—, er, devil out of everybody, and scares the dog and cat foolish." He grinned, touched his cap, and went on toward the swings and the jungle gym. He turned back and said, "Dam—, darn shame Cluny's got her head so full of that ballet business." He pronounced it *belly.* "She's one of the best little hitters I ever saw. She was giving Shannie some practice one day. Must have been feeling kind. Never seen it since. But with her on the team too—good-bye Brigport!"

"Seems as if we've managed to win quite a few games in the past without help from the mainlanders," Joanna said. "I'm not looking a gift horse in the mouth, of course. But if Shannie quits, it probably won't be the end of the world."

"Good stuff in these island kids," George said hastily. "I dunno what's biting that boy lately. You know his mother's kind of *odd?* She comes over every week for my sister to trim her hair, always leaves a couple of dollars in the jar, but never gives anybody the time of day. And Binnie's so good-natured, she just shrugs it off." His bony face softened rather endearingly. "Well, when I figure what she's been through, that makes her easy on the weirdos." He trotted briskly out to the field, which was the lower half of Hillside Meadow, kept mown for sports. He sat on a track hurdle, folded his arms on his chest, and gazed out to sea.

"Dreaming of horses, or baseball?" Philippa murmured. "I wonder what he'll do when there's no more baseball this year. It's a long winter out here as well as a long way from temptation."

"He'll dream of horses and stables and races, and cross off each day of his probation. And concentrate on winning the cribbage tournament. Maybe take up chess. No gambling there."

After his breaking-and-entering conviction—his first (and last, it was hoped)—he'd been released to the custody of his sister. He had come to the island with her and he had been given employment, helping Sky to get back into lobstering.

Sky had always loved the island and had grieved when his family left it. It was new to Binnie, who'd had to give up the successful beauty shop that had supported the family during their worst times; she explained she could not run a shop here that would obey the state laws, but she'd be willing to cut anyone's hair as a neighborly act, or give a home permanent. In the scrubbed, whitewashed shed off her kitchen she was soon barbering. Emlyn Jones, Terence Campion, and Barry Barton were the pioneers, proving that she could give a good masculine no-nonsense haircut. This was as great a convenience as the generator or bottled gas.

She had no set rates, and she did not ask for money, but anyone who wanted to put a few dollars in the crockery jug on the table should understand that it would be banked toward the children's education.

There'd been no objections among the islanders to Sheena Bainbridge's letting the house to a friend who had lived in it as a child, and who was remembered with kindness and sometimes with affection. Whatever had tumbled a bright, kind, well-educated young man into alcoholism wasn't known out here and didn't much matter. It was never discussed. But most of the islanders were silently pulling for him to succeed.

Joanna knew, listening to the ordinary quiet sounds of gulls, the sea, and homecoming boats, that Shannon's accusation and its results might not be simply disposed of in a morning's session in the schoolroom, and presently Philippa would know.

Suddenly the flag overhead snapped out in a random gust, and Philippa said, "Believe it or not, Shannon and Stuart are in charge of the flag and the bell this week. I wonder if one will resign, or if they'll observe an icy silence when they're folding the flag by and by. But come in, Jo. I need a cup of tea."

4

The schoolroom, though greatly changed since Joanna's time there, held the same old essence, like a psychic presence left behind by the crowded and intense day just passed.

"Or maybe it's just the sneakers," she said aloud.

"And we've kept a window open all day, too," Philippa said. "Somebody's shoes had bait on them."

"Nothing changes," said Joanna. "Except it used to be rubber boots. There were always a few who couldn't be parted from their boots. My mother'd been the teacher once, so my brothers had to wear shoes unless it was barefoot weather."

In the back room Philippa put a small teakettle on a two-burner gas plate. "Herbal or the real stuff? I need a caffeine fix."

"Me too," said Joanna. "A good schoolyard fight isn't exciting when you're grown up. It's upsetting. I saw the whole thing from down there by the roses. They came boiling over the wall, and nobody had time to look around, it was so fast and furious."

Philippa filled the flowered china cups; cambric tea sipped from one of these had often relieved homesickness in a small new pupil. The two women sat in a couple of comfortable old chairs donated by the Homestead to the teacher's room.

"Now tell me just what happened," Philippa said. "I settled Danny down to work on his fractions before practice, so I wasn't at the door when they went out—for the first time since I've been teaching here. Wouldn't you know it? And I might have stopped it at the start."

"Don't worry," said Joanna. "You'll have more chances as long as you

18

have Shannon." Joanna paused. "Well, the first sign was Stuart's cap flying high." She went on from there in detail until her throat dried. "Thirsty work, reporting a battle," she went on. "Stuart got in a few good licks when Shannie was down, until Johnny pulled him off. Shannie came up fighting, and there was what they call a spirited exchange, in which Johnny offered to fill Shannie's mouth with loose teeth, as well as promising him a roll in the rotten rockweed. And then you appeared."

"I'd been hearing noises," Philippa said, "but through two closed doors. I thought it was high spirits over a lot of good loot. Danny was such a bundle of squirms, I was about to dismiss him and tell him to come in before school tomorrow, when he said desperately, 'I have to go *real bad*,' and shot out the back door. He came right back in and said, 'I don't have to pee, but there's some gosh-awful hellacious fight going on!' " Philippa smiled. "You know Danny. Like Kate, straight to the point. The first bad time I ever had here was with Helen Campion, and when Stuart went past me trying to clean his glasses, and gave me that look, it was Sky all over again, at eleven. Those eyes!"

Her own eyes flickered, and blinked once. "No place for sentimentality here," she said crisply. "So Shannon called Sky a dirty drunk. I wonder how and what he heard."

"Listening around corners?" Joanna suggested. "In his own house his parents talking after the kids have gone to bed? Maybe he makes a habit of checking on them from the head of the stairs. Myles knew some of the Campions on the mainland. Nils says he knows his own weaknesses and is tolerant about others'. He might have been giving Sky credit for winning a hard fight, and Nan probably wasn't charitable. There may have been times when that woman isn't finding fault, but they must have all happened on the mainland, when she was snug in the Harmon house being a Harmon daughter-in-law, when Myles was skippering a Harmon trawler. And let's not forget her car and her dress-up job in the courthouse. If I sound nasty, it's because I *am*. At times."

"Really? I hadn't noticed." They both laughed. "Shannie must have been surprised when the whole school, from the first grade to the eighth, fell on him today. Imagine being the one that nobody likes. It almost makes you feel sorry for him, doesn't it?"

Philippa sighed and blew hard. "Oh, Lord, I had a feeling he'd be disruptive, almost the minute he and his mother came into the schoolroom. Tracy Lynn was trying all the chairs at the primary table, like Goldilocks.

Cluny was looking at the pictures and plants, the Indian collection, and so forth—a world away, as if she'd turned her mother off. But all the time Nan was talking, Shannon had this fixed sneering grin, as if he'd got himself all prepared to show nothing but contempt. This wasn't a real school, with a paved parking lot and a gym and all the rest of it; this was a shack where a crowd of dim-witted characters collected to make believe they could read and write. Listen to me! I might as well laugh as sneer. And I could be borrowing trouble. After all, he's only one child among many, and he must feel like an outsider. He misses his bike and friends. He's bored and angry. Nobody else is, so he wants to strike out and make everybody else miserable."

"Could be," said Joanna. "And was Nan giving you the talk about the social deprivation out here, and the island children not being fitted for the modern world across the bay? Makes you wonder what our kids are doing over there, doesn't it? Huddling in corners, rousing out of a catatonic state only to forge their report cards and invent lives to tell us about?"

"I'd better give Robin a closer look," said Philippa. "Nan's children welcome *challenge*, you understand; and a large up-to-date school system offers plenty of that, with healthy peer competition," she recited. "So I challenged Cluny and Shannon at once by telling them that nobody had ever graduated from the eighth grade here without having read all the books in that special bookcase, beginning with the first grade. But since they'd come late, and I assumed they'd already done quite a bit of reading in their mainland school, I'd give each of them a list of suitable books to get them through during this year, and I would be expecting a well-written report on each. Shannon dropped contempt for—well, let's call it dismay. Cluny held up *The Diary of Anne Frank,* I nodded, and she signed for it and left. Since then she's read three more. Shannon hasn't started yet, but I have that in mind."

"I didn't see Cluny out there plunging into battle to defend Shannie," said Joanna. "And Tracy Lynn seemed more fascinated than horrified."

"The older girls enjoy making a pet of her. And she loves being the whole second grade. What importance!"

"And she's crazy about the teacher," said Joanna.

"Right now she's as uncomplicated as a kitten." Philippa smiled. "That little hand comes creeping into mine whenever she can make it. I have to smooth Dennis's cowlick several times a day to keep things even—Dennis was the whole *first* grade. Cluny's out the door and across the marsh before the others have argued their way down the steps. She does her work and is friendly with the other girls, though not intimate. And they admire her because she's told them she's going to be a ballerina and practices every afternoon. Shannon is bright enough, but he's not doing his best. I'm about to give him another challenge by starting him on algebra with the eighth graders and anyone else who wants to give it a try." She added wryly, "The trouble is that the other sixth grader is the lad with the Red Sox cap, and he'll eat algebra like cream. Either Shannon will stick to it out of pride, or he'll dismiss it as a load of manure, spelled with four letters.

"Enough of school," she said with finality, putting the teakettle on again. "I'm through with work for the day. What's going on at the harbor? Is there anything I should know from Penobscot Bay's traveling tabloid? I see he's in the harbor." She nodded toward the western window.

"He's just come then, and he's brightening the conversation around the lobster car."

"My, Steve and I miss a lot by living at the Eastern End. All that free entertainment. You don't have to believe a word of it, but he's such a great storyteller."

"Think what the Eastern End has done for you. Walking all that distance twice a day, you're practically as willowy as when you first stepped off the mailboat."

"A despairing wreck. More tea?"

"Yes, please. Any more letters from prospective despairing wrecks?"

"There are always a few letters dribbling in, but most of them are hopeless. They haven't read the description completely or looked on a map to find us. They think of Maine as Summerland, a romantic off-the-planet fantasy. With these letters you don't get résumés or references. I suspect it's because they don't have any; they think they don't need anything out here like experience, the children are probably all retarded because of years of inbreeding. Oh, one woman thinks it's the perfect refuge; her husband could never find her here. Another asked point blank about available men. I don't know how Laurie will answer that." She laughed.

"She and I take turns writing answers. We're politely discouraging to the lunatic fringe, and we explain the setup to the possibles, from the positives to the negatives—like no liquor stores and twenty-five miles between here and the mainland, and you can't simply decide to run into town. So far there's been no rush of returning letters."

"There must be a lot of thinking it over," Joanna suggested. A procession of Campion children passed by the window toward Hillside. The Red Sox cap was firmly in its place. Young Dennis struggled with an assortment of gloves and mitts and two bats. Johnny kindly relieved him of the bats before he could trip himself up.

"Stuart and Dorrie have probably threatened him within an inch of his life if he tells their parents about what was said," said Philippa. "These kids are very loyal and protective."

At the same time, an uproarious confusion broke out in the entry as more equipment was collected. Somebody pulled the bell rope, there were a couple of clangs from overhead, the door slammed, and outside, George's whistle took on a hysterical life of its own.

"I wonder if Shannon's back," said Joanna. "He must know they'll miss him as a team player, if not as their favorite person. What does he do best?"

"Name it," said Philippa. "He's good at everything. Years of Little League and a natural gift too, I'd say. Stuart's so slim and light, he runs bases like the wind. Nobody's a real dud, but Shannon's the best all-rounder since Harry Percy graduated last year." She stretched and yawned. "It's a long time since five this morning. . . . Let's not get onto the Harmons again, and I'm a bit fed up with this search for a new teacher. I want to stop teaching, and Laurie doesn't want to take over, though we'd both be willing to substitute or do some tutoring. But let's face it, Jo, what do we have to offer a young woman except scenery and our unique community?"

"And all the men who are loaded with charm are married, and some are old enough to be grandfathers. We've got bachelors, but Hugo's having a high old time in New Bedford when he's not out on the Banks, and Eric's in Nepal; Richard and Sam are in school and too young anyway."

"Don't forget George and Willy," said Philippa.

"Look, who says it has to be a woman and young?" Joanna demanded. "What about a man, robust, middle-aged like us, seeing it as high adventure? Interested in birds, geology, astronomy. Retired from business or walking away from it, wanting a new direction, as they say. Writing a book in his spare time."

"No men have applied yet," said Philippa, "but maybe you're psychic, Jo. Maybe at this moment the perfect answer is on its way. Let's hold that thought before we can think of anything to ruin it."

They went outside onto the big front doorstep. The late afternoon was warm and almost flat calm, scented by both earth and sea. On the field chaos became order as the teams took up positions without obvious division of sex. Gulls slanted over them, curious watchers as if this were not an everyday scene. Shannon was not there. Over the women's heads the flag briefly flapped and then went limp. Eyes turned often to distances here on the island, as if to seek familiar bearings, and without speaking Joanna and Philippa gazed out at a horizon now crayon-sharp blue as the wind shifted to the northwest.

5

Joanna walked to the harbor by crossing the marsh which had been green in the summer and flowering with its own specialties. Now with its autumn colors and plants it would still hold summer in the springy damp black earth, as long as the weather was mild. The path would be velvet against bare soles; Joanna's feet remembered and wriggled in her boots. She was half-tempted to shed them now and finish the path barefooted. Some day I'll do it, she promised, and I hope I meet Nan Harmon at the Anchor, nipping around the harbor to have Binnie trim her hair.

Somebody's sweater had been flung over the one visible fluke of the great anchor sunk into the marsh. It had been well back from tip-top high water nearly a century ago. In Joanna's childhood there had still been a broad flat space between the beach stones and marsh, where small workshops stood, and there was room for rows of drying traps and for painting dories. But for a long time now beach pebbles had been tossed up into the road by high tides, and the marsh had flooded both from the harbor and Schoolhouse Cove more often than once a year. When Joanna was small, and for the children now, it was exciting to be taken off the school steps into a dory, but even then the older people who knew every cove, and how each had changed in their lifetimes, saw the threat that the island might be divided at the marsh. Then the sea would break through at last to the harbor and destroy that refuge forever.

"It's not going to happen in our time," someone always said. "Not till we're long gone."

"Or blown up. And don't spit in the face of Providence—as long as the lobsters keep crawling."

As for Joanna there was always—if she thought about it—a small spot of grief, like a tiny sore place, knowing the island would not be its perfect self forever, a world without end, as it had been in those days when either Pickie or her father could take care of every menace.

Ahead of her when she turned toward the wharves the waters were in slight but constant motion, so dazzling under the westering sun that she couldn't pick out the boats that were in. Fragmented voices, a dog's barking, a sudden burst of laughter borne on the wind, were assurances that everything was as it should be, even if you couldn't see who was at the lobster car because the sun was in your eyes. It was the satisfaction of homecoming, and if you refused to spoil this weather by saying there was likely to be an early winter, starting anytime now, why worry about the future of the island a thousand years from now?

When she stopped believing the world was flat and it was just luck that all the boats hadn't fallen off yet, she had more trouble with the world-as-orange twirling in space. *Space* was bad enough; and you—not just the boats—could still fall off the Earth when it was your turn to be upside down, and the water would all spill out of the ocean. It hadn't happened yet, but it would. Pretty soon now they'd all drop off, and then the world would really look like an orange. An old one. Gravity, like endless space, was just something made up, like the boys' sea monsters.

What had been the next thing to hen about after gravity? She looked out between the fishhouses and saw Charles coming up a ladder from his skiff, one-handed, with his dinner box and thermos bottle tucked under the other arm, and his skiff painter in his hand. He looked preoccupied, not overtired. He didn't notice Jo, but she was always relieved not to see him making heavy weather of the ladder at the end of a long day.

Rob Dinsmore crossed the road from the Binnacle, looking newly washed and combed, fresh from a mug-up that would keep him going for a few hours' work before supper.

"Hi, Jo!" he called. "Been some elegant day!"

"Elegant!" she agreed. He went into his fishhouse, whistling "Put Your Little Foot Right Out."

She'd had a vague notion of joining Lisa in her porch hammock to watch for Nils to come in, but Lisa was on her way to the store with Vanessa Barton. Van was ahead on the narrow track through the asters; she stopped at the corner of the big shed where Mark kept the propane gas tanks and turned back to speak to Lisa, who nodded violently. Then they both disappeared around the corner. Joanna wondered what stories their children made of the fight in the schoolyard when they rushed home from school to change their clothes and rush out again. Supper was going to be a pretty interesting meal around most tables tonight; disturbing too. If Philippa managed to settle it or at least to quiet it, time should flatten the controversy as the dying storm surge had flattened under the north wind.

She realized then, as she turned up toward her own house, that she hadn't met Shannie on his way back to school, and he certainly hadn't been there when she left. He might have gone straight past home and out through the Sorensen backyard to the woods beyond, to be miserable in private. Or maybe he preferred comfort from his mother, who'd be on his side even if nobody else was. If she had no fresh baking on hand, she'd perhaps give him money for ice cream. But would the sweets and her indignation really solace him? If he made up a yarn about a vicious, unprovoked attack by the whole school, and she went at once to complain, she'd find out what had really happened. Then, Joanna suspected, Nan would not make a fool of herself by insisting they were all lying. Besides— Joanna felt her mouth twitching—Nan wouldn't want to risk losing her hairdresser. Binnie was the only pure beacon of civilization out here among the barbarians. And *besides*—his mother going to the school to fight for him wouldn't make Shannie very happy, and it would make the rest of the children *really* happy. Like it or not, he was stuck out here with them unless he ran away from home—difficult on an island when you didn't own your own boat.

Poor Shannie. He was no older than Stuart, eleven or twelve, just bigger and louder. He was probably hating himself for getting into this as much as he hated the others. She remembered what it was like, the deed done, the word said—you couldn't unsay it, and this was the longest worst day of your life. There had been worst days before, but they had never seemed so achingly awful as this one.

And there was Shannie in person, sitting on his front doorstep, elbows on his knees, and his chin in his hands. George's whistle sounded through the soft quiet air; from the clubhouse among the spruces up the lane, toward the Fennells', there came wisps of music, the Blue Danube Waltz: Cluny was practicing her ballet exercises. Cluny, a self-possessed child, had asked permission to use the clubhouse for two hours every day; she had her own tape player and tapes. She offered to pay rent, but that wasn't necessary, if she promised not to have other children in. She said politely that her practice was too important to be disturbed by children. They wouldn't be allowed even to look in the windows.

The comparison between Cluny and her young brother was a painful one. Joanna stopped and said, "It sounds as if George is whistling in Morse code. Signaling you, Shannie?"

He shifted his stare without freeing his chin or moving his head. His eyes were green under quirky brows, and he must have hated the length of his lashes. His shrug was like a huge convulsive hiccup. *To hell with George,* it said. He looked like his father, with his brown hair falling untidily almost to his eyes, and standing up at the crown. He had a strong freckled nose and a good jaw he would grow up to. He might in time smile like his father; no one out here had seen Myles anything but cheerful. But twelve was not an age for unlimited sunshine.

The radio was quietly playing upstairs; Nan kept tuned to the Limerock station when she was alone, either to block out the quiet or the wind. So she wouldn't be overhearing any conversation from the front doorstep.

"Maybe they can't start till you get there," Joanna suggested.

"It's not a real team!" he said angrily. "It's just fooling around, like little kids playing catch. I'm used to a *real* team, with *uniforms*"—that word exploded—"and a game schedule!"

His face flushed and his eyes glistened. Not with tears, she hoped. "Gosh, you must miss all that like everything," she said. "I know I would. I guess if you can't have what you're used to, nothing else is any good."

"I'm not friggin' with that stuff any more!" he said. "I don't care what *anybody* says!" If you shouted loudly enough you could keep your voice from cracking and your eyes from filling.

"That's right," she said. "Never compromise. I guess they really need you, but it's a matter of keeping your word to *yourself,* that's what counts. That's what I used to tell myself. You may be lonesome, but you have your pride."

A flicker of confusion crossed his face, and he scowled down at his knees. A triumphant shriek from the ball field made him let go of his chin and turn his head eagerly, as if he welcomed the interruption.

"Was that a boy or a girl yelp of triumph?" she asked.

"Tammie Dinsmore." He spoke as if with immense boredom. "She's pretty good. Mostly by accident," he added. "Always surprises the he-heck out of her." He couldn't help a small grin. Joanna grinned back.

"Well, it would me," she said. "I always dodged so I never hit the ball.

After a while I retired. Everybody was relieved, but they were too polite to say so except when they thought I couldn't hear them."

"*You* used to play baseball?" He was startled into amazement.

"Well, sort of. I just told you. I know you think I'm about a hundred years old."

"Not really, but—I mean, *baseball!*"

"They've been playing baseball on these islands since the game was invented. They even used to have two teams here. Bennett's was ahead of the mainland in some things—women and girls could play if they could hit and run. Of course, in the *really* old days the females didn't get to play in the games. It wasn't ladylike."

"Did this school always have a game every year with Brigport?"

"Yes, either here or there, and always on Columbus Day." She turned to go on, but his voice stopped her.

"Do they have a real ball field over there? Not a pasture?"

"Now, *that* was interesting. You might slide without meaning to. Pretty messy, though." This was a pardonable fib, but it worked. He actually laughed. "Yeah, you could *really* slide into home base!"

"Courtesy of a kindly cow," she said, which really put him over the top. He had to wipe his eyes and his nose on his sleeves; a good thing his mother wasn't watching, but if she had been, she'd have called him in before this.

"Do they have a real field now?" he asked, sounding disappointed.

"Nope. They play on the airstrip. Of course that *used* to be the pasture. On the day of the game nobody can land a plane on the airstrip all afternoon, unless it's a matter of life and death."

"*Honest?* And they *do* it? *Really* hold off?"

"Yes, and any Brigporters who are off the island and don't want to miss the game make sure that they're home in plenty of time, either by boat or plane."

"Do a lot of people go from here?"

"You bet. It's for the honor of the island."

"What if it rains?"

"Wait till the next good day, school or not, and everybody comes in early from hauling. But it hardly ever does rain. I hope that it works this time." She held up crossed fingers. "Well, it's been nice talking to you, Shannie."

As she turned away he cleared his throat and said, "Uh—Mrs. Bennett—"

Politely and pleasantly, she said "Yes?" as if her mind were already on something else.

He was painfully awkward but persistent. "When the high-school kids are here, do any of them play in the game? I mean, like Harry Percy and them? If the team's short, I mean. What about Richard and Sam?"

"Oh, no! None of them belong on the team once they're out of the eighth grade. When they choose up sides to play over here, and it's just Bennett's Islanders, anybody can be in it who wants to. But it wouldn't be fair to use the older players against Brigport School. *They* wouldn't put up with it. Neither would we, if Brigport tried it. So we make up with what we have. So long, Shannie." She took several steps toward the gate, knowing that behind her the boy hadn't moved. As if by afterthought, she beckoned him away. He looked back at the house and then came quickly, brightened with curiosity, not apprehension.

"Look, Shannie," she said. "This is a bit of free advice from somebody who's been there, said or done something they wish they hadn't. You can do what you like with it. But if you do go to practice, get Stuart alone and say just two words—you know what they are. I know they'll stick in your throat, but believe me, it's better to say it to one person in private than in front of everybody tomorrow, unless you're lucky and the teacher sends you two outside to do it. Everybody will still *know*. If you take care of it this afternoon, on the quiet, it means *you're* taking charge, you're ending it before it can turn into a big hooraw and the parents move into it."

His blush looked as sore as a burn. "What if Stu won't take it?"

"I'm pretty sure he will. He doesn't want his folks to hear anything. They've already had a hard time. Tell Mrs. Bennett you're apologizing, and that will take care of it. She's fair."

He stared at the ground, and nodded his head twice, or rather jerked it. Then he turned and ran back to the house. She hoped he was not crying. She hoped Stuart was like the gentle boy Sky used to be, not one to hold a grievance. Otherwise Shannie will hate him forever, she thought, and I'll be lucky if I'm not Old Lady Witch. She heard the back door slam next door, and let her breath out.

"*Gramma!*" Sara Jo's shriek pierced her before she reached her own door, and Pip cried plaintively on the other side; he'd been watching her from the kitchen window all this time.

With the jingle of the tiny bells on her red leather harness, the child came running ahead of her parents, up from the wharves, trailing her reins. Shannie seemed to have disappeared from the Earth with the slam of the door. If Stuart felt that a quick apology wasn't acceptable for an attack on his father, there was nothing she could do about it. She had no regrets. Come weal, come woe, Shannie would have to answer for his own mistakes. It had taken her young self a long time to find out there was no escape. She could remember well the words that stick in your throat when you are ten or twelve, but must be spoken.

Sara Jo broke into a gallop, shouting "I'm a norse, Grammie! I'm a norse!" Uttering realistic whinnies, she slapped one thigh, becoming horse and rider both. "Come on Bronc!" she urged, and Bronc neighed petulantly. Joanna waited by the well for the small galloper in overalls to reach her, braced for the usual impact against her legs and the immobilizing hug around her knees. The rush was interrupted when Maggie came out to take in her sheets, and Young Dog Tray squeezed past her. He'd been kept in so he couldn't join the baseball practice; otherwise, nobody ever got a chance to pick up the ball, and most of the runs were in pursuit of him.

He was not a replacement for Tiger—no dog could be—but he had his own talent; he could make almost anyone laugh. He was a large hairy black-and-brown dog of unknown mix, all tireless enthusiasms and exuberant affections. He and Sara Jo raced in demented circles until she tripped on her loose reins and fell down, out of breath but still laughing. Tray had learned a few useful things, such as not holding down a fallen child while he scrubbed its face and ears. So he fell at the feet of Rosa and Jamie, his own four feet kicking in the air while he waited for someone to rub his belly.

"Fool," Maggie said indulgently. She'd been taking in her washing and held a sheet up to her face. "My, this smells splendifical, as Rob's uncle Airey would say. He was the simple one," she added. "But could make up the *best* words!"

Joanna agreed. Tray made urgent little whimpers and wildly waved his feet.

"I'll do it as long as I can, Tray," Rosa said, leaning down. "But don't expect this all winter." She was pregnant for an April birth. Jamie dropped to one knee, and Tray sprang up and leaped at him; Jamie obligingly fell over.

"That's what he needs," said Maggie. "A good wrassle."

"Who?" asked Rosa. "Tray or Jamie?"

Maggie laughed. Sara Jo rolled over, got up, competently untangled her reins, then held out her arms to Joanna. There was no knee-hug if she couldn't come full tilt at her target. Lifted, she put her arms around Joanna's neck and whinnied in her ear.

Joanna recoiled. "*Good Lord!*"

"I'm a norse, Gramma!" Sara Jo explained. She had gray eyes like Rosa's, now about six inches from Joanna's and luminous with health and the pure happiness of believing that the world was perfect and she was the center of it. Her Dutch cut was the color of Jamie's hair, and she had the Bennett cleft in her small chin. She took a breath to whinny again, and Joanna said, "*No.* Polite horses don't try to make their gramma deaf. Why don't you purr, like Pip?"

"I kept Peter all afternoon," Rosa said, "because Carol's papering." Carol was young Matt Fennell's wife. "And there were horses—"

"*Norses,*" said Sara Jo firmly.

"They had fun running around wearing their reins, and Peter taught her to whinny. I could've done without that. Oh yes, norses are different from the regular kind. They *talk* through their whinnies. Can you imagine 'cookies' whinnied over and over? Besides everything else they think of?"

"We had fun."

"Will *I* be glad to get this one into the barn tonight!" Rosa said. "I'm beat!" Sara Jo gave Joanna a hug and a kiss on both cheeks, and wriggled to get down. She rushed giggling to the man and the dog, but the good wrassle was over. Jamie was brushing himself off while Tray, with his chin on his paws, gazed winsomely at him through black bangs.

Rosa began to help Maggie fold sheets as they came off the line. Joanna watched Jamie and his daughter. He was listening attentively as she talked; he could understand everything she said, or at least she thought he could. For Joanna, holding Jamie's child in her arms had not been even a remote possibility for so long that, after two-and-a-half years, the reality hadn't lost its luster. Neither had the reality of Jamie as a deft and humorous father who accepted the facts of burping and diapers with talent and equanimity. If he was awestruck by this small wonder that he and Rosa had created, he never said; being Jamie, he would not. For Nils, there was the deep personal satisfaction of rocking his first grandchild after being the only grandfather of Ellen's children for so long. They were not to know the difference, because he would never change toward them. Even Ellen's stepchildren adored him. Don't we all, Joanna thought with a sudden desire to see him coming up from the wharf at this moment; the longing was almost painful, and accompanied by a subtle brush of cold as delicate as a light breath.

She wanted to scoff it away, to laugh raucously at it as Shannie had laughed at Stuart. She thought, I will *not,* I will *not* again terrorize myself with hearings and seeings and what-ifs. But every imaginative person had them, and they were not always on the side of dread. It's age that does it to you, she thought, and I refuse to bow to that.

"No sense going to the wharf, Marm." Jamie's voice came to her as if through a layer of sleep. "The old man's been pinned too long to the cigarette case by the Ancient Mariner."

"The one without the long gray beard and glittering eyes," Rosa said over her shoulder. Everything righted itself. Joanna laughed with relief as well as amusement. John Haker, of course.

"What is it *today?*"

"I didn't wait to find out. There was a lot of Finnish in it, and Helmi told him once or twice to watch it. When she finally said it in Finnish, it must have been strong enough to get through. So I figured it must have been sort of indelicate. But who else would understand it?"

"*Sort* of?" said Maggie. They all laughed.

"Was Emlyn there?" Joanna asked. "He said once that Finnish was as complicated as Welsh, but John's stories were worth it. Only Helmi won't always tell him what John just said. But he likes the sound of it."

"He wasn't there," Jamie said. "I saw him heading across to Brigport when I was hauling. It was about time for school to let out. Maybe he figured he could walk their new schoolteacher home."

"I haven't seen her yet," said Joanna. "Maybe if she and Emlyn hit it off, we could toll her over here for next year, and then Owen would be even more sure of his sternman."

Maggie knocked on the clothes pole as the nearest wood. "I don't know if she's his type," Rosa pointed out.

"Any woman is his type," said Jamie. "Well, I guess he's choosy enough, but then he can afford to be."

"Let's go home," said Rosa, "and then you can tell me just how you meant that."

He gave her a smile, very much like his father's, and said, "I can hardly wait." He unclipped Sara Jo's reins, handed the coil to Rosa, and hoisted the child to his shoulders.

She clutched at his head and looked around in radiant triumph.

"Now who's on top of the world?" asked Maggie.

"Me!"

"Top of her voice too," Jamie said. His yells as a child were usually re-served for rage; his joys had been deep and mostly silent.

"So long, everybody," Rosa said. Maggie caught Tray by the collar be-fore he could become an escort; he would take too many detours on the way home.

"See you later, Jo," Rosa called back. Jamie said, "*Hey!* Easy with the heels. This is Dad, not Bronc. And let go my ears, too."

Sara transferred her grip to his hair, leaving one hand free to blow kisses, not ignoring Tray, who between that and cries from the ball field, whined in frustration. Maggie bribed him into the house by mentioning supper.

As the others walked toward their house, Joanna heard Rosa laugh, an easy, intimate sound that made Joanna smile. Imagine Jamie being able to make a woman laugh like that. But the woman would have had to be Rosa—Joanna was convinced of that. It could never have been anyone else. It was Rosa who had made it possible for Jamie's parents to hold his child and for Jamie to be the man he had become.

6

John Haker's real surname was one of those long Finnish names that sound extraordinarily musical when correctly pronounced, which seems to be possible only for other Finns or those with an ear for the rich and strange. He and his brother trawled for hake and had favorite grounds all over Penobscot Bay. Everyone knew the rakish two-man trawler *Annie-Elmina;* John claimed that applying new paint too often would have taken away her identity. From being referred to as "the hakers," they had become the brothers Haker, their first names Anglicized to John and Charlie. They were as welcome everywhere as the pack peddlers who used to visit the islands, carrying goods the small island stores didn't stock, turning a borrowed workshop into an Aladdin's cave in a time when most people went to the mainland only for absolute necessities like seeing a dentist or a doctor.

John claimed to know inside facts about people all over the bay—not all of it scandalous—and what he didn't know he was suspected of making up. He was a born storyteller and gave great value for the meals he accepted, as long as nobody tried to find out just where the truth lay in his dense and vivid verbiage. He stopped short of slander, it was hoped, but nobody ever took chances on repeating off the islands any of his more outrageous yarns.

He was a short, stubby man with a round bald head and small pale blue eyes with a perpetual twinkle. He smoked a corncob pipe whose stem he constantly jabbed at his nearest listener. His brother was a lanky, silent man with a sparse white-blond beard. Seemingly morose, he always managed to be somewhere else when John was on stage, even not eating in the same house with him. He said that John embarrassed the hell out of him, that his brother's tongue hung in the middle and wagged at both ends, and that it rested only when they were working. Charlie was quietly generous with fresh hake when they stopped to gas up on the way home, and there were some who preferred the hake to John's latest story. They always stopped at Bennett's Island on their way to a favorite spot outside the Rock.

Occasionally he told a verifiable story that later appeared in the *Limerock Patriot,* if it had enough drama in itself, though he might add dialogue he thought it needed. Therefore they knew on Bennett's Island how the Harmon family reacted when Myles committed an unthinkable act—unthinkable for a Harmon, that is. He gave up the newest queen of the Harmon trawler fleet to go lobstering, so he could be at home on the mainland with his family every night. He wasn't quite excommunicated, but the result was about the same. The islanders also knew about the persecution from certain resentful lobstermen when he set his first traps from his new lobster boat. It didn't end with the immediate loss of those traps and the next, but continued by word of mouth over boat radio and by work of hands after dark. He could stand the slurs and jokes on the air; it was just talk. The vandals were a minority and would give up soon, he thought. But finally his boat was cut from her mooring on a windy night and was picked up the next morning by a homecoming trawler (ironically, a Harmon vessel). She was slamming against Limerock Breakwater in a smart breeze, and everything salvageable had been taken from her. They'd had to leave the big marine engine, but they'd done their best to ruin it.

John Haker's story had stayed close to the facts but with embellishments. David Sorensen gave a tight account; his oldest son-in-law, a winchman aboard the *Nanette Harmon,* was one of Myles's friends. He brought Dave and Myles together, and now, accepted on Dave's references, Myles was on the island. He never talked about his experiences; after the sickness of a defeat such as he had never known before, growing up a Harmon, he mended himself and bought David's boat, *Sweet Alice,* and rented Dave's house. He'd come out to Bennett's Island on a fine summer day, with his son and his first load of traps. He never seemed to look back; he was catching lobsters as he'd dreamed of doing, and he didn't worry about slow times in cold weather, when the lobsters might or might not be out there, but the everlasting wind would keep the men from going out to see.

Right now Joanna wouldn't have been surprised to see John Haker coming home with Nils for supper. Well, she had plenty of stew; it needed only a few more dumplings. Charlie would likely be having a relaxing

meal with Mark and Helmi, Young Mark, and Willy. Young Mark said that
Charlie could tell good *true* stories when he had half a chance, but he
didn't mind listening to other people's, except John's.

She set out another of the mugs Linnie had sent from Sweden, just in
case. But when a sudden long howl from Pip at the front door announced
Nils, he was coming alone through the gate, and Myles was heading for
his own back door. Myles was a big, rangy, pleasant-faced young man,
lightly freckled, with rumpled brown hair and his cap pushed to the back
of his head. It said "Harmons" on it—the name of the fishing dynasty he
had left. He called something to Nils, and both men laughed; then Nils
came on. Pip was clawing at the screen, and Joanna let him out. He ran to
Nils and landed on him at about midthigh.

"Hey!" Nils said. "That's me in there!" He lifted the cat to his chest,
and Pip began bumping his head against Nils's chin. Joanna held the door
open for them.

"Unhook me," said Nils. She did so, one paw at a time, while Pip
rubbed his cheek against hers.

"None of our children were this adhesive," she said, finally getting Pip
away before he could fasten on again. "You see why I don't rush at you and
cling when you come home. Pip's already done it. I'd be an anticlimax."

"Oh, come on, try it." He held out his arms, and they kissed and em-
braced while Pip watched them from a chair with his brilliant gold-
speckled eyes.

"Everybody thinks I'm moderate, but I'm not," Nils said in her neck.
"Let's go upstairs."

"You don't really expect me to take you up on that—"

"No. I need a couple of aspirin and a good cup of coffee. I don't know
what happens to coffee in a thermos bottle all day. It starts out all right,
but ends up the way bilgewater ought to taste." He took off his boots and
went to the kitchen to wash. He took the aspirin while she was pouring
the coffee.

"Hard day?" she asked. "Rough day? *Good* day?"

"All three. She's been dancing ever since we left the harbor this morning, but the gear wasn't in too much of a mess, and the lobsters were
crawling. Jamie and Matt had a snarl, but they didn't need any help. Acting as if it was a big picnic down there off Bull Cove Reef. Took me back,"
he said reminiscently. "When we got our first haulers, we thought it
couldn't get any better than that. Now most of us have so much electronic

cultch aboard, we're asking lightning to strike. It's like shaking a fist at God. And when you're out there working, it doesn't matter how much fancy tackle and gear you're carrying, the sea's the boss and it doesn't let you forget it."

He was matter of fact; didn't everybody, everywhere, live intimately with risk? You knew it was there, and you survived by not forgetting it. Around the water you learned young what respect was. Grandfathers like Gunnar might be tyrants, but the sea was his boss too, and he knew it. "But I thought the sea was friendlier," Nils said absently, and she knew what he was thinking. He picked up his mug and the plate of hermits. "Think he's still around?"

"Either he's given us up as lost, or he's mellowed," she said.

"Somehow I can't see that." Nils sipped coffee cautiously and said, "Ah, that's good!" He slid down in his chair and stretched out his legs, and wriggled his toes. "Simple pleasures," he said. "Makes the whole day worthwhile."

"Don't tell me you'd been wishing all day that you were somewhere else."

"No. Right now I'm being thankful for coming home to something different from *that*." He nodded his head toward the house next door. "I wonder how soon after he went in that he lost that grin."

"Maybe it'll make Shannon happy at least. It'll be a nice change from her. . . . Something happened today. There hasn't been such a brawl in the schoolyard since we were kids, and I can't even remember what the last big one was all about. I remember we were all kept after school—detention, Mrs. Abbott called it, and it sounded so grim."

At that moment Pip landed on Nils's moving toes, which kept Joanna from escaping into a pleasant ramble about the past. After the cat was shaken off Nils's feet and it began eating pieces of hermit, she told Nils in detail, from the beginning, with the first sight of the flying cap. "It's not over, of course. Shannon knows now he can make Stuart cry; Stuart knows it, and he can't help that any more than Sky could when he was that age."

"Myles will have to tend to his boy," Nils said. "And Sky's children shouldn't have to protect him. Maybe he can teach Stuart how to keep from crying. It all belongs to somebody else, Jo. Not to us. Not to you."

"There's more," she said. "I got involved."

"Do I need more coffee to brace me for it? Should we put a shot of brandy in it?"

"Oh, shut up," she said, and Nils laughed.

"Get it over with," he sighed.

"I could have shaken that boy, but when I came home and saw him sitting on the doorstep there, looking so miserable and lonely. . . . When you were a kid, did you ever do or say something you wished you hadn't— wished *violently*—and you didn't know how to get out of it?"

He was looking at her with the kind and thoughtful expression with which he had listened to his children, and she said crossly, "No, you didn't. You never had a chance to. But I did."

His eyes narrowed into the ghost of a smile. "I remember you. But I did have some chances; I wasn't Little Saint Nils. I got into snarls and out of them again. Sometimes with help."

"You never told me. You've been cheating. I want to hear more about the private life of Nils Sorensen."

"Not now," he said placidly. "Save it for under the bedclothes on long cold winter nights. Go on."

"Well, I stopped to speak to Shannon. George was whistling madly on his genuine London bobby's whistle, and I said he must be trying to reach Shannie." She told him how she had talked to Shannon. "I think I was pretty good," she said. "At least I got him to talk back, then smile, and even laugh. He listened when I suggested he could take charge by apologizing to Stuart on the quiet, and when he went into the house I thought I'd reached him. But then I thought, He may have been a deceitful little brat and told his mother he'd been picked on at school, and I'd just been picking on him some more. . . . So God knows what Myles met when he went into the house."

Nils took the mugs and went out to the kitchen. Joanna sat there with her arms folded tightly across her chest, waiting for the mild suggestion that she should mind her own business; she was startled when he said quietly, "Look out the door." She turned and saw Tammie Dinsmore going into the back door of the Binnacle, and Tom J. Percy walking up past the well, swinging his hat. "See you," he called out to someone, and Shannon answered back. He was passing the front doorstep, where he had looked so unhappy, and coming around to the back door. He was carrying his bat, and both his pitcher's mitt and his catcher's glove. He'd been ready for anything, and he looked cheerful.

She was surprised by the strength of her relief; it was almost a rejoicing. Nils came back with the coffee, smiling. "You did it."

"Now don't tell me it was more a hit than any good wit."

"I won't. But don't expect he's got over Stuart this quick. There'll be something else always happening, as long as the reason is there. I can tell you all about jealousy—you know that."

"I know that much about Nils Sorensen, but where does it come in here?"

"Remember the day he and Myles arrived? They had two weeks before Nan and the girls came out. They set that load of traps and hauled them. They camped out in the house; they were invited to eat in other people's houses. I remember a happy kid."

"And a friendly one," she said. "This is what was so disturbing about the fight today. Earlier, when he wasn't with his father he was with the other kids, rowing, fishing, hiking to Sou'west Point or the Eastern End. I've seen him and Stuart getting soda in the store and kidding each other. Nils, what happened?"

"His mother came," said Nils. "You wouldn't have noticed it all happening because you can't see the wharves and harbor all day. But one thing after another stopped. Going to haul with his father, baiting up. Rowing. Not being near the water at *all*. Then school started, and they were all wound up in baseball, but on weekends Stuart was still right under his father's elbow. And he has a new skiff, by the way. And where was Shannon?"

"Is she so deathly afraid of everything out there she doesn't dare let Shannon go near the water?"

"She's not that afraid," he said. "I got this from John Haker, and I don't think it's a load of codswallop. On the mainland Nan worked, and it was fine for Shannie to hang around his father's shop after school, doing anything Myles gave him to do. He'd bait up, if Myles wasn't in yet. When Myles was there, he could row around, go out aboard the big boat and fish from her. Get a chance to steer her if Myles went around to Limerock Harbor for anything. His mother didn't have to worry about him riding his bike uptown with the wrong kids. Cluny went straight to her dance class, and the little one went home with another youngster until Nan picked her up after work. Shannon was safely occupied between baseball and his father. No, she isn't afraid of the water."

"But why stop it out here, where it's the normal life for a boy? It sounds as if she's mad about everything and can't keep Myles from being happy, so she's taking it out on Shannon. She's *monstrous!* Why can't Myles . . ."

He shook his head. "It looks to me—and I haven't been talking her over down on the wharves—that Myles is so damn' happy to get her to come out here, he's not going to raise hell about anything. So Shannon's missing a father, but Stuart's got his."

"Then Myles is monstrous too," she said. "I liked him until now. He can get her two pails of water in the morning and leave the house whistling because he's going to be happy all day doing what he wants to do, never mind what he's leaving behind him: a woman who's fit to be tied and a child who's having to pay for that. With the two of them letting this go on, Shannon is likely to explode someday and go on a vandalism spree, or set the house on fire so they'll have to move back where he was so happy," she added. "Oh God, why did we have to have something like this land in our dooryard? Damn it, this morning I emancipated myself from trying to be nice to Nan, and now I have to see that tormented child going in and out, and each time I'll feel like bashing her. *And* Myles."

"That's my ladylike wife, God bless her."

"Don't laugh," she warned him.

"I'm not. But remember, somebody else's child isn't our responsibility unless he's being starved or beaten or otherwise abused. But what's going on in there . . ." he shook his head. "Sooner or later, it's going to change, I hope not with a house afire. Let's pray for a wet fall," Nils added. "Whatever happens, it's up to them. Of course, if you want to go on trying to captivate Nan to prove that you're irresistible, I can't stop you. But I wouldn't advise it."

"You're right," Joanna said. "But I resent that crack about being irresistible. I thought I was doing my duty."

"As a Bennett," Nils said solemnly, "one of the First Families, after the Indians."

"Noblesse oblige, as they say in books," she said. "Oh, one more thing about this afternoon, I just remembered. Can you stand it?"

"I'll try."

"Young Mark called Shannie a mainland arsehole."

The effect was all she could ask for. "*Our* Young Mark? Little Gentleman Mark?"

"Yep. How's that for noblesse oblige?"

They burst out laughing, and the tension of the last hour dissolved in the flood.

7

To make the most of the shortening days, before it was time to have supper by lamplight, Nils and Joanna ate at a table by the living room windows, where they could get all that was left of the light until after sunset. In clear weather there was an intensity about this flood of brilliance missing from the most spectacular of summer sunsets, when you had so many more to come it didn't matter if you missed one. Tonight, in the hush that set in after the last boat had come home, when the dying breeze had left a calm sea and everyone had gone home to supper, leaving only the gulls, it was as if the world were tilting very slowly into the flames of the last sunset before the last night.

There'd been no letters in today's mail to read and discuss, so Nils and Joanna ate in a companionable silence, not hurrying, their eyes always turning toward the intricate patterning of sun-gilded wings, to Brigport across the water, and beyond the southern end of Brigport, to the blue bay stretching twenty-odd miles to the mainland. It was a satisfying blue, the very soul of blueness. Between them they had seen that stretch for over a century. They knew all its moods and voices; but the color of it before a clear and windless sunset was always alluring because one never knew how long it would last.

The hush of the hour was emphasized by a sudden burst from a chickadee in the nearest tree and the calling of blue jays, a sound that was autumnal even in summer. The crickets were underrunning everything else. In the house the mantel clock ticked, another emphasis. Pip slept deeply on the sofa, full of beef stew as well as his own food. Sometimes he moved and made a small murmur in his sleep. The clock and

41

the cat were enough for Nils and Joanna, who didn't need radio or television to fill the gaps. They would get only the war, anyway. Hardly anyone on the island wanted to have the war at mealtimes, or any other time.
They were sick of it, disgusted at what they saw as the cynical official attitude of people with power and no sense of responsibility. The universal
hope was that it would be over before any more of the boys, anywhere,
reached draft age. On the island, Richard and Sam were the closest, both
sixteen.

Emlyn had been in Vietnam. He didn't care to talk about it; he said
once, in a lapse from good humor, "It's behind me and I want to keep it
there forever. If I'd had the brains God gave a louse I'd have gone to
Canada, or to jail, or to empty bedpans in a hospital. I never thought I
was saving my country; I knew I was wiping out somebody else's. We all
did . . . those poor bastards being driven from place to place with all
they could carry, and the rest of us poor bastards doing it to them."

Nobody ever talked about it after that, and even the children who saw
him as a hero because he'd been in a war, understood it was a different
kind of war than those in which their fathers, uncles, and some young
grandfathers had fought.

Now the sun was going down behind Mark's house on Sunset Point,
and with a burst of engine sound echoing from the harbor walls, the fifth
White Lady came in. She was towing Richard's dory on a short painter,
and her bow strained like that of a rebellious horse. The combined wakes
cut out behind them into a broad V of blue and gold. Abruptly she
slowed, the engine became a mild murmur, and White Lady slipped
across the harbor among the moored boats as easily as the gulls did, and
disappeared into shadows turned very dark by contrast with the blazing
sky above.

The village awoke as if from a community trance. People appeared on
the paths, children first, running like mad and hoping to catch a line. The
adults were leisurely, but still moving toward the wharf. From the
Sorensen house most of that wharf was invisible even in full sunlight.
Joanna was guiltily aware that she hadn't thought of Owen all afternoon
except to suppose he'd gone home past the Head at Eastern End and
around to Schoolhouse Cove, as he usually did; the next day people could
pick up and pay for any purchases Laurie had made for them. Stonehaven
was a very small island town, but it had a good assortment of stores and
services that could save a trip to Limerock.

"I wonder why he came in here tonight?" she said. Nils began to carry their dessert dishes out to the pantry.

"Why don't you go find out?" he suggested.

"Are you coming too?"

"Nope. I've had my thrill for the day." He went on into the kitchen. When he came back, she put suddenly chilly fingers against his cheek. "I think I'm scared. What if he came in here instead of going straight home, to tell everyone at once his bad news? And then say, like Emlyn and the war, that he doesn't want to hear a word about it? More profane than Emlyn, of course."

He dropped an arm over her shoulders. "And what if he came in to leave off that twine Mark wants, because Maxwell's Rope doesn't carry it anymore?"

"Oh, you're probably right," she said. "You usually are. That could make you a real pain if you weren't who you are. But I can't help worrying each time he goes to the cardiologist."

"We all worry. Owen beached would be like—" He broke off and gave her shoulders a tight hug. "He and Laurie live with it, and the rest of us are thinking *It could be me, anytime.* But it's like everything else in life, island or not. We all know a hell of a lot of dirty surprises can happen, and what some of them could be, but not when. And if you're going to dwell on them, then you're either ungrateful, or—"

"You don't have both oars in the water," she said. They laughed.

Nils picked up *The Sea and the Jungle* and lay down on the sofa with his head to the windows, jamming the cushions comfortably under it. Pip spoke without opening his eyes and rolled over out of the way.

"From up here you have very distinguished bones," she said. "Did I ever tell you my thoughts on blue eyes?"

"Git along before I lay lecherous hands on ye," said Nils.

"Just wait an hour or two," she said. "Until it's dark under the table. John Haker calls it 'leechus.' That really sounds more like it, doesn't it?"

Washing the dishes, she saw Myles leave next door, bareheaded, hands in his pockets, no children behind him. Didn't he ever miss Shannon? she thought crossly. "You're the poorest excuse for a father that ever feet hung on and was called a man," she said to his back; it was a variation of one of Aunt Mary's favorite insults.

Tammie Dinsmore and her mother came from the Binnacle's back door, put Tray on his run, and left him whining. Ross and Amy ran ahead of their parents to embrace and comfort the dog. The Campion cousins from around the harbor were racing one another, except young Dennis, who was limping and being kindly escorted by Anne Barton.

Children made the most of any break in the routine, and a boat coming in after supper was an event. Besides, Laurie would have done the errands in Stonehaven. Adults strolled; such a mild, calm, cricket-sounding evening deserved a leisurely appreciation. The light was changing quickly—not exactly failing, but shifting from the afterglow toward the watercolor twilight. Too edgy to read, Joanna knit trapheads from a hook screwed into a windowsill, while Nils read on.

As people began returning home, and lights bloomed in kitchen windows, Nils shut his book and lay quiet, perhaps thinking of the Amazon; he had seen it and been on it in his Merchant Marine days.

The birds were silent now, but the crickets would go on into the night.

Joanna waited to see *White Lady* leave, her running lights reflecting on the water, the dory towed behind. But she didn't appear; Joanna kept her eyes on the harbor, glistening from the last light upon it from the sky, the boats seeming to sleep upon it. She didn't see the group coming up past the Binnacle until they were in her yard. Myles broke away from the others and went up his own steps.

"Are you asleep?" Joanna asked Nils. "They're on their way."

"Fine," he said drowsily. "Who?"

"They're here," she said. And they were. Mark's laugh encouraged another. There were some indistinct remarks, and more laughter. "I'll put the water on," she said. Nils got up and turned on the lights. She was filling the teakettle when Owen came in, scowling in the sudden light. "The more they come, the worse they look. Any grub around here?"

"If you want a meal, I can heat the beef stew," she said. "If you want a mug-up, how about coffee and fresh hermits?"

"I'll take whatever you've got for soul and body lashings," he said. He gave her a squeeze around the middle and a loud, smacking kiss on the cheek. "There! Don't say I never gave you anything, sister mine. You want a kiss too, Nils?"

"I'd sooner jump off my wharf wearing a pair of boots and holding onto a sack of ballast rocks," Nils said pleasantly.

"Besides, he ought to have a new shave before he propositions anybody like that," said Laurie, coming in behind him. She was always euphoric after a good report. "Jo, coffee and some of those hermits sound out of this world. We ate Italian sandwiches all across the bay." Mark and Helmi, Charles and Mateel followed her in, and Philip. The sun parlor was at once crowded. When they came together like this, it was as if they hadn't met for a week.

"So even the Senior is with us tonight, and his lady," said Owen. He gave Mateel a sardonic bow. "Anybody want to play Paul Revere and go get Steve?"

"What's eating you?" asked Charles. "We just walked down to see what the doctor said, if I can mention this out loud without being challenged to a duel."

Owen was not apologetic. "I thought everybody was gathering for the wake." Laurie winked at Joanna.

"It's a little previous to have one for you," Nils said.

"Well, if there's ever a wake for me I want to have it while I'm still around to enjoy it. . . . Say, do you miss anybody? The laddie with the fine plumage and the manners? The Welsh skylark?" His grin was ferocious. Color burned under his dark skin. He went off into the dining room, and Nils and the other men followed him. Mark and Philip had evidently heard something already. Charles was saying, "I'll be damned. When did this happen?"

Out in the kitchen the women worked together from habit—they had been sisters-in-law for so long; they were setting out mugs, getting the two big trays ready for the dining room, with paper napkins, spoons, sugar, milk, a platter of cookies. Pip joined them, sitting on a stool for a better view.

The men's voices masked Laurie's, and she kept it down. "There was a note waiting for us in the store when we went into Brigport to drop off Phillida Robey. Emlyn knew we were taking her along, so he left the note there. It was addressed to me—I was supposed to break the news to Owen, though why he thought that would be better I don't know. Of course, Owen had to see the note for himself."

"What did it say?" Mateel whispered, glancing toward the door into the dining room. Lisa let herself in, carrying a pan with a large frosted sheet cake. It had been cut at the end. "Good thing I made two of these. Tammie's with the kids, and they've all got cake. Why is everyone so solemn? You aren't faking the good news, are you?" she asked Laurie, and Laurie shook her head. "No. The doctor was practically beaming, and that's what counts, except that Emlyn's gone, with no warning."

Helmi's cool low voice came in. " 'The nightingale that in the branches sang—ah, whence, and whither flown again, who knows?' " She smiled at their faces. "You'd never suppose I'd ever memorized romantic poetry, would you? That just flew into my mind when I heard Emlyn was gone. Though the man didn't have to say both 'whence and whither,' one would be enough."

In the other room Owen was being fluently profane about con men and traitors. "Tell us about the note," Mateel said.

"Talk about poetry, it's engraved on my heart," said Laurie. " 'Thank you for everything. I will never forget you. Please give my love to everybody. P.S. Before I left, I fed the troops. Your friend, Emlyn Jones.' I thought it was nice of him to feed the animals, but Owen wasn't impressed."

"I'll bet," said Lisa. "What's he going to do now?"

"Well, he's got Willy for a few days to help him shift some traps."

"Did he put an ad up right away over there?" asked Joanna.

"No, he had to get out before he blew up. There were some women in the store, and he didn't want to lose his reputation for charm." The corners of her mouth quirked up. "Of course my stomach was trying to crawl up under my ribs. He didn't speak all the way across, and neither did I, but the minute we touched the wharf here, he took Mark aside and told him, and got the hire of Willy." She blew hard. "What a relief, but only for a few days."

"This is so sad," Mateel said. "Almost like a death; one minute Emlyn's here—"

"Looking forward to the winter," Joanna said.

"And the next he's gone. He seemed so perfect for the job, and so happy," Mateel said, sighing.

"When anything's too good to be true, it usually is," Laurie said. "But I *hate* it to be Emlyn, I really do! Something must have happened to make him go like that."

"Maybe he got a letter today," Lisa said. "Someone's very sick—"

"He could have told us that," Laurie objected. "If he did get some bad word, he didn't want to share it. The girls were always sure he'd left someone home with a broken heart, or that he was being faithful to a married woman, because he couldn't have been more brotherly with *them,* and always kept to safe subjects. I know they both had crushes on him, even Joss. Well, you know, he was quite a change after Tommy, who was like a slightly dim kid brother they had to bring up."

"How about 'Congratulations, you've just become a father and you'd better get back here pretty quick'?" suggested Joanna. "Either he's gone home or out into the unknown everywhere. Good Lord!" She was suddenly remembering him at the foot of the ladder. "I saw him leave! He waved at me and took off, smashing through a couple of seas as if he was riding high, and not just on rough water."

A meditative silence settled on them, an interval in which Pip got tired of his stool and landed on the counter beside Lisa's cake. Joanna lifted him off, but Lisa said indulgently, "Of course you can have a taste. After all, you're one of the gang." She cut a sliver with a bit of frosting and put it on a paper towel beside his water dish, where he ate it at once. Everything was grist to his mill.

"Anything to drink out there?" Owen shouted.

"It's on the way," Joanna called back. The others picked up the trays, and she followed them with the coffeepot.

"Where are the dancing girls?" Owen asked.

"We always serve coffee in our civvies," said Lisa, "so the customers won't scald themselves when they get excited." There was a shifting of chairs, and others were brought in. Pip got onto Nils's lap for a good view of the table.

8

As they settled down, there was an air, if not of pleasure or contentment, then of rightness, a familiarity—a sense that once you went through the right rituals the rest of life would fall into place. It was an illusion, because nothing about the Bennetts could ever be that simple; but they always started out with the correct moves.

"I wish Philippa and Steve were here," Mateel said. "We haven't all been around the table for a long time." Sometimes there was a little ghost of her early French-Canadian accent, the hint of a dropped *h*. Though she'd come as a baby, the family had always spoken French at home. Charles looked across at her with a little smile, as if he were thinking back.

"Well, now," said Owen expansively, "this is something *like*. Good coffee, *good* coffee, Jo. Nobody will give me a drink, and I can't afford to go back to smoking. Right now I could go through half a carton without stopping. So the worst I can do to feel devilish is go on a caffeine bender." He gave Laurie a sidewise look, which she pretended not to see. "We'll have the house to ourselves for the first time since Joss was born," he said. Who knows what we'll be up to next? Never had much chance for that kind of fun." He lifted Laurie's hand and kissed it. "Think we're past it?"

"Never!" said Laurie, and everybody laughed; the last constraint around the table was gone.

"Settle down, everybody," Owen said. "I have an announcement to make. Emlyn's gone, and that's the end of it. Maybe there's a woman or two involved, or he owes money and somebody's coming after him— every con man has to run sooner or later. I just wish his actions hadn't caught up with him till spring. It's worse than being keelhauled trying to get somebody out here for the winter unless *he's* running away and wants to get under cover. But I've got Willy for the next few days, and longer if Mark'll let him go." He cocked an eyebrow at Mark, who looked impassive. "Don't get me wrong. I miss Emlyn like hell already. I *liked* the bastard. That's as far as my thoughts on him go, except to wonder where he'll be combing his hair next."

He poured more coffee and took more cake. "Elegant, Lisa." He lifted his cup to her as if in a toast.

His nonchalance didn't fool them. He'd had somebody who seemed the perfect sternman, who seemed to be in love with the island and happy to be working in waters unknown to him, looking forward to winter as an adventure. Now he had gone, behind Owen's back, leaving no message except his thanks.

Nobody else needed or wanted a sternman. There were long-standing partnerships, when men doubled up in emergencies or for jobs that needed two; there was the habit of cooperation without which no small community could survive, when everyone turned to in a crisis. Hurt feelings and irritations were ignored during the emergency. The help was always reliable, always *there*. Sternmen were birds of passage, as Nils called them. Really good ones were ambitious, anxious to get out on their own after earning a good bankroll from their 20 percent of each haul, with the boss providing room and board.

Poor men had to be fired for legitimate reasons, or they simply disappeared. But Emlyn hadn't been a poor sternman, and he had left a note, such as it was. The event had been absolutely unexpected, and that had been its impact.

The Bennett's Islanders considered sternmen more nuisance than they were worth. Steady attention to gear was what paid off. For wintering, when they went far out from the island, some boats went in company, keeping each other always in view, neither starting for home without the other. There were pairings, too: two men in the same boat for the winter months, halving expenses and profits. But Owen was the only islander who needed a man aboard with him all year round, not only for his sake but for the boat's, to bring *White Lady* in so she wouldn't go drifting away with a dead man lying on the deck. The others knew the desperation behind his humor, and some believed it was all for the boat, not for himself.

"How about it, Cap'n Mark?" he asked, still jolly. "Going to let Willy take a winter job with me? He's wasted on land: Strong as a horse—not that I want a horse aboard—but he knows what's needed." It was hard to resist a certain tone and that expression, but the family had known him for too long.

"No steady job," Mark said calmly. "We've got a lot of work to do before snow flies. Roofing, painting, carpentering. And what about the first good day in a windy while when everybody's gone out to haul and it's boat day, and the gas boat, the oil boat, and the smack come in all at once? Willy's out with you on the bounding main singing 'A Life on the Ocean Wave.' "

"Christ, you sound as if you never had a hand to help ye. Poor old Mark, trudging up and down, up and down, all by himself, getting closer to collapsing at every step." Mark stayed impassive, but one forefinger was tapping on the table, and Owen watched it. "Besides his 20 percent," Owen went on, "I'll pay for his board and room so he won't cost you anything on days he works for me."

Mark said with commendable calm, "Tomorrow's fine, and so is the next day, but after that . . ." He shook his head.

Laurie laid her hand gently over Mark's. "*I'm* going with Owen until Christmas, anyway. Then we'll see." She took her cup and went out into the kitchen; the other women followed.

They left silence behind them, a shifting foot, the scratch of a match, a clearing throat. Then Charles said, "Well, I guess that takes care of you for a while, brother." There was a suggestive quaver in his voice. "I guess she can put on bait bags, and measure and plug a lobster as good as anybody."

"When it's flat-arse calm," said Owen. "Good stiff chop can bounce her around the cockpit like popcorn. She'll be breaking an arm or a leg, first hop out of the box."

"I don't recollect her bouncing around too much when she went with you before the kids," said Nils.

"Well, hell, sure she can go," Owen said belligerently. "But not for winter fishing. I need a man for that, goddammit!"

Philip said mildly, "Well, Skipper—"

"Don't use that word on me!" Owen flared. "Reminds me of Felix Drake. I heard him spoken of today. Not nicely, you might put it." The conversation settled on Drake like butterflies on a honeysuckle bush, as Philip had probably intended.

Joanna, closing the kitchen door, asked softly, "What did you mean by 'and then we'll see'?" Laurie's grin was like her son's.

"That's when the traps are coming up. He doesn't know it yet, of course."

"How do you think you can manage that?" Jo asked skeptically.

"I don't know. If he won't take me—and believe me, I don't fancy winter lobstering anyway—and he can't get a man to go, he'll have to take up, at least until March, and maybe *through* March. Then maybe I can go with him again. I've always kept my license, just in case. I loved to be with him out there, to have him to myself, but first I was teaching *and* pregnant. Then I got too big, and after that it was one thing or the other—if I wasn't either, I had small children at home. Oh, once in a while I'd get out. Then we had Tommy all those years till last June, and Richard went with Owen until Emlyn." She sighed. "I could have had the whole summer with him if *that* blessed event hadn't happened. It's a good thing I couldn't help liking Emlyn. I could have been pretty miserable to live with."

"Oh sure you could," Joanna teased her. "We all know how mean and ugly you can be."

"What I want to know," said Lisa, "is how you're going to get those traps up."

"Well, I've got from now till December to work on him." She sounded more hopeful than convinced. "Anyway, I'm not worrying about it tonight. I'm glad you didn't take *all* the cake in there, Lees."

Pip pushed open the door and came in brightly and hopefully. The men's voices followed him. Smothered by laughter, Owen's broke through.

"Good-looking, too. She caught me outside the store over there—I'd just put my ad up. She wanted the job. She said she was a damn' good sternman, been going with her old man for years. Vinalhavener. Spending a week with the Bradford girl—they were in college together."

"You know this story?" Mateel whispered to Laurie.

"I know them *all*. Listen, it gets better."

" 'Honeybunch,' I said. 'I'd love to hire you, but my wife won't let me.' 'Oh, that's all right,' she says. 'I'd be no threat to her. I'm engaged to a navy pilot on an aircraft carrier. He's overseas right now, but he trusts me, and besides, you're as old as my father.' "

"So you slunk away," said Philip.

"Looking for a mirror," Charles added.

"I would've if Young Lochinvar hadn't come up to us. I thought he wanted to cut some ice with her, but it was *me*."

"I bet that took the wind out of her sails," said Mark.

"Go on smirking, you idiot. He was everything he claimed to be, plus a few items he didn't bother to mention." His mood was about to change again. "*Damn* him."

Philip said, "Speaking of women, remember that one on the yacht that was storm-stayed here a couple of years ago? Nice ketch, named *Brianna?* The boat, not her. We never got that far."

Mark chuckled. "Ayuh, came into the store while all five of us were standing around getting dissipated on soda . . . pants like a second skin and a peekaboo shirt she'd got fetchingly wet on the way ashore. Poses against the door, shoots out one hip and one breast, looks around at all these rugged toilers of the sea, and says, '*Wow!* It's *true* what they've got out here!' And then Helmi came out of the back room and says, 'Yes, we do have a good inventory. Were you looking for anything in particular?' "

In the kitchen Helmi's eyes were as near to twinkling as the others had ever seen them. "I have to admit I felt pretty smug that day," she said. "They were a handsome bunch of men, and they were all taken. She forgot what she came in for, and went for a walk."

In the other room Charles was commenting on John Haker's latest scandalous yarn about the doings of wealthy summer people; the "new kind," John called them. But as a diversion it was no good. Owen said suddenly, "I could hire one of the Brigport kids who can't go in winter because their boats are too small. He could go home every so often and gamble away all his earnings, smoke pot, and raise hell."

Laurie was looking to the ceiling as if in prayer. Her lips moved, *Over my dead body.*

Mark spoke the unspeakable. "Why don't you take up until March? You can find plenty to do ashore."

"*Take up!*" What in hell are you talking about? Trouble with *you,* brother Mark, is you quit lobstering too soon. Now because you've got arthritis—more likely *rust*—you think we're all over the hill, every goddamn one of us!"

Jamie came in from the sun parlor, noiseless in his moccasins. "What's going on?"

"Your Uncle Owen," Laurie said. "He's fine, but Emlyn's left him in a cleft stick." She tried to sound cheerful, even amused, but the day was wearing on her. Jamie, surprisingly for him, squeezed her shoulders; he had become more demonstrative since he'd married. Then he picked up Pip and stood just outside the dining room door. Owen hadn't stopped yet.

"*Arthritis?*" he said contemptuously. "Our family doesn't have *that.* You wouldn't either—"

"Oh, Jesus!" Mark was goaded into it at last. "No, with you it's always a sprain or a bump or a jolt that makes you sore as a boil. Or the boat fetched a sudden jump or she dropped between two big ones, and you didn't see it coming. She threw you. Or you skidded in the bait shed. Or you—oh Christ, I've been through them all. Sometimes it was the truth, and sometimes it wasn't. If I hadn't taken over the store, where would you all be now? You'd be goddamn sad about something every day of your life, and it wouldn't be about sternmen."

They all knew what could happen to an island store bought by non-islanders who had never been mainland storekeepers: office men, thinking it would be a healthful and totally delightful escape from what they called the rat race. In all except very rare cases they refused to take advice from the customers who would keep them going, and they thought they could run the store like any business, down to the accounting. They were glad to sell out to other romantics and get a good distance away, unlamented.

Mark was still going strong, not letting Owen get a word in. "I'd ought to sell the place to some dreamer or just shut it up altogether and get the hell off the place once and for all. *Jesus Christ!*"

Into the following silence Nils's voice spoke to Jamie like a gentle rain over a dying grass fire. "Come in, son, and sit down. Your uncles are just holding a little prayer meeting."

9

In bed that night, in the reflective quiet after the books were put aside, Joanna said, "We think it would be nice if you all took up for the winter."

"Who's *we?*"

"Tonight in the kitchen, all the so-called Bennett womenfolk, except Philippa and Rosa. After all, none of us is driving her man out to catch every lobster in the ocean and earn her all those dollars. Well, Mark doesn't lobster, but he used to, and Helmi knows it's not the winter fishing that keeps the store going, especially in one of those seasons when you don't get out more than four or five times between Christmas and March." She lay on her side with her arm comfortably across him, looking past his profile at the brilliant stars. They were so thick and the weather was being so fine, it seemed like one long weather-breeder building up to Hurricane Frank, who hadn't yet made up his mind whether to strike inland when he reached Hatteras, or to continue up the coast for a while.

Nils was quiet, but she knew he wasn't asleep. "I think every woman on the island feels the same way," she said. "Especially about those surprise snow squalls, when everything a hundred feet offshore disappears."

Nils murmured ambiguously.

"So what is it?" she persisted. "Do you think if you lose those few days in winter you'll forget how to haul? After all, we went away in the spring once, and the ocean was right where we left it when we came back. And you were setting out the next day." She gave him as much of a pinch as was possible over his ribs. "Or do you think the ocean will run dry if you don't use it? Mateel says when Charles gets out of bed in the morning, the first thing he does is to look out and see if it's still there. Nils, why don't *you* stay in? You always can find something to do when you're on the beach, and not just make-work chores. Lord knows there's plenty of wood to work up, and carpentry jobs to keep the buildings in repair."

"Supposing there comes a pretty day," he said. "One of those blue days that looks and feels like spring, and I've got no traps out there, so no reason to go."

"Would it be so sinful for us to just go out for a sail, not to work? Would that be a criminal waste of fine weather?"

"No," he said agreeably. "But this conversation isn't getting us anywhere. Do you think that if I quit, somebody else will, including Owen? Sweetheart, I was never a bellwether to your brothers. They're Bennetts; they do as they goddamn please. The *goddamn* goes with it, different from plain 'wouldn't'. . . . And Owen's so touchy about anyone telling him to take it easy, how do you think we've kept speaking all these years?"

"Oh, you're right," she said, sighing against his arm. "How many times have I said *that* today? Good night, love." She turned onto her other side, gave her pillow a few punches, and settled down to sleep. Nils lifted the hair from her neck and kissed her behind the ear. "That's nice," she said, turning her face to his.

As they began to sink together into sleep, Pip jumped onto the bed, feeling his way cautiously around and over their feet, and lay down against the footboard, purring. As the purr grew fainter, Joanna almost went to sleep with it. Then all at once she was on the slopes above Sou'west Point on an early July day, smelling the wild roses that thrived on the granite, and the wild strawberries.

"I'll mourn for the strawberries," she said foggily.

"Are you talking in your sleep?" What was Nils doing here? Then she came fully awake. "It's from what I was thinking earlier today, the island a thousand years from now. What it will be like, if the sea keeps chipping it away. Two islands, or just slabs and big junks of rock ten times bigger than what we have now, with nothing green and growing. What if there are earthquakes along the coast? The way there used to be? Real ones, not just tremors, to destroy it as we know it?"

"Do we get ready tomorrow, or do we have to start packing tonight?"

"This is all in a spirit of scientific inquiry," she said.

"It's been a long day," said Nils, and yawned to make his point.

"What if the sun burns out? Stars burn themselves up when they're

old enough. Will there be all new life in the cold dark waters? Giant lobsters, whales as long as the island, sea turtles as big as the clubhouse, the
return of the big cod—*very* big cod. After all the creatures of *now* have
been hunted to extinction in the bright world, who'll be the owners of the
dark one? . . . Am I putting you to sleep?"

"I'm getting there."

"All right, I'll shut up. But when I think of the sun going out, I know
it'll be ages from now unless some unthinkable cosmic disaster is about to
happen. Otherwise, it's nothing as involved as Owen's sternman, so it's
pretty restful."

Nils began one-handedly kneading her shoulder and the back of her
neck. "I *was* feeling bad about the strawberries," she murmured, "and I
don't like to think about you and me being extinct. Maybe our descen-
dants will evolve into seals. I wish I could stick around for *that*."

Nils's breathing changed. Pip had long ago given up, but his tail
flicked as if he were dreaming. From the outer shores the unbroken sound
of the sea came through the woods; it was too even now for a listener to
be able to distinguish the difference in the everlasting voices of those
ledges, this cove, that point. But the noise would never be silent, even
though it might fade to a whisper at times; all day, all night, the waters
poured over the rocks, the tides crept whispering up the beaches or came
charging in. So it had been since the islands were born, and so it would
go on, even if the sun did go out. Or would it? How about the moon?

She awoke suddenly at first light; a squawking of enraged blue jays
below the window announced that Pip was on his morning rounds. The
scent of percolator coffee reminded her, but only briefly, that Laurie would
not have wakened to that perfume this morning; and she also wondered
for an instant or two where Emlyn was. But she had put that aside last
night and expected to leave it there except for idle conjecture in an idle
moment. She could hear *White Lady* coming up Long Cove to pick up
Willy; the sound of each engine was as distinctive as the sound of each
island voice.

Downstairs Nils was drinking coffee and eating a doughnut and listening to the Coast Guard weather report. The hurricane was stalled off
Virginia, and the South was having torrential rains. It looked as if the ball
game would have fine weather tomorrow, but after Saturday night, who
knew? The experts could only report the possibilities. But many of the
children attending mainland schools, coming out tomorrow, would be

hoping it would strike before they could start back after the weekend. Richard and Sam would, certainly.

She took a mug of coffee and a buttered heel of homemade bread to the window and watched the harbor activity and the busy gulls, tinted by the apricot light. *White Lady* came in; Willy would be waiting on the lobster car with his dinner box, as radiantly expectant as any of the children could have been. Rob Dinsmore was leaving the Binnacle, and next door Myles left the house, whistling as usual. Maybe he was whistling away his anxieties, she though charitably.

"You want to go with me today?" Nils asked unexpectedly behind her.

"*Yes!*" Not a moment's thought for anything she should do today, like the girls' letters, and picking the tomatoes before either the frost or the tempest got them. She laid a hand on his forehead. "*Cool.* Did you really invite me? Any conditions, like a vow of silence the minute I step aboard?"

"Not yet," he said dryly. "But there might be if you stand there talking about it, instead of getting squared away. So look sharp."

"*Yessir.* Go ahead, I'll be there by the time you get the bait aboard." He left, taking the gallon jug of fresh water.

She set some eggs on to boil hard, and buttered some bread. Added a half-dozen apples to the canvas tote bag. She made a double lunch of thick-sliced corned beef sandwiches, with tomatoes and cucumbers on the side. There were the hearty raisin-studded hermits for mug-ups, and a quart thermos bottle of coffee.

Pip wasn't around when she let the chickens out. Young Dog Tray was baying after Rob, as if he'd just been marooned on a desert island. Rob, rowing out to his boat, shouted, "Stop that noise, you chowderhead!" The dog drooped like a dying plant, then heard Joanna's step and revived. All flapping tongue and ears, he rushed to escort her out onto the Sorensen wharf, where he stood raptly watching the transfer of food from Joanna's hand to Nils's; watching while Nils stowed the tote bag in the cabin, as if making a note of it in case he should ever be alone in that area.

"Now, Tray, my love," Joanna said, "*Go home.*" Fortunately this was reinforced by Tammie's vigorous two-fingered whistle from the Binnacle.

Jamie was leaving the harbor. *White Lady* had gone. The waves of departing boats caused miniature surf all around the harbor and left skiffs rocking and bouncing at the moorings. The gulls always seemed excited at these times, circling and crying, but when the chorus had begun to fade melodiously into the distance, and Mark went up the hill for another breakfast, the gulls began to settle again. A comparative quiet would lie over the island until it was time for school, and that week's bell ringer went in to pull on the rope. Ringing the bell was more for symbolism than necessity—it was the bell that had hung in the belfry of the first school-house. Every student had a week at it, several weeks in a year as the time rolled around again. The small children aspired to it. It was at once a privilege and duty, as was raising and taking down the flag. They were both significant rites of passage.

10

Nils was famous for not wanting anyone aboard the boat with him. He kept his radio on as part of the responsibility they all shared; a man never knew when he might be called upon. But when everyone was talking, he would turn his radio off. "You'd think they all lived on separate ledges and never got a chance to communicate with another human being except out here."

This was such a day. Only John Haker, who had left while it was still dark and was trawling outside the Rock, was conspicuously silent. It was said that when the two brothers were working, John always kept silent, because Charlie might really hit him this time.

"Jamie's getting as bad as the rest of them," Nils said now, not annoyed but bemused; Jamie and Matt were exchanging stories about what Sara Jo and Peter had said this morning. Joanna laughed. "I don't suppose *you* ever bragged like that about your kids."

"I didn't need to," he said. "Everybody could see how superior they were."

Ralph Percy began, "Puts me in mind of what Harry said one time, right out of a clear sky—" Nils turned him off.

"They don't need us for an audience. The whole bay is out there waiting to hear what Harry said."

"Oh gosh," said Joanna. "Now *we'll* never know unless we ask."

They ran quite a while before the first buoy; the men were gradually moving their gear out away from the island, on longer warps, for the winter.

The boats were scattered on the pastel sea like cattle spread far and wide on blue pastures. Joanna always looked at everything as if she'd never seen it before; she was always fascinated by the way the familiar ledges kept changing shapes and colors, depending on any deviations in the boat's course. Only the Rock remained the same, seen from any direction, having no woods or meadows to clothe it. A great fortress of rock dominated by two towers, that was it, and before the towers it had been the Rock alone, immutable, everlasting. Known to the first Americans, and discovered by the first great ocean explorers, it had had many names, but the Rock it would always be, like the Rock of Ages; the Rock was the image that rose before most island children's eyes when they sang the hymn.

To Joanna as a small child it had been an ancient and dreadful castle with a prisoner left alone in a barred room at the top of the old tower. His rations were brought to him by a silent man who came from somewhere every night to light the beacon. Imagining where the provider came from and *how*, and what crime the prisoner could have possibly committed, was endless entertainment when you were a child and didn't know about really terrible things; and every so often you could make up a thriller about the Bennett children and their friends going out to rescue him because he was really a nice person.

Later she knew it for the family light it was, with three keepers and their wives and children; they had their own teacher when so many of the children were too small to be boarded away from home. The girl who would become Donna Bennett was the teacher. When Stephen Bennett was a young man he had vigorously courted this tall fair-haired girl, and after they were married she taught in the Bennett's Island school for a while. As the family grew they went out to the Rock on fine summer Sundays several times a year, taking a picnic. Joanna had long since given up the prisoner; now she thought she would have given up everything (almost) to be a lighthouse child. This always lasted until they came home to Pickie, the cats, even the cows; Goose Cove and the woods; and the night music of surf on Homestead Point. The lighthouse children liked to visit Bennett's Island and stay overnight, but they always seemed to be as happy to go home as she'd been. She had gone to high school with a few of them, but they were all scattered now. She exchanged cards with some of them. The Coast Guard manned the light these days, with the company of the vast arctic tern colony and the puffins, which had always been protected as long as Joanna's father could remember.

Most of those childhood friends were close to the water somewhere, if not on it, but one girl had married and settled on a ranch in Oklahoma. Joanna used to wonder if she ever dreamed she was sleeping in her room at the Rock, with the foghorn going; they were so used to it for days in a fog mull that if it stopped in the night, they woke up. Did she dream of such wakings now and of the perpetual voice of many waters that never whispered, because the Rock was always under siege? It was as if the sea had been trying to wear it down for millennia, not mere centuries.

While *Joanna S.* was heading out, Joanna covered her front down to her boots with a barvel, a long oilskin apron tied snugly around her waist. She had enough spare cotton work gloves for several changes if her hands got too cold when a pair soaked through. Nils gaffed his first buoy, hooked it onto the hydraulic pot hauler, and it came out of the water onto the washboard as if leaping aboard by itself. Joanna went to work as a sternman; Nils kept the boat gently circling to where he would set the trap again. It was half full of lobsters, most of them keepers.

At midday, they ate their lunch, anchored to another trap. They now had half a crate of lobsters, and their silence was satisfactory to them. There was only the light pleasant slap of water against the sides, accompanied by the harmonizing hum of engines both near and far, the comments of the gulls either in passing or circling close to the boat in hopes of treats like old bait from shaken bait bags. It was one of the pretty blue days Nils had described, when winter was a dream, and so was the hurricane now ravaging the southern coast. It was a time to imagine a square-rigger under a full load of canvas, coming up over the southwestern horizon. Nils sat on the washboard smoking his pipe and contemplating the sea as peacefully as if he were alone, and Joanna considered this a compliment to her. She was no Jonah, though the boys used to make puns on her name. At the end of the day they had a good haul aboard, and she had been efficient to the last trap, handling that one properly, too.

They cleaned up the boat on the way home. Someone once remarked that Nils probably picked herring scales off his boat with tweezers; he wasn't that much of a perfectionist, but he was energetic with a broom and buckets of seawater. Joanna shook out the rest of the used bait bags, loving the descending cloud of beating wings that sometimes came close enough to fan her face. She delighted in the excited—and exciting—cries. One bird rode with them all the way in—Hank? (for Prince Henry the Navigator). He took off over the fishhouses, receiving either salutations or challenges; gulls were never uncommunicative.

There were three boats at the car, and Nils tied up outside Steve's. Joanna could have gone onto the wharf and walked home, but she was in no hurry to end the day. She sat on the stern, placidly tired, listening to the easy voices of the men and watching Young Mark in his long-legged rubber boots, dodging elbows and full crates on the car. He came over *Robin B.* and into Nils's cockpit, his dark face bright.

"Hey, Aunt Jo, we got our T-shirts and caps today! Boy, are they some *flashy!* I'd show you mine, but George says to keep 'em clean for tomorrow." It wasn't often that Young Mark was in full spate; he was usually more like his mother than the Bennetts, so she just nodded to keep him going. "Kate and Aunt Lisa gave them out. George's says COACH so big you could see it from an airplane. If he was lying down," he added. "Aunt Philippa put her cap right on, and it looked real good on her; Sara Jo and Peter were specially invited this afternoon, and *they* got caps and shirts, too." He began to laugh. "Peter was so solemn, he kept looking down at himself and patting his front as if he could hardly believe it. Wow! Sara Jo was so excited, and was she *funny!* It was the cap she was so crazy about; she kept trying it every which way. I'll bet nobody'll get the shirts off those two till they go to bed, and Sara Jo'll want to wear her cap." Suddenly he remembered his manners. "Did you have a good day?"

"Finest kind," she said. "I'd call it close to perfect."

"It's a long time to next summer," Young Mark said with a sigh. "But by then I'll have more traps to set, so it evens up. And maybe," he dropped his voice and looked around, "an outboard. Dad still thinks I ought to get everywhere by oars first. But I know just about everything along the west side already. Either seen it or bumped into it or got stuck on it." He was not bragging, just self-assured. Juvenile lobstermen's gear was restricted to the west side and Long Cove. Sam and Richard had moved out around Sou'west Point for the first time when they set their traps at the close of school last June.

"Well, I'd better get to work," Young Mark said. He climbed over Steve's boat again, in time to seize one end of an empty crate and help swing it onto Myles's *Sweet Alice.*

"Coming to the game tomorrow?" he asked casually of no one in particular.

"Of course we are," Nils said. "You think we're unpatriotic?"

"We'd get up a drum-and-bugle corps if we had time," said Steve on his way up the ladder. "But Robin can bring her kazoo."

"I'm terrific on the spoons," Myles said.

"Gorry, you fellers make me feel untalented," Sky Campion said. "I can play the comb. Anybody else here do that?"

"Just what we've been waiting for," Mark said. "A comb virtuoso. Your wife being a hairdresser must give you a good choice of instruments."

Young Mark lengthened his upper lip, trying not to indulge adult humor by even a smile. "So long, Aunt Jo," he said sternly to her, and went up the ladder fast and passed Steve. They could hear his boots clumping as he ran through the shed.

Mark gave Myles his slip and his money, and Myles, who still couldn't keep from showing his pleasure at how well he was doing after his disastrous year ashore, said, "This calls for some reckless celebrating, and I hate to drink alone."

"It's my Christian duty to save you from that," Sky said solemnly. He went up the ladder behind Myles.

"If he can joke about it, that's healthy, isn't it?" Joanna asked, watching them disappear into the shed.

"Oh, he let go of that tiger's tail quite a while ago," Mark said. "Can't say the same about Myles, poor bastard. His tiger's not rum, it's what he lives with. Damn shame. Good boys, both of them, willing as hell. Shows you what a difference the right woman can make."

"Maybe Myles Harmon the husband isn't the same as Myles Harmon the good feller," Joanna suggested perversely. "After all, nobody's heard her side." There wasn't any way to argue that; Mark began writing another slip. Nils, who wouldn't have commented anyway, finished his pipe, emptied the ashes overboard, and began filling his gas tank.

She knew she didn't want to wait any longer to go ashore. She was growing uncomfortable, so she left the boat, saying, "I'll go home and start the coffee." At the head of the ladder, she met Steve back from the store.

"I heard some talk on the radio today about Emlyn taking off," he said. "It was one of the MacKenzie kids. He says he was in the store when Emlyn came in and left a note, then went off with a dragger that was heading Down East." He looked whimsically from one face to another. "Anybody going to tell me about it? I saw Owen by the Seal Rocks and it looked like Willy with him. I gave him a holler, but he must have been turned off."

"Yep, Emlyn's gone all right." Mark was sardonic. "And if he's headed Down East, that's more than the rest of us know. Too bad none of us was on deck to get the full glory of it all when Captain Ahab got home and found Moby Dick out of reach forever."

"I didn't know it until I heard the same talk on my radio," Myles said. "I suppose my kids are full of it by now."

"Well, I saw him leaving, only I didn't *know* he was leaving," Joanna said. "I didn't have any premonitions, and if Maggie saw it in her tea leaves, I haven't heard yet. I'm going home."

"He's trying to get Willy away from Mark," Nils said. "For the winter. Pull Devil, pull Baker." Mark, scribbling on his pad, grunted something.

"Would you care to repeat that?" Steve asked.

"*No*," Mark said.

Joanna went quickly through the shed, with more imperative reasons than before to get home fast. More boats were coming in, but on shore there was one of those odd, short intervals of quiet when the children all seemed to be busy elsewhere, and no women were out; it could all change when the men began coming ashore.

She was safely past the Binnacle, with Dog Tray yearning at her from the end of his run, and she was just thinking *I made it!* when Ross and Amy burst out at her from the ambush of Philip's backyard. Dog Tray threw back his head in a howl; the two leaped around her in a war dance, chanting, "We're the Racketash Raiders and tomorrow you'll be dead!" They were wearing the shirts and caps designed and given by Ellen. Amy stopped long enough to explain, "We don't mean *you*, Aunt Jo. We're going to kill *Brigport*."

"Blood will run!" Ross slashed a finger across his throat, and the dance went on. Lisa came out the back door, and Joanna put her hands to her mouth and shouted, "Team spirit! I'm happy for them!" Happier when I can get to the bathroom, she thought. The children went home with her, slapping their hands against their mouths, ululating and dancing all the way. The shirt was a brilliant yellow with a heavy black outline of the island across the front, and the word "Racketash" in blood-red. The back showed an Indian profile in black, with one scarlet feather standing up at the back of the head, a red tomahawk horizontal underneath, and above the head the scarlet word "Raider." The cap had the two words together above the visor, red again on that eye-scalding yellow.

Pip came around the corner of the house, took a look, and ran back. The children were winding down; she held each sweaty small face in her hands and kissed it. Ross didn't resist, and Amy put her arms around

Joanna's neck. "Save some breath so you can cheer like mad tomorrow," she told them. They ran silently, and she went into the house to the bathroom, Pip talking behind her.

Washed up, her clothes changed, Pip eating, and their own supper started, she was still thinking about Ross and Amy, a happy escape from the family next door. Out of sight, out of mind; when she'd been aboard the boat, the Harmons barely existed. Now the house was in sight, and her recent impression of Myles was that he hated to go home. Would Nan ever let her daughters wear such clothes? Probably not. But why waste time even idly thinking about it, when Ross and Amy made her smile?

Their pride in their outfits, and their team name shouted like a war cry, labeled them as islanders at last. It was not a matter of the island's accepting *them*—it was their final acceptance of the island. By the time they had first come, when Ross was Ramon, and Amy was Lourdes, they had managed to run away from every home in which they had been placed, no matter how loving and understanding the foster parents had been. It was not to escape to their own home; they'd had no home since they watched their father shoot their mother in the head and then kill himself. They were like little creatures with a blind compulsion to return to the place where they had been spawned. Wherever that was.

Sending them to Philip and Lisa on Bennett's Island, twenty-five miles out to sea and in another state, had been an act of desperation on the part of the agency for which Lisa's sister worked. Sam was already there, starting out as a foster child and becoming a son in every way but the biological one. Even if Lisa and Philip were heading toward grandparents' age, they had good health, good nerves, and a sense of humor. There was an extended family to provide uncles, aunts, and cousins, and there was Sam, the big brother.

But the two orphans were valiant in their fight. Attempts to stow away on the mailboat didn't work; neither did telling visitors that they'd been kidnapped. No one ever left a skiff handy that they could hijack, and even their courage didn't wipe out all common sense; they'd have to learn how to row first, and that was a slow business when the grown-ups kept the skiff on a long line so they could haul you back in. On a school picnic to Sou'west Point the two tied a sneaked-out dish towel to a stunted, solitary spruce to identify them as castaways, knowing that they'd have to get off by themselves and look sad and lonely. But someone always had an eye on them, and the older children were used to looking after the younger ones.

Ramon and Lourdes fooled Tammie Dinsmore, though, when she took them one day to sail toy boats in a big tide pool at the edge of the harbor. They told her they both needed to go to the bathroom and ran back to the house, which was in full view of the pool. Tammie saw them go in; Lisa was at the Circle that day.

When they didn't come back, Tammie went looking for them. They had gone through the house and out the back door. They weren't playing out behind the Sorensen barn or out in the meadow or down at Goose Cove. Meanwhile Dog Tray was having hysterics, and Maggie insisted he was trying to tell them something. Released, he led them up around the clubhouse and out to Barque Cove. Philip restrained him before he could go down to the children, and the surf on the rocks drowned out his frustrated noises. They were building a raft of driftwood, using two of Philip's hammers and an inordinate amount of nails, including spikes. Unnoticed, Philip watched for a while from above, until a badly banged finger made Lourdes give up in tears; Ramon was getting desperate enough to cry himself, and a brisk surf was creeping up on them. Then Philip let Dog Tray rush down to assure them of his love, wash their faces and ears, and have his neck cried into by Lourdes.

Philip followed him down. They were so defeated, he had wanted to take them into his arms, he said afterward. Instead he told them that if they'd managed to launch the raft, they would have been drowned very quickly in the surf.

He would take them ashore tomorrow in his own boat, and maybe the authorities would find them a place they liked better. Whether it was the certainty of drowning, or the word "authorities" that convinced them—it was a case of "the devil you know," and a kindly one. They trudged back to the harbor with Dog Tray cavorting around them and Philip walking behind; alone, they returned the hammers and the cans of remaining nails to the place in his fishhouse from which they'd spirited them. No more was said. They were bright children; it had come to them at last that their home wasn't in the great amorphous *There,* but it could be *here.*

Now they wanted to change their names, and Lisa told them they could have as many names as they wanted, but she said that they'd better not discard what they had even if they never used them. One day when they were grown up they might want to remember what they were named when they were born. But they wanted brand-new first names when they were officially adopted.

They were taken up to the Homestead and left alone to study the albums, helped by Aunt Mateel's frequent treats. After several visits Ramon chose a Civil War soldier named Ross Bennett, one of those brave children who ran away to enlist before their voices changed and who had their pictures taken in too-big uniforms, looking scared and defiant over their rifles. Ross had survived, gone out West, and struck it rich. That didn't impress Ramon; it was the boy soldier he admired. "Amy" was a pretty little girl perched on a big boulder in her Sunday dress and best pinafore, holding a kitten. She had black curls and a dimple in one cheek.

"That will make everyone know we're related," Lourdes said, "because I have curly hair and a dimple too."

There was no need to tell her that this Amy hadn't lived until her ninth birthday. Her grave was not on Bennett's Island for the new Amy to discover one day.

11

On Saturday morning, along with the mail and freight, the mailboat delivered an uproarious crowd of high-school students as well as Holly Bennett from the University of Maine at Orono, with her roommate. Apparently the youngsters had raised Cain with the Brigport students all the way out, and now were hoarse but exhilarated. Mothers and siblings were the greeters at the wharf, except Laurie, who was out again with Owen. Tomorrow Richard would go in her place. Both Richard and Sam were brilliant-eyed about working on Sunday aboard their fathers' boats. Parents on both islands had united to hire Duke to make a special trip out in the mailboat to take the students back to Limerock Monday afternoon.

It was a day for poetry about October's bright blue weather, and behind the Sorensen barn the asters by the brookside did indeed make asters in the brook. It was a day for baseball, never mind Hurricane Frank idling his way up the coast, making mischief as he came. The swells were deeper, but the air was still, with only the murmurous rote like the sound of silence in one's head. It could change at any time, perhaps at the next shift of the tide, but a certain quality in the air and in the occasion produced euphoria.

"We just want a chance to go to Brigport and yell 'Yay, Racketash! Down with Brigport!' all afternoon," Holly Bennett said. "Once we get that game over, old Frank can come down like the Wolf on the Fold!" She seized and squeezed Young Mark. "You've grown a foot since Labor Day."

"Another hand would be more useful," he said, straight-faced.

"Every one of them is hoping Frank will strike while they're here," Lisa said to Philippa, watching Sam hoist a giggling child under each arm.

"Look at those three. I'm not sure but what Sam will be glad to get back to school after a few days of all this attention."

The only person who didn't go to Brigport on Saturday afternoon was Nan Harmon. The rest divided themselves into six boats; Brigport was already a crowded harbor. Myles and the girls traveled with Rosa and Jamie, and Nils and Joanna, aboard *Valkyrie;* Shannon was with the rest of the team and George in Sky Campion's boat. All the dogs had been left in the houses, or secured on their runs, so they couldn't rush to the wharves and mourn their families. "And go gallivanting," Maggie said. "Raise hell is more like it," Rob said.

What would Nan do, having the island all to herself? Joanna wondered. Take the first decent long walk she'd had since they'd arrived? Or huddle inside her house in horror of the great echoing outdoors? Agoraphobia? Were occasional walks to the store or out to the well the only ventures she dared to make?

Out on these blue waters with the easy swells, enjoying the sight of the other boats spread out across Brigport Roads (the nautical name of the stretch between the two islands), she could only be sorry for Nan this afternoon, for being a prisoner when everyone else was out on sky blue waters, under the wondrous patterns of clouds like wisps of down and small curly white feathers. The boats were white, pale blue, dark blue, and green like dark spruce trees, and also dark red. Jamie's, of course, was conservatively white; Rosa was always threatening to paint *Sea Star* hot pink or lilac. Sara Jo in her life jacket was on the stern to see the boats and name them all; she waved and shouted even if nobody heard her, with Rosa hanging onto her. She was wearing her new cap and, under her sweater and overalls, the yellow T-shirt.

All the children, plus George and Philippa, wore their new outfits, and the homecomers had been included. Cluny wore hers, while maintaining her aura of detachment, and her hair was still done up on her neck. She'd wanted to ride up on the bow, the favored spot, but Jamie wouldn't allow it, no matter if some other boats had bow riders. They were all older than she, and used to it. He took no chances aboard *Valkyrie.*

She hoisted herself onto the washboard as far forward as possible, just behind the men standing around the wheel. There wasn't too much width to the washboard, but she arranged herself in an artistic manner that suggested tights and a leotard rather than blue jeans and a gaudy T-shirt. But her being allowed to dress like this and leave the island, if only for Brigport, meant that she knew how to manage her mother. An engrossing possibility was that they had all managed Nan today, and she had been left defeated and weeping.

Tracy Lynn and Sara Jo were now sitting on boat cushions at the women's feet, playing patty-cake. During a placid conversation about the beauty of the day and the wrath to come, the two women watched Cluny without appearing to. As soon as they were well out of the harbor, she had begun to unpin her hair. The pins were slipped into her pocket; a comb was taken out of the other. She took off her cap and began to comb her hair with long slow strokes until it lay fluffy on her shoulders. It was light brown, and the breeze fingered it and blew it back from her ears. It caught the sun like fine silk threads.

As they entered Brigport Harbor, the little girls got up to see; the ball team went past them, everyone shouting. "I don't know how they'll have the strength to play by now," Rosa said.

"Well, they can always blind the opposition with the sun bouncing off those shirts," Joanna said.

Cluny was shaking her clasped hands over her head; by the time she was walking up the wharf with Tammie Dinsmore and Dorrie Campion, Tracy Lynn bounding ahead, the metamorphosis was complete.

The Racketash Raiders won, with Brigport close enough for an honorable defeat. There were some sulks and scowls, but by a courageous effort—and with a few quiet words from their coach-teacher—the team became remarkably gracious, and the Raiders were not obnoxiously triumphant. They did mob George, girls and all, until he nearly disappeared. The Brigport coach shook hands with him and congratulated him. She was a good-looking young woman, and his meager face, already flushed, grew fiery. She and Philippa walked down the road together, into shoptalk before they reached the store.

There was free ice cream for the players and a great deal of treating among the rest. With all of Bennett's and most of Brigport at the store, it looked like the last time the Governor had visited, someone said—except that with all these kids whooping and hollering together, not even the President could have heard his own voice. Adult friends visited in quiet places, exchanging promises to meet again before winter.

No one heard the telephone ring in the back room until Tom Robey went out there for more cold soda. When he came back, he gaveled the counter with a can of baked beans.

"May I have your attention, please?" He was always moderator at town meetings, for the strength of his voice and his use of it in keeping order. Now the Brigporters fell silent out of habit, the Bennett's Islanders out of politeness.

"Duke just called," he said. "He figured you folks from the South Island would still be here." He grinned: being called a South Islander used to be grounds for battle. "He says on account of the latest advisories, he's coming out tomorrow morning. Be out around nine. He won't cut it any finer than that. Looks as if we're getting Frank after all. Or at least he's going to take a swipe at us by Monday morning. No telling what we'll get until it's here."

In the silence before the groans and protests could begin, he said, "God, I never shut down a meeting *that* completely before."

Suddenly infected with a sense of urgency, almost everyone began moving toward the door. Outside, and down the hill toward the wharves, conversations went on, stories were continued and finished. The two ball teams made a compact boisterous group, their excitement replenished by the weather news. At least *they* didn't have to cross the bay and miss out on the excitement at home. The older students growled about the timing, which cost them a whole day of their weekend. They had long since learned that fussing about the weather might let off steam, but otherwise it didn't make the slightest bit of difference. The sea was the captain, and the wind went arm in arm with it. You could only wait, and there was no sense in praying that God would save your father's gear or wharf. But, there was no harm in thanking him afterward for damage not done, just in case. "You'd think He'd have *some* control over His own creations!" Jamie at twelve had once said in disgust. "If He *did* make it."

Joanna had heard the grousing all her life; she had gone through it herself. So far no one was a declared atheist. The weather was in a class of its own, answerable to no power on Earth or in Heaven.

She was walking alone, the family all in sight but scattered. Behind her Holly was saying, "I hate losing a day. Maybe it'll come really fast, tonight, so no boat. Then you'll see something *wonderful*."

From her friend's silence it didn't seem that she could hardly wait for this experience.

"Well, *Gosh!*" said Holly. "On the mainland you'd get live power lines down, and big trees crashing across cars and houses, and flash floods, no lights, no water. We don't have that good stuff happen out here. We just go along the way we always do. Of course, nobody wants a hurricane, because of the boats and traps," she went on, "but at least on the island you get the full power and glory of the sea!"

She was pleased with this. "Besides," she added, "the bay wouldn't be fit to cross for a few days after that, maybe a week. Think of all the work we could get done. Good thing we brought something with us."

Aboard *Valkyrie* Sara Jo was sodden with tiredness but made a token fuss when Rosa settled her on a locker in the cabin. "I'll lie down with her so she won't roll off," Tracy Lynn said importantly. They were both asleep by the time the boat was out of the harbor. Rosa and Joanna observed unobtrusively Cluny's change from Cinderella (somewhat) back to the aloof girl who had boarded the boat a few hours earlier. One aspect remained, to prove that it had really happened; when she was halfway up Nils's ladder, following her father, she turned and smiled, and was transfigured for that instant, as if in memory of a time of pure, untarnished, thirteen-year-old happiness. "Thank you, Jamie and Rosa. I loved the ride. And it was nice to be with *you,* Mr. and Mrs. Sorensen." This was directed at Nils and Joanna, who answered in kind. Tracy Lynn tossed her thank-you from the wharf and then scampered off; the senior Dinsmores had gotten back, and Young Dog Tray was out. Myles said, "Much obliged, Jamie."

"Any time, Myles. I'm glad our kids won." He ducked into the cabin to bring out Sara Jo, who nestled into Rosa's arms, hid her face, and refused to speak to anyone, including her grandparents.

Joanna stepped from a crate to the washboard and thence to the nearest rung of the ladder. "Guess we won't be over to supper tonight, Jo," Rosa said. "She's not going to be fit to live with until she gets fed and put to bed."

"I remember." Joanna nodded at Jamie, who missed it, because he was discussing with Nils some particular traps they would each be shifting tomorrow; they decided to go together. Joanna stood on the wharf, looking around with familiar pleasure at the harbor. The ball team was unloading over at Sky Campion's wharf; they were reluctant to give up the day and its almost unbearable delights. They seemed to think that if they were quiet for an instant, it would all blow away like flung spray.

Rosa came up the ladder. Jamie climbed it one-handed with a sleeping child draped over his shoulder, a common skill for island men, but always good for some tense moments.

Up by the Binnacle, Myles was smoking and watching Tracy Lynn play with Dog Tray; Cluny stood beside her father, looking up steadily to where gulls rode the wind currents in an unceasing flight pattern. Shannon came past Philip's house with the Percy boys and the Dinsmore girls, each still trying to be heard above the others. Shannon shut up abruptly. Without speaking, he joined his father. The other four greeted Myles as Mr. Harmon and called "So long! See you!" after Shannon, who didn't look back. Tracy Lynn left the dog, which now flung himself at the girls, and took her father's hand. Shannon, looking older than his age, walked with Cluny behind the other two. It was a curious little happening.

"No running inside to say, 'We won!' " Joanna said. "Everybody waiting to go in together. It gets curiouser and curiouser." They had all disappeared before Nils and Joanna passed the house, and she said, "I wonder what they met when they went in?"

"An empty water pail at the end of a woman's arm," said Nils. Myles was already coming out with the pail, and he grinned at them. "Wonderful afternoon, wasn't it?"

At the sound of their voices, Pip rushed around the corner of the house with his tail crooked sidewise; he fastened onto Nils's leg and began to climb the rigging.

"At least she hasn't hanged herself yet," Joanna said as they went into the house.

"Did you expect that?"

Together they unhooked Pip. "Not really, but she's such an odd specimen. . . . I just thought of something. She could have gone around and investigated every house on the island except where a dog wouldn't let her in. If she goes ashore on the mailboat tomorrow morning, we'll know she's loaded with loot."

12

Sunday morning the sky was smurry and the air was mild. There was no wind. Public beaches had been closed up into the Gulf of Maine because of the great seas apparently rising out of nowhere. Surfers who defied the restrictions wished they hadn't; a few didn't live to swear they'd never again take such a chance. In Massachusetts two children dancing at the surf and daring it to touch them were swept off their feet by a surprise wave and carried out before anyone knew they had been there, except someone who had seen them from a distance, with binoculars. They disappeared while he ran for the telephone.

Around Bennett's Island the water offshore looked pleasantly ripply, with barely a whitecap; it was along the rocks that the impression of indolent power slowly rousing itself was as palpable as a chill sending cat's-paws of gooseflesh along bare skin.

The men would go out to finish what they'd left undone yesterday by coming in early for the game. Deep swells were fairly common in some spots, even without a hurricane on the way, but when your boat seemed to drop suddenly into a bottomless hole—and the trap you'd been about to haul aboard was now higher than your head—it was time to come in.

Two men together could finish hauling and baiting most of the remaining traps before that time came, and then there'd be no more hauling until the storm was well past, leaving, it was hoped, something to haul. Wire traps weren't supposed to move much—an advantage over wooden traps—but "never" was not an irrevocable condition in any marine business. Under desperate circumstances wire traps could be rolled around and battered against ledges, or actually be crushed by the tremendous forces in the depths.

Nils and Jamie went out about half-past five, when it was still dark. Joanna had a second cup of coffee by the living room windows, watching the moving red and green lights, and the white glare of an occasional spotlight illuminating the breakwater or Eastern Harbor Point as the boats moved slowly out. The breakwater beacon seemed insignificant in contrast, but alone it was a steady gleam in the dark—shutting itself off at full daylight, turning itself on at dusk.

The men would come home tired, disgusted, or philosophical, according to their temperaments. Most would be satisfied that they had done all they could for the time being. In the harbor the ground lines and the mooring pennants could not be more secure. Ashore, anything movable had been stowed back behind the fishhouses. No one would show nerves; it wasn't their way. Prepared for the worst and hoping for the best, they were laconic about it, at least in public if not in their thoughts. Most of the children were exhilarated.

Pip sat on the windowsill beside Joanna's cup, and occasionally leaned over to rub his cheek against hers. "I don't think Maggie can tell from her tea leaves just what it's going to do," she said. "A good thing. Let's start the chowder." A dressed catfish, or wolf fish, had been in the freezer since Nils found it in a trap, eating young lobsters.

Joanna had been cleaning fish, beginning with harbor pollock, from the time she was first trusted with a knife, but cleaning a catfish had never become one of her top accomplishments.

"I don't think God intended for human beings to eat catfish," she said to her father when she was about twelve, handing over her mangled first attempt for him to finish. He remarked that it looked as if Pickie and some friends had been playing with it. But the fine white meat, fried, poached, or in a chowder, made the struggle all worthwhile, as long as someone else did the hard work.

Clarice Hall whistled outside Eastern Harbor Point a little before nine, and by half-past the hour she was on her way back to Limerock, heading past the end of Brigport, straight for the mainland, a wavy line drawn with a soft black pencil on rough gray paper randomly flecked with chalk whitecaps. Duke had stopped at Brigport on the way out and picked up those passengers. Any adult who decided to take advantage of the extra trip would soon regret it; the boat was noisy with adolescent

good fellowship and high spirits. Add the electric influence of the approaching storm, and the only refuge would be in the pilothouse with
Duke. His authority, and that of the engineer and deckhand, could keep
the young pretty well in place. ("For Chrissakes, will you light somewhere
and stay *put?*") After all, as island children, they were supposed to know
how to behave aboard a boat and not disgrace their parents by falling
overboard.

Back on the island the remaining youngsters burst into sight by the
Binnacle, a giddy little flock tagging, running, tripping each other up,
and getting tangled in Dog Tray's line. Finally, somebody unhooked him,
and he joined the two Campion dogs, a stocky little untiring terrier and
a long-legged mixed setter. They contributed their own hysteria, nipping
and barking. Joanna was out looking at her asparagus bed, thinking lust-
fully of all the rockweed she would have available on the harbor shore
after the storm. Pip prudently took to the nearest tree, where he could
still get a good view. Young Mark stood on the big boulder by the Binnacle's back door, like a rooster on a henhouse roof. Hands on his hips,
he contemplated the turmoil below. The big setter knocked little Dennis
Campion off his feet; Tammie Dinsmore hoisted him back up and, with
a whoop, aimed the dog at Young Mark, who leaped off his perch yelling
"Geronimo!"

Everyone was the Tagger and the Tagged, and Joanna knew exactly
what it was like. She could even feel the twitching and tingling in her leg
muscles and a bounce in her feet, as if she could spring suddenly into the
vortex, uttering war cries as she tagged one after the other. "I could amaze
those kids right off their feet," she said to Pip, who was too entranced to
give her a look. She wondered if the Harmon children were watching from
inside. They couldn't escape the noise; on Saturday they'd shared in the
glory of victory, and now they'd probably be angrily envious and resentful.
Obviously they had not been allowed to see the boat off. This isolation
was brutally hard after yesterday's blue-sky triumph. But Nan could de-
prive them of such pleasures, as she'd deprived Shannon of freedom
around the wharves, simply because she had authority over him and none
over her husband. She could excuse it all as a mother's anxiety about her
children in this threatening environment.

Oh, all right, Nils, Joanna thought. There's no harm in giving in to my
own mean thoughts now and then. I'm sure she has plenty of them about
all of *us*.

Laurie and Philippa came around the corner of the Binnacle, skirting the maelstrom of children and dogs. Maggie stood on the back doorstep, laughing and shaking her head. Lisa sat on her porch railing; Ross and Amy whizzed among the others in a fine fiery rapture of pure being.

Philippa and Laurie stopped to speak to Lisa, then came up past the Harmons', and Joanna met them at the gate.

"We didn't want to wait for the party to break up," said Philippa. " 'Touch hands and part with laughter'; crack heads and part with tears—and I like happy endings. We came up for a cup of coffee."

"I'm still dry from arguing," Laurie said, "until the moment Sam dragged Richard aboard the boat, and I *think* I pushed." Pip came across to them and she said, "Aren't you glad this one can't argue?"

"Well, he's pretty articulate, but we're bigger than he is. Besides, he can always be diverted by food."

When they had settled at the sun-parlor table with their full cups, and doughnuts warmed in the oven, Laurie said reverently, "Oh God, this coffee is wonderful, Jo, especially since my son is aboard the mailboat, and he can't argue with me any more today." She held up crossed fingers. "Unless he finds a way to come right back home. I'm glad they're not stopping at Brigport. . . . He sprang this on us last night: He can leave school until his father gets a new sternman ('Because you know, Mum, you can't do all that heavy stuff, and he can't have Willy all the time.')." She mimicked Richard exactly. "He can study at home, he could repeat the year, he earnestly swore that an extra year would make all the difference in his readiness for college. He had it all prepared, but Owen was great, too. He knows it's no good to argue too long before he lays down the law. So he was magnificently calm. But Richard couldn't leave well enough alone. He couldn't say, 'Will you just think about it?' and then shut up. No, he kept on. Well, I was going to end it, might as well do it first as last, but Owen took the wind out of our sails by saying very placidly that he was taking up for the winter, and he didn't know when he'd be setting out again, because he and I would likely be on a trip and might use up the whole spring."

She laughed. "I don't know how I looked, but I saw Richard's face. He was suddenly bereft of speech, you might say. He went out. I guess he ended up at the Homestead with the girls. We were in bed when they came back."

"And did you ask Owen if he really meant it?" Joanna asked.

"I didn't give him the satisfaction. He knows how I feel about winter fishing, and maybe this was his way of telling me he wouldn't go. But I'll be ready if he tries to back out of it. I'll accuse him of lying to his children as well as his wife."

"And he'll point out," said Joanna, "that he said 'likely,' not 'definitely.' He's an expert on that. As you should know. Anyone want to bet on this? He'll say he needs to go all winter to pay for the trip, on account of you poor folks living from hand to mouth all these years."

"On salt herring and potatoes," Philippa said.

"And salt cod for Christmas dinner," said Laurie. "Cape Cod Turkey. I'm starting to make notes of my ideas, and it won't be Florida. You fall over half of Maine there, and I hear the overflow is heading for Arizona." She looked very young and merry, scratching Pip's ears as he kept pushing his head into her hand. "It's Sunday, and Sunday plans never stand. So I'm not saying anything more. But he can't talk about money, because I'm the family bookkeeper."

"You said Richard was arguing with you until the last minute," Joanna said. "Did he start up again with you?"

"Oh, no! This is different. And if he thinks I'm going to break it to Father, he's badly out of his reckoning." She put the cat out of her lap, and took her cup to the kitchen. "Don't worry," she called back, "he doesn't want permission to enlist, and he doesn't have to get married." She came back and sat down. "Well, I'll tell you, seeing as we sisters-in-law have gotten along and been friends all these years because, for one thing, we can keep our mouths shut. But you can tell Nils and Steve if you want to, because they won't mention it to Owen."

"It was self-defense in our family," said Joanna, "to keep mute about our ideas until they were ripe. So say on."

"Well, Richard doesn't want to leave school for just a year. He wants to *quit*. Period. This boy who's been talking marine biology since he was twelve, and reading up on everything he could get on it, has now suddenly decided he's not college material. He knows—very sweetly earnest here—how much we want him to go ahead with it, but he'd be deceiving us if he didn't tell us while it's still so simple to back out. He was in great Bennett form. He even quoted at me, 'To thine own self be true.' " She nodded at them. "Of course I recognized myself there. I think I've quoted too much, and now I'm getting it back. Anyway, we can stay away as long as we want, have the trip of a lifetime because we deserve it, and he'll set out in the spring to get the spring crawl, and then he and his father can be partners. You can see how perfect it will be, can't you? No more hassle about sternmen, somebody always there you can trust not to walk out. Isn't that *great?* Those eyes! Talk about starry! Well, this was all between Hillside Farm and Mark's wharf." Her eyes were wet. "I don't know whether to laugh or cry. I'd been saying 'Yes, but—' and 'Wait till you've been accepted at whatever college, and then think it over—' while he kept insisting on its perfection."

She thirstily drank cooling coffee. "Once in sight of that blessed *Clarice,* I collected my wits. I said, 'When are you going to spring it on your father?' I thought that would make him say, 'Next time I'm home, or Thanksgiving.' Instead he jumped at it. 'If I stay home now we can get it all settled.'

" 'We might get something settled,' I told him, 'but you won't like it.' He skated over that, looking about ten. A wounded ten."

Philippa was slowly nodding. " 'Standing with reluctant feet,' " she said, " 'Where the brook and river meet.' I'm a quoter too. Occupational ailment of schoolteachers."

Laurie's face cleared, but not joyously. "Good Lord! *Cold feet?* Fear of competition, even failure, after all these years?"

"All at once, Laurie, the first step into adulthood is the last step out of childhood. Farewell to everything that's been your life until now."

"And you can't hold on to it. You can't go back," Joanna said.

"I was remembering my first week at Farmington," Laurie said. "It was exciting and I wasn't exactly homesick. But I kept reminding myself that I was eighteen, I was of age, and it was as if an iron door had slammed behind me. I got over it more and more, but—"

"But there was that sinking feeling when you know you have to start acting like a grown-up, and what's worse, *being* one," said Philippa.

13

As she stood at the door, watching her sisters-in-law go down the path, as empty of children and dogs now as if they had never been there, her curiosity about next door began to stir itself. She was determined to suppress it, if with *her* nature that was possible. But she'd have to pretend the Harmons weren't there, and the effort would only make them more intrusive. Better to decide as Nils advised, that what they did or didn't do was of no interest to her whatsoever. Of course it wasn't true, but it was sensible.

For lunch she made herself a large sandwich of sliced tomatoes and onions of her own raising. It was risky to eat while reading. She propped open her book against a couple of heavy volumes in the middle of the table. She was trying to finish it so she could start a new one on the actual day of the hurricane. Pip, who didn't care for tomatoes and onions, didn't bother to join her at the table.

Going to the kitchen with her dishes, she saw Young Mark headed away from the Binnacle toward Philip's. She guessed that he was carrying the word to parents that Duke had called as he entered Limerock Harbor. By now the school returnees were being collected by friends and relatives to finish out the holiday weekend. By tomorrow they would be enjoying the doubtful pleasures of a hurricane on the mainland: the possibilities of flash flooding taking out roads; trees coming down on power lines and smashing through roofs; frozen foods thawing; heaters not working; bathrooms out of use. By comparison the island would be an oasis of luxury.

"Rather you than me, kids," Joanna said cheerfully. She gave a quick thought to Richard; there was no sense in wondering which way that cat would jump, but he was too honorable a boy to try to make his parents wish they'd given in to him.

After finishing her lunch and her book, she wandered out back across the Homestead meadow and watched the seas rolling into Goose Cove and ashore as far away as Schooner Head. No urgent thundering surf yet; the sea was waiting for the signal to attack. Some ducks, too far away to identify, calmly rode the swells. Pip flattened his ears when a few drops of spray reached him, but instantly ran down to flick out whatever was left in the lacework of foam—a chip, a mussel shell, or a sprig of rockweed.

Coming back, she gave a last long look around the barn, the hen yard, and the garden to see if anything had been overlooked. Crickets sounded in the grass as if this drowsy quiet were forever. She walked along behind the spruce windbreak that had shielded Gunnar's field for so long from the north wind. None of the original trees were there, and many others had lived long lives in that line and died. Almost every year some elderly giant toppled, and not always in a hurricane. She laid her hand on several in a farewell gesture as she passed, knowing that at least one could be down by tomorrow night. Others came to the end of their lives deep in the woods, in calm weather, alone. To her it was always sad to find one down after all the years she had known it.

Pip scampered up one of the trees and called to her from above. "I see you," she answered and walked slowly back to the house, among pale lavender plumes of asters. The mild damp air was scented with spruce and fallen wild apples too bruised to save, and there was a sweet hay odor from the last time Jamie had widened the path with a scythe. The crickets chirped on. Scents and sounds melded into a breeze that seemed to blow from the past. It was as if those engine voices blown unevenly through the rote, and the capricious snatches of wind, belonged to a phantom fleet of the past, and the men who would come ashore at the end of the day could be those who were gone like the old spruces. Nothing like a good imagination, she thought. Maybe they *are* all there. Who really knows? But we'd certainly know if Gunnar was one of them.

Pip caught up with her, and she picked up a spruce-scented cat that was probably getting pitch in her hair. When Joanna came to the house, the Harmon children were just leaving their back doorstep, all dressed up for Sunday school.

Nan hadn't prohibited that—yet. It was held at the schoolhouse every

Sunday afternoon, and it was unlikely that Nan would ever volunteer to be one of the women who took it in turns.

Shannon made a running jump off the doorstep and landed a good distance from where he had taken off. Smiling, he buttoned his blue blazer and went down the path whistling, his hands in the pockets of his slacks. Tracy Lynn followed, wearing a pink plaid skirt and a pink sweater, white tights, and black Mary Janes. Her brown bangs were neatly trimmed, and she carried a small purse hooked over one arm.

"You look pretty, Tracy Lynn," Joanna called to her.

"Thank you, Mrs. Sorensen," she sang out, with a hint of a curtsy. Cluny, who had been standing back, now came forward. She was extremely straight and dignified. "Hello, Mrs. Sorensen," she said quietly.

"Hello, Cluny. You look like a model." She wore a pleated tartan skirt and a short green jacket with silver buttons. Her long straight hair shone like dark water on a dull day. She followed them down the path just as Maggie, on duty today, was leaving the Binnacle with her guitar case, while her husband restrained an anguished Dog Tray. Tammie had gone up to get Peter; Sara Jo was too young to sit still for a story. Tom J. joined them, and Young Mark was coming along the path from the store; Amy and Ross were heard leaving the house with their usual exuberance.

All the children enjoyed Sunday school; they liked to sing anything with a good swing to it, hymn or not. The girls loved to dress up, and if any boy enjoyed it he would not admit it, though it was noticeable that they walked differently when they wore their shore-going clothes. Young Ross strutted like a young bantam rooster in his new clothes. His Sunday necktie was sacred to that day because it had once been Sam's. He had never worn such nice things in his life, or had Sunday school either.

"A couple of hours a week won't kill ye," Ralph Percy said to his boys. "There's things anybody needs to know if he don't plan to grow up numb as a turd. And putting on your good duds is a mark of respect to the Lord."

Apart from singing, the sessions were centered on Bible stories and discussions; the students were split into two groups, with ten as the dividing age.

In the late afternoon, when the children were coming home again and the boats were beginning to come in from hauling, Laurie stopped at the Sorensens', looking very cheerful. "Don't put the teakettle on," she said. "I'm going home and start dinner, before all the men set foot on land. I just wanted to tell you I gave in and called Richard at Kristi's, not to mother-hen him, but to finish what I was trying to say when the boat left."

"Sure," said Joanna. "Perfectly natural. You wanted to see if he'd speak to you, right? I've been through the silent treatment, but I can't imagine it from Richard."

Laurie laughed. "He didn't have a chance, because I did all the talking. I had the store to myself for a few minutes. Mark was down on the wharf and Helmi went out, but I told her she didn't need to. Anyway, what my son and I argued about this morning is now referred to as 'Oh, *that*.' "

"Now why does it sound familiar to me?" said Joanna. "I've heard it a lot of times, that's for sure."

"Well, I didn't know if he was just about to discourage me from getting personal, but I scudded right along, told him he didn't have to answer, just listen, and then he could get back to his football game or whatever they were watching. I said he knew we really want him to go on. He's come so far, he really owes it to himself, and to *us*, not to discard it without a long hard look at it." She grinned. "Golly, did I talk fast! He'd take a breath, but he never got a word out. Anyway, I wanted a promise that he'll wait until he's finished one year of college—which gives us a safe two years—and after he's tried one of those summer jobs in marine biology that he's always talked about. *Then*, if he is absolutely sure that he wants to drop it, his father and I won't say a word." She held up crossed fingers. "Speaking for Owen is dangerous, but we've got those two years before it comes up. 'Have I your answer?' I asked. 'All right. Agreed,' he said. I was very calm. I said, 'Thank you. I love you.' And he said, 'Same here. See you, Mum,' and hung up. I could have said, 'Oh, *thank* you, *thank* you, my darling, for this—' "

"And he could have said, '*Oh, that,*' " said Joanna, and they both laughed. "He's probably as relieved about the long gap between now and then as you are."

"I feel as if I could take off and float all the way home. Let Frank roar; it'll be music to my ears!" Laurie leaned forward and kissed Joanna's cheek. "I don't think I've told you often enough how much you've meant to me over the years." She was blinking and grasping through her pockets. Joanna handed her a tissue. They hugged briefly but hard, and Laurie went merrily away.

14

Jamie, Rosa, and Sara Jo came down for fish chowder and went home early. The men were satisfied with the day's work. There'd been few lobsters crawling; they knew where to shelter, deep on safe bottom. What would happen when Frank passed through could not even be guessed at; Eudora had taken a slightly different track and spared them. Men who lived as close neighbors to the elements bore no grudge, though sometimes they wished, profanely or otherwise, that the forces of nature could have gone a dite easier on them.

Nils and Joanna watched a favorite television program, each knitting a stint of trapheads for the new gear he'd build in the winter. They'd be able to follow the hurricane on television, an advantage of supplying one's own power. Before they went to bed they got by radio the official report and advisory to mariners, if any were out there tempting Fate. Frank would hit the Massachusetts coast tonight and move quickly into the Gulf of Maine.

It was still quiet when they went to bed, feeling that this had been an extraordinarily long day. Tomorrow would be longer. Having been on his feet all day in a heaving boat, Nils fell asleep first. Joanna read on, trying to end a Victorian murder mystery that spent a lot of time in the slums.

Pip lay sleeping against her legs. She thought of the seas splashing in and curling back on themselves; they were not loud. There was an eerie quiet, something distinct in itself, separated from the rote. One felt it should have been as visible as fog.

She fell asleep thinking about it and woke in the dark to a roar through the trees, only slightly muted by closed windows and not yet at full strength. It was raining, Nils and Pip were gone, and she could smell coffee. There was nothing more to do to get ready for Frank.

There would be no school because of the holiday. The children would be wild with adrenaline—she remembered it well with herself and her brothers, and then with her own children. When the excitement wore them down, they would return to the things they usually did when they were shut in by the weather.

Nils was walking around drinking coffee, eating a cold buttered biscuit, and listening to the news on the small radio on the sun-parlor shelf. Frank was now whooping across the Gulf of Maine after leaving parts of Massachusetts and New Hampshire well battered. Pip, who had gone out when he first arose with Nils, climbed up the back door to look in the window; let in, he shook one paw after another, complaining, or perhaps merely commenting. Nils built a small wood fire in the Franklin stove for the company of it; the day was mild. Pip rolled before it, passionately grooming himself, his ears twitching when sudden assaults of rain struck the southern windows as if by the bucketful. As daylight strengthened, the sight of the boats and their up-and-down performances would have affected sensitive stomachs with miserable memories of seasickness.

Joanna put on her boots and the long slicker and sou'wester that hung by the back door, and went out to feed the hens. She refilled their water dishes from a brimming rain barrel. Their house was in a corner of the barn, smelling cozily of hay and hen; she had to grab up a couple of foolhardy individuals and throw them back inside. "You wouldn't like sailing out over the harbor," she told them. "Don't you want to live to grow up?"

The trees were tossing broken twigs and sometimes whole branches, but none was near enough to reach the house even if the whole tree came crashing down. There were some grand old sugar maples behind the barn, their last red leaves flying away from them now; she always had it in mind that they could lose one, but they were in a fairly good lee, with a thick belt of spruce between them and the meadow. Here the small birds would be taking cover while the storm whirled and wailed.

She had collected six eggs. "Let's live it up and eat them all right now," she said to Nils. "Annabel sent you one with love and kisses." Annabel's favorite perch as a youngster was on one of Nils's feet as he worked around the place. They'd had a large rooster then; as Linnie said, he wasn't into bonding between father and children, so it's no wonder she preferred Nils.

"Can't hurt her feelings," Nils said. "Which one is it?"

"Oh, damn, I should have initialed it," Joanna said.

With the unremitting tumult outside, you had to go upstairs to hear the delicious music of water running into the cistern. "We're rich!" she said to Nils, then knocked on wood. "Unless this time nobody has a trap left whole, or a rogue wave makes a clean sweep of the waterfront."

"Or somebody's roof is blown off for the first time ever," Nils suggested. "Or the Homestead barn collapses in a pile of splinters, or a tidal wave comes over the seawall and moves the schoolhouse off its foundation and out to the harbor, with the bell clanging like hell until the belfry crashes off. I'm just throwing in these things so you won't have to."

"I'll stop imagining while I'm ahead, I guess," Joanna said, "and settle on something I've been putting off for a rainy day."

Wearing his oilskins, Nils left for the shore; once away from the house he was seized and jostled by the wind until he could brace himself. Myles came out and joined him. Even head-on into the brutal rain he looked as cheerfully anticipatory as ever. All the men would be at the shore for the day, except when they went home to dinner. Otherwise they'd be in their fishhouses or visiting in others', or over at the store with the water smacking and splashing underfoot. They'd talk, play cards, listen to Frank's latest news, do chores they'd postponed. But all the time they would be watching the boats. Even having made them as fast as possible with extra lines, even knowing that the ground lines and mooring pennants were secure— that no chain links were thin enough to wear through—they had to watch. Where else would they be but close to the boats? They'd go home to eat, and some might stretch out for a nap, but not for long.

Joanna was strongly disinclined to clean a closet or go through winter woolens; it was a long way to cold weather. It was more satisfying to write to her children, giving each daughter her sister's news. Linnie was skiing in Sweden; she would be home for Christmas. Ellen's husband was saving vacation time, using none at Thanksgiving, to bring the family to the island for three weeks at Christmas. She wrote news of the rest of the family, Sara Jo's latest, and how the neighbors were. The game was the big news, of course. She mentioned Shannon as the hero but left out his mother—the subject was too depressing. Nils would add to the letters when the storm had gone by and tell them what Frank had left behind.

"It seems like a long time until Christmas," she said to him at noon when he was going back to the shore. "We've got Indian summer ahead and after that, Thanksgiving. Then it's a hop, skip, and a jump to Christmas, and before you know it—"

"You've got three months of wind, and you might as well throw April in. No time at all till spring if you say it fast enough."

"Oh, come on," said Joanna. "What about those pretty blue days you like to talk about? Your reason for not taking up and getting all snugged down for the winter?"

His mouth twitched in not quite a smile. She said, "When you do that I wonder what you're thinking." He leaned over in a rustle of oilskins and kissed her. She drew his face down and gave him another, more thorough, kiss. "If we were all alone on the island now—but we're not. So go along to the Boys' Club. Too bad John Haker isn't storm-stayed out here. He'd make it a lot more fascinating."

"This gives some of us locals a chance to be creative. You'd be surprised at the cuffers they spin, if I told you."

"Which you won't," she said. "And I know all about the Ananias Club."

"How can I prove your brother Owen's lying, when he was out of our sight for seven years?" he retorted. "And if these ex-deep-sea fishermen want to swear to what they've seen—or heard tell about—who am I to differ? After all, nobody's proved the Loch Ness monster doesn't exist, so how do we really know what exists off the continental shelf?"

He went out, and she took her new Ngaio Marsh book and went into the living room. Like the kitchen, it was buffered against the power of the wind by the bulk of the house and the woods behind it, though there were thumps, rattles, and creaks enough. She piled cushions on the end of the couch toward the front windows and lay down with an afghan over her; Pip stretched very long over that, watching her.

She'd borrowed the book from Vanessa and had been saving it for a time like this; putting off the acute pleasure of opening it, she lay there listening. Back in the days when the Rock was a family light, she'd envied the children who lived through such storms out there. She had never been afraid during thunderstorms or hurricanes. Up in the attic of the Homestead she could hear the faint creaking of the hand-hewn timbers and feel the life in them through her hands. "As long as she creaks she holds," the boys said importantly, imitating the old men who had spent their youth under canvas. It wasn't until later that she shared and understood the anxiety about the boats, because they had to stay out there and couldn't be brought into the barn like the animals.

As Pip's eyes closed and he laid his head down, she found herself going to sleep with him. She opened her book to wake herself up.

15

With the first page she was where she wanted to be; the rain was falling in London, and she was there. She had just turned the page when the hammering at the door sent Pip flying off her chest and brought her up all standing, her heart beating hard enough to choke her, or so it felt, in recognition of the undreamed-of disaster that had struck one of the family. *Please, not the baby!* She was on her way to the door without knowing she was in motion. *If it's Nils—if it's any of them—* She was at the door, seeing with a sweet relief that it was Nan Harmon beyond the glass. Her relief was tempered by a clear view of Nan's face; framed tightly by a dark scarf, it looked bloodless, pinched, distorted with either pain or terror.

She opened the door and pulled Nan inside by hands that were cold enough to give Joanna a chill. Nan's mouth worked as if she were trying to speak but had no words.

Rubbing the hands hard between hers, Joanna said, "One of the children?" Nan shook her head. "*Myles?*" Nan was still shaking her head, but her mouth moved into a faint grimace.

"*Me,*" she said. "I think I'm going crazy."

"You won't be the first one to think so out here," Joanna said, brisk with relief. "Especially if the wind scares you. Come on, get out of that coat." Nan's fingers fumbled uselessly, and Joanna helped her out of the wet raincoat and scarf. "What about your feet? Good Lord, you got soaked just between doorsteps." She got her fleece-lined slippers from the stairs where she'd left them that morning, and draped the coat and scarf over chairs before a replenished fire in the Franklin stove, the shoes propped against the hearth. "Now let's go into the kitchen and have tea." She pointed Nan at a chair, set the teakettle on the gas, and went into the dining room for the bone china cups and silver spoons. She'd left Nan huddled in her chair, hugging herself. "I don't use these things enough," she called back. "Today is just right for them." There was also a round tin of thin lemon wafers Ellen had sent. "I've been saving these too," she said, setting the tin on the table. "If I left them out, the men would go through them like potato chips."

A slight exaggeration, but she had a compulsion to keep on talking, saying anything at all. Nan had straightened the collar of her blouse and was trying to smooth her hair. It was the first time Joanna had ever seen it mussed; if she didn't go anywhere else, she went to Binnie Campion once a week for a shampoo and trim. Now she seemed well beyond caring about this slight vanity. She was still very pale and expressionless. Joanna turned to the small bright cans of gift tea on their own shelf.

"Now what would you like?" she asked. Without looking around she began reading the names.

"English Breakfast sounds good and strong," Nan said, quite steadily.

"Then that's what we'll have. Bags are quicker than the pot, I guess, so let's have them." There was brandy in the house, but there was always a question about liquor when the person was both reclusive and unknown. Pip appeared and made a beeline for Nan, and Joanna diverted him with his favorite dry food in his dish. She set the steaming cups on the table and sat down opposite Nan, who would use neither sugar nor milk. "This is really nice," Joanna said, trying not to sound offensively cheerful. "Company in the midst of a hurricane."

Nan slowly stirred her tea in a cup decorated with violets, gazing into the amber depths as if in divination. When she lifted her head, Joanna realized she had never really seen Nan's eyes before; they'd either been behind dark glasses, or narrowed as if against sun or breeze. Now they were wide open, light blue, a very pure flowerlike shade. Her lashes were fair and thick. With her thin straight nose and precisely cut mouth—and those eyes—she had the capacity for being a very striking woman. Joanna realized suddenly that she was staring, but Nan was too self-involved to notice.

She said all at once, "I shouldn't have run. I was never a coward." She lifted the cup with both hands because they were shaking. "I apologize." Really to herself, Joanna thought, because she was a coward in front of me.

"*Why?*" she asked bluntly. "For getting out and speaking to another adult?" Even me, she thought. "It must have done you some good already. I wouldn't have given a nickel for you when you showed up at the door."

"I should have been able to do it for myself, the way I've always done."

"Where are the children?"

"Home, doing their own things. Cluny and Shannon are working on a giant jigsaw puzzle they brought from school. Tracy Lynn's making new outfits for her paper dolls." Her voice became arid. "Myles is down at the shore, happy as a clam wherever he is as long as people like him, and of course they *do*. The children make it harder for me; I keep wanting to slam doors and throw things—*smash* them. *Swear*. Not that I ever did," she said quickly, a brush of color on her sharp cheekbones. "But walking back and forth, staring out the windows and wishing I could stop, until you feel, until *I* feel—*you* probably never felt it in your life—as if something's going off in my head." Her teeth chattered on the rim of the cup. "I had to run, but I didn't know where."

"I'm glad you came here," Joanna said. "And listen, if all the Bennett's Island women from the first of them had kept journals, or wrote their hearts out to their relatives, you'd find plenty who thought they'd never make it through the next twenty-four hours." This was a bit thick, but excusable under the circumstances. "For most, a little stay on the mainland was enough. Being over there to have a baby could be too long, sometimes. And most of those who just up and went came back happily enough to their own vine and fig tree—and their own man, in case he'd moved in a housekeeper while she was gone." She laughed. "But for a few it was never right. The ocean surrounded them like prison walls, even when it was smooth as silk. A long fog mull or a spell of wind made it hell. And some men weren't all that easy to live with. How about a fresh cup of tea?"

Nan handed up her cup. "But what about the women *now?* They're all here by choice, aren't they? Marriage isn't the last resort nowadays."

"Oh, we've all had our bad times. It's the human condition, isn't it? Nobody's fault, really, but it's a good thing the mailboat or the lobster smack isn't here every day, or there'd be spells where there'd be a lot of female coming-and-going. Even my mother must have had her moments, though she'd never say so." Another diversion from the truth, but it seemed to be working.

"You said most of them in the old days came back," Nan said sharply, as if to keep her on track.

"Oh, yes! There've been some stories handed down—call it folklore by now. The place was well rid of two or three of them, bad choices on the men's part. Then there were those whose husbands went to fetch them and came back with, or without, or didn't come back at all; they went fishing from the mainland, for their women's sake. And there was one woman who ran away with a lover. I thought that was romantic as all git-out until I saw him in one of those old group photographs of my great-grampa's fishermen, lined up outside the store on a Sunday. *That* skinny little feller?" She was laughing. "How could he be romantic when he looked like *that*? Her husband looked like a big blond movie star to me. But later my mother told me he came from a super-strict family, and he didn't believe in married women going to dances even with their husbands, so they stayed home and listened to the fiddle music floating down the lane on summer nights, usually with a baby in the cradle and another on the way. And that skinny little feller in the picture was the best fiddler they'd ever had out here. How he and she ever got together nobody knew, or told, but they ran away on a mackerel seiner one night and went out West somewhere."

"What about the children?"

"Oh, she took the baby, and this must have been before she could get pregnant again. She left the rest to her husband, knowing he'd be a good father and that he wouldn't lack long for a wife. Sure enough, when he got the word that she was divorced, he married the schoolteacher of the moment, and she was a good kind woman. One of the grandchildren grew up to be storekeeper, lobster-buyer, and postmaster for years. Pete Grant. Mark bought out the business when Pete retired."

"What about *her*? The wife?"

Joanna shrugged. "Who knows? Maybe she saw some of her children when they were grown up. But you know, most of the women were *for* her, and a lot of them blamed Tom Grant for losing their fiddler. They figured that if he'd taken his wife to the dances like a normal man, the fiddler wouldn't have looked so good to her. They never had one that suited them so well, until the Trudeau family moved here from Cape Breton. Now Ralph Percy is the expert, and both his boys are learning."

She had been thinking of Alec all the while, but he was not to be handed over to divert Nan; she was doing enough to keep this troubled woman from listening to the wind. Nan was gazing at her with a dim, strained smile. Then words burst out like blood from a swollen artery suddenly pierced.

"We shouldn't have come here! His idiotic pride made him run away, but he could have gone to the family and got help even if he didn't want the *Nanette Harmon* back again, or any Harmon vessel. But of course he couldn't go lobstering out of Limerock again, not with the Dallases after the rich boy's scalp." She became sourly sarcastic. "The family was just waiting for him to come back to them like the prodigal son, but *they* were all too proud to come down off their high horse. *Horses,*" she corrected herself with a slight twitch of her lips that made Joanna almost like her.

"That bunch of bandits would never let a Harmon set a trap within thirty miles of what they call their territory. Anybody else fishes there because they don't make any trouble, never steal a trap for a trap. There aren't enough wardens to keep track of ordinary fishermen, let alone that Mafia." She was alive without raising her voice; her energy seemed to fill the room. "You'd need a navy to catch them at everything they're up to. Take licenses away, fine them hundreds of dollars, and there's always plenty more to fill the gap. He'd put so much into that new boat—state of the art he called her, whatever that means—and they vandalized her within two weeks. Stole everything they could off her. All the electronic equipment. Smashed the engine and cut her loose in a northwest gale to fetch up, breaking herself to pieces on Limerock Breakwater. When he borrowed a boat to go haul, none of his gear was left. All brand-new traps. We thought that was the end, he'd have to go back to trawling even if he didn't want to. But did he? *No.*" Her fist came down like a hammer on the table, and the cups jumped. "He was going to show us all!"

Her cheekbones were flushed, her eyes brilliant, seeming to dance. One could be deceived into thinking she was tremendously proud of him, instead of enraged. "He was going to get a loan to go with the insurance and build something even better. Wouldn't do for a Harmon to have a secondhand boat, would it? That's what he's got now, but you can bet he's picked out a new design and the yard that will build it for him.

"Well, he went around to all the fishhouses and the wharves, and called up men who avoided him. He was like a labor organizer with no takers. He kept saying 'In union there is strength,' but nobody wanted to go for an all-out trap war. They just stayed out of the Dallases' way and got even in little tricks they couldn't be caught at; the Dallases have lost plenty over the years. All the rest of them could see was that they couldn't afford to keep replacing gear, but Myles had money behind him, and his family would never let his wife and children starve." Again that harsh burst of laughter.

"Besides, I had a good job, and we lived in the Harmon Homestead. *That's* a joke! My God, his folks signed it over to us for a wedding present, and all it cost them was the deed. It hadn't been lived in since the old people died, and after that it was just mended and patched enough to hold it together. And *they'd* held onto the Point; that's where the money is, so he couldn't sell it and make a fortune. I guess they knew him a lot better than I did. I was such an innocent—I thought, Once a Harmon captain, always a Harmon captain, until he got past it, and then he could live easy in his old age." She wiped her eyes on the back of her hand, and Joanna pushed a box of tissues toward her, hoping something hadn't been set loose in Nan that she couldn't control.

"The family paid the taxes on the land, and we took care of the house; with his work we had plenty for the taxes and insurance on it, and my job helped for fixing it up inside, and then . . ."

The words hurtled forward. "And then when he decided to give up deep-sea fishing, and nothing could talk him out of it, I put the food on the table and new shoes on the kids' feet, though I have to admit the grandparents helped some at Christmas and birthdays. All the boat insurance went into the next new one. And then the bank loan didn't come through." She began laughing again. "*That* was a shock to Prince Charming! He'd been too proud to ask anybody to back him—he'd always made plenty of money. But I guess the bank didn't have much faith in a Harmon who'd give up fishing to go lobstering."

She took a thirsty gulp of tea. "But *I* was going ahead! I'd been doing private tax work, and then I got into the Registry of Probate, at the courthouse. A *county* job. *Me!*"

"I can imagine how you must have felt," Joanna said. It sounded feeble compared to the fierce triumph across the table from her. Nan was more alive than one could imagine possible.

"The only thing ever as good as getting that job was when they launched the *Nanette Harmon*," she went on. "She was built for him and named for me, the way the Harmons always named their boats for their wives and daughters. *Nanette Harmon*," she almost whispered. "I broke the bottle on the first try. . . . I had red roses."

She was seeing it, remembering the shower of champagne, hearing the laughter and applause, smelling the roses. Joanna left her to it, feeling a tightness in her own throat. She got herself more tea and then, sensing a change behind her as if the glory had departed, she said, "Why did he want to leave her? Were there too many times when he thought he wasn't going to make it home? I've seen pictures of those trawlers out there so iced up you can't see how they could stay afloat in a mildly choppy sea, let alone what's in the photographs. Always makes me glad none of my men are out there. It can get wild enough around here, but they're close to home."

"Nothing ever scared him," Nan said contemptuously. "But he came home from a super trip a year ago September, and Tracy Lynn had started school a couple of days before. *That* was what did it. He said he'd missed Cluny's first steps—she'd taken them toward the man I had painting the house, and he was the one who picked her up, *not* her daddy." She verged on sarcasm again.

Ouch, Joanna thought, remembering how she'd cried secretly because Ellen couldn't walk to Alec's arms, and never would. He had been drowned in the harbor before Ellen was born.

Nan was going on. "And he thought he'd missed Shannon's first sentence, when we'd waited so long for him to talk. And he'd wanted to take Tracy Lynn to school her first day. Well, he wasn't going to miss any more firsts. They'd be grown before we knew it, so he was going lobstering so he'd be home every night. The more the family argued, the deeper he dug his heels. I was sick, but I tried not to show it. The kids were so happy. . . . But I thought once he found out what hard work it was—and he was used to making money out there at sea, with plenty of room to do it in. . . . I still don't know why he thought nobody would resent him as a lobsterman. That cussed optimism! Tracy Lynn's like him, Merry Sunshine, but who respects a man who's as hopeful as a six-year-old no matter what's done to him?

"Even when he knew his traps were being hauled . . . When they stripped the boat and cut her loose, I was sorry for him, but I thought he'd go back where he belonged. And I still had my job." She was quiet, gazing down wearily at her cup. "But you don't take Myles Harmon for granted," she said. "He never gets ugly, and he's not a drinking man. Even with the bank turning him down and all . . . One night he brought me flowers and took me for a walk along the shore without the kids, and told me he'd rented a house out here. *Out here.* Away from my job! I was so frantic that if there'd been a way to sneak out here and burn the damned house down, I'd have done it. Does that shock you?"

"Nope," said Joanna. "I'd feel the same way if anyone tried to drag me away from *here,* and told me it was all set."

"But he still needed my money," Nan went on as if she hadn't heard anything. "I worked out my notice, and I still had some savings. He borrowed enough when he got a good deal on some secondhand traps, and he swapped the new hull for the boat he has now, *Sweet Alice.* Got her from the man he rented the house from." Her mouth twisted up one side. "How's *that* name for a loser? And of course you can't change the name because you'll change your luck! As if luck and Myles Harmon didn't part company the minute he gave up the *Nanette Harmon!*" She nodded sharply at Joanna, as if in argument. "Yes, I know he's been making money out here by fits and starts, the way lobstering goes, and nobody's started bothering him yet. But I've been buying the groceries out of my savings so we don't have to eat out of any island store. I want as little to do with this place as possible, and if you're insulted it's too bad."

Joanna shrugged. "I'm not insulted." They all knew about the big orders coming out once a week on the mailboat, from Grier's in Limerock; the cartons were always set thoughtfully in the cool shade of the wharf shed, and Shannon came after school with a wheelbarrow to collect them. He knew better than to hang around for more than ten minutes or so, watching what interesting things were going on at the wharf and the store. Myles must have talked to Mark about the groceries, and Mark had relieved him of his embarrassment; Myles was in and out of the store as often as any of the men, and of course Mark bought his lobsters. The children came in for ice cream, soda, or to brood over the riches of the old-fashioned candy counter.

Joanna wondered how Nan would feel to know she was considered charitably as *odd,* and the island had always been tolerant of the random oddity. At first it had been suggested that she was a secret drinker, but that went nowhere. Getting a regular supply out here, unnoticed, would be impossible unless Myles went ashore to buy it, and he hadn't left the island except for Brigport since he'd moved out here.

Nan spoke suddenly out of her fit of abstraction. It was in a voice of mourning. "*My job.* I'd have been unopposed this year for Registrar of Probate. *Me.* One of Old Eisner's kids an elected county official! And here I am, listening to the wind that never stops blowing, even in my sleep."

"Oh, *Nan!*" Joanna was jolted into shame for her own lack of charity. "I'm so sorry! You have a right to be angry with him, with everything." It appeared that Nan hadn't heard Joanna. She stared across at Pip, sitting in a chair and washing himself, as if he were simply something moving on which she could concentrate without meeting Joanna's eyes. Pip suddenly stopped washing and stared back at her, but he was not tempted to hurry to her as he did when he caught a look that might be cordial to a cat.

"*Winter,*" she said in a faraway voice. "The wind will go on all winter. I know this is a hurricane, but wind is wind, and the bay could be the whole Atlantic when you can't get away from it. And you listen to the wind day and night, when it finds places to squeeze through and howl and wheeze and cry. And if you step out the door, it's ready to beat you up and drive you inside again. And the boats never keep still, until you'd like to cut them all free, except that even if you were that crazy you couldn't get a skiff away from the shore."

"Some winters are worse than others," Joanna said, feeling inane in the presence of all this passion. "Every so often there's a long calm spell—and sunshine—and everyone gets a little drunk with it. We all get cabin fever when the wind goes on too long, but we have our ways. We build up to quite a social life out here. It just takes a little courage. The northern lights make it all worthwhile, when they light up more than half the sky. And if it's cold enough to freeze the ice pond for skating . . . Owen had it enlarged last year."

Nan wasn't listening. "I *hate* it out here. I hated it in midsummer. I'm homesick for my house—I *made* it mine, you know; I worked so hard on it. And here I am out here, without even a bathroom, and I never used an outhouse in my life. Don't tell me this composting rig's an improvement, either." Joanna wanted to say that if Dave Sorensen ever sold the house to Myles, there'd be no reason why they couldn't have a bathroom, and a composting toilet in a shed off the back entry *was* an improvement over an outhouse.

"I've got relatives enjoying my house," Nan said. "At least I didn't have to put all my nice things away. They'll take care of them."

"That's always a help," Joanna said brightly. "How are the children liking it out here?"

"The *children?*" She looked blankly at Joanna. "*Oh!* Cluny's in a world of her own as long as she can practice. *She* doesn't care that she'll never launch a *Delphine Harmon*—Delphine's her name, Cluny's her ballet name she chose for herself. Now Shannon . . . ." There was a little hint of complacence. "He's just like me. He wants everything just right and even better. He had a great future in athletics before we left home."

"Well, he's still got that," Joanna said mildly. "Meanwhile he's the Racketash Raiders' hero of the year, and he seems to have made friends all at once. And Tracy Lynn's a delight."

Nan couldn't quite help smiling. "She *is* a sunny little thing. I always loved that sunniness in Myles, till—well, it's hard to believe a grown man could be so . . . so *kiddish*."

"You forget I've grown up surrounded by men," said Joanna.

"I suppose I can be thankful he isn't crazy about gambling with cards. He does enough of it in other ways."

"I don't think lobstering's any more of a gamble than trawling," Joanna protested. "It all comes down to what's there to catch, and a lot of people think that's all getting scarcer by the year. There are good years—you know that, the shrimpers and the scallopers know it—and there are awful years. I have a nephew who says everybody should be thinking about it *now*. And I guess he's right. . . . He likes to remind us of the last passenger pigeon, which always makes me feel very sad. Did it *know* there was nobody else?"

Nan stood abruptly and went for her coat. "I don't suppose the children have missed me, and Myles won't be back until there's no one left at the shore to talk to." She kicked off the slippers, put on her shoes, and got into her coat with furious gestures, as if it were fighting her. "Thanks for the tea," she said. "Thanks for putting up with me." She tied the scarf under her chin with punishing force.

"I just hope this has been some help to you, and I don't gossip, believe me," Joanna said. "I'd say come anytime, but I have a feeling you wish you hadn't come this time."

"Your feeling is right," Nan said dryly. "But it's done, and all I can do is try to live it down." She went out quickly, head bowed against a blast of rain and wind, and ran the short distance to the other doorstep. Joanna waited to see if she'd look back, perhaps wave before she went inside, but she didn't. Breathing the fresh wet air, Joanna wished she could run out in it and walk somewhere in a lee until the feel of the afternoon was dissolved away. She shut the door and went back to Ngaio Marsh. Pip soon joined her, and it was something like what it had been before. Nonetheless, she knew that nothing concerning her and Nan could possibly be the same again.

16

Someone came into the sun parlor, and Pip used Joanna for a springboard again, roughly awakening her to a quieter afternoon than she'd left a few hours ago.

"You asleep?" Nils called to her.

"No, but I've been a long distance away." She hadn't moved for at least two hours, and she stretched her arms and legs hard, wiggling her toes. She didn't get a cramp and rose swiftly before one could attack. Darkness was coming on early; Nils had a lamp lit and was making coffee. He had let Pip out.

"I might as well be thinking about supper," said Joanna. "We finished the chowder this noon. How about macaroni baked with some of that Vermont cheddar, and our own tomatoes sliced on top?"

"Good. Coffee?"

"Why does it always taste better when you make it in the pot? Yes, but I'll get the pasta going first. Then we can talk about how exciting our afternoons have been. I take it the wharves are still there, and nobody's been swept off Sou'west Point."

"Yes, to the wharves. Not that I know of, to your other statement."

"I suppose you've been housecleaning the shop so we can move down there next summer."

He smiled. "Jamie and Matt and Ralph have been in there all afternoon talking about going back to seining come spring. Looking around this winter for a good rig they can buy."

"Rosa must love that—Jamie out roving around half the night, with the baby due in April. 'Bye, Baby Bunting,' " she sang. " 'Daddy's gone a-hunting . . . You shall have a fishie in a silver dishie, when the boat comes home.' " That was from another song, but Daddy certainly wasn't going to bring back a rabbit skin to wrap Baby Bunting in. "Rosa calls those three Wynken, Blynken, and Nod," she went on. "Sara Jo will sure know *that* song by heart if they keep talking herring all winter. Winter dreams! When I think of what's been hatched up around practically every kitchen table every winter since the start of time—if they'd all been carried through, we wouldn't know the place."

"He won't start till after the baby comes. This time it's three *seiners* talking, not dreamers. I wondered how long it would be before they heard the call again." Taking the Swedish mugs from the cupboard, he noticed the teacups by the sink. "You and Pip been having a tea party?"

"He likes the one with the thistle pattern. . . . You'll have a hard time believing this—I still do, and I was right here. Nan came over just when it was at top screech. She was desperate. She had to get to *somebody,* even me." The macaroni was boiling gently. She poured her coffee and sat down opposite Nils. "Have one of these. Have a handful." She pushed the tin of lemon wafers toward him. "Well, I was handiest. I'm so sorry for her, but she doesn't want that, which makes me even more sorry. I don't know what she could take comfort from, Nils. She's so tangled up in resentments and hurts and rages, she can't let loose. And if she didn't *really* resent me before, she does now, because she let me in on it, and she's sure I'm telling you every single, solitary word."

"Is that how they came? Single—solitary? Must have been a lot of gaps." Pip assaulted the back door again, wailing. Nils got up to let him in and instantly became his favorite person of the moment.

"Most of them came in schools, like fish," Joanna said. "Once she got going, and for a bit there, I felt like that blind cod in a school of herring we keep hearing about. She wasn't whining for sympathy. It all sort of jumped out, as if she couldn't hold back. She *does* have a side, Nils, and there's just no middle ground." She got up and took the cheese from the refrigerator, set it on the counter, and began to cut off chunks, first giving crumbs to Pip in his dish to keep him from landing on the counter beside the wedge.

"Nan had a good job she'd worked very hard for, at the Registry of Probate. She spent a lot of her pay on fixing up the Harmon Homestead while Myles was still trawling. Then when he quit, and ran into all that mess over there, she supported the family. Her grievance is—and she's right—that Myles only appreciated her job when he needed the money."

Nils refilled her mug and sat down again, giving her the courteous undivided attention that was his way. She could always be sure of his complete interest, even if sometimes he didn't get angry as quickly as she wanted. He ate lemon wafers absently, watching her face.

"But Myles has a side too," she went on. "Not wanting to be away from his children so long at a time. If he hadn't run into that . . . that *vendetta*, maybe you could call it, and if she could have kept on with her job—running for Registrar of Probate this fall, imagine!—they'd be getting along all right. *Probably*," she added cautiously. "But, Nils, he rented Dave's house without talking it over with her—sprang it on her as a done deal, and there was nothing she could say. Of course that's never been *my* trouble, but I gather she freezes up. It probably half-killed her to give notice and to leave that house. After all these months she hasn't forgiven him one particle. And how can he be so damn' *happy*, knowing how she feels?"

"Maybe he's not damn' happy," Nils said absently. "Just putting up a good front. Maybe that's why some days when the rest of us are letting 'em lay over, he's out there looking like a breaking ledge when you see him from a distance. Good thing *Sweet Alice*'s a real tough Novi boat, what he puts her through sometimes."

"And Nan hates him more, because she thinks he's having such a good time," Joanna said. "After just so long I'd quit biting off my nose to spite my face and break out of solitary confinement. But then, not being Nan, I wouldn't have gotten into her place in the beginning. . . . For one thing, I'm *home*. Poor Nan," she said softly. She drained and rinsed the macaroni and stirred the cheese into it, turned it all into a buttered casserole, and began slicing tomatoes.

"Maybe there's a lot eating at her besides the job," Nils said. "Last time John Haker was storm-stayed out here, he spent an afternoon in the fishhouse talking and drinking aquavit. Pouring rain. Nobody came in, so he didn't have to share. . . . Well, he'd been to the well during a lull. He wanted some fresh water—yes, he drinks that sometimes—and came face-to-face with her. He'd known her as a kid, and when she saw him she looked as if she'd been slapped, left her bucket, and turned and ran." He shook his head. "Poor old John, his feelings were hurt. He's always wished her well and wanted to say so. But I figure she thought it was bad enough to be exiled out here without meeting somebody who knew what she came from and could tell it. Anyway, he filled her bucket and put it on her doorstep, got his own water, and left."

"And has he been yammering around the fishhouses?" she asked angrily.

"John's decent. He only told me because he was upset, and he knew I was safe."

"Is that why you never told *me*, until now?"

"Don't take it for granted I'm going to tell you now." Then he laughed at her expression. "We don't have many chances to get onto long stories around here, the secret ones. We're too damned popular, and at night we're too sleepy; if we're not, we aren't reporting the neighbors' histories."

She put the casserole in the oven and set the timer. "Well, tell me *now!*" she said impatiently. "I already know one thing. She never had to use an outhouse."

Nils laughed. "With good reason. Her father, Eli Eisner, thought building a toilet was putting on airs. Besides, he said, they were unsanitary. He wouldn't have one on the place. It was either out in the bushes or in a bucket out in the shed. They got a decent one—with windows too—after the old man died; two of the sons-in-law built it. There's not much you can say for Eli except that he was on a minesweeper in the first war and got an honorable discharge. That's when he was young."

"What a sad statement," Joanna said. " 'That's when he was young!' "

"All the kids know about it are the old snapshots, and what he'd tell sometimes to the older ones, before he turned to rum as a career. Maybe he wasn't always a drunk, but that's what his children grew up with—his being fired off one boat and another until he managed to sink himself and the old ruin he had at the time, trying to go it alone. 'Poor old girl,' John told me. 'No boat deserves what that boat had to put up with since she first hit the water.' The aquavit was cutting in and John was a little weepy," said Nils, "but I know how he felt—like these old horses driven until they dropped dead. But Eli went down with her, and the family had a chance. The oldest ones bailed out as soon as they got jobs, but Marm had taken to drinking along with the old man to keep him company, so they lost one drunk and were left with another."

"Where did Nan fit in?"

"Oldest one at home. Eighth or ninth grade . . . Somebody had to be there nights with the mother—she wasn't quite ready to be put away. But Nan swore nothing was going to keep her home on school days. She talked an old friend of her mother's—who'd given up on Marm—into coming in every school day, and then she talked the rest into giving the woman something like five dollars a day. She was a great persuader in those days. She wanted to go to school so much, nothing could stop her. The older sisters parceled out the three youngest and took care of them. And the Harmons made Nan an allowance for clothes and shoes because she couldn't get an after-school job, having to come home and baby-sit her mother. She was proud as Lucifer, John said, bragging on her; she was going to work off that allowance by guess and by gorry, she told them, and they said their payment was to see her do well. This is where John began blowing his nose," explained Nils. 'You wouldn't guess I was such a sentimental son of a bitch, would ye?' he says.

"Ray Harmon and Eli Eisner had been buddies aboard that minesweeper. Before that they'd both played baseball for Limerock High. When they got home, Ray got Eli a job alongside him on one of the Harmon boats, and when he inherited the Harmon acres he gave Eli a good chunk of shore where Eli could build a house and raise a family. But nothing— nobody—could get Eli out of the bottle once he fell all the way in. He was doomed. He couldn't work on the Harmon boats anymore after he brought liquor aboard, and he wasn't reliable with anyone else. But the Harmon youngsters and the Eisners walked up the same road to school, and the two oldest boys eventually went to work for the firm."

"But still," Joanna said, "wouldn't you think Myles's parents would have wanted something more for him than the daughter of a couple of drunks? I'm not downing Nan! Don't think that! But the Harmons were some of the top people in Limerock. Still are."

"They're not snobs—everybody knows that about the Harmons—and they're practical. They had three sons, all learning the business; but Myles was the one the girls were making eyes at before he was thirteen. 'Myles, the living doll,' " he said dryly. "That about breaks up John every time he says it. 'My own girls, for Chrissake!' he says. First they chased him on their bikes, hanging around the wharves, and then they'd drive down in somebody's car when he was due in, to admire his dimples and his muscles when he was unloading fish with his shirt off. John ordered his own girls away before Ray laid down the law.

"Nan didn't have time for such foolishness, but she and Myles were always friends, and John thinks his folks had their eye on her for a long time. She was a pretty kid, if you go by the high-school yearbook, but she was serious, and Myles was always trying to get her out for some fun when she was going to business college. She liked him well enough, probably always had, and there was nothing to stop their marrying; her mother had set her bed on fire one night with a cigarette, and nearly took Nan along with her and the house. Her sisters gave her a good wedding, and Ray promised Myles his own boat, so they could square away with fair wind and no favor." He watched her as she set the table, frowning at the silver as if she had a grudge against it. "Doesn't that make you feel a dite happier about her?"

"Why should it, seeing that she's miserable now? Must make it that much worse. Listen!" She turned to him. "If she could stand up for her rights once, why can't she do it now? *He* comes off as a spoiled kid who doesn't expect anybody to oppose him. It would be good for him if she *did*. Tell him how much she resents his never giving a thought to what her job meant to her and how hard she worked to get that far. Tell him she's taking the kids and going back, and if he wants to be with them so much, he can come along too. There's other work besides lobstering. He could go partners dragging with another man, out in the bay. He could do a lot of things; he's a *Harmon*." She couldn't help the sardonic inflection.

"Can't hold his name against him," Nils said moderately. "Maybe it's the name that keeps her from doing just that; it could be why she doesn't want to call his bluff. Maybe she's like the charcoal burner's daughter being courted by the Crown Prince in the fairy tales. He got lost while hunting, fell off his horse, and she found him and took care of him."

Joanna sat down, rested her elbows on the table, and stared at Nils. "Tell me more! Do you remember all this from the kids' storybooks?"

"I remember it all from my innocent youth," he said with dignity. Then he grinned at her expression. "Grampa tried to keep us from reading anything but the Bible and our schoolbooks, but Gramma had a misspent youth and knew all the fairy tales by heart. When Grampa and Father were out with the seine gang, we had to knit our stint of heads and bait bags, but she kept us entertained."

He tipped his chair back, looked at the ceiling, and tented his fingers. "We never knew what a charcoal burner *did*—this was long before barbecues, remember—but he was always there, deep in the royal forest, whenever somebody got lost. It was usually a prince, and he was always young and gorgeous; so was the charcoal burner's daughter—after a good bath. The royal forest wasn't anything like our woods, you understand."

"Definitely darker, deeper, and scary," she agreed. "But there was always a charcoal burner in the midst of it, I used to hope, for me."

"Well, there was always a daughter who could be cleaned up and presented to the king and queen—"

She picked it up. "Who were usually charmed to think their reckless son had found somebody to straighten him out, and they were prepared to make a princess out of this lucky find. A wonderful ending! I always loved it. But what's it have to do with? . . ." She tilted her head toward next door.

"Well, suppose this pure but sooty maiden thought she was going to be a princess and have a hot bath every day of her life, and plenty of clothes, and—"

"A coach and four," Joanna prompted. "Or even eight? Of course she'd always be good to her parents, but from now on she'd live in a castle."

"And *he* said, 'Now that we've got this cussed fancy wedding out of the way, we'll go back to the woods; I'll become a charcoal burner like your father, and we'll live happily ever after with all the creatures of the forest.' "

She was gazing at him, gently bemused, and he looked back, a questioning around his eyes, not quite smiling, his mouth sober. Pip made a little sound, as if something about the silence disturbed him. Still watching Joanna, Nils began scratching around the cat's ears. "I know Eli Eisner, besides being dead, is no match for the honorable charcoal burner, but he *was* a lobsterman, and there was a time when Nan had to take her turn going sternman with him. So it's not too different from the charcoal burner's daughter, who always hated that life and then found out her husband wanted it."

"That isn't what I was thinking," Joanna said. She went over to him, lifted his head, and kissed him on the forehead. "I was thinking it's wonderful to find out something so . . . so nice . . . and so new about the person you've been living with for over half your life, when you thought you knew all the great things about him. I wish *I* hadn't told you everything I remember, so now I'd have something as beautiful as your grandmother and the fairy stories, and you remembering them, every bit."

"I was saving it. Must have been for now."

"Well, it was perfect. And I just remembered something I never told you—I'll save it for the right time, too."

"What's it about, besides you?"

"Pickie and I ran away for a whole afternoon when I was four-ish, and nobody ever missed us, and I think it changed my life. There's a lot more to it."

"I'll keep reminding you." Pip reached up and possessively fastened a set of foreclaws in Joanna's apron. She freed herself and straightened up.

"What if, once she was made a princess, she didn't intend to become a charcoal burner's wife? and said so? And he was just as stubborn?" she asked.

"Is she going to give up the royal name that easily? Nan knew about all the girls—princesses to begin with—who lusted for him, and she knew that women would be schooling around him the minute he was free," said Nils. "They'd even risk life in the dark forest, because they were all sure they'd knock that damn' foolishness out of his head soon enough. *No.* She's taking no chances."

"Like the women from here who used to leave their husbands but came back because they might move a housekeeper in. But some followed their wives off. I suppose she wouldn't trust Myles to do that. And what if the kids didn't want to leave him?" Joanna asked.

"Can we eat?" he asked patiently.

"Yes, we can. I'm starved. Well, I guess I ought to know by now I can't tell anybody how to live, so why worry?" She felt *good;* from the time Nan had appeared at the door she'd been shocked, saddened, angry, frustrated, and then heavily depressed. Now it was all gone, and she was a fool if she ever let it come back. All she had to do was remember that in this house Gramma Sorensen had told her fair-haired grandchildren wondrous stories while they made trapheads and bait bags, and she went on with her endless knitting of socks. She'd be a far more delightful ghost than Gunnar, and always a comfort.

17

The day after the hurricane was so brilliant it seemed to have been created with cosmic poster paints in every possible gradation of the primary colors. Under the northwest wind the sea was a vibrating impossible blue to the horizon. The rocks glittered; the island that had lain so battered under the storm may have lost most of the hardwoods' foliage, but it still presented October's brightest palette in the green fields, the red and wine of blueberry plants and wild rose leaves, and the waves of asters and goldenrod straightening up as they dried. The black and white of crows and gulls had a special intensity as they cruised over the shores, looking for anything new in the heaps of rockweed and kelp. The chickadees and the other small birds, visiting migrants, sounded as excited as they did in the spring; there was something for all of them.

The crickets were loud this morning. What did crickets do to keep from being drowned out, she wondered. She was glad to hear them, a promise that there was still much good weather to come.

Going to school, the children made an uncommon amount of noise, as excited by the departure of the hurricane as by its arrival. Nor had they yet used up the momentum of their victory on Saturday. Even the Harmon children burst from their back door, Shannon on the run to join Young Mark and Tom J., Tracy Lynn screaming to Amy to wait for her. For this little while, Cluny was a stranger child; she left the house with more decorum than the others until she met Tammie. They spent a few minutes playing with the dog, laughing at him, dodging his kisses, Cluny's hair bouncing in wild escape from the ponytail. When they went along, the dog played by himself, tossing a battered aluminum-foil pie plate into the air, chasing it, pouncing on it with growls and yips.

Nobody would be going out today, but most of the men were already down at the shore to begin clearing away the accumulation of rockweed and kelp flung up on the wharves during the night's high tide. Joanna didn't intend to stay in. She let the hens out of their yard to forage for what the rain had set loose, their version of beachcombing. Across at Schoolhouse Cove, the children would be getting as much done as possible before the bell rang.

Joanna took the mail and set out for the store, leaving Pip inside watching from a window, soon to be entertained by her encounter with Dog Tray and his pie plate. He danced up to her, wagged the foil enticingly until she faked a grab for it, and dodged away, obviously laughing. Then he turned and chased after her. "All right for you," she told him. "I won't play with you no more, Old Dog Tray Dinsmore." If he could have said "Ha ha!" he would have.

Maggie came out the back door with her arms full of heavy clothes that gave off a powerful effluvium of mothballs. The dog backed off sneezing and shaking his head, and ran to the end of his run.

"I went a dite heavy on the moth stuff," Maggie said, "but Rob always swears the Bennett's Island moths are real superior critters, and he's right. He swears to the kids they can open trunks, so I never take any chances." She laughed merrily. "Who knows? Lots of peculiar things out here that you can't find anywhere else."

"Like the people," Joanna said. " 'Here's to us! Who's like us? Damn' few!' That was our slogan when we went off to the mainland to mingle with the lesser breeds in school."

"Funny," Maggie said. "You live in a town, and you think it's a great town—*special*. But once you move onto an island—*this* island, anyway— you think that it's a different country, that we should run up our own flag."

"We were always designing flags," Joanna said, "but we could never agree on one design. That ought to be a good project for the kids when winter gets going hard. Give everybody a chance to vote for the best one, then fly it under the American flag to show there's no hard feelings—we haven't seceded." They both laughed, which encouraged Dog Tray to brave the mothballs again.

Rounding the corner of the Binnacle into the fresh wind, she could hear scrapings, thumpings, and voices from the wharves where the cleanup was going on—an occasional whoop, a whistle, a guffaw, and some cheerfully profane comments. On the way to the store there was a short steep shingle beach between the fishhouses and Mark's big utility shed, which stood half on land and half over water, with the short chop bouncing noisily around the spilings. The beach had been piled high with rockweed, some of it thrown across the path and into the asters.

Good for my asparagus, she thought. Suddenly she could hardly wait to get at it with her wheelbarrow and fork. I'm as bad as the kids, she thought: I can't wait to get my boots on and go squishing and skidding around in the mess.

She went around the corner of the broad shed, whose double doors stood open. Willy Gerrish was inside, singing to himself and shifting hundred-pound gas cylinders into rows against a wall. "Hi, Jo!" he shouted at her. "Some pretty day!"

"Sure is," she agreed. "Hello, Louis." The store cat was always very busy when anything was being moved. "How's the Inspector-General today?" she asked him. He gave her a dismissive look and stalked into the shadows; he didn't allow familiarities when he was on duty, even from old acquaintances. Compared to him, Pip was an undiscriminating extrovert—like Willy, whose gaunt, homely face now radiated even more pleasure than usual.

"Boat ain't coming today," he warned her. "No mail."

"I didn't expect any. Duke's pretty tender with her. She's been pounding across the bay for a long time now. He won't risk her or himself and the mail as long as he can make up his trip the next day."

"Never missed one yet!" Willy said, giving a tall cylinder an energetic twirl across the floor. "Nope!"

Young Mark's dory had been hauled up and turned over on the other side of the path. Her carefully lettered name was We Two. No one, not even his mother, knew if this meant Mark and the dory, Mark and an imaginary girl, or Mark and a hoped-for girl in the future. He was twelve.

She heard women's voices in the store, but she stood outside to listen to the water everywhere—under her feet, under the wharf, around the spilings, and racing across the harbor under the wind to break against ledges and the heaving bows of the boats. After yesterday, they seemed to be sentient, joyous beings prancing among flung diamonds.

At the end of the long shadowy shed, figures moved in and out of sight on the wharf; Mark, Owen, Philip, Matt Fennell—they seemed to be

busy putting the place to rights, as if the gale had knocked down everything that had been expected to stand. Beyond them was a white flare of
surf on the outer side of the breakwater, and white seas came hurtling in
past the far end, where the beacon was. Overhead the gulls rode the wind,
their voices blown away like tatters of foam.

She sat down on the bench and leaned out to get a good view of Eastern Harbor Point, disappearing and then seeming to rise up and shake itself.
Laurie left the store on a wave of laughter, calling back something that
brought another response. With this dry, brilliant weather they all felt exhilarated. Peter Fennell tried to squeeze out past Laurie, and Carol called
"Peter, *no*."

"It's all right," Laurie said. "I'll hang onto him. He's bored with all the
female talk." She gathered up Peter's reins before he could be off down the
wharf. "No, you don't young fella, me lad. Let's sit here, and you can watch
the harbor in case anything happens out there." Peter, a sturdy and amiable
little boy, squirmed around until his legs dangled, folded his arms along the
railing, rested his chin on them, and dutifully stared at the harbor.

"There's Daddy's boat." He pointed. "There's Grampy's." He went on
identifying boats in a dreamy litany.

"It's official. The mailboat isn't coming," Laurie said. "What a relief. The
first thing I thought of when I woke up this morning was that Richard was
going to be out here with Duke, saying the school was closed for the week
until they got something dire repaired, so he came home to help out."

"And talk some more about 'Oh, *that*,' " said Joanna.

Laurie nodded. "I didn't want to put any ideas in his father's head, but
I could hardly wait to get over here and call Kristi. They were already on
their way back to school; Pete was driving them."

"Not me," Peter said, alert.

"No, this is another Peter," Joanna told him. "Grown-up."

"I will be," Peter said with confidence, and turned toward the harbor
again.

"Anyway, I just had the *best* cup of coffee," Laurie said happily. Willy
and Louis left the utility shed next door, Willy whistling. "You're whistling
up another wind, Willy," Laurie told him, "and we like this one, don't we,
Jo and Peter?"

"I ain't calling up a foul wind," Willy protested. "This'll keep it where
it is. Different tunes make different winds." He disappeared up the path
between the dory and the store, Louis behind him.

"I thought I wouldn't get into that," said Laurie. "Willy's explanations often lead into obscurities that only he can fathom. I wouldn't be surprised if that was a charm to keep it just rough enough so I can't go out with Owen tomorrow. Well, Willy's going anyway. He doesn't need a charm. I won't feel cheated of anything but a day of bouncing around the cockpit like a Ping-Pong ball, while Old Damn-the-Torpedoes doesn't even look back to see if I'm still there." She began to laugh. "Well, he does sometimes. But when he sees I haven't broken anything, he says, 'What are you doing down *there?*' as if I'm being eccentric. As soon as I can reach a bait bag, he gets one on the back of his neck."

Peter was entranced; the extreme pleasure of assaulting someone with a well-stuffed juicy bag of salt herring was yet to be his, but it would happen some day when he was one of the big boys working in the bait sheds after school.

"What's the latest on the trip?" Joanna asked, "Or haven't you brought it up yet?"

"I'm biding my time and collecting material. When he starts to take up, I'll be ready for him."

"There's a duck." Peter pointed. "Out by *Wind-dancer.*"

"That's a loon," Laurie said. "Can you say *loon?*"

"Loon-duck," said Peter firmly.

"Right," said Laurie. "Near enough."

All at once Willy made a spectacular appearance around the corner of the store, wild-eyed, his Racketash cap barely clinging to the back of his head. "Hey, look what's coming!" he yelled. He wrenched open the store door, shouting, "She's out there! And she's all winged out some handsome!" He ran into the long shed, and Peter took off behind him, until Laurie caught him.

"I have a terrible feeling," Laurie said, "that Duke's made it after all, and my son is standing up there in the forepeak like Columbus. I don't want to look."

"*Clarice* would have a hard time being all winged out," Joanna said, "having not a sail to her name." The women in the store were coming out, faces lively with anticipation. Carol reached for Peter's reins. "Thanks, Laurie. All right, Peter. Don't try pulling me off my feet." They went off after the others, Peter shouting, "Hurry, Mama! *Hurry!*"

"Come on, you two!" Nora Fennell called back, but didn't wait. Coming out behind them, Helmi said very quietly, "It's the *Conqueror.*"

She was never a broad smiler, but Joanna guessed that she'd been holding back the news to surprise them all; that was why Willy had been practically incandescent with happiness as he got the shed ready for a new shipment of propane cylinders. Because there *she* was, coming past the southern tip of Brigport and heading for Bennett's. If she'd actually been one of the historic schooners of the past come to life, nothing would have been more dramatic than the two-masted tops'l schooner *Conqueror,* black-hulled like the original, tearing along on a fair wind with a bone in her teeth, her canvas booming, her ensign snapping, and the gulls escorting her like attendant spirits.

The island was all at once bursting with people—you would sense this without taking your eyes from the schooner. The men were out on their wharves, except for those coming around the shore; more women were gathering, and the children's voices were echoing like the gulls' all the way from school. They'd been let out to greet this vision from their island's past.

The black schooner was not a stranger. She was always welcome even when she came chugging across the bay under power, with bare poles. But nothing ever lessened the impact of her arrival under sail. Joanna's eyes blurred, and she could hear noses being blown as the coaster came flying toward them straight out of one of the pictures on the old Linen Thread calendars. You'd known that the colors of sea and sky weren't exaggerated in those paintings; you'd seen them in reality. But this was a living ship under a living sky, and her voice was made of the rush of her passage through living seas, and the sound of her sails as she heeled with apparently reckless elegance; she throbbed with life between the uneven temper of the wind and the hurly-burly of water breaking everywhere. Aboard her, you would feel that life beating beneath your feet and hear it in all the little sounds—creaks and rattles and thumps and a humming through the masts. If you were the helmsman, her heart beat powerfully in your hands. And the gulls went careening about her, crying, crying, as if she had come for them alone.

As the wharf grew crowded, Joanna walked around the edges and back to the store. She sat down on the bench again. Helmi was at the wharf, so she could blow her nose and wipe her eyes in private.

The *Conqueror* was a genuine coaster, as the original had been, back in a day when the schooners had been the workhorses of the coast. The vessel seemed to have been deeply loved in a day when more and more of her sisters were disappearing. She had been finally betrayed—sold from hand to hand after her builder and lover had died. She labored hard through seas that should have killed her, and she had never been favored. She had ended her days piled up on a ledge by someone with less seamanship than most of the island children had. There the sea kicked her old bones to splinters with every blow until, mysteriously, she was doused with kerosene on a dark night with an extremely low tide—"low dreen"— and given an honorable funeral.

In her youth and his, Stephen Bennett had seen the old *Conqueror* as dreams made tangible; whenever he was aboard her at the wharf with the other boys, he could lay his hands on those dreams, in the big wheel. He wouldn't have needed to go too far, like the great navigators; sailing his own vessel from the Maritimes to Florida, with side trips to islands on the way, would have been enough. He'd never done it; there were too many responsibilities at home that he couldn't shed, as some of his cousins had done. Joanna used to think it was unfair, but he smiled at that.

"What more could I have? Just think, I might not have met your mother, and somebody else might have got her. Like your Uncle Nate. And where would *you* be?"

"I like Uncle Nate all right," she said belligerently, "but I wouldn't want him for a father. None of us would."

"So you see," her father said. But when she was older she thought she could see him as a young man in one of her brothers, and they had, mostly, set out as they pleased.

The new *Conqueror* was as much like the old one as any creature of dream could be. Three young men enlisted in the marines together in 1941, with the agreement that if they survived they would do something probably impractical but splendidly daring when they got home. They did survive, and their project was a new *Conqueror.* Splendid, expensive, and eminently practical, she had been working ever since. Building her, they'd had more offers of unpaid help than they'd expected, from men who wanted to feel the joy of the work and to see such beauty blooming again, like a rare blossom which opens only once in a hundred years. None of them had ever seen the first *Conqueror* alive, but it was believed that somewhere among the three owners and their volunteers was the group who had given the shattered hull a fiery funeral.

All these years later the godchild had paid for herself many times over. The sons and grandchildren of the owners had all served on her, and some still did. Always immaculate, from ensign to keel, she didn't belong to the windjammer fleet; she was a freighter, built beamy for the job. She relieved the crowded ferries, carrying lumber like the Johnny Wood boats of old and hauling heavy equipment and propane gas in quantities of cylinders impossible to transport when they must share space with passengers and other freight. She carried trucks and jeeps, new engines, livestock, and house furnishings; several times she'd moved everything for building a small house, from chimney to cellar. Barring the accidental disaster that could sink her at sea, when she became too fragile for her work she would be hauled up and set in a cradle in a salt marsh near one of her owners, so she would be safe from vandalism. Some winter, when the marsh was covered with snow, she would be given her suitable funeral.

It was time to go back to the wharf again. The schooner's entry into the harbor and her arrival at the end of Mark's wharf had to be watched for the pure artistry involved. Even when she was tethered to the wharf by the big hawsers, with her sails furled, she would still be alive, just waiting. Joanna was halfway through the shed when there were feet hurrying behind her, a jingle of little bells, and Sara Jo's voice. "Gramma!" Joanna turned and braced automatically for the impact when Rosa let go of the reins. Sara Jo seized her hands in a fierce little grip, and pulled. "Come on and see . . ." It ran into a garble that meant "*Conqueror.*"

Joanna picked her up and carried her out onto the wharf. She tried to gallop, which was hard on Joanna's midriff. "Let me down! *Please!*"

"In a minute Uncle Mark's going to say, 'All children off the wharf.' "

"I'm not children, I'm Sara Jo."

"He'll mean Sara Jo too," Rosa said.

Mark cleared the very end of the wharf of ambitious boys before the heavy hawsers snaked upward. He caught the bow line, and Barry Barton, grinning, caught the stern one. "Skunked you that time, Cap'n Owen!" he called back to Owen.

"Oh, I saw you standing there with your hands out ever since she hove in view," Owen said. "Every boy should have a chance at it and I figure you're old enough now, but I dunno about big enough. Thought that line was going to make a snatch at you before you got a good hold around its neck."

"All young ones off the wharf!" Mark announced in his quarterdeck voice. "This means you too," he told his son, who was trying to slide unobtrusively around him. Young Mark lengthened his upper lip, shrugged, put his hands in his pockets, and walked back toward the shed. The other children dispersed slowly, until one of the men called from the schooner, "Never mind. You can come back after school and kiss her good-bye!"

Philippa's voice followed them. "You needn't come back to school now, but be there at one sharp if you want to get out to see her go. She's got to wait for the tide, you know.

"I'd like to seduce Steve into coming over to have lunch with me," she said to Joanna and Rosa, "but I know where his heart is right now." She nodded at the end of the wharf.

"Come back home with me?" Joanna invited, tightening her grip on a wriggling Sara Jo.

"Thanks, but I'll use my extra time on a walk, I think."

"Gosh, maybe you'll be the lucky one to find a body in the rockweed."

"I'm all tingly with excitement. Give Aunt Philly a hug," she said to Sara Jo, who leaned forward and squeezed her around the neck and gave her a smacking kiss on the cheek. Philippa went on up to the shed. The other women were moving away too.

Aboard the schooner the donkey engine choked and coughed into life. Sara Jo bucked in Joanna's arms, staring toward the noise. Jamie was among the men at the edge of the wharf, and Joanna thought Sara Jo was about to shout at him; instead she turned astounded blue eyes on her grandmother and said, "I saw a *man*."

"Come on, Punkin, you'll be wearing Gramma out," Rosa said, but she was ignored. Sara Jo pressed her hands against Joanna's cheeks and repeated intensely, "I saw a man."

"There are lots of men," Joanna pointed out. "Grampa and Daddy, all those uncles, Peter's daddy—" The child shook her head violently. Joanna handed her over to Rosa. "I'll go see," she promised.

"Gramma will tell you after your nap," Sara Jo's mother said. "When we come back to see the boat go."

"Yes," Joanna agreed, trusting that Sara Jo's man would have melted away in her dreams.

She hoped to pass the time of day with Paulie Dunnett, her favorite among the owners; he'd always been a great addition to the dances, but that had been a long time ago, when occasionally the *Conqueror* had stayed the night and headed out the next morning. Nowadays she usually left at once for her next port of call to pick up another load; she was that much in demand.

The men would all turn to, helping to unload the gas and transport the tanks to the shed. They used Mark's three dollies and several more from around the harbor, delivered by children who, however, would not be allowed to loiter.

It would be an all-adult, all-male occasion. Well, we have the Circle, she thought indulgently, and was about to leave, when her name resounded above the confusion of voices, the creaking of the hoist, the explosive cough of the donkey engine. Over the intervening heads, Paulie Dunnett shouted again between his hands from the *Conqueror's* bow.

"*Paulie!*" she answered, and began to make her way back past the stacked crates.

"I *told* you two not to carry on at the top of your lungs that way," Owen said to her. Nils gave her an amiable smile, but Jamie, who had been too young to know those dancing days, managed a fast glance between Paulie and her; she winked at him, and the narrow-eyed look was suddenly gone.

"Just so long as you don't elope with him, Marm."

"*Elope?* I'm going to run away to be a cabin boy."

Paulie jumped aboard the wharf like a twelve-year-old; a light-footed and tireless dancer, he had always been skinny and had put on very little weight through the years. He wore glasses now, and the creases at the corners of his eyes were more plentiful and deeper, but the eyes were the same. He took both Joanna's hands and squeezed them.

"Promenade the hall! When's the next dance? I'm ready now!"

"I'll bet you are. Why aren't you working?"

"Lame shoulder, dear. See my scrawny double down there? He's doing my job this trip. God, dear, you get handsomer all the time."

"So do you," she said.

He wore jeans and a black sweatshirt saying "Conqueror" in white, and a visored black cap, untitled; as always, a lock of sandy hair fell across his freckled forehead, ending just short of his eyebrows. He squeezed her hands again. "None of that sweet talk, now. Tell me about the dances."

"Come and find out," she said, "but better wait till spring. This is no time of year to go twenty-five miles by water to dance. We've got a new bunch of players, and they're good. The trouble is, everybody's forgotten the schottische. The young ones never knew it, and the rest of us are out of practice."

"I'll come out and give ye a lesson, and get that boy of mine out onto the floor—he *ought* to be a good dancer, dammit, but the kids can't do anything these days but jiggle up and down like those tin monkeys on a string. I'll bring my wife too. She always claims we don't go anywhere."

"You do that, and we'll put you up. Look, I'll let you know in time for the first real dance in the spring, and that's a promise. Now tell me something."

"Anything, dear."

"This may sound foolish, but my granddaughter kept insisting she saw a man—well, the place is full of them, but it wasn't anyone we pointed out. She's only two and a half, any one of you aboard the boat would be a stranger to her. But she's managed to convince me of *something*."

"Fact is, we did bring someone else, and this is where he wanted to come."

She felt as if Sara Jo's knees had just bumped into her midriff. Paulie was talking. "Said good-bye and thanks outside the harbor, so I guess he was planning to jump ship soon as we tied up. I saw him scoot ashore about the time all the young ones came running." He tipped his head toward the far side of the stacked empty crates.

"Did he tell you anything about himself?"

"Nope, except he was looking for the mailboat and then found out she wasn't running today. He came over where we were loading, asked where we were heading, and when Raymond told him he said he'd pay anything to get here."

"*Here?*"

"That's the place. Had a backpack and a bedroll. Nice lad, good handshake, good grin. Raymond took quite a shine to him. When we told him we aren't licensed for passengers, he said how about signing on for a deckhand this one day, and Raymond was all for it. 'Course he had to sign his name in blood and promise he wouldn't sue no matter what happened to him, and neither would his heirs and assigns." Paulie was tremendously amused. "All we left out was division of property rights and custody of the kids. Well, he worked like a regular stevedore, made himself real useful, and then soon as we were outside Monroe's Island, he lay down on the deck and was mighty sick. Blamed it on the breakfast he ate at Collimore's—said he'd been on boats all his life and never been this sick before. The boys put him on a bunk and left a bucket with him, but up he came about halfway across and had a hell of a good time!"

The hoisting operation halted for cold drinks and cigarettes. One of the partners spoke loudly. "You can always trust Paulie to find a woman to flirt with when the work begins. Nils, you allow this?"

"All the time," Nils said.

Paulie's son, down by the donkey engine, pushed back his cap and wiped his forehead. "You guys may not know this, but in some places he's known as the Casanova of the Islands. An old man like that gives a kid something to aspire to, you might say."

"Or makes him take to drink. Catch!" A can of soda was pitched down to Raymond, who said, "Thanks, Cap'n Owen. You're an officer and a gentleman."

"But can he dance a schottische, Raymond?" Joanna asked. "Can *you?* Now *that's* something to aspire to!"

"A *what?*" Matt Fennell asked.

"I don't know about dancing it," Ralph Percy said, "but I sure as hell can play for one. Just give me the time, that's all."

"Well, we're all going to learn it come spring," said Joanna. "That's what Paulie and I have been cooking up. The rites of spring."

"God, those rites went on all year round when I was young," Owen said, "and covered a lot more than dancing."

"Now don't get to recollecting your past," someone said, "or else give us all a chance." Amid a flurry of comment, most of it too fast or too soft for Joanna to catch (though none of it would be new to her), the work began again.

"What does he want? Did he tell you anything?" Joanna asked Paulie.

"Nothing that I remember, dear. Except he wanted to get here."

"Maybe he's running away from a bank robbery, and we'll see him advertised on television," she said. "Or maybe he's a teacher, and he's trying to get a look at the place on his own, not knowing he's already been spotted by the eagle eye of a very small child. Anybody who thinks he can be invisible out here for more than an hour is in for a shock."

He'd had to go around the stacked traps and crates; he hadn't come along the outside of the wharf, head-on into the stream of people on the way down. "Thanks, Paulie."

"You're always welcome, dear. I have to go act like the supercargo now, but I'd rather yarn with you. Let's not forget the dance."

"*Never!*" she promised. "I'll dream of it all winter!"

"Come to think of it, maybe his name's the explanation, according to his driver's license."

She stopped. "What was it?"

"Something-or-other Bennett!" He flipped a hand at her and was off. She hardly saw him go.

18

She saw the backpack first, leaning against a crate, the bedroll beside it. Expecting that he had gone up through the shed while it was still empty and the work of unloading the schooner hadn't really begun, she was painfully startled in her chest to find him here. His body looked as if it had simply been dropped by a great bird—left belly-down, sprawling and limp—and hadn't moved ever since. One arm sheltered the exposed side of his face; his cap lay between the other cheek and the wharf planks. He wore a dark blue nylon windbreaker, narrow jeans, and hiking boots. Thick black curly hair grew over the nape of his neck. Dark glasses lay just beyond the exposed fingertips; his other arm was under him. If he had planned to wait here in this warm lee until the wharf emptied, he must have been suddenly surprised by sleep.

Trying to detect signs of breathing, she saw none. No one had ever yet dropped dead when he set foot on Bennett's Island, but there was always a first time. What about those old stories when somebody died at the instant of beholding his heart's desire? What distant Bennett, whose family had long lost touch with its origins, had discovered old journals and set out on a quest? Only to—

Oh, don't be so romantic, she snapped at herself. *Ghoulish* is more like it. You can trot right back to fetch Nils to feel for a pulse. But this is *your* find, and at least it's not a body in the rockweed that the crabs have been at. She went closer to his head and said softly, as if in fear of waking him, "Are you all right?"

Back by the schooner, laughter broke out, and a couple of dollies took off, racing noisily over the planks; as if the reverberation, rather than her voice, had roused him, he turned over onto his back and laid his arm across his eyes. He stretched and then flexed the arm he'd been lying on. He wore a dark red turtleneck jersey with a large gold H on it. She moved to stand between him and the sun.

"Is that ship *real?*" he asked in a distant, dreamy voice. "I didn't invent her, did I? Am I really *here?*"

"You're really here, if Bennett's Island is what you want," she told him. "The ship's here too. She's neither the *Dead Ship of Harpswell* nor *The Flying Dutchman.* Nor the *Marie Celeste,*" she added, so relieved that he was alive, she wanted to laugh. "And who might *you* be?"

"I *might* be almost anybody. Gives me a lot of leeway." He took his arm away from his eyes. They kept blinking and then suddenly opened wide with the bedazzlement of a small child seeing his first lighted Christmas tree. And she looked back, all at once seeing a child's face in a tiny print, a school picture; the hair was short, and neatly combed, but there had been the same expression around the eyes and the curve of the mouth— and, in miniature, a familiar cleft chin.

"You're Haliburton Bennett," she said. "Six years old, the first grade. You're Hal."

"And you're cousin Joanna," he said. "You really are, aren't you? I'm Hal, how did you know?"

"Your grandmother sent us school pictures of all of you until you moved out West. How did you know *me?*"

"Grammie again. She gave my kid sister and me a big box of old photographs when we moved. We got to know everyone and every place on the island by heart. You look just the same, only older."

"So do you," she said. They were smiling at each other, very pleased with their discoveries. Given focus and direction, his voice had taken on an identity, a shade of family resemblance appearing here and there. He started to get up, then fell back against the nearest crate. "*Whoa!* I'm not drunk, but the wharf's afloat and definitely sinking. Shouldn't we tell somebody?"

"We'd better get off quick, and let them take their chances."

He hauled himself up and reached out to pull her into an embrace and kiss her cheek. Then he stood her off. "I can't believe this. Can you?"

"You're actually Hugo's son—Uncle Nate's grandson—and I never thought to see this day. There's always this feeling that if anybody goes to California, you'll never see them again, and in this case we've never seen you *once.*"

"Disgusting, isn't it?" he said cheerfully. "Tell me the truth, now. Could I pass for a Bennett in a crowd of them?"

"You'll soon find out. You're not quite the image of any of my brothers at your age—or your father either—but it's strong enough so that nobody who knows the family could ever mistake you for anything else. You've got the height and the chin."

The incandescence was back. "God, isn't this *great?*" he exclaimed and hugged her again. A curious gull drifted over them, and still holding onto Joanna, Hal squinted dreamily up at the sky. "The gulls do sound different here! My dad always swore they did, and he's right! They were different around the ferry landing this morning—had a Down East accent, I'd swear to it. Then when the island gulls picked us up, they sounded different still. Listen to them!"

"We could go around the crates, and you could meet most of the men at once, or you could walk home with me and have something hot to drink while I get dinner on—they'll all be going home for that soon. You'll have plenty of chances to meet everybody, unless you're just going to take a look at the cemetery and the Homestead and leave on the *Conqueror* with a couple of photographs to prove you made the pilgrimage."

"I'm going to stay until I get kicked off!" he protested. "I've been all my life getting here! But I wouldn't miss a cup of tea or coffee. I think when I lost my breakfast I lost a lot of me too."

"Come on, then." He picked up his backpack, and she took the bedroll. They walked along behind the high ranks of crates. On their right, as scraps of wind hit it, the water flashed and danced between the wharf and the steep climb of rock toward the high point where Mark's house stood.

He stopped to look up at the house before they went into the shed. "There must be some view from that roof," he said. "I'm not afraid of heights if anybody needs a roof patched. That place fairly makes my mouth water."

"Anybody with a strong back and a head for heights is always welcome. More so if he can use a hammer."

When they went into the shed, he sniffed loudly. "Just the way my dad talked about it—as if you could smell everything that had ever been in it, especially those cod livers in the hogsheads. Before his time, he said, but the ghosts were here." As they came out by the store they were met by crickets and warm pungent air rising from soaked earth drying out, mixed with the herbal and fragrant scents of autumn. Hal inhaled deeply, lifting a smiling face toward the sky.

" 'October's bright blue weather,' " he said, and she turned to him with pleasure.

"Did you have that in school? I didn't know it was taught anywhere these days, except maybe here."

"Not out there, either, but my dad would recite it every time a certain kind of day came along. And then there was 'What is so rare as a day in June?' If I'm lucky I'm going to know about that, come June."

They walked quickly by the store, but she guessed it was empty; Helmi would be up at the house getting Young Mark's dinner. She was relieved—and amused—at herself the way she wanted to keep her secret for a bit longer. Hal paused by Mark's dory and ran a hand lightly over her side. "Beautiful," he murmured. "Was she built here?"

She shook her head. "Times have changed in that way too. We've had crackerjack dory builders in the past. Now there's an old man on Brigport who does it. But we have hopes that some of the kids, at least one, will be a boat carpenter someday. Maybe even Young Mark—he's half of *We Two*. Or should I say half of *Them Two?*"

Hal grinned. "Who's the other half? It should be the dory."

"Probably is." Back at the wharf end of the shed a couple of dollies rattled and rumbled on their way up. "Come on before we get caught," she said. Around the corner of the big shed the place was apparently empty again, though she had no illusions about being unseen. Lisa's cat watched from the porch railing, but Dog Tray was in the house.

" 'Asters by the brookside make asters in the brook,' " Hal recited, trailing his fingers through them. "Where's the brook?"

"Behind the barn," she said absently. Nils was at the well, and she wondered if he'd known she was over beyond the crates. He saw them with no apparent expression and went on pulling up a pail of water. He took it off the hook and set it on the well curb, and waited for them to come to him.

"Did you know I was back there?" she asked him, and he smiled.

"I heard about the passenger. I figured you'd be on his trail." He held out his hand to Hal. "Hello. I'm Nils Sorensen, and you're a Bennett, but whose?"

Hal dropped his backpack. "Hugo's. Haliburton, but I'm Hal. You're one of the kids in the old photos Gram gave us. It was a school picture.

My dad named everybody; your brothers and sister were in it too, you were the only blonds." He was beaming again. "He even told me—" He stopped short, blushing.

"About my grandfather," Nils said. "That's all right, you can mention him. We do. Often. Now he's been mellowed by time into a picturesque old character."

"Which he'd hate," said Joanna. "Too bad he can't know it, and go around snarling to himself."

"Careful," Nils said. "If you go in and find some plate you love fallen out of the cupboard on its own, you can't always blame it on the cat. What are we standing here for? Hal must be ready to eat." He picked up the other empty pail to hook it onto the pole, and Hal said eagerly, "Can I do that?"

"I won't stand around and watch," Joanna said. Pip rushed through the gate to meet her; she dropped the bedroll to pick him up, and he kept craning his head past her shoulder to look at the stranger with Nils.

"It's a cousin," she told him. "In his first half-hour or so on the island everything's been perfect. He'll probably turn out to be dangerously allergic to cats." Pip wiggled to get down as if to go and find out at once. She took him into the house so he wouldn't disturb the experiment by winding himself around legs, and he hurried to sit on a front windowsill to watch. She put the teakettle on and started the thick pea soup to heat slowly; she had made it last night, with a meaty ham bone saved in the freezer. At the well Hal was drawing up the pole, scowling in concentration. When the brimming pail appeared, he lowered it slowly to the curb without a spill, then slid the hook away from the bale. Nils nodded, and Hal's grin was again full-blown. He shut down the cover and laid the pole across it.

When they came in, each carrying a full pail, Hal stood back watching as Nils set his pail on the counter without a splash, as if it were no more than a child's sand pail. For fifty years or so, except when he was at sea or at war, he had been bringing pails of water over the same doorstep, or its replacements, and around the same corner into the same kitchen, knowing from the age of eleven or so that he'd better not slop if his grandfather was around.

Hal now repeated the maneuver, slowly and with the impression that he was holding his breath. He just missed tapping the bottom of the pail against the counter edge. He gave Joanna a small, prideful glance, and she nodded. Nils said, "You're initiated."

"This is better than getting my Cub Scout pin," said Hal. "I'll go get my backpack now." He went out, and began to whistle as soon as he was across the sill.

"*Hugo,*" Nils said with a smile.

"Yes, and he quotes him every other breath. I'm having a hard time taking this all in. . . . Sara Jo kept insisting there was a *man.* What was there about him, I wonder?"

Dog Tray hallooed from the Binnacle back door, and Maggie, fastening his line, stared as Hal crossed the doorstep. Tammie joined her mother and gazed too; Rob and Myles, coming together around the corner of the Binnacle, didn't quite stop walking, but Rob scratched the back of his head and tilted his cap forward. Myles came on toward the house next door, smiling and curious. Hal, unaware except for the dog's salutation or warning, said, "Fierce, is he?"

"Take your arm off as soon as look at you," said Nils.

"Yep, I can tell. What about you, Old Stocking?" He leaned down to Pip, who stretched his neck toward a knowledgeable hand. Nobody knew where "Old Stocking" originated, but it had been used a long time on the island, and Joanna and Nils could hear it now in Hugo's own blithe voice. He had been the lightest of heart among all the Bennett boys.

"Where can I wash up?" Hal was asking, and Nils showed him where the bathroom was. Hal whistled. "I was going to offer to paint outhouses to work my board. Any left?"

"A few," said Nils. "Come in handy if the cisterns get low and you don't have a composting toilet. But if you're thinking of an old shack half a mile from the house, think again. Your father must have told you some tall stories."

"Didn't you go around tipping them over at Hallowe'en?" Hal sounded disappointed.

"That used to happen, but by our time, the toilets were likely to be in the woodshed or the barn."

"And a good place where you could disappear to finish a book," said Joanna. "If nobody caught you at it when you were supposed to be doing something else. Tipping over toilets would be tame compared to the joy of risking a hernia by hoisting a seine dory up on the schoolhouse roof."

"Gosh," said Hal. "Well, I'll carry my disappointment like a man."

Pip just missed getting into the bathroom with him and sat down outside to wait, every so often standing very tall to hit the doorknob. While Nils washed up at the kitchen sink, Joanna set the table in the sun parlor, where the windows were full of sky. The tall clouds, like the tall ships, sailed serenely over the island and into the southeast, endlessly patterned by the crisscrossing flight of gulls flashing white against gunmetal, or with wings translucent against the sun. Down below, small birds flashed and chattered in the alders, and ran about on the grass, their voices amazingly vigorous for their size. Three robins shared the birdbath.

Joanna made grilled-cheese sandwiches to go with the soup. Hal came out, to Pip's pleasure, wearing clean jeans for him to smell and sneakers that were even more fascinating, wherever they'd been last worn. He wore a plain yellow T-shirt, very clean. His hair had been dampened and combed back, which had no noticeable effect on its curliness. Now *that* comes from his mother, Joanna thought; no Bennett was ever that curly. I hope his sisters shared in it—and the eyelashes. He's got the chin, and the eyes are almost black, but he didn't get the widow's peak. Oh well, it would be too much for him to have everything.

He rubbed his chin. "I should have shaved. . . ."

"Why?" asked Nils. "We've sat across from them in all stages. You could be growing a beard. They're on and off 'round here all year long."

Hal rejected tea or coffee in favor of the soup, and they sat down to eat. Pip got into the fourth chair and watched him with a gold-speckled glistening gaze. "Ignore him," said Joanna. "He's trying to hypnotize you. It works on weaker subjects, but he's not supposed to be fed at our meals. Only he somehow manages to get in on all the mug-ups."

"I think it's neat to have a cat in the house. We've never owned one, but Dad's always had a cat down at the yard, Old Bobby, and we could play with him there."

He stroked Pip's head. "Later, chum. Jo, this soup is arregorical."

"That's one of your father's words!" Joanna said. "And your voice even sounded like his just then."

He was delighted. "What about a John Rogers soup? Who was John Rogers?"

"Who knows? He's always been around."

"Maybe he was the original Old Stocking. Or wore it," said Nils.

Hal put down his spoon. "I can't believe this! I have to say it again. I *can't believe it.* I'm here! I landed on that wharf down there and heard 'em all joshing each other—that's what he calls it, joshing. Among other words . . . And I've hauled water from an island well, and I'm eating in an island house, with people I was almost afraid to believe in because maybe they weren't real. And I'm talking too much." A sidewise glance at Nils and then away, as if Nils's peaceful silence made him uncomfortable. "I guess I'm a dite drunk. Did I use that right?"

"You use them all right," said Nils. "Look, we'd know you were your father's son even without the words."

"But you're sizing me up, right? This maverick from California?" The flush ran from the neck of his T-shirt up into his hair. "Would you say more if I gave you the chance?"

"Right now we're giving you a chance to eat. The third-degree team will be around here tonight. They've got a lot of years to find out about, besides being just plain nosy."

"Thanks," Hal said with relief. "I guess I can keep my mouth shut and just answer questions."

"You're one-up on all of us," said Joanna. He was startled.

"How? Don't say it's coming from California. The island's got it all over that. I knew the minute I came ashore."

"You came out on the *Conqueror*," Joanna said. "Nobody else has, under full sail too. As if it was all laid on for you."

"It was all an accident!" he protested, laughing. "I knew she existed— there's been enough written about her. Dad was pretty excited when she was launched. But I didn't even see her name when I went down to ask the guys where the Bennett's Island boat left from. I thought she was a cruise schooner, till I saw the trucks coming—all that gas, and a load of lumber for Isle au Haut or somewhere. Then I saw her name." He slapped his forehead. "My God! I didn't know what it would take to get aboard her when I found out that gas was bound for Bennett's. . . ."

"You managed," said Joanna.

"I think it was the name that managed," he said soberly. "You've always lived around here—you must know what it's like to have people's eyes open up when you say what your name is."

"Not always with respect," she told him. "After all, we've had more than a century to pick up some hard feelings along the way."

"You'll have a lot to tell your folks," Nils said. "You're not only here, but you came out in style. I can hear Hugo now."

"Did they know you were heading for here?" Joanna asked. "Or were you planning to surprise them? I want to be around to hear Hugo whoop across three thousand miles. Why didn't we ever get reckless enough to call him ourselves? All those years . . ."

"I didn't exactly tell them," Hal sounded subdued. "In fact, I didn't tell anybody when I left, but I called my kid sister when I was more than three looks and a holler from home." Nils smiled at that; he could hear Hugo again. "They thought I was safe on campus, half-buried in engineering studies. I'd been talking all summer about a year on my own, but I couldn't spin a thread, so I just went." He turned eagerly from one to the other. "There wasn't any other way I could do it. If you knew about us all, you'd understand." There was sweat on his forehead. "It's better like this, believe me."

"I hate to make mother-noises," said Joanna, "but they have a right to know you're alive." Of course, they all knew Vivian's ideas.

"Can't you talk to your father alone, away from the house?" Nils asked. "Catch him at the yard? You don't have to say anything more except that you're safe with the family—"

"And that I'm staying as long as they'll have me," Hal said with sudden fire. "I'm of age. I can do as I want, and I'm going to work my board. Heck, I might get a chance to build a dory! He'd like that. . . . Can I help myself to coffee, Jo?"

"Anytime. There's a mug set out for you." As he went around the table toward the kitchen, she saw that his face looked set and older. When he was out of sight she rolled her eyes toward Nils, who lifted an eyebrow in response. Hal wouldn't be the first boy to set out to see the world after a family row. How many thousand years had it been going on? But not to let them know would be cruel, unless he thought it would be a surrender. But even Owen, who had gone away for seven years, had sent postcards— albeit at long intervals and from far places, with nothing said on them except that he was alive. And his father had said, "Well, he's not the first, and he won't be the last."

Pip had followed Hal into the kitchen and was making loud interrogative sounds, which Hal answered with considerable imagination. When he came back, his pleasure was as unblemished as it had been from the start. "I need a walk more than coffee," he said. "Just looking out at those blowing clouds—and the way it smells out there! California never smelled like that! There must be crickets out West, but I never noticed them before. Shall I wash the dishes before I go?"

"You don't have to start working your board yet," said Joanna.

"Nils, anything I can do down at the shore? Sweep the fishhouse or something?"

Nils smiled. "You're welcome any time, and if there's anything you can do I'll let you know, don't worry. Go on out and have a good time. The *Conqueror* should be heading out around four."

"I won't miss that." He picked up his jacket. "Anywhere I shouldn't go?"

"No, except across people's dooryards. If you go into the woods anywhere, follow a track you can follow out again, but you'll always come to water if you've got a nose for it. If you still get lost, we'll put all the dogs on your trail."

"Hey, they wouldn't fall upon a stranger and tear him to pieces, would they? Any Dobermans or Rottweilers in the bunch?"

"No, and none of them are desperate characters," said Joanna, "but they like to collect at school and join pretty strenuously in the schoolyard action, so they're anchored until the kids are all home again. Some of them are pretty noisy, like Dog Tray, but they're about as savage as Pip."

He stopped at the front door, looking from one to the other as if there were something else to be said, but he couldn't think how to begin it; then he smiled, looking as uncomplicated as the six-year-old in the school picture. "See you!" He went out, whistling again—"The White Cockade"; he'd have learned that from his father. It was one of those tunes always played at the dances, along with "Soldier's Joy," "My Love Is But a Lassie Yet," and "The Devil's Dream."

"I'll bet Hal knows them all," she said. "Nils, I have this terrible feeling that Hugo's got chronic homesickness, and here we've neglected him all these years. I guess knowing how Vivian felt about his family put us off." She couldn't help smiling. "Remember what Aunt Mary wrote us about her? The Haliburtons might have been just ordinary Down Easters like the rest of us—not that any Bennett was ever ordinary—but she acted as if she'd married beneath her. She'd never visited the island. According to Aunt Mary, who could be pretty funny if she was mad enough, Vivian thought she'd have to sleep on cornhusk mattresses, in sheets made from grain bags, in a shanty chained to the rocks so it wouldn't blow away. She figures she'd done enough for Hugo by getting him into the Haliburton family. I guess she never listened to the stories about old Billy-be-damned Haliburton."

After Nils went out, she went upstairs to make Jamie's bed for Hal. Pip was in her way, diving under the sheets as she unfolded and spread them, pursuing his ghostly prey, grabbing her hand through the fabric. The cat went under the coverlet to the foot and back, and emerged with his eyes very big and black. His foolishness was a relief; he could always make her laugh, and that was restfully ordinary after the extraordinary morning. The excitement and elation were fast ebbing away. Just what were they taking into their house? Somebody who was a storm center in himself? She had always been inclined to accept people at face value but had found out often enough that the face wasn't the person, and charm might be disarming, but it was dangerous to trust. They knew nothing of this boy since the time of those school pictures.

"Oh, I don't believe he's a mass murderer," she said to Pip, who stopped rolling to give her his attention. "But what if he left home under a cloud? *Really* ran away from something, not just an argument about college?"

He hadn't smoked a cigarette when Nils took out his pipe, but supposing he smoked marijuana? Could she recognize the scent? No, but Jamie could, from the time he spent at Brigport before he became domesticated. Smokers called it "whacky tobaccy." He had once tried it, when he was in the navy, but hadn't been attracted to it. He saw no reason to chase after new sensations and reactions; he liked himself as he was.

A luxuriant small plantation had been discovered in the Brigport woods by a state police flyover. Naturally no one claimed it, and the owner of the woodlot had threatened the planter—if he ever found out who it was—with cutting his tail off behind his ears.

No more was grown, and the smokers had dwindled; it was expensive to buy on the mainland, and perhaps the smoking of it had been a rite of passage.

No one had smoked it on Bennett's. It might have been tried away at school, but none was brought home; the village was too small to have any secret meeting place, and besides there was that scent, which the off-island students would recognize. Linnie had broken off with a boy whom they'd never met, because he wouldn't stop smoking.

"He's a good kid and a smart one," she said. "He should *be* something if he doesn't fry his brain first. Maybe once in a while is all right, but he doesn't know how to be moderate. It's more and more, and I couldn't sit around and pretend I didn't notice."

She'd been sad about it for a while, until she'd decided he was his own problem, not hers.

Why not take Hal exactly as he presented himself? "The way we take you," she said to the cat, "and Young Dog Tray." That made her smile. Hal seemed as ingenuously friendly as both animals, and so had his father been, while Jeff always seemed to have something on his mind. His bursts of fun had been infrequent enough to always surprise. He left home because of a mainland girl who claimed he'd gotten her pregnant. Whether it was to marry her or to escape her was never mentioned, and now he was an insurance executive in a Texas skyscraper, with a gaggle of daughters who all talked Texan. Hal had told them all this at the table.

Rachel, Nate's and Mary's oldest, had never seemed to really belong to the island, perhaps because Aunt Mary never considered it home; apparently, though, she'd been loyal to it in facing her daughter-in-law.

Rachel had gone to Oak Grove Seminary and to Bates from there. She visited home rather like a summer boarder and had gone a great distance from Maine to begin teaching. Now she was a dairy farmer's wife in Michigan, with five children who had graduated from the state university. She was a tireless Grange member and substituted in the local schools. It was hard to imagine that she and Jeff ever dreamed of surf and seagulls.

It was Rachel who sent Joanna a card and a note every Christmas, giving the news of her family as it grew. But she never included anything about her brothers, whereas Joanna touched on all *her* brothers and their families, all the while feeling that Rachel didn't really care. But she deserved something for her rigid sense of family etiquette.

19

"Let's think of something ordinary," she said to Pip, closing the bedroom door behind them so he couldn't go in and lie on Hal's fresh pillow-cases. Pip was always agreeable to most of her ideas, and said so all the way down the stairs.

She put on her boots and went out into the bright day to replace the sides of the wheelbarrow; she laid the pitchfork across it and started for the shore. "Rockweed for the asparagus," she told him. "You're crazy about asparagus, so think of next spring and be patient."

You could read resignation in the way he sat down, if you wanted to be that whimsical. She left him there between the gateposts. The children had gone back to school, and Dog Tray was in the house. Even Lisa's cat, Tabby, that indefatigable watcher of harbor affairs, was absent.

The bare-poled *Conqueror* was alone except for the gulls atop the masts and along the bowsprit; the crew would have had their dinner and would be in the store, in someone's fishhouse, or taking a nap. Across the harbor Vanessa Barton was trying to capture sheets that were blowing wildly on the line; one got away and went sailing out over the meadow to-ward Hillside, and Kate Campion helped her chase it. Joanna had some lee here, and the sun was warm; she was close to the surf breaking on the harbor ledges as the tide came and to the gulls flying low over her as if discussing her.

"Hi, Hank!' she called to one who came really close. Diane Dinsmore went away to high school now, but she swore Hank was always there to fly over the mailboat as she came home; never mind explaining how she knew.

Joanna pitched rockweed into the wheelbarrow with such energy that the load was soon too heavy to move, for her anyway. Myles hailed her from his wharf, the nearest. "Lots more of that good stuff over here, Jo, after you get that load home. It's for your asparagus, isn't it? That likes salt."

"I was just about to pitch some off."

"No problem. Leave her right there, and I'll fetch her up when I go home to supper."

"And I'll owe you a good mess of asparagus come May."

"Finest kind!"

She hadn't given much thought to Nan since Hal arrived—was it only *this morning?* Now she marveled at what an odd couple they were: unpleasantly odd, with Myles forever buoyant, unless he lost that the instant he went into the house. "Some pretty day," he was saying, "and there's that beautiful lady over there just waiting to take wing again."

"Yep," said Jamie behind her. "And I heard she had a stowaway, or else a rich paying passenger."

"You don't say," said Myles, in a manner that suggested he had seen Hal with Joanna and Nils at the well. Probably at the fishhouse next door Nils had been having visitors with questions, and the schooner's crew wouldn't have kept Hal a secret either.

"Yep," said Jamie again, very crisp. "I'll take this load up, Marm. You lug the fork and I'll lead off."

"Thanks anyway, Myles," Joanna said to him. "You'll get your feed. It's the thought that counts, you know. Oh, the passenger's a cousin of ours, who came to see where his father grew up."

"Good for him! He chose a crackerjack of a day, didn't he?"

"Pure luck. More of a hit than any good wit."

"I'll bet," Jamie muttered under his breath as they turned up by the Binnacle.

"I heard that," said Joanna. She waved the fork at Maggie Dinsmore, who was keeping Dog Tray from charging the wheelbarrow like Don Quixote charging a windmill. At the gate Pip backed out of the way and followed alongside around to the garden.

"You want it spread now?" Jamie asked his mother, as if delivering a challenge. She was both amused and annoyed. Once in a while the old Jamie showed up—the family xenophobe, Linnie called him—but he was too old for that now and certainly too secure in himself for his hackles to rise at the sight of a stranger. It was neither a Bennett nor a Sorensen trait; it was pure Jamie.

"I'll spread it myself. I need things to do outdoors," she said. "But thanks. I'd have made three trips out of it, if Myles didn't do it. Come on in."

If he refuses I'll feel like kicking him, she thought, but he came along to the back walk. They took off their mucky boots, Joanna talking to the crowding hens. "It's too early for supper," she told them. "Oh, sure, I know it gets dark early these days—but I'll give you a mug-up if you'll let me have mine first."

Jamie finally yielded to Pip and picked him up, the only thing to do when the cat stretched up as tall as he could and hooked one's belt. Lifted, he snuggled into Jamie's neck; he'd spent a good part of his youth wrapped around that neck.

"Should have made you wipe your feet," Jamie told him. "Wipe your nose too. What've you been poking it into?"

The chill left him as he followed his mother into the house. "Who's he belong to?" he asked, quite amiably. "I heard he's a Bennett."

"He's our cousin Hugo's son. Your psychic daughter saw him slip ashore and kept talking about him till I had to go look. That's what Paulie and I were talking about, except when we were planning a dance for next spring."

"She was running on about a man all through dinner," he said. "She got annoyed with me when I said, 'Sure, there were lots of men down there.' She went to sleep mad with me," he added.

And I'll bet she looked exactly like you at that age, Joanna thought. Went to sleep with her lower lip pushed out.

"I'm making tea," she said.

"Milk for me." He took the carton from the refrigerator. "All right, Marm, so he's from Haliburton Boat. He could have chartered the *Conqueror* with one of his credit cards." He poured a glass of milk, got himself a handful of cookies, and broke one up for Pip.

"He was wandering round the ferry landing when they were loading this morning, and they told him *Clarice* wasn't going out today. They were short a man, and he worked his passage by helping them load, and besides, Paulie's son took a liking to him. *And*," she said emphatically, "they couldn't charge him because they're not licensed for passengers, but he signed a promise not to sue if something fell on his head or the ship sank or anything."

Jamie hadn't given up yet. "How'd he cross the country? In his Porsche?"

She took her cup to the table. "He came on foot, on trucks, sometimes by bus. He's been on his way since September, after a family touse. Remember when you went into the navy?"

His mouth turned up at that. "It wasn't a touse as I remember. I just came home from Limerock and dropped the news in the middle of the dinner table, like a brick in a kettle of soup. Maybe I was trying to see if I could surprise the old man for once." His smile broadened. "I did, for a second or two, didn't I? Of course there wasn't any war going on then, no hot spots to rush the fleet to. I had a pretty good time, except there were too many other people around."

"So you were glad to get home and have your own navy, no bigger than the seine gang."

The smile left his eyes. "It's different now. He may be running away from the draft."

"So what?" said Joanna, watching his reaction. "You're scared sick like the rest of us that Richard and Sam'll get sucked in and be killed in Vietnam before they're even grown up."

"And what could they do if they're called? *His* father probably knows half the people on the local draft board. Or he went to college long enough to have a student deferment."

"If he had one, he's lost it. He left school. He wanted to see where his father grew up."

Not willing to give up completely, Jamie scowled at his glass. "But he got that *chance* the rest of us couldn't beg, borrow, or steal; Jesus, we could live out our lives without ever crossing the bay on the *Conqueror,* and under full sail too, unless somebody broke a leg or a woman was having a baby, and they were heading straight back anyway."

"Knowing the Coast Guard could do it faster," she said, exasperated.

Suddenly Jamie looked at the ceiling and said softly, "*Sleeping?*"

"I wouldn't have let you run on like that. No, he's out trying to see everything at once. But he'll be back when she goes."

"Just taking a look at the Homestead and Hillside and the cemetery and then off again, thankfully leaving the poor and primitive relations behind."

Joanna sighed. "He says he's staying until he's kicked off, and he'll work his board. He swears he's even prepared to clean toilets. I guess he's been living his father's youth, and he's perfectly willing to take everything as it comes, just to be here."

"Nice of him." Jamie was only slightly sarcastic now. "But *why?*" He gave her an austere Swedish-blue gaze. "There has to be something else. If it's not his draft board, it could be the police—six months of traffic tickets, hit-and-run, driving O.U.I.—or there's a girl who thinks he should marry her."

"I don't know all the answers, Jamie," she said, more uncomfortable than he knew. "He's only been here a few hours. I'm taking him at face value until I have a reason not to."

"What does Dad think?"

"The only time we've had to talk about Hal is—"

"*Hal? Like Little Hal and the Seal King?*" He was lighted up like Sara Jo when anything made her laugh. "He has curly hair too, like in the pictures, but longer."

"I'm sure if he ever read that book he hated it," she said. "Anyway, your father and I had a few minutes while Hal was cleaning up, and *he* didn't immediately develop a prickling in his thumbs or a tightening of his scalp or feel a weird cold draft."

"All right, I know I'm a suspicious bastard."

"You're definitely not a bastard, but you do have a suspicious nature. I won't say paranoid."

"Thanks, Marm." Jamie's full smile, when it eventually arrived, made up for what had not been there before. He removed Pip from his thigh and stood up. "I'd better go home and make up with my daughter. Maybe I should take her down and let her dabble in the bait butt and try to stuff a bag. It's her life's ambition right now, next to being a horse."

Joanna nodded her head toward the house next door. "Tell Nan about that; she'll shudder for a week. She won't let Shannon set foot inside the fishhouse."

"He manages it now and then," Jamie said dryly. "Gets out on the wharf too. He must know enough to stay away from the bait. I guess any day now he's going to blow up, push off a skiff, and row like hell across the harbor." He dropped a comradely arm around her shoulders. "Beats joining up or setting off across the country. But just the same, Marm, don't be taken in. Just because his father's your cousin doesn't make him one of us." He was pulling on his boots.

"Words of wisdom from the sage of Bennett's Island," she said. "Go home and apologize to your daughter. Bring her down by and by to see him, if you think it's safe."

"I'll hang some garlic around her neck," he said, and went away laughing. Then the hens reminded her of their mug-up.

20

By four the *Conqueror* was preparing to leave; everybody who had missed her arrival that morning was there to see her go, including Mateel, who was arthritic enough to walk with a cane these days. And nobody, family or not, made a secret of wanting to get a look at Hal. Not only was he an intriguing stranger, but he was a Bennett; he came from California, and even though there were distantly related Bennetts strewn here and there, they knew none of them. But a son of the island was head man of Haliburton Boat, the western branch; the whole company, on both coasts, produced vessels that were written up enough in maritime publications to attain star status. The cover of the latest issue of the *National Fisherman* showed a Haliburton-built trawler battling a seventy-mile gale off Alaska. If his coming from California was simply coincidence, and the stranger had no contact with the yard, his glamour would be severely tarnished, except in the eyes of the youngsters, who thought of California as the golden coast of movie stars and heroes on surfboards.

But Hal hadn't shown up at the wharf. Joanna told everybody who asked that he'd planned to see the ship go; he'd gone exploring, and had no doubt miscalculated his time. He wasn't going right back. He'd be out in public soon enough.

"You don't suppose he *could* be lost?" she said to Nils when he arrived on the wharf. "It's possible. I thought he was dead when I first saw him this morning. People *have* dropped dead like that. So, he could be lost."

"If he's that numb, he deserves to be lost," Nils said unfeelingly. "Want to get a search party started?"

"Oh, I don't think we're going to find a pitiful skeleton deep in the woods a few years from now, wearing Hal's clothes, his bony fingers still dug into the spruce needles. Besides, you can't get deep into the woods anywhere on this island. I just didn't want him to miss this."

Then, watching and listening, she forgot to regret. After a sudden calm, the wind had risen southwesterly, and gusts came irregularly down over the woods to hit the harbor and contribute to the challenge involved in getting the schooner outside, as it was always done before the days of auxiliary engines. She might have been towed, but today it was an ensemble of lifting canvas, puffs of wind, voices relaying orders in the particular language of sail. Paulie was the man at the wheel, constantly looking up at the fluttering pennant and ensign; one had to watch his hands to realize the subtle movements of the wheel and the ship's response to it, as if she were as light and sensitive as a dory.

The adults were quiet. The younger children were hushed into silence by the older ones, who knew what was going on. Even the gulls seemed subdued, until she slid gracefully out between the two harbor points; once she was outside and felt the wind aft and began to lay on all her canvas, the cheers and the gulls all went up together.

"Let's go home and get a cup of coffee," Nils said predictably. Some would stand around and talk awhile, others were going up through the shed, and the more long-legged children had gone racing over to Long Cove to see the *Conqueror* as long as they could without watching her out of sight.

Joanna wished she were one of them; failing that, she'd like to be free of people for a time before the family gathered tonight. Up by the store they met Rosa, with Sara Jo pulling at her reins like a nervous colt. She shouted joyously at the grandparents, and Nils picked her up. She held him by the ears and kissed him loudly on his cheeks. "I've heard from Jamie," Rosa said. "I can hardly wait to meet Hal. I feel like one of the schoolkids. Can we bring down supper tonight? I've got a *big* chicken pie started; it was going to last us a couple of nights, but heck, nothing's too good for the cousin from California."

"I guess not," said Joanna. "Yes, yes, *yes*. Bring it!" They both laughed. She let Sara Jo lean over and hug her, and then they went on. What's the matter with me? she wondered. I was always up and down, but now when I start to go down, it's too fast and too steep. *Maybe I'm getting old.* She almost spoke it, but the thought of saying it to Nils made it ridiculous. He'd have only to give her that kindly look, which either comforted or irked, and she was never sure what reaction it would be. The maddening thing was that he probably knew just how she felt, and he was reasoning with her by using silence.

"Jamie wheeled up my rockweed," she said, to break the mood.

"Good. Trying to find out more about the visitor, was he?"

"Naturally." The tension was gone. "If he looks like a Bennett and maybe sounds like one, he's still not like that famous duck—he's not necessarily a Bennett except by name. If a cat has kittens in the oven, you don't call them biscuits." She was suddenly cheerful. "Maybe we should call Hal "Biscuit" for short, before Jamie starts remembering out loud how thrilled he was by *Little Hal and the Seal King* when he was seven or so."

Pip had come in with them, wreathing himself around their ankles, needing to be spoken to and then to be fed. Nils went for a fresh pail of water. They were sitting at the sun-parlor table, looking out at the late sunlight when they heard whistling outside the back door, and Hal came in. He sniffed loudly.

"All the perfumes of Araby," he said. "Fresh coffee and . . ." his voice faded out as he went for a cup. "I missed it, didn't I? I wanted to say 'So long' to the gang. Maybe I can write to them." He didn't seem too downhearted. "Raymond anyway, and he can pass it on and give the lady a pat from me." He sat down at the table. "I did something I didn't expect, and it was *great*." Looking from one to the other, he gathered them both into an aura of serene happiness, far from the morning's high spirits. "I fell asleep in the cemetery."

"That seems the right place for it," Nils said.

Pip crawled onto Hal's lap, and without looking down at the cat, he cuddled him up, all the while talking. "I was reading the stones and thinking it was too bad my grandparents weren't there—Grammie probably felt at home over in her family lot, but my grandfather should have been got back here with *his* family. Well, it was too nice a day to begin grousing about that, but I know he must have often remembered it the way it was today: birds singing like mad, the surf on the rocks not far below, flowers still blooming around the graves. I saw the stone for the shipwrecked sailors," he said abruptly. "And the stones for babies and little children and the old people who'd lived here so long—back to Charles James and Pleasance—and, oh yes, the ones who never grew old. They probably didn't come willingly."

He stopped to drink. "Then I lay down in a sunny place to watch the treetops and the gulls against the sky and to smell the good stuff you get when you're that close to the earth—now and then a little sweet whiff from some flower—and I thought, "I'm *here!*" I know I kept thinking that the minute I stepped onto the wharf. But it was a different *here.* This was the ultimate. The place where they all came when the physical part of them was ended. And I thought . . ." He colored. His eyelids flickered, but he kept his open gaze steady. "This is what Dad really wants. And I do too. It's home."

"Yes," Joanna said. Nils, leaning on folded arms, nodded.

Hal sat back in his chair and let out a long breath. "*Good.* You believe me, or you know what I'm talking about. Same difference. I wouldn't tell anyone else but you two—" He broke off, shaking his head as if in a frustrated search for a word. "You're not too young and you're not too old, but you've been through a lot in your lives. And you've both been away and come back. It must have been even more special when you came back. This island is like a separate planet with its own atmosphere. There must have been times when you thought you couldn't breathe out of it. I don't know how Dad manages."

"Your father's a busy man," Nils said. "He builds things. There's nothing better. If you can't have what you want, turn to what you've got. Now, I don't know how eaten with homesickness Hugo is—maybe building boats is almost as good as being aboard one. It's *creating,* anyway. It's not sitting down in your life like a rock in a puddle."

"I couldn't have said it better," said Joanna, "but Hal's right, Hugo has to have moments that come over him or dreams from which he wakes up."

"He used to take Nicole and me around with him a lot, when we were small enough never to get tired of what he told us. We'd take that box of photographs—sneak them out, really—and this would be on a Sunday when the yard was closed. He'd take us where we could get Maine lobsters, fresh boiled. We ate at long wooden tables outside, and those California gulls were mad for Maine lobster!" He laughed. "You didn't dare look away for a second—there'd be one swoop down and grab a lobster tail from your hand unless you fought him for it!" He was hilarious with the memory. "Dad called them all these colorful names—I used some at school once and a note was sent home. I won't repeat them, Jo, but you probably know them all." She nodded. "If we were lucky, they'd have blueberry pie—real Maine blueberries, big signs out shouting it. Then we'd go down on the shore. We had some favorite rocks, and we'd sit there and talk about the pictures all afternoon. And look at charts, too, and hear what happened at this ledge and that reef. My God, we thought our father'd lived in Paradise."

"What about the other two?" Joanna asked.

"Quietly brilliant, as far back as I can remember. And the big kids were always into so many damn'—darn—things that took up their weekends. Chorus, band, Scouts, sports, school projects, and politics. Nicole and I were the mavericks. They'd shove us into things, and we'd shove right out until everybody gave up. Nicole liked her dancing lessons and I liked being at the yard, so neither one of us was running wild; we did all right in school. In high school Nicole decided to be a vet—I kidded the hell out of her, telling her she just wanted to tack 'doctor' on her name to impress Leslie and Will."

"What about you?" Nils asked.

"It was always the yard. But they thought an engineering degree wouldn't do me any harm, just in case the yard wasn't always there—or Dad wasn't." He grimaced. "I could do the work. I'd always done well in the subjects I'd need. But I couldn't see the sense of it. I was willing to start at the bottom at the yard; I didn't want any favors. But," he shrugged and held out his hands, upward, empty, "I'd still be the boss's son. Nepotism? Anyway, I put up my last big fight this summer, and I decided it *would* be the last one, by God. I tried to talk Nicole into coming with me, but once she got into her courses last year, she was out of my life. This summer was my last try. The 'Us-ness' of Us is no more. She says I want to stay a kid forever. Maybe she's right." He had the proud and shining face of the first grader, scrubbed and combed, wearing a new sweater, and beaming at the camera. Then he slapped his hands palms-down on the table, startling Pip, and got up. "I'm going out and walk around the harbor before supper. I haven't been out on that point yet." He gestured toward the far side of the harbor.

"Supper at six," said Joanna. "Jamie and Rosa will be here; that'll get you ready for the rest of them."

"Is that like going up before a Board that'll decide whether I'm fit for Bennettship or not? They can't reject me. I fell asleep a stranger and woke up a Bennett; all I need now is the baptism, and I don't mean headfirst in the rain barrel." He didn't seem worried when he went out.

21

Rosa and Jamie came down at dusk, with Sara Jo and the fixings for the chicken pie. A big casserole was three-quarters filled with a mixture of chicken, carrots, peas, onions, potatoes, and green pepper slivers, in a thick, savory gravy. The dry ingredients for the baking-powder biscuit topping were all mixed in a bowl, needing only to be moistened, then gently patted flat on a floured board—never rolled—while the gravy mixture came to a bubbling boil in the oven; then the biscuits were cut out and placed on the mixture, and the casserole was pushed into the oven again. When the biscuits were browned, supper was ready. Rosa always had another pan of biscuits ready to go in, and no dessert was necessary besides fresh hot biscuits with wild strawberry or raspberry jam.

Hal was not home yet. "Do you think everybody dropping in will overwhelm him?" Rosa asked Joanna. "Is he nervous?"

"No. He's very self-confident, I think. He's been brought up by his father to think the Bennett's Islanders, especially the Bennetts, are a race apart, and he's just come into his own."

"What about his mother's people?"

"Of course *she* thinks we're a race apart too, but not the same way he does." Joanna laughed. "The Haliburtons have nothing to be ashamed of. They've been master shipwrights from way back. Hugo was lucky to get in with them, but I think California's too far away from the Gulf of Maine for a good old island boy. It looks as if Vivian was pretty anxious to go a long distance and outrun some of *her* family skeletons. She hasn't got any, really. Her grandfather Haliburton was famously known as Billy-be-damned because of his fancy language. But he was an honest man."

"I know I must have heard my father speak of him," said Rosa. "I think he knew him."

"He probably did," said Joanna. "Billy's a legend along the coast. He chewed tobacco all his life, bought a brand-new Chrysler every year—the top one—and kept a coffee can beside him on the front seat to spit into. Maybe that's what Hal's mother has been trying to live down."

"My God, the *disgrace* of it—" Rosa began, and then they heard the music; not obtrusive, not loud, but suddenly *with* them. It came from outdoors, but close. In the sun parlor Sara Jo sat on the floor staring entranced toward the door, and beside her Pip stopped grooming with one hind leg pointed at the ceiling; he was also staring. In the living room the men's voices stopped; the whole house was listening to a single strand of music so pure and so poignant it took a moment to realize it was being played on a harmonica. It was deceptively simple, and then suddenly it was not. Just as a phrase seemed about to declare itself, it turned to something else; the resemblance was gone like the shadow of a bird's wing on the grass.

Joanna and Rosa had turned in its direction but hadn't moved otherwise. Rosa, a musician, seemed to be holding her breath; Joanna knew she was holding her own. What was it like? Those elusive phantoms of old, old songs that could put tears at the back of the throat? Yet it was complete of itself, with the singleness of a flower.

When it finished, there was no other sound outdoors except the distant closing of a door, as if the Harmons had been listening too, or some of them.

"I'd better start the biscuits," Rosa said softly.

Hal came into the sun parlor, and he and Sara Jo beheld each other with mutual surprise, while Pip leaned against Hal's legs in greeting.

"And who's this?" Hal asked softly of Sara Jo's uplifted face.

"I'm Sara Jo," she said, as if answering a challenge.

"How do you do, Sara Jo? I'm Hal." He put down his hand to her, and suddenly she was overcome. She scrambled to her feet, ran in to Rosa, and hugged her mother around her knees. Hal followed the child's flight. "What did I do?" he asked quizzically.

"Nothing," said Rosa, "except she saw you this morning, and nobody else did; then you weren't there anymore, but now you are. Does that make sense?"

"Perfectly," said Hal.

"Rosa's my daughter-in-law," Joanna said. "Rosa, Hal Bennett."

"The cousin from California," Rosa said, smiling. "It's nice to meet you."

"Nice to meet you—and Sara Jo. It'll be nicer when she shows me her face. What smells so good out there in the yard?"

"Night-scented stock," Joanna said. "You hardly notice it all day, and then at dusk it lets you know it's there."

"Well, it hit me in a wave as I came up to the house, and it was enough to stop me—not too much, just right. It seemed a good time to sit on the doorstep and play something to celebrate being here."

"It was so sad for a celebration," Rosa said. "A homesick sound, home-sickness for something you can't touch."

"*I* wasn't sad. I haven't been so purely happy since I was a little kid. But it felt just right for the scent of the flowers and the harbor all mixed together in this quiet dusk, this *island* dusk, and the sea's deep breathing under it all."

Jamie came out, looking amiable if serious. He put out his hand. "I'm Jamie Sorensen—"

"You're *Daddy!*" Sara Jo shouted, transferring her hug to his legs.

"You and I are first cousins once removed," Jamie said, "or something like that. No, second. I'd know you from your pictures."

"You mean I don't look any older now than I did then? What's the use of being twenty-one when you don't look any older than a tall six? That's how your mother recognized me too."

"Don't worry," Jamie said, "if you stay around here long enough you'll begin to age. It's not Shangri-la. What was that tune you were playing? I kept thinking I knew it, but I didn't."

"I learned it from a man at the yard, the first year I had this harmonica." He took the case out of his jacket pocket and opened it. "The first thing I learned to play well. She's a chromatic job with a range of three octaves." He seemed modestly proud of the instrument. "The name of that tune is 'The Flower of Portencross,' and the man who played it was a Scot. It always made him sad, but he never said why, and I wouldn't ever have asked. But he knew a lot of fast ones too."

"Could you play for a dance, and give the fiddler a rest?" Jamie asked.

"Oh, I guess I'd manage," Hal said. "Hamish told me I'd do, and I felt as if I'd just won Eagle Scout."

Nils appeared in the living room doorway. "I thought we had a wandering minstrel on the island," he said.

"Thank you," Hal said seriously. "I'd rather be called that almost more than anything else. I played for my meals a few times crossing the country, so I qualify."

If Jamie hadn't yet given up on the Porsche and the credit cards, he had at least admitted that Hal was pretty good with a harmonica; they hadn't had a real virtuoso on the island since Pierre Bennett joined the Merchant Marine. If Hal could play his way unwinded through the "Lady of the Lake," Jamie's approval would be unqualified on at least one level.

"Everybody goes through a harmonica stage," Joanna said. "I mean *wanting* one. There must be enough old ones around the island to stock every man, woman, and child. But not many of us ever got beyond what I call the push-pull stage. And you'd never get *that* kind of music"—she pointed at the case—"with one of the little ones."

"If you're serious you can do a lot with one of the little ones," Hal said. "I stuck with mine because I had this superstitious idea that if I didn't, I'd have to take piano lessons. Not that my mother was crazy about harmonicas, but I guess she knew making me practice the piano would take more work for *her* than she wanted. When my father gave me the big one for my birthday, even she had to admit you could get real music out of it. Especially when the older kids said so."

Supper was ready. They sat down at the table; Sara Jo was in her high chair between her parents, across from Hal. Rosa had put the girl's supper to cool in Jamie's Peter Rabbit porringer, and she was a good eater, managing to hit her mouth most of the time while staring at Hal. When he winked at her, she blushed and lost track of what she was doing, and once tried to put her spoon in her ear.

They were all busy with their food at first, after complimenting the cook, and the family was too mannerly to ask Hal personal questions while he ate with such concentrated enjoyment. When the meal was over and the table cleared except for the coffee cups, what Nils and Jamie wanted to know was everything he could tell them about the recently launched *Ariadne;* she'd appeared on the cover of the *National Fisherman,* going through an extremely rough baptism somewhere off Alaska. There was a story about her in the magazine; it was disappointing in that Hugo was not in any of the photographs, though he was mentioned often.

"Has your father got camera-shy or lost his looks?" Joanna asked Hal.

"Neither. Mr. Bennett hasn't lost a thing in the charm department. The ladies love to have him coach them on the best way to smash that champagne bottle. He was along on that trip," Hal said to the men, nodding at the cover picture.

"*Jesus!*" said Jamie, then gave his daughter a guilty glance.

"Jesus loves me," she told him. And he said seriously, "That's right, honeybunch, and don't you ever forget it." Sara Jo sang it loudly, climbing out of the high chair onto his lap and then over to Nils. She folded comfortably into place the way Pip did, with her head against his chest, where she could listen to his heart and grow drowsy. Jamie pulled the magazine toward him and studied the photograph.

"Why weren't *you* there?" he asked. "Didn't you want to go?"

"Sure I did," said Hal. "But I wasn't asked. My dad's the good-luck bird in our flock. And I wasn't one of the guys who worked on her. Professional courtesy doesn't extend to the builder's kids."

"Your dad has to know about the *Conqueror.* . . ."

"Who doesn't?"

"So are you going to tell him you came out on her?" Jamie persisted.

"I don't know if it'll be a kindness to tell him," Hal was not smiling. "He's got pictures of her in his office, and he talks a lot about the old *Conqueror*—seems he never got to sail on her either. There's an old snapshot he's had enlarged, showing him and my uncle and you," he nodded at Nils, "and Owen, and a Trudeau, all lined up on her bowsprit with bare feet dangling and big smiles on their faces. Ten, twelve or so?" he asked Nils, who nodded.

"That was a day," he said, smiling. "We all seriously discussed stowing away on her. But they were onto us."

"One could have done it better than five," Hal said. "Never take a gang along when you want to disappear."

"We didn't exactly want to disappear for good," Nils said. "We wanted to go Down East with her, maybe to Nova Scotia, where Maurice came from."

"I never heard this story before!" Joanna said. "Of course Owen couldn't brag, because it never came off." She looked happily at Nils. "It's still great to find out there are secrets left about you. But I wish you'd made it, even if you'd had to be fetched home from wherever they left you. You'd have all been heroes to the rest of us." And you were willing to risk your grandfather, she said silently to Nils, who showed by a slight creasing around his eyes that he knew what she was thinking.

"Well, Owen and Maurice and I all went to sea eventually," he said, "and Hugo ended up in California and Jeff in Texas. But the voyage not taken—that's the one you'll remember hardest."

"I guess that's what the picture means to my dad, then," said Hal. "The day *he* almost went to sea."

"I think I can figure what you're getting at, not telling him you've sailed on her," Jamie said. "But when are you telling him you're on Ragged Arse?" It was the early settlers' irreverent version of the Indian name *Racketash*.

Hal burst out laughing. "When he told us kids that, we could hardly wait till we used it in the house. We spent half a day in the brig for foul language and got chewed out later by the Old Man for not knowing when to keep our mouths shut." He tipped his head toward the drowsy Sara. "I don't need to tell you how picturesque some of his words were for 'blabbermouth.' We didn't use them around the house, but they sure brightened up the neighborhood and a couple of schoolyards for a while. They spread like measles, and yet using them wasn't really dirty, like knowing all the really important four-letter words in French, Spanish, Chinese, and Portuguese, as well as good old Anglo-Saxon English," he added. By then even Jamie was laughing, and Joanna had a feeling that Hal had just carried out a successful diversion. But he'd misread Jamie, who from his first trip across a room on hands and knees, had never lost sight of a target.

"You can invent a hell of a trip out on the mailboat," he suggested. "I can give you real vivid details."

"I don't doubt that," Hal said, "but I'm not sure when I'll tell him where I am." He spoke easily, but it seemed as if his windburn had deepened to a stronger color.

Rosa's eyes widened. "You mean they didn't know where you were *bound?*"

"Not exactly, but my sister Nicole may have told them by now. I tried to get her to come with me. She wants to get here sometime, but she won't leave her studies. Going to be a vet. Well, look," he spoke to the table of them. "I told her not to say anything to upset my mother; I'd let them know when I got here." He was cheerfully confidential. "My reasons are good ones, and I'm pretty sure she's respecting them, or there'd have been a letter waiting for me here when I arrived."

Jamie was unreadable. Sara Jo slept against Nils's chest. With his head back and his eyes half-closed, Nils watched first his son's face and then Hal's, handsomely flushed and animated, eyes blackly bright under familiar peaked eyebrows; the boy was leaning forward, vividly intent on making his point. It was a face Nils had been watching for many years; there'd been many tables for the Bennetts to gather around, beginning with the big kitchen table at the Homestead. There'd been years of separation during the war and after, but eventually they were all back, and the meetings around whatever table was handiest went on as before. These gatherings served for family rows; family griefs; family news, good or bad; and for the winter dreams that would disappear with the first intimations of spring, even with a couple of chilly months to go. All the passionate arguments for and against, and their violent, usually witty, language, would vanish like the smoking vapor that rose from the sea on freezing mornings, to be gone by noon.

They'd laugh about those rows, much later. "Remember that goddam foolishness about mortgaging everything and buying Pirate Island, and how we'd keep the Brigport bastards from fishing it and still keep out of jail?"

Some brilliantly new figure of speech flung across the table, like a flaming brand cast from the spontaneous combustion of someone's skepticism and contempt, could break up the most passionate row in one huge storm of laughter and slaps on the back, the whole issue gone for the time being and maybe forever. The new invective would pass into the family lexicon as too good to lose, and later into the island language.

Right now Hal could be one of the brothers in his youth, explaining how his wonderful idea would work and make them all rich if only everybody would cooperate. Of course it was all done with mirrors, so to speak; closely listening and watching, you heard and saw Hugo at first, filtered through his son, who was an unknown quantity. You couldn't even pick out what came from his mother, except his curly hair.

"It's hard to reach him sometimes," Hal was explaining. "When he's so busy, he's fast as a flea. They were almost ready for another launch; she might even be out on her shakedown cruise. Calling the house is *out;* I don't want to get into it with my mother and either hang up on her or say something I shouldn't. Or they could be out for the evening. I can write a good letter telling him about everything and everybody, and send it to the office. After I've looked around and seen the house at Hillside and so forth."

"But still," Rosa argued, "you could just leave word somewhere—with your sister even—to let them know where you are and that you're safe. Let somebody hear your voice, even if it's on a machine." She colored and was suddenly a little flustered. "Oh gosh, Hal, I'm not saying this to be a pest, and if I sound like one I apologize. But now that I'm a parent, I feel for them and for you, too. I can't help thinking about when Sara Jo's grown up—and the new one. No matter what kind of a touse it was when you left, they've been worrying. Unless," she paused hopefully, "you've sent somebody a card now and then?"

"Not really," said Hal, somewhat dimmed by her honest concern. "But this is how it is with me. I hardly know I'm here myself yet. It's not even been a whole day, and for a couple of days I just need to think about myself and get my island legs under me—something like sea legs—when you get to a place you've been dreaming of for your whole life, and it's *real,* and everything's coming at you so fast you can't stop blinking or catch your breath. And . . ." his voice went low and he looked down at his hands as if they belonged to someone else. "I don't know how I'd be, talking." There was the faintest suggestion of a tremor in his voice. "If I'm going to bawl, I'll do it in private."

The ticking of the mantel clock suddenly increased in strength and volume, as it did in silence like this. Rosa left the table, carrying dishes and looking straight ahead, her eyes full of tears just short of spilling. She went into the kitchen and began energetically rinsing and stacking. Joanna felt a familiar stress in her throat. She stood up, carefully looking at nothing but the sleeping child; she could feel Nils watching her. This did the most to stop her eyes and nose from wanting to run. Jamie got up and took Sara Jo from his father's lap and carried her to the living room sofa and put her down. Joanna knew he was both embarrassed and moved. Behind her she heard soft whispers and movement as Rosa joined him and tucked an afghan around Sara Jo. Would they, for just a moment, clasp hands tightly in the dark?

Hal still sat there, head bent, playing with his teaspoon as if he'd never seen such an object before. And he's furious for showing weakness, she thought. She wished she could tell him she understood that. Across the table Nils arose and stretched. "I'm going out to smell the stocks," he said.

"So am I," she said. She pulled a sweater off a hook in the sun parlor as she passed by it. Somehow Pip was at the door before them, going out into the night with a chirp. They left the doorstep and went around the opposite corner to where the night-scented stocks bloomed along the foundation. It hadn't cooled down enough to quiet the crickets. The seas had flattened considerably to a gentle but constant susurrus, heard across fields and through woods. The lighted windows from the Binnacle and from Dave's house across the yard shone with the almost rosy brightness they showed at this hour, before complete dark.

"There's nothing we can say to him at this point," Joanna murmured. "Except 'Go to bed.' He must have been going on nervous energy for so long, he's running down even if he did have a nap in the cemetery. But there's no way to call off the others."

"He won't need to talk. They've always been their own best audience."

"You're the best of all, because you never interrupt or call somebody a Down East chowderhead, and then they can't stand it—especially Owen—and they have to ask you what you're thinking." She put her hand through his arm and hugged it. Across the yard the Harmons' back door opened and shut, and Myles called over to them.

"Fine large evening, huh? That was some nice music a while ago! If he'd kept on, my young ones would be out here yet, driving their mother crazy." He chuckled. "If he'd played something fast enough and started walking, they'd all be following him to one end of the island or the other, like the Pied Piper." He went across to the well, stopping to lean down to Pip and call him a good old pussycat.

"Who's getting all that love talk?" Steve's voice called from down the path. He and Philippa came into the light from the Harmons' front windows. There was some jokey talk loud enough for Nan to hear it, if she was just inside; did she ever miss this kind of chaffing, or had she ever experienced it? Steve stood by the well, his flashlight pointed down into it, while Myles insisted he didn't need to *see* the water; he could let the pail fill in the dark.

"Oh, let my kid brother play with his new fancy bug light," Joanna said.

"Come on in," Philippa said to Joanna. "I want to speak to the cousin from California before the crowd gets here."

"I hope he's not asleep with his face in his plate," Joanna said, hoping Hal had taken himself off to bed for at least a half-hour's nap. But when they went in, the house was hardly the silent place they'd left. Sara Jo still slept, but Rosa was washing dishes in the kitchen, and Hal was leaning against the counter drying them, and talking about volunteer firefighting in California forests. Jamie was in the living room with the television turned low, getting an evening weather report and finishing off one of Nils's trapheads. Hal left the kitchen to meet Philippa, looking as if he'd never had an uncertain moment in his life. Steve and Nils came in as they were shaking hands. Pip was with them.

"Hello, Hal," Steve said. "We came early to get the good seats and first grab at the mug-up."

"Whatever makes you think you're getting a mug-up?" Joanna asked him.

"As if your cupboard's ever bare. Never mind, my wife baked cookies after school and wouldn't let me have any.

"I'm not going to ask you any foolish questions," he said to Hal. "If you were your father I'd be saying, 'Welcome home.' "

"You can say it anyway, because it feels like home to me," Hal said. "Haliburton Bennett. And you're Steve, and your wife's the schoolteacher."

"She's after your hide, that's the real reason we're here early, plus it's a far reach from here to the Eastern End."

"What'd I do to get the schoolmarm after me?"

"It's what you're going to do."

"Fresh coffee?" Rosa called, and Philippa said, "Not yet." Joanna took the large tin of cookies from Steve and put it in the kitchen. In the slight confusion of the settling-down, Rosa murmured, "He's fine. We all pretended nothing happened. But I felt awful there for a few minutes, and I know it really threw Jamie, realizing anyone could feel like that about a place he's always taken for granted. It's always been here for *him,* as it was in the beginning, as it is and ever shall be, world without end." Joanna joined her on the last three words.

"I guess because we all know we can always come back; it'll be here like a fortress in the sea, with the Rock out there on guard. We don't think about being deprived of it. Well, that's happened to his father. But I'm glad Hal made it home."

The men had gone into the living room, but Pip climbed companionably into Hal's lap, and joined him in gazing across the table at Philippa. Both were all attention; Hal looked again like that school picture.

"You wouldn't know this," Philippa said, "but island teachers from way back have muckled onto anyone who'll have anything interesting to tell their students. 'Muckled on' is a good island expression, by the way."

"I've heard it," said Hal. "I just haven't got around to using it yet. What do *I* have to tell these kids?"

"They know a lot, they're all good readers, and they've met a great many people over the years whom they wouldn't be likely to meet anywhere but here, because the islands attract so many amateur and professional experts in so many different fields, and they're always willing to share. We have school trips away from home, and of course there's television, and I use as much of that as I can. When they're through the eighth grade here they go away to high school, but we want to make the first eight years just as rich as possible."

"But where do *I* come in? I haven't done anything; my father's the star."

"Oh, they know all about him and about practically every vessel built in the western yard. But out in *California!* You, Hal, are already famous in your own right; you're the Cousin from California."

"Oh, good Lord," he said in dismay. "Listen, I don't surf, I don't hangglide off mountains. I've seen a movie star by accident a couple of times, but I guess you could see as many or more around the Maine coast in the summertime, so that's nothing exciting."

"You've been firefighting in some of those horrendous forest fires the kids see on television. I heard you talking about it to Rosa. They'll ask about that; they learn fear of fire along with their first words. You wait and let them ask questions; even the slow-starters will get up steam. Being mute was never an island trait. Expect a lot of questions about the boatyard, and *Ariadne,* and even older vessels the yard's built."

"I'm intimidated already," Hal said.

"Listen, how many people do they know personally who've crossed the continent by guess and by gorry? You must have had adventures. You'll be a modern chapter in their history of the island; you're somebody to add to the list that begins with the first Indians to find their way here and continues with the English and French, and Italian explorers, who all knew the Rock out there that these kids see every day. And let's not ignore the Norsemen! They wouldn't give *them* up for anything."

"I'm feeling smaller and smaller," said Hal, half-smiling.

"Don't," said Philippa. "You're part of the comings and goings in this harbor that have been happening for centuries. There are no pirates that we can discover, though there've been plenty in the stories of other places.

There's the age of the coasters like the old *Conqueror,* and then you arrive on the new one, bringing the past to life. And let's not forget the era of the peddlers, who went from island to island with anything they could find to sell and made new lives in a place completely alien to what they'd escaped in Russia. Some started businesses on the mainland and did well, but a few took to the saltwater life and came to know Penobscot Bay almost as well as any fisherman. Mr. Judah still comes here a couple of times a year."

"I've heard about *him*," said Hal. "He brought a lot of stuff you couldn't get in the store. As good as Christmas, my dad said. Dad had us convinced that this place knocked the rest of the country into a cocked hat, cowboys and mountains and all. 'Let's go back there and live,' I used to beg, and I never got a really satisfactory answer, till I figured that everybody here was so smart, they all built their own boats so Dad wouldn't have a job. All right, Philippa, I'm on. When do you want me?"

"How about Friday afternoon, about two?"

"Done." They shook hands on it. "How'd everybody get to know me so quick? Until Jamie and his family showed up for supper, *I* didn't know anybody but Joanna and Nils."

"Kelp line," Joanna said, coming from the kitchen. "We don't communicate with drums, but there's nowhere you could have snuck ashore on this island without everybody knowing it in a couple of hours."

"That's right," said Mateel's soft voice from the sun-parlor door. "I saw you walking across the meadow this afternoon, and I knew you had to be a Bennett, but from where?" She smiled at Hal, who had arisen at her presence to take her hand; he was very tall in comparison.

"You're Mrs. Charles."

"And Charles found out from Nils about you. I'm such a nosy old critter, I had to stub on down to the wharf to see if you'd be there when the *Conqueror* left, but you weren't. All the children were looking for you, as excited as gulls over a weir full of herring."

"I *think* that's a compliment," said Hal.

Owen and Laurie, Lisa and Philip, came in right behind her and Charles. "Mateel, you'll have to let your kids get you that Jeep if you're going to take to the roads," Laurie said. "Down the hill twice in one day!"

Mateel laughed and held up her cane. "This old nag will do me for a long time. Today's special. I'd do it once for the *Conqueror,* God bless her, but twice only for a Bennett coming home. Or a Trudeau."

"I hope you'll be meeting one pretty soon," Joanna said while the new arrivals were greeting Hal. "Maybe your Hugo will suddenly get tired of scallops."

"Before this winter, anyway," Mateel said. "He must know all the girls for miles around New Bedford by now. If we're lucky, our new school-teacher will be another one to marry and stay here."

"We should be so lucky," said Joanna. "First Laurie, then Philippa. If marrying's the way to keep a teacher, I'm out of brothers but ready to start on cousins. I think young Hugo would make a great husband and father."

The house now seemed to be revving up to head out; the energy given off by a houseful of Bennetts, even though none were shouters, was formidable. In the midst of it Hal's face was transfigured by an almost blazing happiness. Nils said once that two Bennett men meeting on the road constituted a family reunion. Hal, in the midst of this—and the cause of it—was now realizing an enormous, life-altering truth: He'd always been right. This was where he belonged.

Mark and Helmi came in finally, and were saluted by all as if with raised glasses, which reminded Joanna they'd all be soon dry enough for coffee. "It's a good thing we've all been weaned onto decaf at night," she said. "Remember that old ad where Mr. Coffee Nerves was the villain?" Mateel did.

Sara Jo slept on as if she were in her own crib at home; Pip had left Hal for Jamie. The women were all in the kitchen. "Tell me," said Helmi. "Is this really exciting, or is it because everybody craves more and more thrills after the ball game and the hurricane and then the *Conqueror*? Hal looks like a nice boy, and he's handsome too, but it can't be just California, can it? My son just shrugs."

"It's exciting not just because of Hal, but because of his father," Joanna told her. "None of you except Mateel ever knew him. We grew up with him; he was almost like another brother. But he didn't come back after the war. We only heard about him through his mother, and by the time she died he was in California. We figured he'd turned himself and his life around completely, and we were the Past. The *Dead* Past. Hal's already changed that. It's never been the Dead Past to Hugo, and he's going to know he hasn't been dead to us, either."

There was a natural break for coffee, tea, and Philippa's thin butter-scotch cookies. Everybody crowded around the table now, and there were scraps of individual conversations about other subjects besides Hugo. Hal sat with his elbows braced, his chin in his hands, watching around him from under drowsy lids, stupefied with contentment and weariness.

Charles put down his cup with an unmistakable finality, and sat back in his chair. He didn't speak but seemed to expect that he wouldn't have to ask for the time. He wore glasses and was whitening at the temples now, which was very becoming against his dark skin. The fine creases of the weather and the years added to his distinction. Sometimes he looked so much like his father that his silent presence was silencing in itself. It was now.

"Harken to the Chairman of the Board," said Owen.

Charles smiled, lost years, and said, "Now I *like* that. Let me hear it more often. I hate to pull rank on you critters, but I'm still the oldest."

"No chances of promotion in *this* outfit," Steve said.

"Listen, the youngest is privileged," said Philip. "How'd you like to go through life labeled 'next to the oldest'? "

"If nobody else has any comments," said Charles, "I simply want to point out that we're all looking at a long day tomorrow, and I'm about ready to crawl under the kelp. But there's something I want to know while it's still today. Hal?"

Hal came alive. "Yessir?"

"Are you running away from the draft?"

Hal's cheekbones went dark red and his shoulders braced. "No, sir, I am *not*," he said.

"*Good.* I just wanted to be sure we won't have a U.S. Marshal showing up out here. It wouldn't be the first time, but it was never a Bennett they were after. Listen, son, I think the whole country ought to be rising up in its millions and marching on Washington, straight to the capitol. We ought to tell the Congress that *it* works for *us*—we pay enough goddam income taxes, and we aren't paying them so somebody can tell us every day what the body count is in Vietnam. It makes a man ashamed of having a good day, for God's sake, when he thinks of how many live bodies we've sent over there to come back in body bags, let alone the piles of dead who once lived there." He didn't raise his voice or speed it up. "We've got no damn' business being there, and if this was our government, we could get us out of it, not next year but *now.* But the law's the law, and until our patriotic Congress repeals it, anybody who objects to being offered up as a human sacrifice is breaking that law. So it would be nothing against you person-ally, Hal, if you refused; but we've never had the law come yet looking for a Bennett."

"And it's not coming for this Bennett." Hal's eyes had a watery shine. "If I ran, it would be somewhere else, not to bring dishonor on this family. But the truth is, I'm not eligible for the draft. I got a broken knee, playing soccer when I was fourteen, and I limp sometimes now. It's not serious, but I failed the physical and just managed to keep from doing a dance of joy when I got the news. Seems that if your dream is to fill one of those body bags or come home alive but in pieces, you have to start out as a perfect specimen. They only want the best." He looked around the circle of faces. "I didn't want to go out and shout 'Hurrah for Ho,' and all that. . . ." He stopped and then went on. "I didn't think our guys were *all* like the bastards who massacred whole villages; they're the ones who plug along scared out of their wits, wondering what they're going there for, who they're supposed to be mad at, and whether they're dying because they weren't lucky enough to have student deferments or trick kneecaps or because their old men didn't know somebody on the draft board. *My* old man knows plenty of people, but he'd never use them to get us out of anything. My brother just got his MD; if they don't bring all our guys out of there pretty soon, he may enlist—because he's a doctor, and it would be to help life, not death."

He glowered around the table at them, then left the table and went to the bathroom, blowing his nose on the way.

He left behind him an unusually quiet room, considering the occupants. Charles pushed back his chair. "Ready?" he said to Mateel, who nodded but was deliberate with her last sips of tea. Two by two they were getting ready to leave when Hal came back and said mildly, "I sure know how to clear a room, don't I?"

"It's time to go," Philip said. "Charles was right about a long day tomorrow, the first time out after a hurricane. I'm going with him." They both shook hands with Hal again.

"You said it as well as any of us could," Charles told him. "Proves you're one of those good Bennett talkers. Who're you partnering with, Steve?"

"Myles," said Steve. "We're set pretty close together in some spots. Good-night, Hal. I'm glad you're going to stay awhile. We'll be seeing you down at the Eastern End."

"You'll be seeing me all over the place. Everybody will. I don't plan on missing a square foot of the island."

"Hal, I'll see you Friday afternoon if not before." Philippa patted his shoulder. "You'll do fine once you get warmed up."

"I think I'm looking forward to it," he told her.

Joanna and Nils went out on the doorstep to say their good-nights.

Pip streaked out between their legs and headed to the nearest fence post, where he stretched tall, drove in his claws, then scampered off around the house. When they went back in, Joanna already bemused by the prospect of lying in bed with her mystery story, Jamie was coming out of the living room with a limp woolen bundle over his shoulder, and Rosa was carrying her dishes.

"Hal," Jamie said. "Once my father and I get all this trap mess cleaned up, you're welcome to go out with me anytime." He wasn't jolly about it, but he wouldn't have said it if he hadn't meant it, and Hal's response was equally toned down.

"Thanks. I'd like that very much."

Rosa kissed Joanna's cheek; she was not ordinarily demonstrative, but tonight had touched her in some new way. Jamie, too. They went out the back door.

"I think I'm going to have a cup of tea in tranquillity," Joanna said.

"Where's that?" Laurie asked from the kitchen, where she and Helmi were washing and drying all the cups and spoons. "That place on the moon? The Sea of?"

"Funny girl," said Joanna. "Ha ha. Who else would like something I can make with hot water?"

"Not me," Laurie said. "I'd rather wait till I'm home and ready for bed, and make it hot chocolate."

"Same for me," said Helmi. Neither Mark nor Owen wanted anything.

"You'll sleep hard tonight, Hal," Laurie said to him, "and you know what? *While* you sleep, everything will be changing for you. Because, as a certain poem says, 'Once you have slept on an island, you'll never be quite the same.' "

"The metamorphosis has already begun," he said. "I've had part of that magic sleep, in the cemetery this afternoon. That's why I missed seeing the schooner go."

"I'm about to make more of a change," said Owen. "Hal, you want to go out with me tomorrow?"

"Gosh, sure!" Hal roused up again. "Hey, I could be some help with those snarls!"

"Hold on! Willy's helping me with all this heavy stuff. By law you can't touch a trap if you don't have a license, and just because the warden hasn't been flying over us much these days doesn't mean we can tempt Providence. Oh hell, I guess you can grab aholt now and then; we could always say you were saving somebody from being dragged over-board."

"Gosh," Hal said, as if for once he had run out of words.

Getting up from the table Owen told Joanna not to fix a dinner box for Hal. "Laurie likes to think she's feeding a regiment. I'll be at Mark's wharf at six sharp to gas up and collect Willy, and *you* be there." He pointed a finger at Hal. "He can wear Emlyn's oilclothes. Practically new, and he left them lying in the dory that day. Whatever his plans were, they didn't include foul-weather gear or rubber boots either." He tilted his head to get a look at Hal's feet. "You can wear Richard's boots. I see you've got those big Bennett feet."

"That's what my father calls them. I always thought it was a com-pliment."

"And so it is, so it is. You'll do, then. Tomorrow morning, six. 'Night, sister mine and spouse." He swung an arm around Laurie and headed her for the door. She slipped free of him and turned back to the rest, showing the mischievous face of one of her children.

"Sad about finding those oilclothes like that," Laurie said. "Finding the human skin and clothes left behind when Emlyn turned back into a seal and swam away." She winked at Joanna and Helmi. "I wonder where our seal swam off to. The Celtic islanders say seals can sing. He's probably leading a glee club out on some distant ledges."

"Jesus, I wouldn't put anything past him," said Owen and swept her out. Mark was laughing. "Come to think of it, did anybody actually *see* him on that dragger leaving Brigport that day?"

"Let's go home so these people can settle down," Helmi said, picking up her jacket. "Hal looks as if he'd fall over if you gave him a push."

"I'm reaching that point," Hal admitted. "Am I remembering this morning or was it three days ago I boarded the *Conqueror?*" What happens to time out here? I guess I'll go to bed and think about it."

Joanna got him a flashlight from the radio shelf in the sun parlor, and tried it. The batteries were good. He thanked her for it, then stood in the doorway to the hall and said, "Good night, everybody, and thank you for making me feel so welcome." He turned toward the stairs, and Mark said, "Come back."

"*Me?*" Hal turned, and waited politely, one eyebrow tilted.

"When did you plan to call your father?" Mark asked abruptly.

The color flowed into Hal's face. He fumbled the words, wetting his lips first. "I hadn't—well, I just got here—I haven't had time to think about it."

"You should've thought about it," Mark said severely, "as soon as you got some good grub into you and your legs under you. That's what I'd expect of *my* boy. Or girl, if I had one. Any young one that set off across the country." He compared his watch with the mantel clock. "Let's see, will he be home yet, or still at the yard?"

"I don't know." Hal sounded on the edge of stammering. "Some . . . sometimes he stays late at the office for a while to do pa . . . paperwork while it's quiet, or he could be on his way home and be stuck in traffic." He seemed to catch up with himself and then spoke calmly. "They don't eat dinner until seven, and sometimes they go out. I don't think he'll be home, Mark."

Mark was in a good humor but was bluffly persistent, as if Hal weren't much older than Young Mark. "There ought to be a place where you can leave a message if nobody's home. Has he got an answering service or a machine, just so you can say you're here and safe, and everybody says Hello, and Why the hell aren't you here too, Dad? That would give him a prod, coming across three thousand miles, wouldn't it?" he said to Nils. "Come on, son," he said to Hal, "you can have the store to yourself, and I promise we won't be listening up in the house, in case you or your folks want to say something personal."

"You might as well go, Hal, or he'll stay right here," said Nils, "and we'll never get to bed."

"And we have a long day tomorrow too," Helmi said.

"The call's a gift, by the way," Mark said. "A little token of welcome, you could call it. So you don't have to be sparing if you want to run on about how handsome and prosperous we all are."

Or if you get emotional, the way you're afraid of, Joanna thought. *Go along and get it over with, so you can sleep tonight with a clear conscience. . . .* As if he were getting her message—or knew he was outnumbered and possibly acting childish—he pulled on his jacket. "Take the flashlight," Nils prompted him.

"And don't worry about disturbing us," said Joanna. "Take as long as you like."

Pip came in when they left, finished his supper, and went right upstairs. Joanna and Nils were not far behind him. Joanna had meant to lie awake for a while in this exquisite silence and comfort, and discuss the day with Nils. But he was prudently asleep first—or apparently asleep, which was also prudent of him. She found that the only coherent observation she could make about the day behind her was that if Hal notified his family, it would be a relief to all of them who were parents.

She turned her head toward Nils's shoulder. At the foot of the bed the purring became uneven and finally stopped, and all the sound left to her was that of Nils's breathing and, beyond the house, a nearly quiet night. With crickets.

22

She didn't hear Hal come in, and when she woke up it was her usual time, around half-past four, dark but with bright stars and no wind. That would arise with the sun. The water was always there, of course, but it seemed at a distance this morning. The scent of coffee came to her; this was when it smelled best. Hal's door was shut, and she hoped she wouldn't have to keep calling him to get him started; maybe he was one of those who wake themselves at a set time and come up all standing before their eyes are open.

She and Nils didn't discuss last evening; each was focused on the day ahead. "They give ten to fifteen sou'west," he told her. "With higher gusts. The seas haven't flattened out much yet, so that little breeze will give Hal a good ride, especially down around the Betsy Ross Shoal. If Owen didn't move them all out of there last week."

"If he did, there are enough other bouncy places so Hal won't feel cheated," Joanna said. "I'm glad Mark bullied him into calling Hugo last night. He'll enjoy himself with that off his mind, and when Hugo wakes up this morning out there in California, he can think of Hal going to haul with Owen off Bennett's Island. And if he's homesick, he deserves to be. If you bring in some lobsters, we can have them hot tonight; I'll make a good big chowder tomorrow night."

Nils always filled his own dinner box and thermos. While he did that, she wrote Hal a note in large black letters and propped the pad up on the table, where he couldn't miss it. It invited him to take anything he wanted for breakfast, from inside the refrigerator or outside. She and Nils walked down to the shore in the chilly predawn light; it was not a silent hour,

161

with engines starting up. There were lights in every house and out on Mark's wharf.

Jamie had already brought *Joanna S.* to the Sorensen wharf; the engine pulsed almost silently by the spilings, and the cockpit was lit up.

" 'Morning!" Jamie called up to them. He happily anticipated going out, and was even happier to confront a good brisk chop, as long as he could find his buoys. For both him and Nils, doubling up was all right in an emergency but not as a permanent partnership, and they would both be glad to keep to themselves again aboard their own boats. It didn't show, of course; they appreciated one another, they worked well together. If Nils thought Jamie was reckless, and Jamie thought Nils was careful, neither said so or even looked critical. Nils said once that if they were ever forced into a permanent arrangement, they'd have to hire an independent skipper to run the new boat they'd have to build, so they could own her half-and-half.

Sea Star moved restlessly at her mooring a little way from the wharf, on waters stirred by departing boats; the last of the darkness was shattered by lights and their trembling reflections. Joanna felt as if *Sea Star* were pulling at her mooring chain, harder and harder, desperate to go, too.

Joanna S. had been cast off, and Nils was at the wheel, taking her slowly away; Jamie called back merrily, "Tell Prince Hal not to let a seal snatch him out by the Gunning Rocks!"

Pip went back into the lamp-lit house with her and immediately jumped onto the heavy, turtlenecked, fisherman-knit sweater that had been dropped on a chair. Hal was at the table eating a bowl of cornflakes. "Pip, get off that sweater with your wet feet," she said. "Good morning, Hal."

"Hello!" He looked as if it were the day before Christmas and he was still six. "What a morning! Did I disturb you last night?"

"Not even Pip. He probably heard you but thought, Oh, what the heck, and turned over again."

"Wow, did I sleep! But my little clock," he tapped his forehead, "got me up. That's a good thing for a fisherman, isn't it? Not having to be called. Of course I couldn't tell right off what the tide was, but that'll come after I've been an islander long enough," he said contentedly. "I wonder if anybody's ever done a scientific study on these men who now live a long way inland but can always tell when the tide turns, back where they came from."

"*If* they know," said Joanna, "or if they just say so to show off. Hal, I'm giving you something extra for mug-ups and more water, because no matter how much you start out with, it's never enough. And two pairs of gloves, in case you get one wet."

"Thanks, Jo. You're a good person."

"Not especially good, I just know about lobstermen. Now get going. Better for you to wait for Owen than for him to wait for you. Willy's probably already on the car, with bells on."

"Okay!" He carried his dish to the sink and tried for a view of the harbor from there; of course it was limited. "He's not in yet, then?"

"No, but—"

"I only need a minute." He turned back to her, the anticipation wiped from his face. "I can't go without telling you, because you're too nice to poke and pry. I didn't get Dad last night."

"You can try again later today. You'll catch him."

"No, it's not like that. I didn't try." He didn't fidget or look away, now that he'd made up his mind. "Mark put on the light and told me that when I was through talking to turn it off and fix the latch so the door would lock behind me. They said good night and left. And I stared at the telephone as if it was this deadly creature that would attack if I touched it and kill me by poison. Then I left too." He kept swallowing.

"All right, Hal, don't blame yourself. I know you wanted to get it over with, but you will, sooner or later."

"It's more than that," he said. "I went down on the wharf and sat on a crate for a while; I looked at all the lighted houses around the harbor, and I looked at the stars. They were so thick—oh, I even saw a couple of meteorites—and I listened to the water talking to itself around the spilings, I heard a lot of other little noises, and I thought, 'Here I am on Bennett's Island at last, alone in the night, and I'm not going to spoil it.' The telephone call would have done that."

"I can see how you felt," she said, thinking how many times she'd put off something so as to keep a perfect moment. "But the duty's still there, and you know it. It's a fact of life, and you'll do whatever the chore is and get it over with."

Suddenly he swooped toward her and kissed her cheek. "So long, Marm. I know that's Jamie's word I'm borrowing. Wishful thinking. Makes me feel I'm a real islander." He gathered up his supplies and his sweater and went quickly toward the door, but there he stopped with his hand on the knob. He didn't look back at her but straight ahead, out the door. "I was afraid he'd be drunk," he said bleakly, "and he'd cry, and I couldn't take that." He went out and set off at a run down the path. Owen was just coming into the harbor.

For a moment Joanna felt winded with shock, and then she was very angry, "I knew it, I knew it!" She didn't shout but felt like it. "There always has to be *something*—no time to be sentimental for a few seconds. No, I have to be left with a picture of Hugo, who was always ready to laugh, weeping drunkenly over three thousand miles. *Damn it all!*" Pip jumped, then came over to inquire. She hauled the lean leggy cat into her arms, and he tried to cuddle into her neck. "How am I going to get rid of this, Pip?" she asked, and he sounded loud as a bumblebee in her ear.

Nils was gone for the day, so she couldn't tell him. She couldn't tell any of her brothers that Hugo was a drunk—and a tearful one; they might feel bad briefly, then they'd be philosophical, or they'd say he shouldn't have gone out West or got mixed up with the Haliburtons in the first place. According to their natures they would be loud or soft in their comments. Mark was over there in the store, but he had no patience whatever; she'd be mad with him in no time. She'd have to unload it on Nils.

She couldn't escape now in a long walk, because Hugo would be right there with her; Hugo as he used to be, Hugo as he was now, and Hal's voice and expression as he told her. The usual gathering of the women in the store while they waited for the mailboat wouldn't take place today because they'd all meet at the Circle this afternoon. It wouldn't have freed her mind anyway; somebody would be sure to notice she was absent-minded if not outright disturbed. They all knew each other too well, and there was a code of manners about asking personal questions unless someone was obviously terror-stricken or suffering grief, physical agony, or great strain. She certainly felt that, with all the rage and disappointment. Refuge with her Ngaio Marsh book, started and interrupted during the hurricane, was not possible. If she didn't show up at the Circle, that would bring someone to the door, especially if she hadn't been over to get her mail.

Right now she would begin making bread. She was not a dedicated once-a-week-without-fail baker, but she always enjoyed it. She found some light classical music on an FM station, and once she was into the routine it was wonderfully tranquilizing. How about a study on *that*? Was the yeasty scent slightly intoxicating with Strauss waltzes? By the time she sat down with a cup of coffee and some crackers and cheese, waiting for the loaves to begin their second rising, she was lecturing herself on the impossibility, not to say foolishness, of taking everybody's troubles to herself. Whatever had twisted Hugo's life out of shape, it was not her doing, any more than Nan's problem was. She'd done so well with that, she had actually forgotten Nan since the *Conqueror* came, and that was only twenty-four hours ago.

"Well, they can all dree their own weird," she said to Pip as she got up to put the bread pans in the oven. "Or should I say 'weirds'?" Pip cocked his head intelligently.

But like it or not, Hal would have to notify someone. He didn't want to talk to his mother—they all knew that. What about Nicole? They'd had her school pictures, too, and Jamie used to have a crush on her, maybe because she'd refused to smile for the photographer; her determination was obvious. What was she like now? It sounded as if she and Hal and their father had been a happy trio once.

When she headed for the Circle, she left four handsome loaves cooling, scenting the house.

The Circle had begun with Pleasance Bennett, as soon as she and Jamie (whom she always called Charles because he had been Jamie to his first wife and first love) moved into the new Homestead from the cabin at Bull Cove. It was important, she thought, that all the women of the island meet once a week for tea and sociability, instead of having the population divided on a caste basis, wherein she and the teacher-minister's wife represented the aristocracy, and the wives of the hired fishermen were "the others." After all, she was responsible for their presence here, arranging it so the men could live with their families instead of being tempted by rum smuggled in against Jamie's orders and by gambling with cards. The schoolteacher first taught in the back parlor of the Homestead while the school was being built. Then they had a place for church, too; the schoolteacher was also a graduate of the Bangor Theological Seminary. When the school was officially recognized, a post office was granted, and Jamie Bennett outraged the population of Brigport by naming the post office "Bennett's Island" instead of "South Brigport." A few Brigporters never spoke the new name, calling it either the South Island or Ragged Arse as a joke on its Indian name.

Pleasance herself had gone from house to house to invite the women.

Some were prickly with pride, afraid of being looked down upon, but Pleasance—in spite of having grown up in a fine house, with a naval captain for a father—swept them in with her mixture of charm and practicality. They could bring their knitting, their darning, their mending, and their children, and they could chat and laugh and drink tea. Pleasance's hired girl was always there, and the women's first remarks were addressed to her, as someone closer to themselves; eventually most of them learned to talk easily with Pleasance. Older daughters were welcome, and Pleasance paid them to tend to the toddlers, either outdoors on the beach or in the big kitchen with a variety of the Bennett children's toys.

Over time, some families left the island, new ones came, and the Circle stayed alive. If someone felt shamed because her baby came too soon after the marriage, or a woman was terrified of the island itself, the charter members could usually bring her in and win her over. There were a few failures with women who were as rigid as Nan Harmon; they isolated themselves from everybody else on this place they loathed. But there were enough successes to justify Pleasance's first ambitions. Friendships began between women who would have never made it on their own. Religion was no problem; if you didn't want to go to the services at the schoolroom, your husband wasn't discharged. But until they built the first clubhouse and began having dances and suppers, church-going was the one lively kind of sociability for the whole family.

They sewed through the wars; they clothed burnt-out families, not only on their own island. They knit warm woolens for refugee children. Other Mrs. Bennetts poured tea or coffee at the Homestead, and the women took turns contributing their own baking. There were no officers, and the only rule—self-imposed—forbade gossip.

Nowadays the small children—Peter and Sara Jo, and the youngsters from the primary grades who shouldn't be left on their own after school— were looked after by Tammie Dinsmore and Dorrie Campion, who were paid by the children's mothers. They played outside the school in good weather, inside when it was wet and cold.

From the time the schoolhouse was finished and the back parlor freed, there'd always been a quilting frame set up there. Usually the quilt was for an island daughter or granddaughter about to be married, but in recent years the quilts were auctioned off at the joint fair held with the Brigport women every summer. Each island kept what its quilts had brought. With summer people and a harbor big enough for a half-dozen visiting yachts besides its own fleet, Brigport could always guarantee a good crowd. The quilts' earnings were high and would usually be spent on the school and the clubhouse.

No one was obliged to work on a quilt, but everybody wanted a hand in it, literally. "Proof of solidarity," Lisa had said. "And we can always convince our children we did *something* for the island."

Today there was a lively interest in Hal, which Joanna thought she managed very well, considering that the thought of Hugo was like a sore tooth she was trying to keep from touching; she kept reminding herself how sensible she had been while she made the bread. No one else here had known Hugo but Mateel; she and Charles had named one of their boys for him. When the conversation left Hal for something else, it didn't return; there was always plenty to talk about.

She walked across the meadow with Helmi, Nora Fennell, and Philippa, who was going to the harbor to ride back home to the Eastern End with Steve. The talk was light and cheerful.

At Nora's they helped take in her washing and fold the sheets, then went on down the field to the lane that ran by the clubhouse, passed Jamie and Rosa's trees and the Percys', and arrived at the big wharf. Walking by the clubhouse they heard taped music from inside, something that speeded up their steps and made them smile at each other. "I *love* a good polka!" Helmi exclaimed, and the other two laughed aloud, not used to such a burst from her.

"Cluny's practicing," said Philippa. "I'd love to see her, but that would be sneaking. If she ever makes it in ballet, I'd make a special trip to Portland to see her."

"Maybe she'll make it to New York," Joanna said. "She may really be a great dancer someday, if dedication has anything to do with it." A little crowd of chickadees flew across the path before them.

"I've missed the geese this year," Philippa said. "I wonder if they've all gone south without too many widows and widowers in the crowd."

"Not to change the subject," Joanna said, "which I'm doing, but you were pretty ho-hum about the schoolteacher when Binnie asked, and Laurie got awfully involved with her snowflake pattern all at once. No new candidates?"

"A couple that Mr. Crane didn't even bother to send on to us. Listen—both of you—while we've got some solitude." They stopped in the lane; the chickadees took this as a gesture of sociability toward themselves and whisked among the alders close to the women's heads. "Good thing they don't speak English." Philippa said. "Think what they could whisper in all the available ears. Look, I didn't tell this at the Circle, because I don't want to talk about it until I hear from Mr. Crane. But there won't be any more applications sent to us. This morning, about three, I was up writing a letter—wrote it three times to cut down on the wordiness—and it was to Mr. Crane, to tell him I'm withdrawing my resignation. Steve mailed it this morning when he came up to get Myles. So it should be on the way to Augusta now."

"I hope he's as happy to get it as I am to know about it," Helmi said. "Mark won't have to have a new teacher for his last two grades here—you know how long it takes him to get acquainted. And I won't have to give up my spare room next September. I could *hug* you," she said uncharacteristically and did so.

"All the kids should be happy," Joanna said.

"Well, I think most of them like me," Philippa said modestly. "Of course the Harmons were an unknown quantity—not Tracy Lynn, but Cluny and Shannon. Shannon looks me in the eye now, since he became a hero. Cluny? She may always be a mystery, but I have no complaints, and I appreciate her uniqueness. The new Campions were disposed to be friendly when *they* came, because I was their father's friend when he was in school. The rest haven't ever known anyone else, except when Laurie substitutes. I've told her."

"When will this be public?" Joanna asked.

"As soon as Mr. Crane agrees. He ought to be relieved, but what if an absolutely perfect specimen shows up he can't bear to throw back? My ego will completely disappear."

She laughed and went on with a kind of easy humor. "You all know why I decided to quit—or guessed, because I refused to bore any of you with my menopause megrims. Steve was a gem, you all know that anyway, but he must have done an ungodly amount of worrying and wondering. It's a good thing we were way down at the Eastern End. Not that I raved and wept and otherwise carried on, but there were times when I just didn't want to see anyone. Finally I decided it was time Steve and I had a life of our own. Robin's growing up too fast, Eric's his own man, and suddenly I just wanted to shake everything off, never give the school a thought when I woke up in the morning—*if* I'd been asleep. Oh, I was a sorry critter sometimes."

"I never heard that the children noticed anything," Helmi said. "And Young Mark's pretty observant."

"Because the instant I got to school each day, it all dropped off as if I'd left this other person behind. Of course she'd still ruin my nights." She made a face. "But you know, when I actually resigned and then had to begin reading letters from all those no-hopers, I got to feeling possessive about turning 'my kids' over to a stranger. And last night when I was talking to Hal, it suddenly hit me in so many words. *I'm not ready to give up my school yet.* And I was sleepy at bedtime for the first time in months, because I'd made up my mind. I didn't tell Steve then; I kept it to myself. But I went to sleep and woke up to a new world. Then I wrote my letter."

23

The wind had dropped rapidly, leaving a hush that was almost complete; the run on the outer shores was diminishing to a murmur no more audible than a light stir of wind through spruce boughs. Everybody was in after a long day. The boats lying quiet at their moorings, with gulls paddling around them, seemed to have a conscious attitude of repose. Now and then a gull perched on a bow or stern, or went down into a cockpit to see if anything had been missed in the cleanup. Young Mark's dory had been launched, and he and Willy were towing a string of ten loaded lobster crates out to Mark's buoy. Young Mark was rowing, but Willy was leaning forward to push on the oars, giving him some help. *Robin B.* lay beside the car, and Steve was in the store with Mark. Not at all self-conscious, he put his arm around Philippa and they lightly kissed. Knowing now what they had gone through in the early autumn—in which the rest of them had ignorantly shared—Joanna was touched by the gesture without allowing it to show. Mark set out their bundle of mail, tied up with string. Philippa collected fruit and groceries.

"Got the island business all squared away, have ye?" said Mark, setting an empty carton on the counter.

"You bet," said Philippa. "What do you think the Circle *is?* We make a chain every week, holding hands, closing our eyes, and chanting. And that's what keeps the island from tipping up and falling over."

"Pleasance found that out," said Joanna. "And don't ask us what the chant *is,* because we'll never tell."

"Swore in our own blood," Helmi said in a deep voice. "And when you think you hear a heavy engine throbbing in the distance, but it never comes closer, that's *us,* chanting till our brains vibrate."

"By gorry, Steve," Mark said. "We'd better mind our failings with all this power flying around."

"You just finding that out?" Steve took the carton. On her way out, Philippa looked back and winked at Joanna and Helmi.

Nils had taken the mail home, along with a half-gallon of milk; Joanna couldn't think of anything she wanted except fresh fruit. "Hal get hold of Hugo all right?" Mark asked her.

"I didn't hear him come in last night, and this morning he was in a hurry to get out with Owen. He'll probably tell us all about it at supper time."

She had escaped without telling a lie, though there would be no real escape until she'd gotten Hugo off her mind. A little gentle splash on Eastern Harbor Point remained from *Robin B.*'s passing. There was a game of catch between the Binnacle and Philip's house; Tammie was kindly lobbing easy balls at Ross, who pitched them back with a mighty windup and a wild aim that kept Tammie running for the ball.

"He's getting better all the time!" she shouted at Joanna from over by Philip's porch.

"I can see that!" Joanna called back. Tracy Lynn and Amy sat on the Binnacle boulder, hugging Tray between them until he saw and heard Joanna, then he was off to meet her. He was learning not to jump, but he trotted with her as far as his line would take him, just short of the well. Myles came across to get water, cheered Ross on, and spoke impartially to Joanna and the dog. He almost always looked happy outdoors, and now, after a day with Steve, his traps all located and baited for tomorrow, and some lobsters brought in to sell, he looked as if he had never been scarred by events.

She couldn't help liking Myles; but now, knowing some of Nan's grievances, she marveled at his insensitivity. Completely spoiled, of course, even to his reputation as a lucky skipper. The charmers in her own family, and she included Hal's father among them, had ended up paired with women strong enough to keep their own heads above water. If this meant pushing a husband's head *under,* it was up to him to get it out again, and to both of them to have a conversation neither would ever forget. It had happened with her and Nils.

Pip met her inside the gateposts and was discouraged from climbing her by the lumpy plastic bag of bananas and oranges. A large bucket of lobsters stood on the doorstep. In the sun parlor Nils sat at the table drinking coffee from a Swedish mug, eating the heel from a loaf of new bread, and sorting the mail. The house smelled wonderfully of both the fresh coffee and the bread. She leaned over the back of his chair and kissed the top of his head; he tipped it back far enough to see her face upside down. "Just wanted to be sure it was you," he said.

"Is that bread good?"

"Was there any doubt?"

"I'm going to have some." She put the bag of fruit on the floor out of the way and hung up her jacket.

"You want a piece of this heel?" he asked. "I'll save it."

"No, eat it, love." She went into the kitchen and turned the gas on under the big canning kettle he had set on the stove and half-filled with water. When Pip heard Joanna slicing the loaf on the kitchen breadboard, he hurried over; she gave him a piece of buttered crust, buttered her own thick slice, poured coffee, and went back to the sun parlor.

As she sat down, Nils gestured with his thumb backward past his shoulder toward the front door; she didn't know what he meant until his lips shaped the word "Boots." In the corner where he left his, there was another pair beside them; their shining black newness had never yet been touched with anything, wet or dry, outside the store. If she picked one up and held it to her face, it would smell as new rubber boots smell before their life with sweaty socks began.

"The first long-legged boots," she murmured. "My first pair went to bed with me that night, standing where I could keep touching them, and I slept on my side, facing them so I could smell their newness while I slept. The next day I christened them in the bait shed and never took them up to bed again. When I couldn't hide the truth that they'd gotten too small for me, they were in good enough shape to pass on to Mark, and of course you know what they looked like after a week with *him*. I took every cut and gouge personally." She sighed and bit into her bread. "Finest kind."

"Bread or boots?"

"Both, I guess." They'd been speaking softly, and now she whispered, "Where is he?"

"Sacked out on the living room couch. They came in just ahead of us, and as soon as Owen left him on the wharf, he went in and bought the boots. When I came in, there they were, and he was flat out on the couch; he never heard a thing." He grinned. "He was a dite late getting his first long-legged boots, but he was smiling in his sleep. He'll have a lot to write home, when he can sit still long enough."

"Nils, I need to tell you—" She could see into the hall, and Hal was just coming from the living room. He waved at her. "Hi! Whatever that is, can I have some?"

"All you want," she called back.

"I'd better wash my face first. It's still got spray on it." They heard the bathroom door close.

"What were you going to say?" Nils asked her. "Any sensational news at the Circle? John Haker hasn't been around, so it makes things sort of flat."

"Among the fishhouses, you mean," she said. "We don't go for that X-rated stuff. I'd better slice that bread. I don't think he's used to cutting a new loaf."

Hal was limping slightly when he came out, but otherwise it could have been the first thing in the morning for him, after a long sleep. He smelled scrubbed. He sat down with his coffee and bread and butter, re-fusing jam or jelly. "This is *perfect*. Gosh, I've been eating all day, when we weren't working on a snarl or skidding up and down the cockpit trying to keep our footing—Willy and I, that is. The big man had the wheel to hang on to, and he was laughing at us most of the time. But anyway, *nothing* tasted so perfect as this." He held up his mug in a toast. "To *us!* May we always be as happy together as we are right now!"

They touched their mugs to his. It was a good moment; they were hu-moring him, yet she knew by Nils's eyes and her own reaction that they both recognized his passion of gratitude for what the last two days had been to him.

"And *now* . . ." He set down his mug. "I have something important to say." He was trying to be solemn, but not succeeding. "A Bennett of Ben-nett's Island should have his own rubber boots, and now I've got those. I don't mind wearing Emlyn's oilclothes; he's gone, and what the heck, maybe he *is* a seal by now. Didn't somebody say that last night? But the most important thing, Owen says, is to have your own lobster license, and tomorrow I'm sending for my birth certificate at Cape Blue, so I can prove I was born in Maine. Mark's got the license application blanks right over there in the store. I'll fill one out and have it ready to send with the money as soon as I get proof of my birth. So . . ." Merry eyes, Hugo's eyes, utterly sure, utterly happy. "Owen says they're pretty quick up there, but just in case, he knows people in the Bureau who'll hurry it up."

Owen says . . . Owen says . . . Nils was reaching across the table to shake hands. "Welcome to the brotherhood, Hal."

"Thank you," he said seriously. "I hope I always live up to it." Then Hugo intervened, irrepressibly. "Isn't there a secret handshake or a wink or a code word?"

"No, but we've been thinking of a flag," Joanna said. She put out her hand, and he took it in a hard grip.

"Designing that ought to be a good project for a winter night," he said. "And I was super at inventing secret handshakes when I was a kid. Look, I'm going out before supper; I've got to work off some adrenaline. Can I do anything first?"

"Bring in the lobsters," said Joanna.

"Done! Where do you want them?"

"In the kitchen."

Whistling, he brought the bucket in; still whistling he pulled on his jacket and got his harmonica from where he'd left it on the radio shelf. "I'm not going anywhere," he said on the way out. "Just out around here." The tune he'd been whistling was picked up on the harmonica almost instantly: "The White Cockade," followed by familiar tunes with strangers interspersed. Joanna promenaded the sun parlor with an imaginary partner, turned at the far end into Nils's arms, and they swung into the next step with the skilled abandon and swift, perfect recovery that are only possible for those who learned to dance in a schoolyard—and to a harmonica— over forty years ago.

Hardly winded, they ended up at the table and drank what was left of their coffee, pleased with themselves and each other. "We've got to have a dance soon," she said.

"What about that schottische? Going to call up your old dancing partner?"

"This time we won't forget it. I'd better check on the lobsters." She adjusted the burners, set the timer, then remembered what she'd been going to say before Hal came out. Nils brought out the mugs to the kitchen, and she said rapidly, "What I need to tell you is that Hal never called his father last night. He told me this morning. He said we'd been so good to him, he couldn't lie about it. But he never even tried. He went for a walk instead."

Nils said equably, "Afraid Hugo would light into him for taking off the way he did? I don't think he would, knowing where Hal was. He'd be wanting to talk to everybody."

"It's not that simple. Nils, Hal was afraid his father would be drunk. And that he'd *cry*." Just saying it nauseated her so, she half-expected the cold coffee to come up. "*Hugo*," she said. "Our Hugo." She was blinking, the tears smarted, and his face was a blur. His hands warmly cupped her cheeks.

"Listen," he said. "That was what you like to call a happenstance. Maybe Hal's not ready to talk with his father yet. We'll likely never know that story. Maybe he knows Hugo's going to be emotional about this, and he doesn't know how to handle it—in case Hugo's had a drink too many." He pressed his fingertips gently on her temples. "If I thought our son could be dead, and he called me, I might choke up a bit myself, and I wouldn't need to be half-drunk. Hal knows this could happen with his father, and he doesn't think Hugo can handle it—for Hal to be alive and on Bennett's Island with all of us."

"You think that's all it is? An excuse not to face him?" She removed his hands from her face and held them. Outside, "My Love Is But a Lassie Yet" conjured up a roomful of whirling dancers, tireless musicians, and occasional whoops.

"I could be wrong," Nils said. "But so could you."

"And often am," she said bitterly. He smiled, and kissed her.

"My wife, right or wrong. Let's go for the easiest ideas first, because we don't know one cussed damn' thing about their life out there."

"I think Vivian's a witch. I didn't say 'bitch'; that's an insult to a dog. Don't tell me I may be doing her a wrong. She's always looked down on us and she had no call for it." He was still smiling, and she couldn't help answering that. "Witch, witch, witch!" she chanted. "There, that felt *wonderful*. Are you going to keep on being reasonable?"

"Here's one more reason not to blow a gasket over this. Hugo's heading up a million-dollar business out there, even though we never thought of him as that bright. There's no way he can spend his nights as a falling-down drooling drunk and still be at the office before anybody else in the morning. Not for long, anyway. The parent company has a board, and I understand from the chief gossip tabloid of the Midcoast region that Hugo's brother-in-law, running the Cape Blue yard, wanted the California business all those years ago. But Vivian worked on their old man because she was in a hell of a hurry to get Hugo away from here before he started acting like Billy-be-damned."

"Good Lord, how'd John Haker get all this?"

"You never get the direct source from John, but he traveled a lot to the west'ard when the hake were thin around here."

"How true do you think it is?"

"I heard about Jarod Haliburton from other sources. He's still sour about it. Paulie Dunnett, your dancing friend, met him at a boat show in Portland; Paulie began talking about how well the western branch was doing and got a dirty look and no answer. This was a long time before the runaway prince showed up on these shores." He began to laugh. "Be funny if Mrs. Jarod turns out to be town clerk down there. The word would be out then, unless she just throws Hal's request away and pretends it never happened."

"What do you think about Owen telling him to get a license right off?"

"*Owen* thinks God's sent him a new sternman."

"I didn't want to put it into words. Poor Laurie, she's been waiting all these years to get him to herself, and she thought she'd made it. No winter fishing and a trip in the spring. . . . Well, we don't need to tell her, do we?"

Nils grinned and called on God in Swedish, a habit that made Sigurd's most simple utterances sound thrillingly dramatic to anyone who wasn't used to him. "We don't tell anybody anything. We just follow our course, with due attention to the set of the sails, and enjoy life." Outside, the music had turned to a waltz. It was "Over the Waves," an old favorite. Hugo must have taught Hal everything he remembered.

"May I have this dance?" Nils asked. She moved into his arms, and they waltzed gravely the length of the room, moving together perfectly as they always had. Nils never talked while he danced, but waltzing with him one didn't need talk; when they passed the kitchen door on the way back, the lobsters were boiling over.

"Farewell, sweet prince," Joanna said on the way to the stove. He came after her with the bucket, saying, "Would you mind just trying this shoe on?"

24

Hal ate his lobsters like a veteran. All Hugo's children knew how to open a lobster and extract everything from it, even if, with their advancing years, they no longer bothered to chew on all the little legs. Their taste for tomalley had been cultivated young, and they knew how to pick out the good nuggets in the body. Melted butter was fine but not necessary. Homemade bread on the side was better than potato chips. Joanna had fixed Pip's own lobster for the sake of peace, and she gave it to him when they sat down to theirs.

These lobsters were hard-shells, and breaking open the big claws called for certain skills, but Hugo had taught his children well. "I don't like to get it all picked out and then eat it," Hal said. "It goes too fast. It's better to eat it chunk by chunk as you get it out, and then break up the tail, and eat the tomalley with a spoon. Or scoop it out with your finger. That's even better. Have you seen that spelled 'tamale'? It always makes Dad snort." He seemed perfectly happy *talking* about his father.

When they were done and the table was cleared away, the shells went into the bucket, to be delivered to the hens in the morning; the rest of the lobsters, well cooled on the doorstep, went into the bottom of the refrigerator. Tomorrow, early, they would become chowder, to ripen all day for supper.

There hadn't been much room for serious conversation while they ate. When Hal came back from washing up in the bathroom, while they used the kitchen sink, he said contentedly, "I almost forgot what I was going to ask you. I must be a pretty simpleminded character. While I was out there falling around in the boat, skidding on rockweed, I thought I couldn't be

177

happier. I felt that way when I woke up in the cemetery yesterday; and tonight, into lobsters up to my elbows, I felt it again." He helped to serve dessert, a fruity gelatin dish that went well after lobster, talking all the while. "I've slept twice—no, three times counting my afternoon nap today—on an island; *the* island. I've been out on these waters, and now I've eaten lobsters from them. What more, you may ask?"

"*You* may ask," Nils said.

"Well, how do I go about *becoming* one of the Brotherhood, as you called it? I know I'm going to have my license—that's like a passport. But I can't freeload on you or make the rounds of the family for too long. How can I get a place of my own? If I can get a boat with a good cabin, I could live aboard her, like the hakers. But first I have to *get* the boat, and how does that happen when you haven't got any real money?" He was as disturbed as if he were watching all his visions disappearing like phantoms in strong sunlight.

"First," Joanna said, "you can stay here until you have a corner of your own, and don't worry, I'll find something for you to do, so you won't be freeloading."

"Second," said Nils, "what else did Owen say to you besides advising you to get your license as soon as possible?"

"That bothers me, now that I think about it. I don't know how I'm going to get started as a lobsterman even after I'm licensed."

"Did he say anything about going over to Hillside, sleeping in your father's old room, and so forth?" Nils asked.

"Yes, but that's up to Laurie, isn't it? Having somebody else in the house?"

Joanna thought this had better be quickly passed over, and maybe he wouldn't notice it. He was going on. "Oh, he did tell me not to mention getting my license until it happens. There's no reason why I shouldn't get it, but he said something about not counting chickens before they hatch. Does he mean somebody can put a spoke in my wheel because they don't want me here?" He looked youthfully hurt and worried. "Everybody's been so friendly, and I figured that the ones who hadn't known my father just liked me anyway. Or maybe it's because I'm a Bennett."

"If they've been open-handed it's because they feel that way," Nils said. "Don't worry about that. Time enough to worry about your status as an island lobsterman when you're ready to set your first traps, and that wouldn't be now, even if you had gear already."

"Being a Bennett doesn't cut much ice around here nowadays," Joanna said. "Not like the days when you didn't get out here without permission from old Jamie. But he wasn't that tough, except on liquor and gambling. Nobody's a Bennett tenant now, and the few rules we've all made up among ourselves apply to everybody. Like not eating short lobsters, trap limits, and so forth."

"But traps and my boat," Hal protested, his cheekbones red. "I could start out with a heavy dory like Richard's and a big outboard, but my God, that runs into a lot of money! And I'm not hinting for a loan or for anyone to sign for me at a bank. What about the Small Business Administration? That's been a help to some fishermen back home."

"*Wait*," said Nils, very softly, as if he were gentling Sara Jo. "*Just wait.* It's not time to worry yet. Wait until your license comes through, and then, if something hasn't fallen into place, we'll work on it. You don't know what's just around the corner, so shorten your sails."

The release of tension was palpable.

Joanna said, "There's an island saying: 'When Nils worries, it's time to worry.' So go along with him."

"Of course it might be that Nils hasn't the brains to worry when he should, sometimes," said Nils, "so don't go trusting in that as if it's Holy Writ. But I'm right this time. You've been here two days, and if there's anything we're rich in, it's time, especially in winter."

"Thank you," Hal said quietly. "There's nobody I'd rather listen to than you." He reached out to Nils and they shook hands. Then the ebullient personality took over. "Well, I guess I'll go out. Unless you want me to wash the dishes first?" he asked Joanna.

"No, no, I haven't even put on the dishwater to heat yet."

"I'll bet you're surprised I already have a place to go."

"You could drop in almost anywhere and they'll welcome you," she said, "especially if there are kids, so they can get first crack at you before Friday, when they can go to school bragging."

"Well, there are kids, but I'm not going to see them. You know yesterday afternoon just before supper, when I took a walk around the other side of the harbor? Well, I gave a hand to a skinny little guy hauling a big skiff up the beach."

"Jockey George," said Joanna. "George Baxter."

"It was pretty empty over there, with the kids all scattering for home, and there was just this good-natured mutt playing around us. Well, we got to talking, standing there on top of the beach—*Jockey* George?" Hal asked. "He's small enough to be one."

"He always wanted to be one," Joanna told him. "He's crazy about horses—and riding them—but there aren't many jockey jobs going in Maine. Is that what you'd call them?"

"Don't look at me, I'm not in the trade," said Nils. "But he's making the best of it out here, where there isn't even a workhorse left. He coached the Racketash Raiders to their first win over Brigport in a long time." Neither would mention that George was on probation.

"He works for his brother-in-law, he told me. But when he gets enough money saved up he's going to buy him a horse and go in for harness racing. He said to be a rider he'd have to go down south and try to get taken on at some big stable, and someday he might make a jockey. But harness racing is the big thing in Maine, and he'd be called a horseman then. He was proud of that. Funny thing," Hal said, "standing there with the twilight coming on and hearing the water so gentle on the shore and taking in the smell of the marsh and drying traps—it was pretty near perfection for me. But here's the little guy talking about racing as if it's a religion. I guess it is, with him. He's even got his horse picked out, a mare from a great family of trotters, if she's not sold before he can afford her. I hope he does get her. Anybody who wants something that much ought to have his wish. I'm getting mine, I think." He grinned and raised crossed fingers. "Yep, I remember—shorten sail. George thinks he'll have her by next summer."

His year of probation would be up then. "When he gets ready to race her," Joanna said, "whatever horse he gets, I'll be tempted to make a special trip to the mainland for the event."

"I'll have my rig by then too," Hal said, "all paid for, or mostly. . . . Anyway, I'm going over to Campions' tonight and play chess with George. He was telling me about all the tournaments in the winters, and he'd like to play more chess so he'll have a better chance. His brother-in-law helps him out now and then, but the youngsters are working on their cribbage, so they get first call on their folks' time."

"So you're a chess player," Nils said.

"A pretty fair one, too. I'm not being modest, but I was tops in the chess club at high school. . . . Look, I won't be late. We had a long day, and he'll be out early tomorrow too. Oh, I forgot again. Owen says he has this deal with Laurie, where she goes with him every good day this time of year, when there's not heavy work to do. So I don't expect to go again—with him—until the weather's a lot worse and I have my license, so I can legally do more. Take Willy's place." He went out.

"And I'll bet Owen told Hal not to mention the license to Laurie," Joanna said softly. "No tempting Fate. I'd like to take a hammer to his head. When she asks him why all his traps aren't up by Christmas, he's going to present her with a full-fledged sternman and move him into the house so he'll be handy! With any ordinary man—I was going to say *normal*—he'd talk it over with her first."

"What makes you think he won't do that?" Nils went out the back door for a pail of rainwater. She didn't intend to answer with the obvious, and he knew it. He turned the water into the big kettle used only to heat rainwater and went into the living room to turn a lobster-drugged cat out of his chair, light his pipe, get the news, and begin his evening stint of trapheads. She brought the mail from the sun parlor and looked it over at the kitchen table. Over half of it was made up of appeals and catalogs. She laid aside the requests they always answered, and she saved the catalogs from which they ordered and which had their own place on a bookshelf where the beloved Montgomery Ward catalog used to live. My, but life was simple then, she thought. In all ways.

"Are you talking to yourself?" Nils's fair head came around the door. "Or swearing?"

"*Thinking* the swears," she said. "At my age I don't want to get into a habit of cussing out loud. I might do it sometime where I'd be embarrassed, and someone would say, 'See? She's losing it. Must be the change of life.' "

He laughed, and went back to the news. She thought vividly of Philippa, who wasn't going to announce her decision until she was sure of Mr. Crane's acceptance. This island, Joanna rambled on in silence (dishwashing was always good for a soliloquy), must be seething with secrets that can't be even breathed for fear of summoning the Great God Jinx. He, She, or It was always waiting for the right moment to smash everything, and it's always been so, she thought. How much of it is superstition, because we're saltwater people, and we've grown up in that tradition? We each have plenty of little private rituals that we honor without thinking, even if some of us don't see *something* hiding around every corner. And how much is plain common sense about talking a thing to death, wearing it out before you can do it? And how much is simply a way to hold onto privacy?

This was all so reasonable, so probable, it was enough to soothe her irritation like witch hazel on a summer rash. Now she could turn to creative ideas for ridding the island of unwanted catalogs, which would be coming thicker and faster from now to Christmas. A bonfire would be it. They burned paper trash every so often at low tide on the shore when it was damp and quiet enough, but what about a giant of a ceremonial fire? Who said the Fourth of July was the only time, especially when the conditions often weren't right then? Other countries had festivals of fire. Why not bring in the New Year with a tribute to the millions of trees murdered to make the catalogs—like the captives killed in the arena, "butchered to make a Roman holiday," a phrase taken in its context that had long haunted her after she spent a snowy afternoon picking her way through an elderly volume of Byron's poetry left at the Homestead by a visitor long before she was born.

To her the woods of Bennett's Island had always had a private life, full of individuals. Even now when she was in the woods, she quietly mourned the passing of the fallen ones that she had known since they were in their prime. A Christmas tree, beloved not only by children, had a significance in its dying, and it was never thrown out, forsaken, with bits of tinsel pathetically hanging on. Long ago someone, whose name no one was alive to remember, brought the custom of burning the Christmas greens on "Little Christmas," Twelfth Night—January sixth— and the islanders, never ones to pass up any new source of blessings, had done this ever since. As the saying went, "If it'll do you no good, it'll do you no harm. And who knows?"

She was smiling as she finished hanging up the dish towels, imagining the island's reception to her ceremonial bonfire of catalogs. The epidemic had been very light in those days. Twenty years ago she couldn't have imagined the way it was now. She expected a good response to her idea; you couldn't pile them out of sight and turn the woods into a dump or toss them overboard, either, to be washed out to clutter the ocean or come back onto the beaches, a sodden mass. They could all wheel their collection down to the harbor beach—she checked the tide calendar hanging by the sink; yes, there'd be a good low tide, a low dreen. She could hardly believe the luck of it. Now if the buildings and hauled-up boats were comfortably wet with snow, and the wind was easy, the wheelbarrows could be dumped almost at the water's edge, and layers of the stack doused with kerosene, maybe by Mark in his position as constable (and justice of the peace, and notary, when one was needed). Fire for destruction was terrible, but for a celebration it could be glorious. This one would be. She was ridiculously elated. The prospect filled her with happiness, not only in anticipation of its beauty (and getting rid of the catalogs), but also in the realization that it could be a tradition born for the children to carry on. They would never forget the voices singing "Auld Lang Syne" and the golden showers of sparks.

It was a movable festival, because if they had to wait for a suitable night, it wouldn't make the celebration any less. It would be their own Bennett's Island occasion to bring in the New Year at their own time.

When she poured the dishwater over the feet of the lilacs by the back walk, she heard a tiny rattling in the bucket of lobster shells and knew a mouse was dining well. They had no other four-footed wildlife. Somebody's night-prowling cat might be in the shells before morning, but whatever scraps he got wouldn't hurt him. Nothing was spoiled. "Blessings on thee, little man," she said to the invisible mouse and went inside again. As she sat down in the living room, she wondered if she would tell Nils about her idea, and then the old caution instinctively took over. *Not till Christmas,* she answered herself. *And all those other things should be solved by then, too.* Nils's attention was divided between the screen and his work, but some instinct made him look again at her, with humor around his eyes. "What are you smiling about?"

"I'm happy," she said, defying Jinx.

25

When Joanna walked home from seeing Nils off the next morning, it was still before sunrise, but in the east the light rising from the sea had begun to blush. Orion had sprawled huge overhead when they first went out, though his lesser stars were dimming. Now more were gone, and Saturn, which had burned with a dazzling tawny fire, was still visible but dull.

Behind her all the voices of morning—of men, of engines, of gulls— would soon die out until they became the voices of late afternoon. The gulls were always around, but they seemed to share in the excitement of the boats going out and coming back.

Joanna had slept well, and she was still very happy about her festival fire. There was no reason why she had to let anything extinguish it; it was a great deal more pleasant than to imagine Hugo getting drunk, Owen plotting behind Laurie's back, and Laurie reacting if she found out. *If* was the significant word. None of it was fact yet. Nils's common sense deserved all the credit for this outlook, but the fire festival was all hers.

The birdfeeders had been filled and the hens let out to find the lobster shells in their yard; their fanfare had been so great, it took Pip's mind off himself for a few minutes of greedy staring through the wire, but he hurried to go in with Joanna. Hal was cooking bacon and scrambled eggs, which made him interesting to the cat; Hal offered to fix a plate for Joanna, but she had eaten with Nils. She sat down opposite Hal with a fresh cup of coffee and a slice of toast with Vanessa Barton's marmalade.

"Nils is *great,*" he said. "Sometimes I feel as if I'm running like a lunatic trying to catch up with myself, and I'm always out of reach but still in the same place, somehow. Makes you feel a little crazy, you know? It's always been my problem. I'm not dumb enough to take to booze or drugs to calm myself down, but . . . well . . . *people,* including my own, think I'm pretty flaky because I go from one thing to another." He gestured with his fork, which Pip watched with a hypnotized stare. "The fact is, I get myself wound up like a top till there's nothing to do but just put it out of my mind."

"Eat while your food's hot," Joanna said. "Excuse the mother-noises, but I've been making them for too long."

"From you, Jo, they're wonderful." He sounded joyously young and uncomplicated in spite of his confession. "Well, when I got up off that wharf the other day, I knew where I'd been heading my whole life; but right away I'm racing again, worrying about one damn' thing after another—like a boat, for instance—and Nils said just the right thing, that *I* should have thought of." He moved one hand, palm-down, in a flat, slow gesture. "Just *wait.* It'll happen when it's meant to. Why can't I say it to myself? Why can't I quiet myself?"

"Just being with Nils is restful sometimes," she said, "and that can help your brain and your heart to slow down. Not that I haven't thought a few times that he was a dite *too* relaxed."

"Have you ever seen him good and mad?"

"Of course I have. I've known him all my life and lived with him over half of it. He's human, and he's not a saint or a martyr." She didn't say any more, and he didn't pursue it.

"I think he's one of the best men I've ever met," he said. "And now I'm going to write my letter." He finished his breakfast rapidly and thoroughly, and carried his dishes into the kitchen. "I'll wash these dishes afterward," he said. "Have you got something I can write on?"

He reached for the notepad that stayed on the sun-parlor table with an assortment of pens in a glass mug, but she said, "There's something better in the desk."

She showed him a tablet of good writing paper and pointed to where the envelopes were. "You'll want to include a stamped and addressed return envelope. The stamps are in this little box."

"Listen, I'm going to pay for all this," he said.

"*Rats,*" she said. "Consider it a tiny donation to the cause. Mark can donate the zip code, and then it gets to go ashore for free on the mailboat tomorrow. It should be in Cape Blue Saturday." She went back to put on her apron and start the chowder, but he came out behind her with the tablet and sat down at the sun-parlor table. By now the sun was filling the room with light and heat.

She had brought the lobsters out earlier, to take some of the chill off. Pip was helpfully in the way as she spread clean newspaper on the counter and collected her tools, importuning her in his many voices.

"Pip, I wish you had a club to go to," she told him. "Why don't you go out in the barn and have a safari? While you've been minding everybody else's business, the mice have probably colonized the place."

"And built a replica of Fort Apache," Hal called. "With armed sentries along the walls. All them little mousies in their blue cavalry blouses out to get you, Pip! Jo, do you think they charge?"

"Who, the mouse cavalry?"

He laughed. "Town clerks. For birth and death certificates and stuff, making copies and so forth."

"I should think so."

"I've got a five-dollar bill. I'll put that in. Shouldn't be more than five, do you think?"

"Good Lord, no. Are you telling anything more than your name? Like who your relatives are, and so forth?"

"No, I am *not*," he said severely. "Just my name and my date of birth. People who work in town offices shouldn't talk about business outside, and there were always enough Haliburtons around there so my first name shouldn't stand out."

She agreed, remembering Nils's mischievous suggestion that the present town clerk could well be his uncle's wife and might call her husband at the yard with the news. Or she might simply throw the note in the trash, just to show what her family thought of Hugo Bennett and his brats. What would she do about the five dollars? Maybe put it in the collection plate at church?

"See you!" he called; then, halfway out the door, he was in again. "What's going on over there? What's that boat?"

She looked out the window and recognized the lobster smack *Julia May* coming in. By now the harbor had been left to the skiffs and the gulls, and as *Julia May* swung toward the wharf and disappeared behind the fishhouses, she left the skiffs rocking in her broad wake, and the gulls took to the air.

"It's the lobster smack," she told Hal. "Mark's dealer's smack. It's about time, the way they've been catching lobsters lately. I don't know how many crates he's got out there by now."

"Hey, if everybody's out but Willy, maybe they can use me!" He was off at a good rate, even if he obviously favored his "soccer knee"; yesterday he'd been limping with it when he came in from a day of keeping his footing aboard the boat. Dog Tray rushed at him and he gave the dog a shout and a flap of the hand, keeping it out of reach; then he circled out around the school-bound youngsters, who yelled, "Hi, Hal!", waving madly as if he were in a marathon as he disappeared beyond the Binnacle.

Mark, Willy, and the men on the smack worked together like part of the same machine, but they would take pity on someone so anxious to be involved. If he could just go rowing he'd be happy, but he'd learned enough from his father not to take a skiff without permission. She'd have told him to take Nils's, but it was out on the mooring, like most of them.

The lobster meat was now heating in a little pork fat in the big iron skillet, slowly acquiring the rosy color that would enhance the chowder, and she sliced the potatoes and started their boiling. The rest of the lobster shells went out to the hens; Pip watched their noisy flurry of fresh excitement with what one could read as greedy resignation. He knew by experience he couldn't get into the hen yard, and he wouldn't if he could have; when there had been a rooster, and Pip had been an adventurous kitten who found a hole to squeeze through, he'd been terrified before he was rescued. "You'd never admit it now, would you?" she asked him. He gave her a look over his shoulder and went out around the barn toward the woods, where a couple of crows announced his passage. Gulls circled anything that looked remotely edible, but they merely cocked their heads as they flew over and kept on going toward the outer shore.

A walk was a good idea. Why should the cat have all the fun? She went into the house, thinking where she wanted to go. She hadn't been for a good walk since before the hurricane, and now anything looked fine; she had a sense of great riches. She was guiltily glad Hal was absorbed over at the wharf, either watching or getting a chance to do something; if he'd still been home she'd have felt obliged to invite him along. She liked him—who wouldn't?—and he was Hugo's son. But she felt about walking alone as Nils felt about being alone with his boat.

When Joanna went back inside, Laurie was standing at the kitchen stove, pouring boiling water into a mug. "If I have galloping indigestion all day it's because I've been drinking coffee practically since midnight, and decaf doesn't make any difference."

"For heaven's sake," said Joanna. "I thought you were out to haul. What are you doing here? Is Owen all right? What's going on?" The familiar wee voice said, *I knew it, I knew it; I slept too well, felt so good this morning. But if it was Owen, the Coast Guard would have been out here by now to take him, and she'd be gone too.* . . . With reasonable calm she said, "What's wrong?

"I wish," said Laurie bitterly, "that I were way out on Georges Bank somewhere with Owen. That's the only way we'll get a chance to talk. Coffee?"

"Tea," said Joanna, shedding her jacket. "I started about 4:30, and it wasn't decaf." They took their mugs to the sunny table where Hal had written his note. Laurie glared at the sugar bowl as if she hated it for personal reasons.

"At ten minutes of three this morning," she said very carefully, "Richard walked in, wearing his bright and shiny morning face. Wasn't this a John Rogers surprise? The brat actually laughed at our expressions. That I just called my son a brat shows my mental state." Joanna let her sip some coffee, and kept from asking questions. The answers would quickly come. As if the first tight knot had dissolved, Laurie's manner began to loosen up.

"He and Sam haven't been expelled for having a pot party, and he didn't come home because he couldn't wait to tell us he has to get married or because he's suddenly got so patriotic that he wants to enlist. Oh, no, it's really simple. They've got measles in the school, and the entire academy is dismissed for two weeks; nobody is to return without proof of having had measles or a certificate saying he has just been vaccinated."

"That's simple," said Joanna, "but how in the heck did they get here at that time?"

"They got down to Kristi's in the afternoon, they went to the movies last night, and they met the Hakers on the street on their way back to the boat to sleep it off. John, that is. Charlie was piloting. They were leaving at midnight, so the boys hitched a ride. They got off at Mark's wharf, and *Annie-Elmina* went right out again to set trawl. Richard left his books at Philip's and came on home."

"Crossing the bay with John Haker must have improved their education," Joanna suggested.

Laurie's mouth quirked up. "John slept the whole way, and they got an astronomy lesson from Charlie. They'd never crossed the bay in the middle of the night, and Richard said it was as if he hadn't really seen anything before; it's so different from on land and with someone who knows his way among the stars from all points of the compass."

She had sloughed off her first bad mood. "They ate Italian sandwiches and watched for whales; Charlie had some whale stories that, if they weren't true, ought to be. There was a meteor shower, and he knew which it was. They'll never look at Charlie in the same way again."

"That's nice; he deserves it," Joanna said. "It sounds as if they had a good time."

"Richard wants to have them over for baked beans," Laurie said. "Brown bread, too, if I can manage it. . . . You know, if the Dazzling Duo had waited to come out on the mailboat tomorrow, I'd be outside somewhere right now, in happy ignorance with my husband, even though that would be shattered by tomorrow. Do you realize how little I've been alone in that house with Owen? How long has Emlyn been gone? And Richard and Holly were home Saturday and Sunday. Now I've got a chance to go with him as I used to between babies and before the heart scare—just until Christmas—and Richard's going to be here right through Hallowe'en and probably all the good weather."

She put her head in her hands. "I know all those good old, all-purpose four-letter words the men find so handy to express various frustrations, and right now I'm *thinking* them."

"Are you too bushed to go for a walk?" Joanna combined the chowder makings, except for the milk, and set the hot kettle on the counter. "Let's go, I don't know how long Hal will be out, just when I'm counting on him to get involved in something."

"Like Richard. Sure, let's go out." Laurie cheered up when they left, sniffing the air like Pip. "I was so mad on the way here, I'm sure it smelled as good, but I could only think of the way I felt. Anyway, talking to you helps me let off steam, and I feel a lot better outside—I always did. When you're indoors with your mad, you forget the island. But there it is, like Jo, waiting, and you begin breathing again."

They went across to Goose Cove and sat on a long thick silvery log that must have been at sea for a long time. The hurricane had left it. It would lie there through the winter, it would sit among the pink bindweed and blue flag of summer, and with any luck it might not go out again for a long time. It would become something with a name, a personality in its own right, and if another hurricane should remove it, it would be missed; it would leave a painfully vacant place until tide rubble and blue flag filled it.

They were in sight of the Homestead windows, but Mateel, if she should look down and see them, wasn't the sort who would rush down to join them.

"I love Richard," Laurie said. "Not more than the girls because he's a boy; he doesn't have a golden aura around him, to set him off. I love them all because each one is mine and Owen's, and I love them for what each is. But when I finally argued Richard aboard the boat last Sunday, I thought he'd stay put until Thanksgiving, and I was going to have all that time to talk to Owen. I've been keeping a notebook of travel ideas; I've sent for more material. He never bothers with the mail. I could receive a passionate love letter every boat day, and he'd never notice unless I left it open on his plate at supper time." They laughed, and she was more herself again. "I'm expecting a big batch from Goodhue's Travel tomorrow, but I asked them to send it in a plain envelope, so nobody will conjecture until I have something to tell. I won't spring it on him cold; I'll give him some idea of it and ask him if he'll just consider it."

"And like Richard you don't expect a cold 'No, and that's the end of it.' "

"What I expect and what my child gets are two different things." Laurie said. "He knew full well that he couldn't expect a 'We'll see' for a good long time. I made a deal with him. I am not only his mother but his father's wife. I don't have to go to college—I've been, and I've worked— and this trip, or a trip, has been due me for a long time. I shouldn't have to argue for it. My God, Jo, I've asked so little when you count it up! And this isn't something Owen would hate; already I'm listing more of what he'd like to see than my choices, besides London and anywhere in Scotland. And it shouldn't be a surprise to him either. He knows I want to go while we're still young enough, and now Richard's old enough to tend the traps—" Suddenly her voice thickened as if her nose had stuffed up, and she blinked her eyes as if they hurt. "I didn't mean to do that," she said thickly. "I don't want to go all emotional about this, but . . ."

Joanna laid a hand on her arm. "Listen, we all do it. I was never an easy weeper, but nowadays things take me by surprise and make me teary, and I hate it. Tuesday night Hal was sitting outside playing the harmonica, and of course that was a surprise, because we didn't know he had one or that he was such an expert. He played a song I'd never heard before and, well, what with everything all together that day, it nearly did me in. I want to ask him to play it again, but not if I get that reaction. . . . It must be what it reminded me of without my ever giving words to those thoughts."

"Gosh, I'd like to hear it, but I'd better wait until I'm wildly happy with something to knock 'old, unhappy far-off things' out of my head, or I'll dissolve."

"Speaking of 'wildly happy,' " Joanna said. She gathered up a handful of pebbles and aimed one at a violet-blue mussel shell just left by a retreating ruffle of foam. "You'll have all the time and space after Richard goes back to school. Until Thanksgiving, unless they quarantine the place before that for something else."

"But the thing is, we need to get our tickets now for the *Queen*. They'll be loaded in April."

"The real *Queen*?" Joanna backed off to get a better stare. "You mean the QE 2, herself? Dear Lord, I'm going to work on Nils!"

"Oh, I wish you would!" Laurie grasped her arm with both hands and squeezed it. "Owen would say yes like a shot!"

"When we go again, it'll be Norway and Sweden and so forth. But Linnie'll be home this spring, so we wouldn't go then anyway. Nils's idea is a freighter that takes passengers; it'll take some time to locate one. But we're talking about *you*. Look, don't worry about the tickets. *Get them.* You've got enough money in your own checking account, haven't you?" Laurie, looking hypnotized, nodded. "Then get your tickets, and don't say anything, and you can take plenty of time to seduce Owen. And if by evil chance you can't use them, you can turn them back."

Laurie giggled, looking and sounding very young. "I've already got the brochure. I take it out and breathe hard over it, secretly, like a miser. I'll show you when I can. It'll be Transatlantic Class, with an outside cabin. I suppose they dress for dinner every night in First Class and have fancier rooms, but Transatlantic looks great to me. I know he worked on big vessels when he was at sea, but being a passenger aboard this one should appeal to him, don't you think?" Suddenly she hugged Joanna. "Jo, I don't know what I'd do without you."

"I don't know what any of us would do without each other. Wouldn't this place be *hell* if a lot of us hated the rest of us?"

"Like Nan Harmon," Laurie said soberly. "Nobody's done anything mean to her out here, everybody welcomed her, now the young ones get along, and the men all like Myles. So is she a genuinely paranoid person, or is there a special name for anyone who carries a giant grudge against the world? That chip's so big it's going to crush her like a falling tree one of these days."

"I hope not," said Joanna, wanting to change the subject before she was tempted to talk about Nan. Laurie would be sympathetic, almost everyone would, but that would be cruelty to Nan. "She's not for us to worry about," she told Laurie. "It's a waste of time."

They walked back across the meadow in a little while, leisurely; at times, they'd crossed it when the wind felt strong enough to blow them about like kites. Now everybody unconsciously slowed down when the wind was light, with just enough chill to remind the senses of March, when the edge of cold was left over from winter but the first comer of spring was close. "I'm glad I came over, Jo," Laurie said. "You made everything so simple. Why didn't I think of getting the tickets anyway? Maybe they'll be good luck, have some psychic influence on Owen."

She refused lunch. "I'll stop in and talk over this measles business with Lisa. Hannah MacKenzie came over here in the big measles year, remember? Philippa never had a full classroom until the thing ran its course. Hannah said it was measles, no doubt, and Dr. Swift's been around on the *Sunbeam* since then and vaccinated all the little ones. They may have to have boosters in case there's an epidemic, it gets into Limerock, and somebody brings it out here, but all the schoolchildren *that* year had the real thing. Hannah keeps pretty complete records, so she can write out something for Sam and Richard." She drew her face down into a long prim mask. "Like a good conscientious mother, I'll carry some of Richard's books home so he can begin studying the minute he gets in. But maybe I'll let him have a night's sleep first after his trip over with Charlie."

Pip came around the barn, vociferously, and Laurie picked him up. "How's Old Talker today, huh?" He pushed his head against her chin, and over it she said, "It makes me mad sometimes to have to sneak around, when there's absolutely no reason—" Pip struggled to free himself. "Sorry, Pip; I didn't mean to shout in your ear. Anyway, Owen gave up winter fishing without a visible qualm, once his sternman was good and gone. Now he just has to leave the traps on the bank for a few months more and spend the spring with his wife in another country. I shouldn't be afraid of its being spoiled. It shouldn't be *spoilable*."

I'm afraid he's going to spoil it, Joanna thought. The process is underway—or will be when Hal's letter boards the boat. Oh, Cap'n Owen's being very cagey, telling Hal not to talk about it. . . . Suddenly Laurie turned back, her face brimming with laughter, resembling Richard when everything was going his way. The boy had probably looked like this when he greeted his parents at three this morning.

"You know, this is a perfect time for Mum to go ashore and leave the boys in their glory for a good long weekend."

"Maybe *you* could hitch a ride back with *Annie-Elmina*."

"I might at that!" She went her way, singing "A Life on the Ocean Wave." But the optimism with which Joanna had begun the day was drizzling away into a puny stream with hardly a glint left to it.

26

She did not want to go back into the house again, and it was not only because of the quality of the day itself. And she didn't want to talk to anyone but Nils; it would be simply making conversation. But even with Nils she would balk at letting him know of her fresh anxiety for Laurie. He must be tired of her gratuitous concern for all her causes, knowing full well that there was nothing she could do for them except worry without their knowing it; so much good it did them. She was getting tired of it herself. But Laurie was different from the rest, and she had reasons enough to love all her sisters-in-law; they had been through so much together.

Laurie had become the younger sister almost from the day of her arrival to teach on the island, when, in all her rosy innocence, she had met Owen. Only a few years ago she had admitted to Joanna that she had never been quite sure of the way Owen loved her, but she'd at last given up dreading whatever it was he was waiting for. Maybe he ought to know that, Joanna thought, but it wouldn't humble him any. Besides, he had known what it was, and he had given it up for Laurie, and this was something she must never know. So I guess I ought to forgive you, Owen, you old son of a sea cook, she thought, even if you only mended your wild ways because you were afraid you could drop dead anytime.

Instantly she saw Owen's grin, and heard him: "How'd you guess?"

It was infuriating and refreshing. She went into the house, sunny and full of the mantel clock's ticking—and now Pip's voice. She got out four cans of Norwegian brislings, a box of saltines, and half a new loaf wrapped in foil; she picked over the tomatoes for six just-ripe ones. She wrote a note telling Hal to help himself; the lobster smack was gone by now, and

194

she hoped wherever Hal was he wasn't on the way home just out of sight around the Binnacle. She put a tomato in one pocket, a can of sardines in another, and a section of crackers and an apple in a small brown-paper bag. She filled Pip's dish, and as an afterthought set a jar of wild strawberry jam on the table beside the bread. Then she went out the back way, taking the small binoculars. Over at Schoolhouse Cove the children were erupting from school.

She cut straight across the field toward the lane and the clubhouse without being hailed by anyone; Dog Tray, all his senses aimed at the oncoming children still out of sight, never glanced around to see her pass by the windbreak trees.

Behind the clubhouse there was an agreeable jungle of wild apple trees and blackberries, scavenged equally by children and birds. There was also a little-used trail through ferns and rosebushes down to the shore of Barque Cove. There were clear, easier paths to the cove from other directions; she hadn't used this one for a long time, and she knew that she couldn't be seen from anywhere else. No one at all was likely to guess where she was, unless she was seen from a boat, and there were none anywhere near.

The island was now blessedly hers. On such a day there could be walkers later on; Nora and Carol sometimes brought Peter out, to climb over the gentler slopes of rocks and along the beaches, where the water bubbled and glittered among the stones that always looked more precious wet than when they were dry. Peter couldn't get too many into his overall pockets, but he tried, and he fought against giving anything up. The compromise was to pile up all his beauties in little nests of grass, to be brought home next time. Next time, of course, these were forgotten for the new treasures. Joanna kept coming across them. Usually there'd be small heaps of driftwood beside them, anything Peter could carry or drag up the slope; he was already a dedicated beachcomber. A buoy, of course, had to go home with him; one didn't leave gold nuggets lying around in plain sight.

She ate her crackers and sardines on a ledge at Pond Cove, and watched the bird life tranquilly in possession of these waters while listening to the voices in the woods behind her, around the small freshwater pond that named the cove. Herons lived down here on their tall trees, and there was an osprey nest in another treetop where there'd always been one as long as she could remember; osprey generations simply kept repairing the family homestead. At least she liked to think it was the same tree, the same nest surviving. The herons and the ospreys had gone south now; on a day so like spring one felt they should still have been here.

"But you'll always be here," she said to a gull that coasted down to take a look at her. She left him her last sardine and put the tin and her paper napkins in the bag to take home. She'd have liked to go on to Sou'west Point, but she needed time for that—and more food. Eating *by* the sea, if you couldn't be *on* it, had always been one of the greatest pleasures known to Joanna.

On her slow way back she found a bright red handful of cranberries gleaming at the edge of the turf just above high water. They were too pretty to pick, they wouldn't make more than a couple of spoonfuls of sauce, and she had cranberries from Long Cove ripening in the catchall closet under the stairs. A crow watching her now from the trees would fly down behind her and eat the berries.

As if she'd been granted the cloak of invisibility she used to wish for (only Pickie would know she was there, of course), she'd gone and returned without being seen. Dog Tray was inside. The children had gone back to school; it was that somnolent hour when most mothers would have their feet up and books in their hands, sometimes falling asleep over them or wishing they could read straight through the rest of the day without stopping till the end. When school was out, and the boats began coming in, the silent hour would have been as a dream.

Hal had been in, had eaten well, and had tidily cleaned up his place. The *National Fisherman* lay open on the table, and Pip lay on the magazine. He stood up to greet her, stretching and yawning, and got off the table with all deliberation to embrace her ankles, commenting on where they had been. There were light pencil ticks here and there on the magazine text, as if Hal had been preparing for some hard technical questions from knowledgeable children tomorrow.

Supper tonight would be simple; Joanna always made huge chowders, to provide more than one meal, and they were always better the second day. There were enough pilot crackers for tonight, but she put them on her store list for tomorrow.

Then she went for her book and the living room couch. She'd given herself a holiday from useless anxieties this morning, and she wasn't ready to gather them in again. Besides, the law of surprises could work in beneficial ways, couldn't it? She might as well cling to that while she could. "Anyway," she said to Pip as they settled down, "I can think the way I want to for the next hour or so and keep the holiday going. . . . And I'll wash tomorrow before we get a week of fog." This gave her a warm sense of having propitiated the household gods.

She didn't fall asleep but strong-mindedly broke off when she'd still have plenty left to read when she went to bed. Tomorrow she'd have to pick the next book; not having one ready was equivalent to facing a blizzard without extra water, fuel, and food in the house.

She washed her face, combed her hair, and went outdoors. The day was still quiet in these last few minutes before school let out. She walked toward the harbor, and Lisa called out from her front steps, where she sat with her bright scarlet knitting, a sweater for one of the children. Joanna sat down beside her.

"Did you get up at three, too?" she asked. "Laurie was in, looking pretty frayed."

"Oh yes! I woke up with this horrid feeling that Ross was sleepwalking. He did when he first came, but I thought he'd gotten over it. What a sensation, wondering what was bothering him and how I'd find out. Philip heard it too; he told me to stay in bed and said he'd handle it." She stopped to count stitches. "Of course I had to get up and listen at the head of the stairs, and there were Sam and Philip, trying to whisper quietly. I went back to bed and let Philip surprise me. I actually went to sleep again. I saw them off to haul before the children woke up!" She put down her work and stretched as comfortably as a cat. "Oh, it's lovely having Sam home again! Bless the measles. What a nice boy he is! I can't imagine him grown up, graduated, and going to sea. Thank God it won't be for some years yet." She began to laugh. "I wasn't going to tell the little ones until they'd had their breakfast, but they saw his dunnage, and I thought I wasn't going to get them through eating and off to school without throwing a net over them."

All at once school ended for the day. Across the harbor the Campion dogs began to bark on cue, and Dog Tray picked it up inside the Binnacle. Lisa's cat, successor to Leo, came out from under Philip's fishhouse, streaked across the road, and flowed up over Lisa and onto a porch railing. She was a large, part coon cat, and the children had named her Tabby after a very small cat in a favorite book. She liked them and was impartial as to whose bed she slept on, except when Sam was home. Any prudent cat would have dodged, as she did, the traveling game of catch that went back and forth between home and school each day, and it was coming now.

Joanna left Lisa with a promise of Ngaio Marsh soon. The beneficial aspect of the law of surprises was still working, she hoped; she went to Nils's fishhouse, inspected his tidy housekeeping, and thought, as she often did, how nice it would be to live here in summer with the tide rising and falling under her feet. She sat on a crate outside, her back against warm shingles, and basked in the sun with her eyes half closed, as Tabby had probably been doing. Sometimes she felt the breeze of a gull's wing as it dipped to see what she was. "Hi, Hank," she murmured, always just in case. Engine sounds were coming nearer. She identified them like bird calls and opened her eyes all the way when she heard *Joanna S.*

Nils came around the breakwater, followed by a flutter of gulls, though he must have finished emptying bait bags long before this; the birds were always hopeful. The boat moved smoothly through the billowy swells at the harbor mouth and glided toward Mark's wharf. Nils could have been any anonymous figure under the canopy, except to her.

While he and Mark were swinging a full crate of lobsters from the boat onto the scales, Matt Fennell came in and was slowly approaching the car, Terence Campion and Ralph Percy side by side behind him.

Nils's skiff lay on the big boat's mooring, but he must have seen Joanna by the fishhouse, because he came directly across to her. He slid almost silently alongside, took hold of a ladder rung, pushed back his cap, and tipped his head to look at her. "Waiting to ride out to the mooring with Daddy so you can row back?"

It called for a classic imitation of Linnie at seven or so. "Oh, *can* I? Please, please, *please!*"

"Get yourself a jacket and we'll take a little ride." She went into the fishhouse and picked an old wool shirt off a hook. "Are you sure you can wait any longer for your coffee?" she asked when she went down the ladder into the just vibrating boat.

"I'd just as soon ride around with my wife for an hour, and to hell with the coffee."

"That's one of the most gallant speeches I ever heard."

"Want to steer?"

"Back her away and everything?"

"Everything," he said handsomely. "I'll grab aholt if she goes astray."

"She might, out of pure peevishness. I know she's pretty conscious of being the other *she* in your life. She feels her importance." With uncomplicated pleasure, she backed the boat slowly out and around, telling her she was a good girl. "I suppose Nils tells you in Swedish," she said. "It sounds prettier."

She headed for the harbor mouth, waving at Young Mark and Tom J., out on the breakwater for some arcane reason. *Joanna S.* curtsied gracefully into the tide rip, and then they were outside. Joanna ran toward the long sand beach on Brigport, considering whether she'd turn eastward and make a loop around the high, small island called Tenpound; Nils sat on the washboard, smoking his pipe, leaving it up to her. She decided to run in the other direction—to Sou'west Point—and out around for a look at open ocean. There was always a higher lift and a deeper fall to the swells out here; blindfolded, you would know the ocean rhythm when you felt it. They saw a big trawler to the south'ard, and outside the Rock a small oil tanker was not hurrying, evidently expecting the pilot who'd been waiting at Brigport to be brought out to take her upriver. In the westering sunlight the Rock had its enchanted-fortress-built-of-gold look, and the tanker partook of the enchantment.

"I hate to go in," Joanna said to Nils, "but I suppose we have to."

"Run far enough, and we'll be out of gas," he said agreeably. "And she's hell to row."

Back around the point, they met Barry Barton and refused to race him home. Joanna didn't want to shorten her time. An hour wasn't much, but she was as happy as if it were a feast; if she'd done as she wanted, she'd have hugged Nils right before the eyes of the whole village as they went into the harbor.

He set her ashore on their own wharf, took the boat out to the mooring, and rowed back in. Rosa and Sara Jo had just arrived to meet Jamie, who couldn't be far behind his father. Between expecting her father, seeing her grandmother on the next wharf, and spotting her grandfather rowing in, Sara Jo was reduced to speechless rapture and hid her face in her mother's shoulder.

"I keep thinking of that harmonica," Rosa said to Joanna. "With Ralph's fiddle and my guitar and Maggie's, we'd make a terrific combo. I can hardly wait for the Hallowe'en party." She would be stately when she got farther along in her pregnancy; now she was like a tall young girl, ingenuously happy in her anticipation of making such music. She jigged Sara up and down on her arm, dee-dumming "The Rakes of Mallow," and the little girl giggled. She looked over Rosa's shoulder at Joanna and asked, "Where's Hal?"

"I don't know," Joanna said. "Maybe he's taking a walk." Nils's skiff grazed the ladder, and his head appeared at the top to a fanfare from Sara Jo. She sent them kisses as they left the wharf, and she was shrieking "There's Daddy!" as they crossed the road.

Hal was at the well, with Dog Tray yearning at him from the limits of his run. "I feel like a time traveler," he told them. "I've been up at the Homestead, going through all the albums and the scrapbooks of newspaper articles from the early 1900s, Sunday feature and magazine pieces, stories about the artists who used to come, pieces on local characters, which takes in about everybody on the island. But why am I telling *you?* You must know them by heart; you're related to a lot of the people—Hell, so am I!" He had to stop talking to lift out his full pail and set it carefully on the curb. "What an afternoon! I have to go back. There's a lot I want to read. And all the photos! God, what a life it was! Everything I look at now—even this well—I'm seeing it in all these different eras, as if I've lived here through all of them and never anywhere else. *Wow!*" He shook his head. "You'll be calling *me* Old Talker, instead of Pip. Seriously, do you think I'm nuts?"

"I'd say you were no more so than the average citizen around here," Nils said.

"Average citizen under twelve, you mean?" Hal was suddenly self-conscious.

"Average citizen, period," said Joanna. "We all go by fits and starts, depending on what takes our fancy. Has Mateel been feeding you cake all afternoon?"

"No, chocolate jumbles," he said seriously. "But hey, if you're going for coffee I'd love a cup with you, and I promise I won't wear your ears off about what you already know."

But he couldn't repress it all. He sounded as if he'd been gazing at Eden all afternoon. Joanna and Nils listened, nodding, sometimes filling in a name or supplying a fact. If Hugo was as desperately homesick as they suspected, he had made a passionate addict out of this son.

Gradually Hal slowed down and had nothing more to say. He took his mug out to the kitchen and headed for his room. "I may read," he said, "but then I may just shut my eyes and think about all those faces I saw today. I guess I've *said* enough about them to give everybody a rest for a while." He kissed Joanna's cheek. "Thanks for listening. I'd kiss Nils, but . . ." He grinned and ran upstairs.

"Ellen could get this enthusiastic," Joanna said. "And Linnie can still do it. But Jamie never ran on like a waterfall."

"Hugo was a pretty fast talker when he got wound up to it," Nils said. "Must have got it from Aunt Mary's side of the family, not Uncle Nate's."

"Nils, Hal's so romantic, and he's fed on his father's stories. And the island itself is so beautiful, we can't half imagine what it means to him— every sight, every sound."

"If it lasts through the winter, we'll know it's the real thing," Nils said.

At supper Hal devoted himself with a passion to lobster chowder and pilot crackers. "I remember them when I was a little kid, but I never saw any in California, not even at the place where we used to get the Maine lobsters. I think Dad actually pined for them." He was affectionately amused. "I'm going to send him a case—to the yard—as soon as I get my license so I can tell him what's happened to his most troublesome kid. I wasn't a juvenile delinquent or anything," he told them hastily. "But they got more notes from my teachers than they did about the other three put together. Dad once said he wished he'd saved them all; he could have made a scrapbook to give to my wife.

"There's something I want to ask about. It's all this Bennett land. Does Charles own it all, because he's the oldest son, or something like that? Or does everybody in the family have a parcel of woods and shore beginning out here and going down to Sou'west Point?"

"No, it's never been cut up in any way unless the family agreed," Joanna said. "Charles doesn't have the Homestead because he was something like the Young Squire. When he and Mateel came back here to live after the war, they didn't have a house. They'd rented a small place from Mateel's family at the Eastern End when they married, but they didn't want to go back there, and they had a family by then, too. There wasn't any trouble about the rest of us signing off our rights in the Homestead to him."

"I'm guessing there's some land that goes with the house, but what about all those other acres going down to the western end? Do you think that as a descendent of Jamie Bennett I could build a camp on it some- where? Or is it true that it wouldn't do me any good—that you have to have a shore privilege if you want to lobster out here?" He slumped back in his chair, dejected. "It seems to me that Owen wouldn't have encouraged me if there was no possibility at all, but maybe he's that kind of a joker."

"*No*," Joanna said. "He's a joker but not a cruel one. You are a part of the family, he needs a man he can trust to stay, and he's hopeful you're it."

Somebody had to warn him. She felt too hot and very angry with Owen. "But he doesn't want any talk about it until he's somewhere near sure."

"When I get my license," Hal said. "I suppose it would be better for me to live with him, considering all the work—I know how much George does. Until . . ." he paused, and Joanna wanted to fend off what she was sure would come next. *Until I want to go on my own.* "But I'd love to have that cabin in the woods," he said. "I could be up and over at Hillside as early as he wanted me in the morning." She was relieved that he was sensitive enough to change direction, at least aloud. He looked across at Nils, his eyes twinkling and one eyebrow tilted in a very Bennett manner. "What are *you* thinking? That there's plenty of time yet?"

"There is," said Nils. "You're getting into the winter-dreams class. Some of them come true; some don't. If you've made it through a year, and you still want to do it, well, they say nothing's impossible."

Nils could advise moderation without being dampening, and though sometimes Joanna disliked being thus cautioned or advised, she was glad of his gift now, because Hal was neither dampened nor flattened. "There's nothing to keep me from designing my cabin."

"Nothing at all," Nils agreed.

There were thumps and inarticulate cries outside, and the laughter of boys temporarily mindless with euphoria. Talk about the Rapture of the Deep, Joanna thought. Sam and Richard fell noisily into the room and wrestled their way to their feet, still trying to trip each other up. Richard suddenly reached for Joanna, hauled her into his arms, and hugged and kissed her. Sam was less violent in his approach, but in the way he said, "Uncle Nils," and shook hands and then turned to Joanna, one could see past his smile to the twelve-year-old at last realizing that Richard's family was his, and he was theirs, and nobody could ever separate him from them.

"Aunt Jo!" It wasn't like Richard's bear hug, but she could stand that. She always wanted to say "Sam *dear,*" and never did. Richard was introducing himself to Hal, and they began talking as if they'd just left off a short time ago. Sam became part of the trio, and as they pulled out chairs and settled at the table, bumping into each other and laughing, there seemed no age difference among them, no hint of condescension from twenty-one to sixteen. Hal had become at once part of the happy foolishness that had come in with the two younger ones. Now that the six feet under the table had temporarily quieted down, Pip began his inspection, was gathered up by Sam, and went to each of the others, contentedly answering their nonsense. He finished in Nils's lap; Nils sat quietly enough to give a cat a chance to settle down on his thigh.

It was a pleasure for Nils and Joanna to watch the three; for so long in the past the house had resounded with boys. Richard was big and growing handsome, with his father's build and his mother's blue-eyed coloring; his sisters had the Bennett dark eyes and hair. In certain lights his face took on an elusive Bennett cast, gone as quickly as it was recognized; a gesture, an expression, could bring it out, always ephemeral but always there, never obvious when you looked for it. There were certain intonations, too, especially in his laugh.

Sam was shorter; his slim, dark good looks were not exceptional, except that his appearance gave as much pleasure as Richard's more vibrant aura did. From the time Sam came to Philip and Lisa as a foster child, Richard had taken him for granted as something priceless, a boy cousin his own age, to be instructed and guided by him. Besides, Richard was the youngest in his family; his elders were girls. Tommy was fine, but he *needed* Sam. Sam was willing to be guided and instructed, but he became his own man in a very short time.

Hal was willingly answering questions and asking a few of his own. Richard now held forth about the field of marine biology and his place in it, as if he hadn't been trying to convince his mother that his choice was probably a mistake.

"They'll always need us," he said expansively. "There's always something new to find out and to fix. The resource will always need to be protected."

"What about the merchant marine?" Hal asked Sam. "This country's not building commercial vessels the way we used to. It's criminal, the way we leave it to other nations. Do you ever worry about getting a ship when you graduate from the Maritime Academy? I've heard a lot of professional gossip at the yard from men who turned to fishing because they couldn't get a job at sea."

Sam shrugged slightly, not rudely. "I hear it. I read it."

"Talk's cheap. Takes money to buy rum!" said Richard, and slapped Sam on the shoulder. "If Sam worries, it's not out loud. He just thinks 'Sail on!' like Columbus in the poem we all learned at our Racketash alma mater."

"Well, I do think about it," said Sam, "and I *want* to go on one of those big vessels and travel those oceans and see those ports. But if I can't, then

I've got more choices than most guys. I've got the island. I can always come home and be a lobsterman. When I came here, that was all I wanted, anyhow."

"Hey, Sam!" Richard said. "You could teach school out here someday and go lobstering on the side. Or you could be running the mail, if Duke ever retires. We could all kick in to get you a new boat—maybe have her built by Hal's kin down at Cape Blue and get a discount."

Hal applauded. "Super! You could name her *Pinafore* so everybody can break into a chorus as you come up the wharf. 'He is the captain of the *Pinafore*,' " he sang, and the other two joined him. " 'And a right good captain too!' " They went on to the end of the chorus. Pip left; Nils and Joanna applauded.

"We did that at school last year," Richard said. "Hey, Sam, I'll be your right good crew. I forgot to give you a message from Mum, Aunt Jo. She's going in tomorrow, and she wants a list from you two. Hal, come on up to the clubhouse and play pool with us. We've graduated from Kids' Night; we're trusted not to go sliding on the dance floor or try smoking or coast down the cue alley board—"

"Or duel with our pool cues," Sam said. "*That* was fun." He sounded wistfully reminiscent.

"Gosh, I'd like to," Hal said. "But I can't tonight. Can I have another chance before you go back to school?"

"Sure, but you could play with just about anybody," Richard said. "Just ask."

"I'd really like to play with you guys," Hal said, which pleased Richard. "Only George is looking for me to play chess with him tonight."

"Friday is Kids' Night, so how about Saturday night?" Sam said. "Bring George too. He's good. He must have played a lot of pool before he," Sam's hesitation was almost too brief to notice, "came out here with Sky."

"Great baseball coach too," Richard said. "This year was our first win over Brigport in a long time. We always used to say it was because Brigporters had unnaturally long arms and legs and because most of the eighth graders were old enough to leave high school—except they could never get *out* of the eighth grade. They didn't like some of our names for 'em."

"We didn't either," said Joanna, "so don't repeat them."

"We wouldn't think of it, Aunt Jo," Richard said virtuously. "Some of my best friends are Brigporters. Come on, Sam. So long, Hal. I'll tell everybody we've got the table for Saturday night. No smoking, no drinking, no serious gambling."

"How much is serious?"

"Anything over a quarter a game. And everybody puts fifty cents in the kitty toward heat and lights."

They said good night all around and welcomed Hal again to the island. On the way to the back door Richard said, "If we weren't going out to haul tomorrow, we'd be over to the school to hear you talk."

"Don't come even if you can, for God's sake!" Hal said. "I've just got up the courage to face a batch of thirteens-and-under. A *smart* bunch."

27

On a clear cold morning (but no frost yet) Joanna remembered her promise to do the wash and got off to an early start, as soon as Nils had gone. Hal offered to wash his own clothes, as he'd been doing all across the country. "Throw them in the hamper," she said, "unless you're modest about showing your underwear." He laughed at that and offered to strip his bed.

"It's too soon for that," she said. "You've only slept in those sheets for three nights, and you've showered every day."

"Three nights," he said. "Is every day here the length of a week in the real world? Or is *this* the real world? I'm beginning to think so. Everything away from here is in a mist. And no, I'm not parting my fasts."

"I didn't think so. I've heard the island called the Land of the Lotus-eaters, where it's always afternoon. Or seems so. But that was only in summer. And only by visitors."

"Summer," he said softly. "I can hardly wait. But I don't want time to go so fast I'll miss something on the way. Well, I'd better go." He was going to help George this morning. Sky didn't need a sternman except when there were snarls to work on, and George was handy ashore, whether it was working on the property, on gear, or in the vegetable garden. Today he was replacing a couple of bad planks in the wharf.

On the way out Hal said, obviously casual, "Well, my letter to Cape Blue will soon be on its way."

And he thinks the license is almost in his hand, or as good as, she thought.

All the washing was on the line when the mailboat whistled outside the harbor. She hadn't planned to join the unofficial female caucus this morning because she was going over later to see Laurie off. She and Nils hadn't come up with much of a list between them. She wrote down things for the Hallowe'en party, items that Laurie had probably included already. Owen had given his wife a considerable list—mostly for the hardware store and Limerock Boat, down on the waterfront.

"You're going to be running around like a hen with her head cut off," said Joanna, as she and Laurie stood outside the store.

"*Not*," said Laurie, "until I get my own absolutely private business done." She looked as happy, though not as drunkenly so, as Richard had last night. They were alone for a few minutes; the official time of departure was "around noon," and no new passengers had showed up yet. Duke and his crew were in the store while Mark closed the mail and padlocked the bags. Somewhere in one of those bags was Hal's request for his birth certificate; she hastily discarded the thought. She would not even *think* anything negative, in case it might dull Laurie's fine luster. Laurie was quite capable of asking suddenly, "What were you just thinking? That this is a fool's errand, and you're humoring me?" She herself had often seen the sudden change or shift in a glance that had been brightly straightforward until that particular moment.

"It'll be a wonderful chance in," she said.

"It's one of those times when the mainland looks so beautiful as you approach it, and you have the feeling that it's a place where you've never been before, and it's full of wonderful things for you. Of course when we nose up to the wharf, and I see Kristi beaming at the top of the ladder, I'll be happy to see her; then the strange and wonderful can wait until we get to it. Look what came today." She waved at the two large cartons of pumpkins outside the store. "Pete's annual Hallowe'en tribute to the young of the island. He says nobody can raise a decent pumpkin out here because there's no horse or cow left to provide the manure, and *nothing else* works. He's always homesick, you know, and so is Kris, even though they love the farm and he's happy fishing. Maybe they'll retire out here, and he can raise his prize pumpkins on the spot. Bringing his faithful old horse and cows with him to contribute."

"And a few pigs to liven us up," suggested Joanna. "Didn't Gunnar always swear by pig manure?

"Pete won't raise pigs now," Laurie said seriously. "The kids always named them and made pets of them, and the end always felt like murder."

Joanna didn't watch the boat out of the harbor. Laurie was happily settled on a camp stool up in the bow, with her back against the pilothouse. She'd probably be *in* it after they left Brigport.

Joanna picked out a pumpkin. The cartons would be about empty by nightfall, as the children came around after school for the happy anguish of making the right choice. She hoped that the Harmon children would be among the choosers. The two biggest pumpkins, which would grin from on either side of the clubhouse door on the night of the party, had come marked in their own box. If Pete had been at sea fishing when it was time to put his pumpkins aboard the mailboat, a neighbor had done it for him.

Joanna walked home with her pumpkin. The children were all inside eating their dinners, so she didn't create a sensation. Dog Tray would have wanted to know what she had, but he was inside. Pip was alerted before she reached the gateposts. She set the pumpkin on the doorstep so he could give it a closer inspection. What a treasury of scents for a cat, and he didn't need to know the meaning of any of them, except that they were *there*.

Hal came close behind her, so quietly, without Dog Tray to announce him, that she hadn't known he was there until he said, "What's with the pumpkin? Did I make you jump? I'm sorry."

"I was alone in the world with Pip, thinking what a feast life must be for these characters with the sensitive noses. Of course Pip does pretty well feasting by mouth." Pip went to greet Hal, then returned to a particularly thrilling spot on the pumpkin.

"I brought it to you to make a jack-o'-lantern," she said. "Did you ever make one?"

"You'd better believe it. They wouldn't let me have a knife when I was a little kid, but my dad made them for us. About two years ago Nicole and I drove out in the country and got a good batch of pumpkins; we carved out enough jack-o'-lanterns to put them on either side of the walk to the front door. We don't get homemade pumpkin pie at our house, but we saved all of them for a woman who works in the office at the yard. She sent a pie and a cake home by Dad, and she was going to use all the seeds for the birds." He smiled, stretching for the sky as if to take it into his arms. "We kept those lanterns lit at night as long as the candles lasted, and we got a lot of compliments, especially from the kids in the neighborhood. We liked to go out and stare at them ourselves. And that pie and cake were *some* good. Did I say that like a native?"

"You did. You sounded *some* natural. Let's have lunch." He picked up the pumpkin and held open the door for her.

"Hold your horses, Pip, I'll give it back to you. I'll start work on it tomorrow. Look, Jo, don't get any lunch for me. Binnie was frying dough-nuts this morning, and I must have eaten six at least. I'm going to clean up and then fall down flat until it's time to go to the school."

"Is that from stage fright or doughnuts?"

"A vicious combination. But the doughnuts were wonderful going down, and I hope the performance will be half as good." He went upstairs and shut his door.

About half-past two he came down and went into the bathroom.

She was on her way out to take in the wash, and when she had a full basket—everything shaken and folded—he came out to carry it in. He had showered and shaved, and he was lightly but pleasantly scented. He wore clean chinos and a blue turtleneck jersey with an inscription in white.

"Well, you look properly glamorous for the cousin from California," she said. "What do the words mean?"

"It's Gaelic," he said. "I found it in a book about the clans. It means 'Listen, O! Listen!' "

"Listen *to* what or *for* what?" she asked.

"I don't know what it meant to them, but to me it means you should always be listening. The sniffers use their ears too, remember." He smiled. "I went through a romantic period, when I was listening a lot to Hamish at the yard, and he told me about Bonnie Prince Charlie. I went through piles of books trying to make the Bennetts into a Highland clan."

"Devon's our place," she said. He nodded.

"I found out. But I got something out of my research, that it was al-ways a good conversation piece with the girls." He tapped his chest. "Wish me luck, Marm." He kissed her cheek.

"You can't fool me," she said. "You've never had stage fright in your life."

"Just as long as they keep the questions coming, and we aren't all left staring at each other, scratching our heads or ears, and making nervous little noises like 'Well,' and 'Are there any more questions?' "

"There won't be any long blank spots with these children," she told him. "Most of them aren't a bit backward about speaking up. And if there's a gap, Philippa will take care of it."

"I could always give them a concert." He patted the pocket where his harmonica was.

It was well after four when he returned. Nils was in, and he and Joanna were having coffee. Hal came in talking, in typical Bennett high spirits. "I went around by the cemetery to have a word with my ancestors, to tell them what I've been up to. They approved." He was too exhilarated to sit down and refused coffee or hot chocolate; they'd had punch and cookies for him. "If I lean sidewise I slosh, or did until I took the long route home for obvious reasons." He lifted Pip out of a chair and sat on it, cuddling the delighted cat.

"They were great! Even the littlest. They must think California's Little Jack Horner land. The others didn't miss a trick: earthquakes—was I ever caught in one? Then it was back to the gold rush, and on to the yard, of course. Had I ever been out off Alaska in one of our vessels? What about whale migration? Did I know anybody who'd been killed by a shark? What about firefighting? I think they'd still be asking me questions if Philippa hadn't saved me. They even got to surfing, but a history-minded kid in the eighth grade—Johnny Campion—wanted to know more about the Spanish who named all those places. Luckily it was one thing I paid attention to in school. But where did all those people *go*? No, we didn't wipe them out like Hitler, but I said it was too much to tell at once, and promised I'd give him a book. I don't know where I'll get it." He looked worried.

"The Bangor Public Library," Joanna said. "A couple of us have memberships. They can provide books about *everything*."

"*Honest?* You know, those kids even know about California writers and artists, for God's sake. I swear, putting it all together, they know more about California—north and south—than some people born there."

"Well, a lot of people born in Maine don't know as much as the incomers who've read everything they could find on the state before they even move. And they keep it up."

He was slowing down now. "I'm winded, but I had the time of my life. They all thanked me. Fortunately, they didn't call me Mr. Bennett; Mr. Bennett's my father, and I don't *ever* want to be Mr. Bennett."

Peter Pan, Joanna thought. And he said with an impish grin, "I don't want to grow up, right? Why should anyone rush to grow up when he's enjoying where he is right now? I guess I'll have some coffee." As he carefully dislodged Pip he said, "We all left at the same time, and this little guy came after me. He reached up and touched this," Hal patted the pocket where his harmonica was, "and said, 'Tracy Lynn says you play *good*.' How

could I disappoint those eyes? So we had a little concert on the front steps
of the school, with them calling the tunes, until I was dry as a cork leg, to
quote my dad, and a bit uncomfortable in other ways. I guess Philippa
wanted to get home to the Eastern End, so she saved me once again."

When he came back with his mug, Hal said, "I got one last question,
from Thomas Jefferson Percy: 'Where are you going next? Home?' I said
this is home, and this is where I'm staying. Bennett's Island. And I not only
got a round of applause, I got a cheer! To tell you the truth, I think it was
all meant for the harmonica."

"Don't be so modest," Nils said. "They think you'll make a great addition to the winter. They can ask you about every state you passed through
on your way here. The harmonica won't hurt. Emlyn promised them a
glee club."

"There must be plenty of California left that nobody touched on," said
Joanna. "Even if you have to read it up for yourself beforehand."

"Go on, you two, kid the pants off me. Nils, what are you about to
come up with?" He looked as nearly blissful as a grown man could be, if
you could truthfully call him a grown man, Joanna thought affectionately.

Nils shook his head, just barely smiling. "Nothing," he said, "except
what I do best."

"I guess I won't dig into that," Hal said, "but my dad always said you
were a deep one. . . . You know, I'll never be indispensable the way you
two are, but already, in four days, I know I'll find a way to be useful so
everybody will be glad I'm here. I'll know it when I come to it." He
blushed. "I'd better go outside and calm myself down before I say something foolish."

He went out the front door, and almost at once there was a long im-
posing chord on the harmonica. "The White Cockade" began.

28

The chowder was heating very slowly. The table was set. Outside in the soft dusk, after the children and Dog Tray had gone in, Hal was still playing his harmonica. He had quieted down to slow tunes now, some of them old and well known, some of them strange to Joanna. She kept hoping he'd play "The Flower of Portencross" again, but she was oddly shy about asking him, in case it meant something too personal to him.

The harmonica was always with him, marching him around to chess practice in the evening or down to the wharf. When he disappeared on a walk she visualized him perched on a rock somewhere, making music for the gulls and the ocean. He might play that song then; she had a feeling that it belonged to his solitude and that he was not as simple as he seemed. But then, who was? There was something complex and probably painful about his family relationships, far beyond what little he said or did not say.

Jamie came in the back way, returning *Time;* Nils passed him in the doorway with an empty water pail, going out around so as not to interrupt the music. "Want me to get that water?" Jamie asked, reaching for the pail.

"No," Nils said amiably. "I've been sitting too long." He kept on going.

Jamie shut the door behind him and said, "Yep! After standing from five or so till about four, putting your feet up for a couple of hours seems sort of sinful."

"You do the same," Joanna said.

"But I'm his *kid!*" Jamie protested. "Makes a difference!"

"Not if he's not lame and stiff in the morning, and he doesn't have arthritis in his hands. He knows how to take care of himself. Are you trying to retire him? He's a young man, Jamie. Younger than a lot of them around here."

"Suppose I wanted to take up for a couple of months in winter—what in hell would I look like with my old man out there alone pounding around and liking it?"

"You planning to take this up with him?" she asked mildly, turning off the gas under the chowder kettle. "A little well-meant sonnish advice?"

The front legs of Jamie's chair came down with a crash. "*Me,* give my father advice? *Anybody* give Nils Sorensen advice? Did *you?*"

"A few times," she said moderately. He didn't need to know that the few times she'd seen Nils at a loss had been because of his children—usually Jamie.

The harmonica had stopped in the middle of a tune, and she could hear men's voices, quiet, as if Hal and Nils were discussing the fine evening. Then there was a rise in volume as someone opened the door, and it was Myles's voice, sharp and clear, not so much angry as anguished.

"We don't have to do anything like that, Nils. Nils! I just wanted the boy's word, that's all."

"You've already had it." Hal's voice, clipped and older. "I don't sneak around looking in windows, either by day or by night."

"Come in, Hal," Nils said. Jamie walked noiselessly to the door, took the pail of water from his father and carried it around into the kitchen. "You too, Myles. Jamie, bring out a lamp, will you?" Jamie was already on the way back with the shaded Aladdin from the dining-room table. He set it on the sun-parlor table, checked the burner, and seemed to dissolve backward into the shadows. Hal came in past Nils; he gave Joanna a look she couldn't interpret and didn't want to. There was a sickening emptiness where her stomach should be. Misery? Rage?

It was obviously misery with Myles, who tripped coming in and more or less fell into the chair Nils pointed out to him. She could see the sweat on his forehead; he was bareheaded and kept running one hand compulsively through his hair as if it were in his eyes; it wasn't. Hal refused to sit; he stood rigid against the wall by the door into the kitchen, and Pip welcomed him in vain. Nils took a chair across the table from Myles.

"Now let's have this straight," he said pleasantly.

"Yes, Myles, you go first," Hal's voice was gentle, with a deadly courtesy. He seemed to have grown much older all at once.

"Well, as I said," Myles began too fast, "it likely doesn't amount to a hill of beans . . . just a misunderstanding. Oh, Jesus, Nils . . . Joanna," he broke out. "Drop it, drop it for God's sake!" He started to get up. Joanna had been right about the anguish, and she now guessed that Nan was outside, pressed close against the crack where the door hadn't latched when Nils swung it shut behind them. "Listen, can't we just make like it never happened?"

"Like what never happened?" Hal asked. "What never happened, or are you telling Nils it happened?" He hardly moved his lips. "If you don't want to tell it again, to all of us, bring your daughter in to do it. She's had some practice."

"All right, Hal," Nils said. "Come on, Myles, the sooner it's out, the sooner it's over."

He was a man willing to commit himself to desperation, no matter what it entailed. "*All right!*" He kept looking at Joanna. "Delphine . . . I mean Cluny, that's what she wants to be now . . . you know how girls are. . . ." His attempt at a grin turned into a grimace. "Well, she claims she was practicing away up in the clubhouse, and all of a sudden when she made one of those fancy turns, she saw a man on the porch looking in at her. She didn't know how long, but it gave her quite a turn, the way he kept staring." He never glanced at Hal; his eyes kept shifting between her and Nils, always returning quickly to her, almost in appeal. For me to believe him? she wondered. Or to understand why he's doing it?

"We never had to worry about anything like that before," Myles said weakly.

"You don't have to worry now," Hal said in that clipped and deadly manner. "Not about me. I'm not into drooling over nymphets in leotards. I never put a foot on that porch."

The door swung open and the screen door slammed behind Nan. She wore a long dark coat over her shoulders like a cloak, and above it her face and hair looked bleached to a dead whiteness, flat and featureless, except for her eyes.

"*My daughter does not lie.*" She walked forward on the words, and the dark cloak became her raincoat. Her features took on distinctive contours and some color. She had looked more than strange, she had looked weird, but now she became simply (if anything about her could ever be simple) a gaunt, outraged woman who'd been distraught with one rage or another for too long. Now she had a legitimate reason to break out.

"Come and sit down, Nan." Nils, all sober gallantry, was putting a chair forward. She ignored it. "My daughter does not lie," she repeated. Myles was frantically mopping his face and neck while staring at the floor between his feet; Joanna wished she could hand him a dry towel. Hal remained stiff against the wall, and Nan didn't look toward him.

"Nan," Joanna said gently, "why don't we have Cluny come in and tell us in her own words what happened?"

"She's afraid to be in the same room with him," Nan said steadily, and Hal exploded.

"*Afraid!* My God! Let's finish this . . . this *circus* once and for all. I won't offend Joanna and Nils by using the right word for it in their house. But I—not you—will tell them what I did this afternoon." He turned his back on her and Myles. "I went from the schoolhouse up around by the cemetery. I came by the big house—Mrs. Fennell was outside, and we talked a minute—and when I'd got down the field to the gate, Carol was there, watching for Peter. She'd let him go to the store alone." His voice warmed and loosened. "She asked me how I got on at the school, and I told her, briefly, then came on through the gate. We could hear the music from the clubhouse. It was one of the Strauss waltzes when I walked by, without even glancing at the building because I was looking for Peter. And Carol was watching me the whole time . . . I saw Peter sitting on a boulder, this side of Jamie's; I turned around, waved to Carol, and pointed. She waved back. Peter had a loaf of bread beside him, and he was eating a Hershey bar Willy gave him . . . I told him he'd better start moving and watched him going up the path." His smile was gentle. "And I'll give you my word, *he* didn't go up on the clubhouse porch either, but I can tell he was tempted. By the music," he added.

Myles shut his eyes and sank back in his chair. Nils was nodding in his slow, encouraging way. Nan said again, "My daughter does not lie," her voice inhuman, mechanical.

"I'll go and get Carol," Joanna offered. If I don't get out of here in the next minute, she thought, I'll scream. No, I'm not a screamer, but I'll do *something* that'll bring them all up standing. For Nan, she did not exist when she went out around her toward the door. As Joanna took hold of the doorknob, it was taken from the outside and turned strongly in her hand; the door was shoved open. She and Shannon looked at each other in mutual shock. Behind them, beyond Nan's tall motionless figure, Myles said very tiredly, "Well, Nan, I guess that's it. Let's go home and let these people eat."

"My daughter doesn't—" she began.

"She does, too," Shannon said, dodging out around Joanna. His cheeks were a burning red, his hair rumpled in all directions.

"Hello, son!" Myles called, practically boisterous. Nan seized him by the shoulder, gripping hard through his sweatshirt; Joanna saw the whitened knuckles.

"*Where is your sister?*" Nan tried to shake him, but with his feet planted wide apart and his hands in his pockets, Shannon was not movable.

"Which sister?" he asked, on the edge of insolence.

"You know." As if the name was too holy to mention.

"You mean my sister *Delphine?* Ayuh, she lies when it suits her. Nobody has to go and get Mrs. Fennell. Tom J. and I were just coming down from his house, and we saw Peter drop his bread when he was trying to peel his Hershey bar. We kidded him a little, and he went along and sat on a rock so he wouldn't keep dropping his bread while he ate the candy. Hal was coming down the lane from the Fennell gate, and we were talking about his visiting school today. He came straight on past the clubhouse, and he waved back at Carol and pointed at Peter. He was talking to Peter when we went over to the well; Mrs. Percy wanted that water right off. Hal came along after us. *Whistling.*"

There followed probably the noisiest silence Joanna had ever heard; it was so full of things unsaid. Myles sighed robustly. "Thank you, son. That about clears it up, and I'm sorry as hell this ever happened." Without glancing toward Nan, he walked directly toward Hal. "I don't know as you'll accept my apology, but I'm making it."

"All right, Myles. But it seems somebody else ought to be apologizing, not you." He put out his hand to Myles, who wrung it hard. Pip climbed up into Nils's lap, and Nils caressed him absently while watching the others as if he were only remotely interested. Nan suddenly snapped into life.

"Just how much do you know about this cousin of yours?" she demanded of Joanna. "I understand you never saw him in your life till he showed up here."

"Oh, for Christ's sake, Nan!" Myles snapped. He took her arm and tried to swing her around toward the door.

She managed to twist free. "Do you know *why* he left home? What's he told you?"

"Enough," Joanna said. "Thank you, Myles. Thank you, Shannie."

"Anytime," Shannon said in a deep voice.

"I'm sorry," Myles said again.

"It's over," Nils said with a slight lift of his hands.

"Good night, everybody!" Shannon shouted from out in the yard as Joanna shut the door. When she turned back to the room, Hal had left it. Nils was standing and stretching, and Jamie had reappeared.

"Good for Shannie," Jamie said. I almost lost my head and clapped like hell for him. That would have cleared the place in a hurry. . . . Well, it was either one in the eye for his mother or for the ballerina or for both. I wonder what's going on across the yard now."

"I don't want to know," said Joanna. "If we woke up in the morning and found they'd all moved away in the night, I'd go over to the school and ring the bell. I'm sorry for Myles and for the kids, Shannie especially, but she poisons everything."

"How about supper?" Nils asked. She went into the kitchen to begin heating the chowder again.

"Well, I suppose my wife will be wondering who stole me between here and there," Jamie said. "Now she'll tell me to never be within a hundred feet of that little girl without a batch of witnesses."

Hal came out of the bathroom. He'd doused his head and was still drying his hair. "How do you feel?" Jamie asked him. Neither Nils nor Joanna would have asked that, but it must have been the right thing, at least coming from Jamie.

"A lot better than I did a half-hour ago," he said. "And I don't know if I'll ever want to laugh about it. Inside I was singing Hallelujah when Shannie came in with his story, and I never loved any two kids in my life the way I love him and Tom J. for being where they were." He took the towel back into the bathroom, and his voice came out to them. "I never said many prayers of thanks in my life, but I guess it's not too late to start."

"How about lobster chowder?" Joanna asked him when he came out.

"A while back, no. But now I'm ready." The hands that turned and settled the collar of his polo shirt were not quite steady; Nils was bringing the lamp in from the sun parlor and didn't notice, but she knew that Jamie did.

"Hey," he said, then stopped. "I've got to quit that, because my daughter's begun calling me Hey. Hal. Sir. We're going over to Stonehaven tomorrow for my wife to see her doctor. How'd you like to come along? Going to be a good day, and Stonehaven's quite a place to see, with the old quarries, the gallymanders, and so forth. And, they've got a big fishing industry besides lobstering. We're taking Sea Star," he said to his father.

"Rosa thinks she's being neglected if we don't take her across the bay every so often."

"You're sure she won't mind?" Hal asked.

"Rosa or the boat? Neither. We'll be leaving at eight-thirty. Marm, Dad, make a list if there's anything you want us to pick up."

"We couldn't even get up a good list between us for Laurie," Joanna said. "I'll know by morning."

"I need a few more clothes," Hal said. "Some cold-weather gear."

"All right, then. See you in the morning. Good night, everybody." Jamie went out the back way. Ladling the chowder, Joanna was appreciating her son more than ever. He was not very patient sometimes, but he was always kind when it mattered, and it mattered to Hal right now. Hal ate well, but he was very quiet, very much closed in upon himself. Delayed shock? She knew she'd felt the accusation as if it had been about Jamie. What if Carol hadn't been at the gate, and the two boys hadn't been watching Hal? Cluny might have said anything; the shock of the attack would have made Hal look guilty, and how could he have proved he was not?

And how would *we* know? That effectively destroyed what appetite she had and wiped out any ideas for a supper conversation. She couldn't leave the table with her supper half-eaten, nor could she do what she wanted—force a discussion to release Hal from himself. Why aren't you a mind reader, Nils? she thought crossly. But perhaps he was doing exactly the right thing, telling Hal how Rosa had come to the island alone in *Sea Star,* by dead reckoning in a thick fog; she'd had her father's marks. Hal was listening. He was trying to concentrate. She hoped he still planned to play chess with George tonight. That should be therapeutic.

In the dining room they hardly heard the tap at the sun-parlor door, it was so discreet. "Come in, come in," Nils was calling on the way out there. But the tap came again, and he had to open the door. Joanna, more for something to do than curiosity, had followed him. Myles stood on the threshold. He was not smiling. Cluny was looking past his arm. Her long dark hair hung lank past her cheeks; she was as colorless as her mother had been, but hers was a child's face, that of a forlorn waif brought in out of the night. At the other end of the room Hal opened the back door to leave, and Myles said curtly, "Wait up, Hal. Cluny has something to say to you." He put his arm around Cluny and propelled her into the room. She was as stiff as if her feet weren't working on their own, and she kept pressing back against him. She had been crying. Joanna felt pity like a twisting pain in her midriff and tried to resist it; the child had lied and been caught at it. With no witnesses, what could her lie have done? And *been?* She turned to leave the sun parlor, seeing Hal motionless at the back door.

"You should hear this, Jo," Myles called after her. "The lie was repeated in your house." She wanted to keep on going and make a noise in the kitchen, but of course she couldn't. She took a deep breath and turned back.

"I did lie," Cluny said suddenly. Her voice was very clear; she was looking past Joanna and Nils at Hal. "I saw you go by. I wanted you to stop, but you didn't. I ran out to look, but you never looked back." It was a recitation, as if she had to recite it like that or cry. "I apologize."

"I accept your apology, Cluny," he said, unsmiling. "It's hard to do sometimes. I was always having to do it. It's over now, so let's forget it."

"Thank you. I apologize to you too, Mr. and Mrs. Sorensen." Color was warming her face, and her voice trembled slightly. "I don't know why I did it. I hope I never do anything like that again." Her voice came young and fast. "My mother called Shannie a liar for what he said in here, so I had to tell her it was true. I've already apologized to him." The thirteen-year-old came all the way through. "He's an awful trial to me sometimes, but he's not a liar."

"I know about brothers," said Joanna. "Three older and two younger. I was an awful trial to them sometimes, I guess."

Cluny nodded, ducked out of sight behind Myles, and was out the door. Myles said heavily, "Thanks, everybody." He turned to follow her.

"We appreciate you and Cluny coming over," Nils said. "How about a cup of coffee?"

"I'll take a rain check on that, if you don't mind."

"We've got plenty of time."

The two men shook hands, and after a moment Hal came forward. He didn't say anything but put out his hand, and Myles shook it hard, looking fixedly into Hal's face. "I'm sorry," he said several times.

"It's all right, Myles," Hal said very gently. "It's in the past now. We'll leave it there." Shaking his head, Myles went out. Joanna felt sad for him, and Nils was thoughtful. Hal's expression could have illuminated a neighborhood.

29

For several weeks, many of the adults and the older schoolchildren had been watching a public-television documentary about archeological finds in Maine dating back to a time before the supposed arrival of the Red Paint people. Every scholar had a firm, reasonable, and exciting theory about ancient travelers. Joanna's favorite involved the Phoenician mariners, sailing right out of Bible days to the Gulf of Maine and leaving chiseled messages for other Phoenicians about good harborage and so forth. If not on Bennett's or Brigport, you could see such a carving on Monhegan—if that was the history you liked best. Nils was more impartial but agreed the Gulf of Maine had been amazingly well-traveled for a comparatively young sea, and if all the men drowned in it over the last five thousand years or so were to be suddenly resurrected, the mixture of languages would beat the Tower of Babel all hollow.

Tonight Joanna couldn't make herself sit still to watch and listen, and she was angry at being cheated out of that. The harder she willed herself to relax, the more aches she developed. Lying in bed with her book, she kept going back to the scene in the sun parlor, studying one face after another like portraits in a museum, faces with voices. In daylight it will all be different, she promised herself. Try not to get riled up—you'll never go to sleep. She was thinking what she would like to say to Nan—after all her sympathy less than a week ago; she knew, however, that she would never use those slashing words but be forever polite. And that's all, she thought. Now what else can I do?

Pip hadn't come up with her, and she missed his sleepy presence and voice. Good heavens, I'm addicted to a cat! she thought, and found herself smiling. She went back to *Night at the Vulcan* but kept herself from rushing to the solution. Finishing a book without reading at least one chapter of another one was a sure way to keep yourself awake.

Nils came up and told her he hadn't yet found out where the ancestors of the Red Paint came from. "Good," she said. "I couldn't stand any more excitement tonight."

Hal hadn't come in yet. Usually his chess evenings weren't late because George and Sky began their day early. They could be having a mug-up with Sky and Binnie, who would be wanting to know about California and the business there after hearing scraps from the children.

She went to sleep but woke about four and knew she couldn't stay in bed any longer. She hoped she'd never be bedridden, because she couldn't stand it, especially when she woke very early when everybody else was sleeping. Pip didn't get up with her. He murmured in his sleep, stretched, subsided again.

Hal's door was closed. Did you think he'd drowned himself? she thought scathingly. She heated water for coffee and buttered a thick slice of her own bread by the light from the gas burner. She took a fat candle from the lamp shelf, set it in a holder Jamie had made from a net cork in the fifth grade, put it on the sun-parlor table, and sat down to eat. The house was chilly, but she wore her winter bathrobe and woolly slippers; she didn't want to stop to build a fire in the kitchen range. She pulled the writing pad to her, found a pen in the mug, and sternly wrote a list of things she didn't really need. But they could always use supplies for the medicine chest; neither she nor Nils had prescriptions to be filled by the Stonehaven pharmacist. Maybe a couple more of these writing tablets and a box of envelopes and half a dozen pens before they were all used up. She ordered two cans of Nils's favorite tobacco, though he would say he had plenty. As an afterthought, but a nice touch, how about a dozen fresh pears? She'd just as soon have green ones. Mark's last batch went too soon—kids kept buying them up as a change from apples.

Children reminded her of extra candy for Hallowe'en. Mark always had plenty in, letting Young Mark make the choices. But she needed some in the house for the children coming around. Some of those miniature chocolate bars would do it, a change from candy corn and marshmallow pumpkins.

Writing letters or lists of any kind when she was the only one up always gave her satisfaction. She knew it was absurd, but it worked. She blew out the candle and went into the living room, curled up under the afghans on the sofa, and went to sleep. She was awakened by Pip standing on her and touching her nose. When she opened her eyes and gazed into his gold-speckled ones, he began to purr.

Nils was in the kitchen and had built the fire. "I'm up," she called to him and went upstairs to dress. A few minutes later, washing her face with cold water in the bathroom, she remembered the last thought, the last decision, that had tipped her into so sound a sleep. She was going to call Hugo, and she wouldn't tell Nils. Oh yes, Hal was going to call as soon as he got his license; he did not want to call, and so there would always be an excuse to put it off another day. A parent ought to know where his children were, no matter how they parted, and it wasn't as if Hal were in jail. Besides, his father had been dear to her long before Hal existed; who was to say her claim, or her brothers', didn't come before Hal's? Auld Acquaintance has got some rights around here, my beamish boy, she told Hal silently.

"You look bright and shining this morning," Nils said.

"There's a lot of good sleep in that sofa," she told him. He'd already had the weather forecast, and it was going to be a fine day for lobstering—or going to Stonehaven. "Coming out with me?"

"I can't," she said, not as rueful as she sounded. "I'm baking beans today, and I'll have Sara Jo for the afternoon. We're going for a nice walk somewhere. Maybe we'll go to the Eastern End, call on Aunt Philippa, and play with Robin's dolls' tea set. That's the real attraction."

"Another time then," Nils said.

Aren't we the deceivers, she thought cheerfully. But I'll tell him afterward about the call. I can't keep that to myself. It occurred to her that this might be a Saturday when Hugo didn't go down to the yard. Never mind; there'll be someone to take a message. She composed it while Nils was busy getting his dinner box ready. *Hal is safe on Bennett's Island. I'll talk to you when I catch you. This is Joanna.* So Hugo would know about Hal, which was the important thing. But she still wanted to hear his voice over all those miles and those years, as if this would prove he was still their Hugo. . . . I should leave Mark's number, she thought. Maybe Hugo will call.

Going back from seeing Nils off, she came face-to-face with Myles and Shannon, just coming to the fishhouse. Shannon was dressed to go out with his father. He was trying to look grimly duty-bound, but his grin seemed to explode forth like the sun from behind a cloud. She pretended she wasn't surprised, as if he went out anytime he could. Myles said, "Morning, Jo." His smile was haggard; he looked years older than at any other time since she'd known him. It was almost as if his good nature and his capacity for happiness were the only young things about him, and now he'd lost them. Last night must have been a hard one in Dave's house; that Shannon was actually going out to haul with his father was an extraordinary happening. At least Shannon was a winner, no matter what happened. *What about Cluny?* For a stricken moment she thought she'd asked it aloud.

"Jo, I have to apologize again," Myles said. "I don't know what possessed the girl. Seems as if she cried half the night. She went straight up to bed from your house, so Nan . . . so nobody said anything to her." Meaning Nan hadn't talked with her. "I haven't spoken with her this morning. I want to thank you all for being so nice to her. But not knowing the *why* of it . . ." He shook his head as if against blackflies.

"Shannie, will you give your father and me a minute alone?" Joanna asked the boy.

"Sure. Dad, I better see if the skiff needs bailing. She leaks a dite," he said to Joanna, and went on down the wharf to the ladder. He carried the two lunch totes.

"Myles." She spoke softly, though no one was in sight along the road. "Little girls get crushes, and Hal is pretty glamorous for almost all the kids right now. None of them are very shy here. They won't be bashful about talking to Hal, but Cluny's not like that, is she? She wouldn't know how to get him to notice her, even just to say, 'Hi, Cluny,' and kid her a bit."

"You're saying she did it to get attention. Well, it's a hell of a way to do that." He reddened with anger. "And how am I going to be sure she doesn't try it again, with somebody else, with a lie that's even worse? How will I know who to believe? What kind of a name will she get for herself?"

Joanna put her hand on his arm. "I can promise you that *this* won't go outside the Sorensen family. And maybe this is the only time it will happen. Maybe once—and being caught and having to apologize—is enough. Oh gosh, I don't know anything! I'm not an expert, but I think she ought to be able to talk with . . . with parents who understand a little about being between hay and grass but who still don't excuse the lie. It's not the first real lie that makes you a liar; it's only if you keep on telling them."

"And about other people," he said. "Ayuh. That's what scares me."

I wish you would all move away, Joanna thought behind her sympathetic expression. I'm not being a hypocrite. I'm just defending myself.

Shannon came back. Last week after the ball game he had looked this radiantly happy. "The skiff's all ready to go, Dad, and *Sweet Alice* is waiting with a big smile on her face."

He was actually laughing at his own whimsy. Myles put his arm around the boy's shoulders and gave him a squeeze. "Then we'd better get going. Doesn't pay to keep a lady waiting. Thanks, Jo. I hope Hal's not holding any bad feelings."

"All he's thinking about is seeing Stonehaven today."

"That's a *neat* place," Shannon said. He clumped off in his rubber boots.

Myles looked around quickly. Shannon was already out of sight on the wharf beyond their fishhouse.

"Nan's gone," Myles said very fast and softly. "Before dawn. She never slept all night, and neither did I. But there was no talking. *God,* what a night. She was like a woman possessed." He himself looked as if he'd been fighting demons. "*Annie-Elmina* came in around two. Nan was out walking around. She went over to the wharf where they were gassing up and told them she was riding in with them. Then she came back and told me." His mouth twisted in an unhappy grin. "Hates John but hates staying here worse."

They were both watching for Shannie to show up again. "Maybe some time inshore is what she needs," Myles said. "I hope so."

"I do too," Joanna said. "So long, Myles. You and Shannie have the finest kind of a day."

"We will!" He dropped a few years. "A *happy* one."

For Shannon such a happy day had been a long time coming, and perhaps it had come now only because of the family touse begun by Cluny. The privilege might be snatched back anytime if Myles reverted to his policy of not opposing Nan, after the first giant opposition. I wish I knew the right god to remove people from one spot and set them down in another one, safe, a good distance from me, she thought. Since there was no hope of this, she decided to stop thinking about them. She was going to talk with Hugo in a few hours, or find out when she could, and in the meantime she'd have contacted him even indirectly.

It wasn't yet sunup, but Dog Tray was out, and they passed the time of day. When she went into the house, Hal really had a shining morning face like Shakespeare's schoolboy and like Shannie today. He was scrambling eggs; tomorrow morning she'd take him out to the henhouse and let him gather eggs from under warm hens.

She sat down with him, tried the eggs, and congratulated him. He gave her a few moments to drink some fresh coffee and make a piece of toast, then said, "Did I make any noise last night? This morning, really. It was almost one."

"You and George must have had quite a match, or that was a long mug-up afterward."

"No," he said seriously. "We finished around ten—George is getting good. He beat me. I wasn't ready to settle down right off; I felt as if somebody had been at me with a giant eggbeater. . . ." He grinned. "While I was concentrating on chess I didn't think of it. But once I was outside and walking around, I couldn't think of anything else. Young Mark told me I could borrow *We Two* anytime, and she was tied there at the car, so I went out rowing around the harbor. I never saw anything more beautiful than the phosphorescence shining around everything it touched. *But . . .*" He put down his fork.

"It's not last night," he explained. "That's over with. But it's what comes next. Oh, I know—no serenades out on the doorstep. I can always go out and serenade the hens. And the only way I'll walk by the clubhouse when she's practicing is in a well-documented crowd. But how am I supposed to *treat* her when I meet her? Pretend she's not there? I don't want to snub the kid, but I'm a little afraid of her." His laughter was embarrassed. "I mean, what could she say next time? And I can't always be sure of witnesses."

"Well, I wouldn't single her out by ignoring her. Just treat her the way you do the rest. Her father said she's really miserable—maybe she's learned her lesson, and she won't want to be like the boy who cried 'Wolf.' "

"But in the end there really was a wolf," he said.

"I guess that's a bad example," Joanna said, "and I'm not too sharp this morning."

"I'd better go brush," he said on his way to the bathroom, "and shave, too, before I go to the metropolis."

She forbore telling him that his beard was hardly noticeable. "Why don't you let it grow for the winter?" she called after him. "We usually have a couple, ever since they found out what a good barber Binnie is—and expert with beards. They have so many in her hometown, and it was cheaper than going to Limerock every so often."

"I don't want a beard, but I was thinking of getting her to give me a trim so I'd look more like a lobster fisherman." Pip pushed open the bathroom door and went in. "Hello, Old Stocking," Hal said. "I suppose whiskers like yours are some real use to you."

When he came out, scented with toothpaste and aftershave, he said, "Anyway, I won't be nearby once I start working for Owen."

She was startled enough to set her cup down hastily before she slopped. "Is this *definite?*"

He was delighted to be talking openly about it. "I'd say as definite as it can get without a written contract. I know he needs a man, and I'm in the family, and I want to stay here."

The only thing she could say to such ingenuous anticipation was a rather weak, "Are you short for cash, for going to Stonehaven?"

"I don't have much of what I started out with, and I'm pretty proud I've done this well. My folks would never believe it. But I've got a credit card I can use to get my duds with and put something extra in my pocket. I wouldn't use the credit card unless I was really between a rock and a hard place, because I got into a real mess for going so far over my limit when I first had it. I thought Dad was going to pounce on me, grab it, and cut it up himself." Evidently his memory of the crisis had become hilarious with time. She wondered if Hugo had paid the debt. As if Hal guessed this he said, "I'll pay it back. I couldn't do it very well sitting in a classroom, but now I'm going to be making real money, judging by what Mark's paying out on the car these days, and how close George is to his Dream Girl."

"You're not fishing yet, so don't count on making a lot of money this winter," she warned him. "I've known times when the men were lucky to make it out twice in one month."

He was irrepressible. "But I've been hearing about the big winter prices and then the spring crawl! Is there a bank in Stonehaven where I could raise some money with my card? If Jamie's along to say I'm who I say I am? Is that good grammar?"

"Who cares?" said Joanna, somewhat giddily. "Just about every major bank in Maine has a branch in Stonehaven. Take an extra jacket; you'll need it on the water."

She could hardly wait for him to be out of the house, and he could hardly wait to get started. She walked down to the big wharf with him before eight, and Jamie was already warming up *Sea Star* at her mooring. All the other boats had long since gone, and Mark was back in the store.

Rosa stood alone, calm and handsome in her shore-going outfit of lightweight heather-tweed slacks and jacket; her rose-pink turtleneck picked up the healthy flush across her broad cheekbones. Pregnancy became Rosa.

"It's going to be a grand trip. It's just like a March morning when you think you can really smell spring even though it may turn out to be a weather-breeder. I'm glad you're coming along, Hal."

Joanna gave her the list and a fifty-dollar bill. "If it comes to more, I want to know. Let's have no false delicacy about asking for what's due you, especially with little He or She listening."

30

Now she had nothing to do until she called Hugo. *Sea Star* had gone, with Rosa at the wheel, the boys sitting on the washboard, and ahead of them blue seas and morning sunshine and a sky that looked polished down to the mainland hills. If she could be strong-minded enough, she could forget for the day what Hal had said about Owen. She didn't. Right now Laurie would be waiting for the travel bureau to open; just an hour from now she would have her reservations for the *QE 2* in April. Richard was also out on this summer-colored sea, somewhere a good distance from the harbor. All of them would be in happy ignorance; the present hour was what mattered, and if they looked ahead they saw only a chain of such hours. Of course Richard had apparently given up gracefully his idea of leaving school, but if all went well he should be hearing about setting out his father's traps in the late spring and fishing them until Owen was home again.

Joanna was not that optimistic; she was simply glad that everyone would be happy for today. Now if Rosa's checkup didn't show something nobody'd expected—Oh, you crepe-hanger, you worrywart, you *idiot!* You bird of ill omen! Severely insulting herself, she walked home rapidly to start the beans.

There was still time before eleven; she thought eight o'clock out there wouldn't be too early, from what Hal had told her, but she was going to make it eleven on the dot, here. She put clean sheets on the beds, dry-mopped the bedrooms, and swept down the stairs. The mantel clock began to strike the hour as she reached the hall.

"*Good,*" she said loudly. Pip ran to her and she said, "No, you stay here." She washed her face again and combed her hair—Binnie's last trim was still looking good. Outside, the children were over in the schoolyard, extending the baseball season. The little girls with their doll carriages were probably being an audience on the steps—mothers at the park. She wondered how Cluny was—feeling better away from Nan, she hoped—and then dismissed her. Maggie must have taken Dog Tray for a walk around the harbor to visit those dogs. "He's a social individual," she said once. "He needs to see his friends."

At the wharf Willy was repairing doors on crates, watched by Louis. Mark was doing paperwork in the post office; Helmi was knitting one of those handsome sweaters that were her specialty, with complex patterns no one else had the courage to try. It was not an hour when the store was busy.

"Either of you or both," Joanna said. "Can I use the extension at the house for a long-distance call?"

"Help yourself," said Helmi, who, after studying her instructions, resumed silently counting.

"Unless you're calling Paulie Dunnett," Mark said. "I owe it to Nils not to let his wife carry on over my telephone."

"Thanks," she said on her way out.

Mark called after her, "Come to think of it, Paulie's up around Eastport right now."

"My virtue's saved again," said Joanna. She went around the corner of the store onto the steep and twisting path up to the house. She knew the other two wouldn't listen, and they wouldn't show curiosity either, even if they felt it.

The kitchen, like any space of Helmi's, was spotless but also comfortable. A young tiger cat was tightly curled up asleep in a rocking chair; she looked like a round plum pudding with stripes. Now she sat up and gazed at Joanna with drowsy eyes the color of green apples. "Hello," Joanna said. The cat blinked and yawned, sat and stared. Joanna had written a number for the western Haliburton yard. She didn't expect it to be answered in Hugo's office, which should be reachable from wherever it was picked up. She was actually startled when a young female voice said, "Mr. Bennett's office at the Western Haliburton Boatyard. Who is calling, please? I will take your number, and he will call back when he can."

Long-distance calling still held for Joanna something of the miraculous, though she would never admit it; and she had never before called across three thousand miles. But the idea of the Hugo Bennett of their youth occupying an office—no, *offices*—and being called Mr. Bennett by this prim young voice was very funny. It was as if he were playing Big State Executive up in Augusta, with his feet on the desk. When they were children, everyone with an office in the state capitol sat with his feet on the desk and smoked cigars.

"Ma'am?" the young voice inquired. She could hear male voices in the background. "Are you still there?"

"Yes, I am," said Joanna. "Will you tell him his cousin Joanna Bennett Sorensen is calling. If he can't answer now, I'll wait here a half hour for him to call, and if he can't make it then, I'd like him to call this number and leave word as to when we can talk. This is the number—"

"*Jo?*" He shouted it. "Joanna Bennett, my cousin on Bennett's Island?"

It was Hugo in her ear, Hugo in this room. Her hand wanted to shake, and then triumph took over. "I'm in Pete Grant's house, only it's Mark's house now. Don't worry, everything's all right. Nobody's dead or anything." She knocked on the wooden table, and the cat got up to look.

He said more quietly, "What's 'or anything' mean, Jo?"

"Hugo, Hal's here. He arrived on the *Conqueror* on Tuesday."

Silence. Then he said incredulously, with a slight stammer—she'd already heard Hal do the same thing—"*Hal* is there, on the island, and he came out on the *Conqueror*? My God. All my life as a kid I'd have given my soul for that, and he hits it—"

"The first day in Limerock. But the old one didn't rise up and rebuild herself. This is the new one, since Korea."

"I know, I know. But it knocked me galley west, thinking of him and her together and at the island. I'd never have dreamed it. And I'm jealous as hell." Obviously turning away from the receiver he said, "Kim, do you want to take your break now while I talk family business? Thanks, dear." A door shut somewhere, and he was back. "Why *didn't* I think it? When they were kids I brainwashed them, and he was the youngest so he got the most."

"So we gathered," said Joanna. "He may not have wanted to call, but you've been very much with us."

"Why didn't he want to call? Did he say?" She skipped that.

"We all got after him the first night—"

"*All?* Who's 'all'?"

"Charles, Philip, Owen, Mark, Steve, Nils, Jamie, and assorted wives.

He went home with Mark, who left him alone in the store with the telephone, and it was Mark's treat. Mark and his wife went up to the house, to bed, and Hal locked the door behind him and went for a walk. Nobody else knows, but nobody's asking him what his father said that night; maybe they suspect, like us, that you and he parted after a touse about his leaving college."

"Well, that's part of it," Hugo said. "Near enough. But he could at least have sent a postcard now and then. You know, when I heard your name I thought, This is something about Hal. Then I thought I was crazy, but I wasn't. I was *right*. Tell me how he is."

"He's so excited—even about the gulls. He says they sound different—"

"They do. What else?"

"He's covered most of the island in a couple of days—first with fast walks, next with slow ones. He's been at the school and answered questions about California and the boatyard and—oh, yes—the *Ariadne*. He's been out one day with Owen, and it was some rough—"

"You've just had a hurricane there. I get my Maine weather fix every day, tides and all. Excuse me." He was blowing his nose. "Listen, this call will cost enough to lengthen the Maine Turnpike, but I'm paying, so don't make excuses and hang up. But first give me the number there."

She did. "It's not like putting all your calls through the Coast Guard base in Limerock."

"What about him and Owen?" he asked greedily. "How'd he do?"

"He was crazy about it. He's sent for his birth certificate."

"Has he got his eye on some kind of boat?" Hugo was sounding alarmed. "What'll he do for gear? Good Christ, it's coming *winter*! This is no time to begin, he doesn't know anything; what kind of hell is Owen raising with him?"

"You don't think we'd let him do anything foolish, do you? He's hoping to go sternman with Owen, who's the only man who needs one. You probably don't know—how could you?—but he can't do all the heavy work anymore because of his heart. What seemed like the perfect sternman flew the coop one day when Owen and Laurie were away. A few days later Hal arrived."

"Well . . . " It was grudging. "I guess it's as good a way to learn the business as any. Owen's been around this long, he must have quit trying to live dangerously. . . . Anyway, I'm so damn' glad Hal's safe, why quibble? Where could he be better off? What's it like there right now?"

"October's bright blue weather," she said, and he groaned.

"Oh God, I can see it . . . smell it . . . hear it, and the colors are always fresh. Everything's the same except for the missing faces and the different boats—and maybe some different houses."

"Not many," she said. "The schoolhouse is the same except for improvements. Fresh paint every two years, and the belfry's been rebuilt, but the bell is the same. Your son's been in the schoolhouse, Hugo. Why don't you come and see everything for yourself? You couldn't have *not* thought of it all these years, or do all your plans fetch up shattered on the Reef of Hugo's Woe?"

He laughed at that. "I can still recite 'The Wreck of the *Hesperus*,' but since my kids all grew up, there's nobody to impress. Why don't I come? Maybe I'm a yellowbelly, Jo. There've been a few times when I could have left with nothing to stop me—*Ariadne* and the rest would've been built without me. This is a yard full of shipwrights, but there have always been things to stop it. Maybe I let them come up, with Vivian or something unexpected here. I guess the point is, I could have come home, but I'm a goddamn' coward. I'm glad the Coast Guard switchboard isn't monitoring this call."

"I wouldn't have been calling California then," she said practically. "Remember? If anyone wanted to make a really private call to anywhere, even just in Maine, you saved it for the mainland. Besides, you never could be sure of being alone with the telephone here in the store. Mark's got an extension in his house; I'm calling from there. And Mark and Helmi aren't listening; they're too honorable. You don't know any of the wives, so you've got a treat coming. So think about it."

"I'm going to think about it. If I could I'd get a flight out tonight *before* I stopped to think. . . . But if Hal is there, and he's finding himself, as they like to say, I'm not going to come crashing onto the scene and drive him away."

"He said he'd write you when he finally got his license. Listen, Hugo, I've got to get home and take a look at my beans, and somebody might be trying to get Mark. So I'm going to quit. But Hugo, the neglect isn't all on your side. One of us could have called, but somehow nobody thought of trying to reach you at your office, and the Christmas cards just petered out. We felt you'd gone completely over to . . .." She was blushing; she felt like stuttering. "We were at least partly wrong, and I won't let the ice freeze in solid again."

"Oh, hell. I'll keep on bashing it from this side. I love you, Jo." He had to blow his nose again. "Tell them all I love them. I'd say tell Hal too, but I have a feeling you're not going to tell him about this call."

"No, he might see it as a betrayal. I think he wants to do his own talking. Today he's gone to Stonehaven with Jamie and his wife."

"I'll be satisfied with not hearing yet, if I can check with Mark from time to time." He chuckled. "I keep trying to see him as Pete Grant."

"One last question, Hugo," she said seriously.

"Ask it, darlin' mine."

"Are you *fat?*"

"Oh, my God! Do I *sound* fat?" This time his laughter came in loud enough to make the cat sit up again and stare at the telephone.

"No, you don't."

"I may have a few pounds on Hal, but he's still a stripling, you might say. I wish I could be there for beans tonight. We never have them." He sounded wistful. "Brown bread?"

"No, johnny cake. And new sauerkraut."

"I just may go jump out a window, except I'm on the first floor. Love you, Jo."

"Love you, skinny Hugo . . . Look, somebody's got to stop, or we'll be at it all day. Haven't you got a trawler to build or something? This time I'm *really* quitting."

"But now you've got a line to me . . . we'll both hold on like hell. No, wait." His voice dropped. "I didn't know whether to ask about Nils or not. Is he . . ." the sudden uncertainty made him sound like Hal. "I mean, you never can tell."

"Nils is fine, at least he was when he went out at the crack of dawn this morning." She rapped a knuckle on the table, and the cat stretched over from her chair to look closely. Hugo's deep sigh was audible.

"Okay, I'll let you go, darlin' mine." Had he ever called his wife that? she wondered. But surely his daughters . . . "If everybody's out to haul this morning, God's in his heaven, and all's right with the world. Remember when we learned that? I guess I'll sit back for five minutes with my feet on the desk and my eyes closed and see it all. No good-byes, we're not going to say any good-byes."

"No," she agreed as she heard him replace the telephone, very quietly. She thought she might cry when she was decently alone. Right now Mark and Helmi were down there, but who might have come in since? She took

some tissues from a box by the telephone, just in case. It had been exhil-
arating after the first shakiness; even with a nation between us we'll never
be really apart again, she exulted. We're the same as we ever were. She
didn't doubt that against his closed eyelids, he was seeing the island and
the boats scattered across the bright seas of autumn; the boats might be
new to him, but the places where the men hauled their traps—every reef,
shoal, and ledge—had names as intimate to him as his own.

No good-byes, we're not going to say any good-byes.

It reminded her of something, and she didn't want to go rummaging
for it now. "Good-bye," she said to the cat, who blinked but made no
sounds; they joked that she was silent because she was a Finnish cat. Outside a puff of breeze caught her up here on the hill, as if summoned up by
some sea spirit to whip away her megrims. She looked across the island
to the school and beyond, then down across the harbor past Eastern Harbor Point to Long Cove. She saw the harbor skiffs moving very slightly in
the wake of the little breeze and saw the gulls idle among them as if they
were letting the water take them where it would. There were no human
beings; it was strangely quiet for almost-noon on a fine Saturday. Where
were the children?

"All gone to Sou'west Point," Helmi told her. "The boys organized an
all-male hike down there. So the girls got up their own affair and called it
a picnic. They took the woods trail. They all went loaded with food, from
the stops they made in here."

"I told them, No fires," Mark growled from behind the post office windows. "No showing-off: no jumping ledges or dodging surf. No going off
alone and no losing track of anyone. Those little tykes are like minnows,
some of 'em."

"I'm sure there were enough orders from every house so nobody will
forget anything—as if they could with Tammie and Johnny in charge. And
Young Mark's pretty efficient, even if he *is* ours," Helmi said.

"I wonder if the Harmon girls went," Joanna said, then remembering
for the first time they were all free, for a few days, at least. "I called Hugo,"
she said quickly. "He sends his love, and he's got this number. I've got to
get back to those beans, so I won't go into detail now, but the fact is Hal
never called that night you left him alone here. He told me the next day."
Helmi's needles paused, and she looked up calmly at Joanna, waiting. Mark
pushed his office chair back with violence and came out into the store.

"What the hell's the idea?"

"No explanations," she said untruthfully. "But I gather there was some trouble when he left, and he couldn't make himself call. He promised to write, but he says he's waiting until he gets his lobster license, so he'll have something to say."

"Be nice if he had something to go in and something to catch," Mark grumbled.

"Getting a license is like getting your citizenship, I guess," Joanna said. "Makes him an instant native, and you can't tell when a license might come in handy."

"Are you going to tell him you called?" Helmi asked.

She shook her head. "It's his job. I just did it for my own peace of mind; I thought his parents should know he was safe even if Vivian does think it's like living with the Jukes and the Kallikaks we used to read about."

Helmi laughed, and Mark allowed a grudging hack that was nowhere near a chuckle. He went back into the post office. "I'm going up to make us some sandwiches," Helmi said. "Want one with us, Jo? Oh, I forgot your beans."

The beans weren't in any real danger, but having a pot in the oven was a great convenience, because everybody respected it. She had been gone less than an hour, and she didn't hurry walking home; there would be too few of these days left. She looked forward to spending this afternoon with Sara Jo, and she thought benignly of the children spreading out their picnic at Sou'west Cove, cooling their soda at the edge of the surf. There was no sign of life except drying dish towels outside the Harmons. Dog Tray wasn't out either.

She was so relieved about the telephone call that the teasing impression of something close, like a sad presence, had disappeared. So had the earlier image of a Hugo who had too many drinks of an evening and could become maudlin. Maybe that was too strong a word, but Hal was afraid of his father's being tearful and sentimental. She couldn't even remotely associate this image with the man who'd just talked with her; even when he said "No good-byes." She hadn't wanted to say one, either.

Pip went out as she went in, giving her a word in passing. The beans were fine. She filled a sauce dish with the new sauerkraut, buttered a slice of bread, and made a satisfactory lunch of it, then lay down with *Time* to rest up for an afternoon with a two-and-a-half-year-old granddaughter.

31

Sunday was a fair-to-middlin' day; it might breeze up and then it might flunk out to dead calm until sunrise the next morning and blow like a man, as they termed it. Nils got an early start, so did they all; Mark's wharf, wearing a Sabbath atmosphere, presided over an empty harbor. Hal had gone back to carpentering with George; he'd done some work on the jack-o'-lantern before he left, and it sat on a newspaper on a chair in a corner of the sun parlor. Joanna was preparing the vegetables for tonight's pot roast, watching fresh activity around the feeder and birdbath, and listening to the Mormon Tabernacle Choir, singing with it when she knew the hymn. Laurie came in the back door. She was so happy that her good cheer seemed to precede her into the room like the scent when the lilacs were all in bloom.

She didn't want anything to eat; she'd had breakfast just before she came out on the plane with Hannah MacKenzie, thus halving the fare. Then Lad and Hannah had brought her across, into Schoolhouse Cove. She was anxious to get home, put her secrets away, and sit down and gloat in private.

"But I wanted you to gloat with me first," she said. "After all, you cheered me on. I have our reservations, and after he's conceded, we need to go ashore to get our passports. Once he's given in, he won't mind that, and the Goodhues can book us into a hotel in London, where we can decide what we're doing next." She hugged herself. "If I can just keep from boiling over until the boys go back. They're not due until a week from Wednesday, but they want to go on the Friday boat, stay with Kristi, and see some local soccer games and a football game. Boy, am I all for it! Hannah's going to give them an official paper about their measles. How's everything been?"

Joanna laughed. "I suppose you'd have heard already if somebody got drowned or went mad with an ax. You wouldn't have to wait for John Haker to spread *that* news."

"Yup, the only good stuff's been happening on Brigport. They had a kerfuffle at their Friday-night dance when a couple of draggermen staying in the harbor got drunk and thought they were going to take over Dodge City. It'll be in the *Patriot*. Oh, how'd the boys get on with Hal last night?"

"Fine. Any reason why they shouldn't? They all had a mug-up in here afterward. Lots of fun, I even heard George laugh once or twice. They didn't really wake us up, and it was fun to hear them; it reminded me of the days when Jamie brought his seine gang in the middle of the night. Hal told me this morning he taught them snooker."

"Well, that's good," Laurie said with satisfaction. "All getting along." She lifted her zippered tote bag and hugged it. "This is *full* of great stuff, all about the ship and so forth. I'll get it to you later, but first I'm going to do that hard breathing over it." She went out.

"I hope the gulls haven't got at your food," Joanna called after her.

Not for the first time Joanna wished Laurie had some sort of early-warning system so she would not be taken by surprise. And for the first time she wished that Hal had not come. But he had come, and he was lovable; there was no point in wishing Owen was not the way he was. He *was,* and he too was lovable, if infuriating.

All right, Nils, she thought. I'll do as you say and drop it.

Sunday night Hal practiced up at Jamie's with Rosa and Ralph and Maggie, who sometimes took over so Rosa could dance. He came home so exhilarated she thought he'd keep himself—and them—awake until dawn. "My God, that was *fun!* I never get to play with anyone at home, and they're terrific. It was fantastic, the way we all came together, as if we'd always been doing it. I can't describe the thrill." He stopped to drink from the large cup of hot chocolate Joanna had mixed for him. "That's *good.* Thanks, Jo. It never tastes like that at home; it must be the water. I can hardly wait to be dancing. They always start off with a good rousing 'Lady of the Lake,' they tell me, and I can be right out there if I take the waltz next." Another deep drink. It should have scalded his gullet, but he was beyond that. "*Not* to be out there on the floor at my first Bennett's Island dance would be the worst kind of sacrilege. I hope I can find a partner who'll shove me in the right direction."

"Oh, I guess somebody will take pity on you," Joanna said.

"I'm a good swinger, anyway. Nicole and I used to swing until we'd fall down like a couple of drunks. Of course I realize that's not ballroom etiquette, but . . . I've got a new thing, like that poem that says once you've slept on an island you'll never be the same again." He waved his spoon at Nils. "This is it: Once you've danced the 'Lady of the Lake' on Bennett's Island, you'll always have magic feet. Magic feet," he repeated softly. "Ralph says he could make up a good fiddle tune for that."

On Monday night he came home whistling and stopped to talk to the finished jack-o'-lantern, which he'd set on the wheelbarrow so he'd see it all the way home. He called it Joselito. Another evening of music had him as elated as he'd been about the *Conqueror.* "No mug-up though," he protested. "Those girls believe in stuffing the musicians to keep up their strength. Good night!" he sang out as he headed for the stairs. Then he stopped halfway, came down, and bowed to Joanna.

"Aunt Jo, will you do me the honor of being my partner for the first dance? Unless you always have it with Nils. . . ."

Nils waved his hand. "You're granted the honor this time."

"Thank you, sir," said Hal. "You're a true knight." They heard him talking to Pip all the way upstairs.

"If he was ten," Joanna murmured, "he'd need tears or a temper tantrum to bring him down. Oh well, he'll sleep it off." She went out to extinguish Joselito's candle.

There were no passengers on the Tuesday boat; Nan would have had a moderately pleasant trip except that she'd be returning to her place of exile. Among the unloaded cargo were the materials Laurie had collected for the party, which couldn't come out with her on the small plane; there were special paper napkins—cups for the punch, bright-colored cardboard bowls for the ice cream—all paid for out of the quilt funds. The ice cream was now stored in Mark's big freezer. He was supplying the apples for bobbing, the popcorn, and the coffee for the adults. Cakes and cookies would be donated.

Along with the napkins and dishes, Laurie had bought replacements for the more aged of the jointed cardboard skeletons, witches, and imps that had been hung around the clubhouse for so long they'd been named. Each year some fell apart when taken out of the chest where they'd lain dormant since last year; they were given an honorable funeral by fire.

Early Tuesday afternoon Joanna, Laurie, and Nora Fennell decorated the clubhouse as richly as possible. There were gaslights now, instead of lighted lamps, at intervals along the walls, but the early lessons about fire were never forgotten, which was one reason crepe-paper festoons were never used for any occasion. Smoking had never been allowed in the clubhouse, though it was reasonable to expect that in the days when the men wore their rubber boots a good part of the time, they *had* smoked when they played pool, tidily dropping their ashes into the deep folds of their turned-down boot tops.

Cluny would practice this afternoon among the skeletons and witches dancing in the drafts created by her turns and leaps. After supper Jamie and Young Matt would set up the sawhorses and the tabletop of planks; the first women to arrive with their plates of cake and baskets of decorated cookies would roll out fresh white paper for a tablecloth. This was all at one side, close to the kitchen and coatroom wing, so as not to interfere with the children's games.

The sixth, seventh, and eighth graders insisted they had all outgrown the visits from house to house, but most of them obligingly escorted the youngsters and dressed up for the occasion. The Homestead and Hillside were the farthest from the village; Steve and Philippa always came up from the Eastern End and waited for the masqueraders to come to Hillside to be guessed at. By seven that night they were all converging on the clubhouse in their costumes, greeted by the huge illuminated grins of the two big pumpkins on which Johnny and Stuart Campion had worked all weekend. The pumpkin pies that were later eaten at their houses had a special savor, as if the artistic satisfaction were not enough. They'd made the faces wonderfully different and expressive.

Everyone was there for the children's section of the party. The older ones and young adults joined in traditional stunts and tricks, bobbed for apples, and became generally hilarious. The teenagers also indulgently joined in the round games to make the circle bigger, and Hal played the harmonica for "Going to Jerusalem," which turned into a scramble full of squeals, skids, tumbles, loud gloating, and just-as-loud disgust. By half-past eight Peter and Sara Jo, who had been too excited watching the games to get sleepy, began talking about ice cream; at least Peter did distinctly, with Sara a very loud echo. Everyone was also thirsty.

The food was uncovered, the dishes set out, and Sam and Richard went for the ice cream, with Young Mark carrying the keys. He believed that a gang from Brigport could come ashore at the harbor and steal the ice cream as a masterpiece of Hallowe'en humor, and Mark, looking back on his own youth, agreed on the possibility. So did his brothers, but they would never explain to their young their cryptic scraps of reminiscence. Nils never hinted, but he always smiled.

In the kitchen the coffee was started, and the punch was stirred in a large stainless-steel mixing bowl, for want of a classic punch bowl.

Wearing a variety of paper hats, the children were settled at the table, and the adults took their plates and drinks wherever they chose. At the clubhouse nobody ever had to drink tea or coffee out of a paper cup, or eat ice cream with a useless wooden paddle; there was a cleanup, sweep-up, washup detail for the next day. Nonstop pool went on in the comparative quiet of the room off the left side of the dance floor. Fathers who had been present to watch the party now went to get a game in before the dancing began. A nest of sleeping bags had been made in one corner; when Sara Jo and Peter fell asleep, they would be deposited here. In this dim, snug nook, with the quiet sounds of the game and the soft light, they would sleep as if in their own beds. A first grader might voluntarily join them instead of trying to curl up on a hard bench, with the dancers going by within touch.

For the dance Hal had produced a white shirt and a necktie to wear with dark slacks, making him appear incredibly dressed up; he'd enchanted the children, and now he was about to play for a dance on what he'd called, laughing at himself, his Island of Dreams. The sad thing was that Laurie—looking not much older than Richard tonight—would soon have to know that *her* dreams were just that, and Hal would have innocently participated in their disappearance. She would have them until Richard went back to school the next week; she had her mind made up to talk about what she called the Maybe Now or Never Holiday on the first night she and Owen were alone again. Meanwhile we all dance and sing and are merry, Joanna thought. Richard certainly didn't look worried and was probably one of the merriest people at the party. Of course he was sympathetic about his mother's concerns, but he was a male; he was beginning to understand what that meant, and he half-guessed—without putting it into words—what drove his father.

"Hey, where's the music?" Barry Barton demanded. "Come on, fiddler, let's get going, or do we have to light a fire under ye to get you started?"

He executed a Buck-and-Wing step that both embarrassed and delighted his daughter, especially when everyone applauded.

"Keep your shirt on," Ralph drawled. "Give me a chance to answer a call of nature." He went out. Joanna had last seen Hal eating cake and ice cream amid a cluster of children who wanted to hear more of the magic harmonica. Then Nora Fennell spoke to her, she had gotten into conversation about the Circle tomorrow, and she hadn't spotted Hal since. She was looking forward to seeing him through his first "Lady of the Lake"; she'd never had that pleasure with Jamie. Ellen had prodded and bullied him through it by threatening to send photographs of him to the younger sisters of her school friends. His cousin Holly had taught him to waltz, when he was afraid his mother might insist on teaching him. Tonight he'd play pool while Rosa played with Ralph, but all her free dances were for him, unless someone else got there first.

Ralph came back in, and he and Rosa began to tune up. Couples were forming, but Hal hadn't appeared. It occurred to Joanna that his leg might be aching from his soccer injury; he hadn't been sparing it, and he might have gone home across the field for some aspirin. Perhaps George went with him.

Nils appeared from the pool room. "Where's your partner?" he asked Joanna.

"I don't know. Maybe it'll be you, if Hal doesn't show up pretty soon."

Sky and Binnie took the floor; Myles chose Cluny, to Tracy Lynn's delight; and Shannon allowed himself a grin. They probably wouldn't have been here if Nan were home. Sam moved around the edges, as if trying to decide between Dorrie and Tammie; Dorrie might be prettier, but back when he'd been learning the dances in the schoolyard Tammie had been Sam's favorite partner, young as she'd been. Richard was heading for his mother when Joanna beckoned him to her.

"Listen, Hal must have gone home to get something for that soccer knee. Will you go over and check on him? He asked me for this dance. Besides, I think you've lost your mother to your father."

He grinned. "Yep, look at him. He's all winged out. Hal told me about that knee." He went out by way of the kitchen. She and Nils took their places beside Binnie and Sky.

"Where *are* those boys?" Binnie said. "George is so bashful, but Dorrie got a promise out of him, and now she's waiting, scared she's been stood up."

"I've been stood up too," Joanna said. "I've sent Richard to look for them. They probably started talking and lost track of the time."

"Yarning about George's horse and Hal's boat," Binnie said.

"Choose your partners for 'Lady of the Lake'!" Ralph called and began at once with the familiar "White Cockade"; the children scattered to the sides, clapping and cheering. Everyone was in the mood; it seemed months since the last dance. It was as if the fiddle itself was sharing in the joy, and the guitar strings would begin steaming at any time. Peter was still up and cuddled against Anne Barton, watching his father and mother dance; Sara Jo was presumably sleeping deep in her nest in the pool room. Joanna began glimpsing Richard in the open porch doorway, but she lost sight of him every time she was swung, until Myles let her go after a really energetic whirl, and on her way to Nils she came face-to-face with Richard. He pulled her out onto the porch, and Nils came after them.

"What's going on?" he asked. Richard shut the door on the joyous noise within.

"Hal's not there," he said in a carefully moderated voice. "Neither is George. I even went up and looked in Hal's room. Pip too. But he didn't need to tell me anything, even if he could." There was a pause that for a flashing moment seemed to Joanna like the halt before the announcement of a sudden death. "He's not there, and neither is any of his stuff."

Joanna shuddered suddenly and violently with cold. It was chilly out there, and the hall had been warm, but this was the terrible inside cold of disaster. Nils put his arm around her. "What next?" he asked calmly.

"I went down to the harbor, and *Sea Star*'s gone. I listened—it's some quiet tonight, hardly any motion—but I couldn't hear an engine."

"What else is gone?" Nils asked.

"Some of the crates out on Mark's mooring. I didn't stop to count."

"No sign of George?"

"No. I figured Hal wasn't alone; he doesn't know anything. But George knows the course across the bay to all those harbors and gunkholes just below Limerock. It's full moon, flat-arse calm, and *Sea Star* can really go when somebody lets her out."

"They've got to have a customer waiting for those lobsters," Nils said. "This couldn't all be fixed up in a day or two. And tonight's a perfect gift to them. The lobsters will likely be gone by the time any of us get in there. We could call the Coast Guard to look out for them. Let's see if we can get Mark out quietly. It's up to him." He kept hold of Joanna's elbow and steered her around the corner to the kitchen door. "You need your jacket. Coming, Rich?"

"No, I'll wait till Sam gets through cavorting, and we'll go down to the wharf and wait." He couldn't be poised and mature any longer. "*Judas!* I can't believe it! But I was *there*—I saw for myself—and oh, yeah, Uncle Nils, they used your skiff to get out to her, and they never bothered to make her fast. She was drifting out of the harbor. I'm sorry I couldn't go after her."

Nils took hold of his shoulder hard and gave him a little shake. "Never mind. It doesn't signify right now."

He and Joanna went into the small kitchen and were in luck; Mark was getting a cup of coffee. "My God, I'm winded!" he said. "I hate like hell to admit it; my wife's going strong. I hauled my boy in to take my place, and he couldn't stop grinning. He can jump around to beat hell, but he's got to be a dite taller to improve his swinging. . . . You two been out enjoying the moonlight?"

"Not so's you'd notice it," Nils said, "but somebody's not wasting it. Hal, George, *Sea Star,* and some crates—Richard didn't know how many—are gone."

There was an overhead gaslight, shedding a cold white downward illumination that was worse than the half-dark on the porch had been, outside the windows. The three faces looked like masks chopped crudely from wood, all angles and small black pits for eyes. Definitely less attractive than the jack-o'-lanterns, Joanna thought, trying to anchor scraps of what could hardly be called *thought.*

"*Jesus.*" Mark said at last, softly. "*Hal? Hal Bennett?* I've been robbed by my *own flesh and blood? Hugo's* boy?" He sounded more astonished than outraged.

"If you want to call the Coast Guard we'd better move," Nils said.

"The hell with *that,*" Mark said, still keeping his voice down. "I'm not advertising to the whole Gulf of Maine that the Bennetts have raised up a crook."

Suddenly "The Devil's Dream" ended, and so did the dance. There was manic applause from the children. "Do some more!" Dennis Campion shouted. The dancers scattered, laughing, wiping their faces; they headed back to seats, the pool room, outdoors, toward the cloakroom for more cake, or straight for the kitchen. Joanna had a glimpse of Richard pulling Sam by the arm out the front door. Just as Young Matt Fennell reached the kitchen, Mark said savagely, "There's not a hope in hell of getting Jamie and Sky out of here on the quiet."

Matt opened the door and looked at them with amusement. "What's this, a special meeting of the Board of Governors?"

"Yep, and there's about to be a special message, too," Nils said. "Might as well do it, Mark. Get it over with."

"Yes, and let Nils do it," said Joanna. "With you, every other word will be a cuss word, and there are children in there. I don't mean you, Matt."

"Thanks. Can I have a drink of water? I'm glad I don't have to cover Peter's ears; he's picking up too many words as it is." He took the mug of water Joanna handed him, and she and Nils followed him back onto the dance floor. She knew without looking around that Mark had gone.

"Where's Hal?" Ralph called to them. "He's taking the waltz. Or has he got stage fright?"

"Can I have everybody's attention, please?" Nils asked; he didn't have to raise his voice. He had brought something new into the room full of skeletons and witches; it was a silence in which small children were quickly hushed.

"It looks as if Hal and George have taken a boat and gone joy-riding in the moonlight," he said. "Maybe they've broken down somewhere, maybe they're on their way back. We're not calling the Coast Guard; there's no use making a fuss for nothing. It's flat-calm and bright out. They can't come to any great harm."

Across the room Sky and Binnie stood close together, motionless, as if George's name had paralyzed them; Stuart and Dorrie moved close to them, Dorrie holding Dennis's hand.

"Whose boat did they take?" Sky asked, without expression.

"Not yours, Sky," Nils said. He looked over at Jamie in the poolroom doorway; Rosa appeared behind him, she'd been checking on Sara Jo.

"They took *Sea Star,*" Nils said. Joanna saw the shock on Rosa's face, as if she'd just been savagely slapped, and then she disappeared, followed by Jamie. Sky and Binnie were getting into their jackets, speaking to the children, evidently saying they could stay a while longer. Kate joined them, nodding in reassurance and patting Binnie's shoulder.

"Choose your partners for a waltz!" Ralph called, and Maggie moved into Rosa's chair with her own guitar. Joanna went outside; Nils was right behind her, and Helmi spoke from beyond him.

"You can stay awhile," she called back to Young Mark.

"I don't want to!" he retorted angrily. "You coming, Willy? All right *then!*" He came out in a rush past his mother and the Sorensens, and was off down the path after his father.

"It's more than joy-riding, isn't it?" Helmi said to Joanna.

"Some crates of lobsters more," Joanna said. "I don't know how many." She felt very odd, as if she were trying to catch up with her thoughts; whatever had happened, she wasn't finding the time to see it clearly, to recognize its contours, to realize its validity as a genuine occurrence and think: *This has happened, and there's no doubt of it.* It wouldn't be any help, but it needed to be done before she could move on. Move on to *what?*

They went down the path, Nils holding her elbow. She had the sense of many people behind him. The family, of course. Jamie and Rosa cut out around her, Jamie carrying Sara Jo.

"See you later, Marm," Jamie said. Passing her, Rosa said, "If they've put one scratch or bump on her—so help me. . . ." She caught up with Jamie, and they turned off onto the path to their house. Helmi came up beside Joanna.

"My son thinks Willy's no older than *he* is sometimes," she said. "He's insulted because Willy's staying awhile."

"Sam and Richard are down around the wharf; that'll suit Young Mark," Joanna said.

From farther behind, Philippa said, "I have a feeling this will be a long night. I'd better go back and cancel school for the morning."

The news of the theft had flown quickly through the family; they must have all been feeling the same incredulity, the alternating waves of anger differing in intensity from rage to the pain of betrayal. Sky and Binnie were somewhere in the group, but she didn't hear their voices among the other wry or profane comments—mostly from Owen. Joanna felt for them; unless the boys lost their courage and came back, George would be guilty of violating his probation, and they would have to report it.

Thinly, sweetly, over everything but fading fast into the distance, Ralph's violin played on; it was at one with the dying scents rising damply about them in the path, like a long wordless farewell to a dying year. She wished she could strike off from the rest, cross the field to the house, shut herself in with Pip, and cry as she used to when she was a child. But she wouldn't be able to, and besides, Nils's fingers tightened around her arm as if he were reading her thoughts.

The wharf and the store were lighted up when they all got there. Some of the men headed directly for the wharf but met Mark coming back. "Seven," he said. "She'll be riding low, but she's able, if they had the sense to distribute the load."

"And if it stays flat-arse calm," Owen said. "And if they don't try to establish a speed record. And if . . . I can't think of anything else fit for ladies' ears. What are those three doing out there?"

The boys stood on the outer end of the wharf, hands in their pockets, apparently gazing at the constant shimmer of moonlit, moving water and the glimmer of the white sand beach beyond it on Brigport.

"Hoping she's on her way back, I guess," said Mark. "You know you can hear anything if you wish hard enough for it—like engines." He rubbed his hands. "It's getting cold. Let's go inside."

"Frost before morning," Charles said. "I can smell it." Mateel wasn't with him; he'd left her at the clubhouse. But the other wives were here, and Jamie and Rosa arrived before they were all inside.

"Marjorie's going to stay with Sara Jo," Rosa said. She put an arm around Binnie, who looked small and frail beside her. "You're shivering. Buck up. *Sea Star* might be pretty mad with them, but she won't drown them."

"That's not what I'm worried about," Binnie said dryly.

"Roost, everybody," Mark said. He began to build a fire in the pot-bellied stove. Helmi always handily left a full teakettle on the gas plate at night, and now she lit one burner. "If anybody wants a soda, it's on the house. So is tea, coffee, and hot chocolate in an envelope."

Nobody answered at once. They stood around uneasily as if waiting for someone to begin, but nobody knew exactly what to say—not so much about the theft but about its being committed by one of them. Joanna doubted that anybody except Sky and Binnie was giving George a thought. He was still the tough little baseball coach and the dreamer known as Jockey George. But *Hal?* Somebody had once remarked there was no such thing as an obscure Bennett, even among those who were so distant that they were unknown to the island family; they *had* to be distinctive in whatever they did, good or bad. It was inescapable; it was in the genes.

In the time he had been here, Hal had been anything but obscure. It was like the old seagoing statement: He was in everybody's Mess and nobody's Watch. His arrival had been spectacular, and his departure was turning out to be more so. He had scattered charm wherever he went, he had amused where he didn't actually dazzle, and he was Hugo's son. When the impact of this night had worn away, and they were no longer trying to come to terms with it, he would not be loved. But he would still be Hugo's son, and Hugo had been as close as a brother. This was the pain of it, and it had only just begun. "It looks like a long night," Philippa had said, before she knew just how long it would be.

Charles said, as if to himself, "Seven crates. Thirty-five hundred dollars at least, and that's modest. *Good Christ.*" It sounded reverent.

Mark said harshly, "I've already said I'm not calling the Coast Guard, and I'm not bringing charges. This is a family mess. Any opposition? It won't do you any good—I'm the one standing the losses."

"We'll all kick in," Stephen said, and looked at Owen as if expecting a growling *What's-this-we-business?* or a four-letter equivalent. The growl came, but it was a surly agreement; then he opened the door and went outside into the chilly moonlight. The others made various sounds of agreement, wives too. Joanna slid her gaze toward the door and then toward Nils, who answered it and then began getting his pipe going. Owen had just lost what he must have seen as the perfect sternman, and his disappointments always seemed far worse than anybody else's. It must have been an instinct for survival that had made him take the heart problem so well; that was one time when he couldn't enjoy making himself and everyone in his vicinity miserable. Now he would have to endure his defeat in silence, and Joanna couldn't help a spark of humor—which surprised her—at how upset Owen would *really* be to know that she and Nils knew all about his plans for a new sternman.

Mark was saying gruffly, "Thanks, everybody. The intent's as good as the act, and I won't forget it. But I've got insurance that ought to cover it. However," and he grinned, "I'll be the first to let you know if they won't pay because I didn't do anything to bring back two omidoms that between them aren't worth two cents and a fishhook. Sorry, Binnie." He gave her a warm smile. "I still respect him as a baseball coach."

"Thanks, Mark," she said. "I think I have to agree with you about the two cents and a fishhook. Could I have some tea, Helmi?" She took one of the mugs off the shelf where they and the sugar were kept.

Sky and Jamie had been standing off to one side, around behind the candy counter, talking quietly. Now Jamie tapped with a coin on the glass top, and as the faces turned toward him he said, "Sky and I are going in right now. We'll take my boat; she's fast. He thinks he knows where George is headed, and if the lobsters are gone when we get there, we can at least bring back the boat." He nodded at Rosa. "And we let that little crook fill her up so she'd be all ready," he said almost reverently.

Rosa ignored that. "I should be bringing her back," she said, "across the bay in the moonlight." Her smile was an adult version of Sara Jo's. "Oh, I wish I could go!" she said. "But this would be the time when the baby woke up and missed me."

32

In the space of an hour, an outward mantle of peace had descended upon the island, gently, as the moonlight covered it. The sea remained calm, the air growing colder but without an increase in the wind. *Valkyrie* had been seen off by a subdued group of adults and children from around the harbor. By the process of osmosis peculiar to small communities, everyone knew what had happened, if not all the details. When *Valkyrie* was about to disappear beyond the southern tip of Brigport, as if traveling a visible road marked out by *Sea Star,* everyone not directly connected with the theft and the family went home. This had been a Hallowe'en party the older children would never forget. The candles in the clubhouse guardians had been thriftily blown out, but the big pumpkins would appear in public somewhere else the next night; they were too good to waste. Around the harbor a few family jack-o'-lanterns were still burning brightly against the blacks and silvers of the night.

In every house someone would be listening for *Valkyrie's* first call in about two hours. They knew some lobsters were gone but not how many. No adult would go around to ask about a family matter; they knew they'd find out soon enough, if not by the first call from *Valkyrie,* by the next day when the crate mooring would be in full view.

Young Mark had been ordered to turn in; Willy had come home and offered to play cribbage with him after he got into bed, to help him fall asleep. Young Mark accepted the offer but denied he was tired. Binnie had gone home after *Valkyrie* left Mark's wharf; the boat was well rationed with a supply of doughnuts and extra thermos bottles brought filled to the wharf by Rosa, Lisa, and Joanna. Helmi supplied bread and cold cuts. Mark filled the gas tanks.

Sam was sent to collect Ross and Amy and see that they went to bed, brushing their teeth first, with no mug-ups after all they'd been eating; Philip and Lisa would remain at Mark's until they were sure *Valkyrie* was safely in and had found *Sea Star.* Richard went with Sam, and they would listen for the rest of the evening to the voices both near and far that filled the night when you found the right spot on the dial. Outside, the island seemed to be dreaming under its silvery veil, the harbor quietly flashing diamonds from every ripple. But each house contained the separate night belonging to that other world of men and vessels.

Except at the Homestead. Charles had taken Mateel home and come back again. "She threw me out," he said. "She says if I'm going to listen for them, I can do it with the gang down here, instead of pacing the floor up there. She's going to say her prayers and go to bed, and whatever the boys have done they can always make up for. The important thing is for them not to be drowned." He hesitated, then said more quietly, "When you've lost a child to the sea you never get over it, even when you stop dreaming about it." He turned away from them and scratched Louis under the chin. As if talking to the cat he said, "We got some news today. She'd wanted to wait until after the party so she could have all day to taste it, you might say. Hugo—*our* Hugo—is coming home. To stay. He's got no plans besides fishing with me this winter."

It was something wonderfully positive to smile about, a reason for the men to shake his hand and slap his shoulder, for the women to hug him and kiss his cheek, and for him to hug back, saying, "Gorry! I dunno but what it's been worth it, him being gone all this time. I didn't know the old man was going to cash in on it like this. I miss anybody?"

"Not even me," said Helmi.

"Yep, I had my eye on ye," Mark said.

For Hugo to be scalloping so far away, out of New Bedford in almost all weather, had never seemed right to the rest of them; they also knew what it meant to his parents, who had lost their oldest son in a snowstorm right out here in Penobscot Bay.

"He bringing a wife with him?" Owen asked. "Surprising you with a ready-made family or one on the way?"

"Nope! Boat was sold, and the new skipper fired all the Maine men. He says they think they know such a hell of a lot more than anybody else. Island men in particular."

"Well, we do," Philip said. "And with good reason. This isn't the first time I've heard it."

"And you sound so proud of it, dear," Lisa said.

Stephen lifted his mug. "Here's to us! Who's like us?" Mugs clinked to the combined shout, *"Damn' few!"* The store was suddenly comfortably, warmly crowded with good company. They were all here, weren't they? The same as it had almost always been. No one had killed or been killed; and, as Mateel said, the important thing was that no one drowned out there, even though you might be calling the boys everything under your breath. The anger, the disbelief, the sick surprise of it—there was plenty of time for that. Time for everything, Nils said, and he was right.

They all moved up the hill to the house, where it would be more comfortable to wait out the next few hours. Louis was left to go back to his favorite banana carton; he hadn't needed to get out of it, but he had a strong instinct for keeping an eye on his own property. At the house, the kitchen cat went from lap to lap until Young Mark, scowling, stalked out, took her back to his room, and shut the door behind him. Willy'd given up trying cribbage as a sedative and was knitting bait bags in the living room, where he could hear the radio in the kitchen.

They were listening to a profanely witty dialogue between a couple of herring seiners, whom they all knew, when John Haker's unmistakable voice came in. "You boys ought to watch it. Not only can you be heard over the whole coast, but the authorities are going to shut you down clip 'n' clean one of these nights."

"How come they never shut you down, John?"

"Because I don't talk dirty. No law against honest talk."

"Depends on how honest it is."

"He's always honest, don't you know that?" Charlie broke in. "It's only when you get obscene they shut you off."

"And John, he can always buy his license back with a fifth of the expensive stuff, can't ye, John?"

John signed off with dignity. "Oh hell," the other man said. "I hope they never do get after Johnny. He's better than one of them late-night show hosts, they call 'em." He signed off, so did the other seiner, and it was as if all three boats had suddenly been obliterated from the night.

"When I was seining," Owen said, "one little 'goddamn' would have them on my neck. Of course they had it in for me."

"Oh, don't be so stuck on yourself," Laurie said, and he grinned at her. Joanna wondered if he'd already gracefully accepted his defeat and was trying to hatch out new ways and means. Laurie was still innocent; the only thing on her mind seemed to be what burdened them all, a Bennett turned thief.

"Good thing John isn't in on this," Philip said.

"*Yet*," Mark grunted. "If they pick up *Valkyrie* . . ."

"Give Sky and Jamie some credit," Helmi said. "They aren't going to mention lobsters, or even *Sea Star* by name. He won't make any sense of it."

"But he'll bust a gut trying to make up something to fit," Owen said. "Ought to be kind of interesting. Never thought we'd be the source of one of his fascinating fables."

Helmi said gently, "John's loyal to us. Besides, they like going in and out of this harbor, having a mooring they can use, hanging out here. Even if they do find out—maybe from one of the kids—I don't think John would advertise it."

"Oh, gosh," said Lisa. "Does this mean we won't get into the In Crowd?"

Just as Joanna was beginning to think they'd gotten trapped in some comic whirlpool from which they'd never escape, while her head wanted to do its own spinning, the call came. First, *Valkyrie's* identification, and then, through the cluttering scraps of voices and engines, Sky's light pleasant voice.

" 'But I am as constant as the northern star,' remember that, Philippa? You made us learn it by heart when we were reading *Julius Caesar.* And what about 'There is a tide in the affairs of men'—"

"What a show-off," Jamie broke in. "How's this for poetry? 'Empty is the kennel, Tiger's stolen.' Anybody reading us?"

"The whole island," said Mark, "and most of the Gulf of Maine. Just burst into song, and they'll be sure you're drunk."

"We're heading up to Limerock now, making merry all the way," said Sky. "Slow trip following the channel, because the tide's covering the rocks. We'll give you a call when we get there and when we leave. Good night, wife and bairns. Go to bed and I'll wake you up for breakfast."

"Rosa there?" Jamie asked.

"Home with the baby," said Nils. "But she'll be listening."

Not for Jamie to become personal across the bay. "Yep," he said. He signed off.

"Who's going to wait up to see them in and out of Limerock?" Mark was as expansive as if it were still the shank of the evening, and he hadn't just been robbed.

"We're all in it one way or another," said Owen. "I don't know about my wife, but I'm sticking until I see *Sea Star* and *Valkyrie* home again."

"We know one thing," Mark said, "or maybe a couple. The boat's safe, and where that other pair is, only they know. I'd like to think this is the end of it and cheap at the price."

"Maybe for you," Philip said, "but it's not over for Sky. He'll have to report to George's probation officer."

"If there's no stink of thievery about it," Steve said, "it shouldn't add anything to his sentence."

"What about 'unlawful flight to avoid prosecution,' or something like that?" asked Philippa. "Or however it's worded on those notices you get, Mark, as if everybody who's wanted *anywhere* is on the way to Bennett's Island by hook or by crook."

"I feel sorry for Binnie," Laurie said. "She's alone over there with the kids, trying to put a good face on things. The older ones will know, of course. Kate's probably there, maybe Van. But having your kid brother or your uncle on his way to jail, or he *will* be . . . And even if we could turn Hal off like *this*," she snapped her fingers, "and we can't—no matter how much we'd like to—Hal's father has to know." There followed one of those formidable silences that manage to be very loud. Willy came out from the next room, rumpled and looking dazed from a nap; he didn't speak and went out the back door.

Joanna wished *she* had gone out as soon as she knew *Sea Star* was safe—not *out* for Willy's probable reason but to head for home. No, I am not going to talk to Hugo, she thought. I refuse. Categorically, whatever that means. Here's a roomful, five brothers, and Hugo was their buddy. It's true that island men, especially those named Bennett, think they're so damned smart. Let one of them show it now. She stood up before Mark could catch her eye and said, "Good night, everybody. I mean Good morning." She put on her jacket.

"We can't catch him in his office till the middle of the morning here," Mark said thoughtfully. Meaning *Go home and get some sleep, and then come back.* She wanted to ignore that, but she couldn't.

"Mark, he was dying to talk with *you* the other day. If you're not going to mention the lobsters, just say that Hal's gone. It should be simple." She was halfway into the hall. "I don't intend to wake up till noon." That was a fantasy; she'd be lucky if she dropped off for fifteen minutes. "Or maybe there's a volunteer," she said and was all the way out.

Behind her, through a stir, a shuffling, a clearing of throats, Owen said crankily, "Oh, the hell with it! Why does he have to know today, anyway? Wait a couple of days; the boy may be back with a good story, and we can all act as if we believe it. Hell of an easy way out."

She knew by his voice he was more tired than he should be, and Laurie would be trying not to look worried. Not my business, she thought. *None* of it. Finding Hal behind the crates that day was just my bad luck. I don't have to cherish it.

Nils was with her, pulling on his jacket. "I'm going with you. That's easier than wondering if you've skidded somewhere on that frost and are making it home on your hands and knees."

"What a picture!" she said. "This weird creature crawling along in the moonlight. Woman or beast? And where is it bound?"

Back in the kitchen Steve said, "The only reason I'm still sitting is because it's easier than moving. And *I* haven't promised myself a morning off."

"Oh, take it—we won't go bankrupt," Philippa said on a yawn.

Helmi came out into the hall. "I suppose I won't get to bed until the serum arrives at Nome."

"You must be about ready to drop," Joanna told her. "I'll come over in the morning and wash all the dishes for you, if you can bear to go to bed without leaving the kitchen spotless."

"I'm not *that* neat!" Helmi protested. "But don't come. I'll get out my Finnish music tapes and wash the dishes in style."

"Doing polkas all around the room, I hope," said Joanna.

Nils went out ahead of her. Helmi said in a low voice, "I'm so sorry about this, Jo. It will be harder for you because he lived in your house."

"Yes," Joanna said. "But it happened, and now it's over." And I won't be the one to call his father, she thought, and try to talk all around the subject. "If he died," she said aloud, "and I hope they don't have one of those accidents from driving too fast, I'm sure Hal would send us a ghost, to keep life as interesting as it's been this week."

Helmi laughed. "Just the type, isn't he? Funny, I'm still astonished because it happened, but I'm not mad with him. As long as he doesn't show up here again," she added. They kissed good night, and Joanna went out into the crystalline hour of moonlight and frost.

33

Nils and Willy were talking on the path, their breath vaporous. "Some pretty night, ain't it?" Willy said to Joanna. He was suitably long-faced. "I'm awful sorry, Mrs. J. He was such a *nice* fella. Seemed so, anyway."

"I suppose we need a big surprise now and then to shake us up," she said. "How was the party?"

"Finest kind for the young ones, and it was mostly their party anyway. I'd of come right along home if I'd known what was going on."

"There wasn't anything you could do," Nils told him. "We're all just holding turn, waiting for Sky and Jamie to come back. The boys and the lobsters are long gone."

Relieved of guilt, Willy said it had been a good dance, a corker, until the bad news got around. He'd done the "Portland Fancy" with Maggie Dinsmore and the "March and Circle" with Kate Campion. He had a lot of partners in the "Liberty Waltz," but he could never get the real hang of that step. Tammie Dinsmore had said he'd better learn, *or else*. "Well, g'night, and I hope the guys don't meet up with any trouble on the way home."

"What kind?" Joanna asked him. "Vietcong submarines?" He grinned but muttered something about the science-fiction movies he watched with Young Mark. "Some of those things *could* happen. We don't know what's out there."

"Well, if there was ever a night for an alien invasion, this is it," Nils said. "For God's sake, Willy, don't take that for gospel!"

"I won't," said Willy. "But I better really say 'night." He went around the house, frosty grass crunching under his feet.

They went cautiously down the steep twisting path, Nils ahead. From up here the harbor, with its motionless boats, and the black woods beginning behind the white-gleaming house at Hillside all looked unfamiliar. They weren't frightening but *different,* a setting for dreams one was not anxious to know.

The air was sweet and cold in the nostrils, sharp in the throat, and the stillness seemed to ring like the echoes of a bell. Under every dwelling-house roof, white as if with a light snowfall, there was at least one yellow or orange window. Someone was awake there and listening. The lamps would not go out until the boats were home. It was a fine night, but there was danger in being safe; thus it was too fine to take for granted. It would not be the men running the boats who would worry. They were *there.* They knew what was going on. Those who waited always thought the time was stretching out too long, and if they were too imaginative for comfort, they'd be listing possible events: A collision with a whale or with some undersea object that had drifted a long way were two of the favorites. Joanna knew, wryly, that engine trouble was the least of it. One boat could always take the lame boat in tow—providing she hadn't sunk in the moment of impact with the mysterious Unseen. Of course it wasn't going to happen tonight, but how many times had it already actually occurred to boats both large and small, everywhere? Deliberately, as they made black footprints in the frosty grass between the Harmons' and the Binnacle, Joanna concentrated on the expectation that this frost could be the one to finish off the night-blooming stock.

Joselito grinned on the wheelbarrow, but uncertainly: his candle was guttering and Nils blew it out. She was unprepared for the emptiness when they went into the house. Pip came thumping down the stairs in his usual passionate greeting, his bliss compounded by scents of Louis and the house cat. Nils lit the hand lamp on the sun-parlor table, and they sat down. "I don't want anything to eat or drink," Joanna said. "Do you want me to fix something for you?"

He didn't, but Pip did, and she restocked his dishes. "Thanks for walking me home," she told Nils. "I'd have been careful, but I've just been thinking of expecting the Unexpected, and well, you know how I am. Why don't you go back to the gang? I just want to lie down with or without my book and stop thinking, or hearing, or wondering, or imagining. This night has been two weeks long and so stuffed with voices that sudden deafness could be a mercy. I don't really *mean* it!" she said.

"I see that warning quirk that means you're about to tell me to be careful what I wish for."

"You make me sound," he said amiably, "like a pain in the . . . choose your location."

"You aren't," she said, "but I know I must be, sometimes. I'm going onto the couch in the other room, and I can read by flashlight if I want to." She didn't want to go upstairs for her book and pass the door of Hal's room. "There's plenty to read down here." Nils blew out the lamp, and after an instant of intense blackness, the windows filled with moonlight again. They kissed, and parted with mutual pats of reassurance. "*You* be careful!" she said after him. "*You* could take a skid and end up with a sprained knee or ankle."

"Pip, can't you shut her up?" he called back.

Every room in the house was illuminated by moonlight; the living room had four windows. If she hadn't been so tired, she'd have settled for a while by each, just to see how the ordinary had become the extraordinary. She picked up a paperback collection of Sarah Orne Jewett's stories, took off her shoes, and settled herself on the couch. She pulled up an afghan, and when that was arranged, Pip moved onto it.

Her eyes felt too tired for reading, but in her mind's eye the faces came and went, crowding together or standing out singly. Hal was never once looking straight at her; he appeared as he did in "Going to Jerusalem." Slumped in his chair, tapping his foot, hunched over the harmonica with his hand half-hiding his face; between it and his hair, his eyes were hardly visible, but he was always laughing when he suddenly stopped the music, and the jumble of children sorted itself out. Then he would begin to play again. How would he have described this occasion? As another rite? Like his first pail of water drawn from the well, his sleep in the cemetery (if that had really happened), his first time out with Owen. When had he decided there'd be no more firsts except for the grand one that he dreamed up for Hallowe'en? The impact of that, each time she came to it, was like a fist driven into her belly; then, like the ripples spreading out from the pain, there were all the questions. Just when was it planned and how? How did George contact the customer who, presumably, had taken the two thieves away with him? This would be talked over endlessly in the days to come, as all the *supposings* and *what ifs* were jumbled together again and again, and tossed out for new reading—like casting the runes.

And if she didn't stop fussing about it now, she was a fool. It will be harder for you, Helmi said, because he lived in your house. Yes, she would have to deal with this, and she could never truthfully say to herself what she'd said to Helmi then: *It happened, and now it's over.* It wasn't over. It would be one thing after another, and she knew already that the worst of it would be wondering when he had been sincere and when he had been wooing them. She knew now that when he had asked her with such charming formality for the first dance tonight, he had known he wouldn't be there.

I suppose one thing that keeps stinging me is the idea of being made a fool of, she thought drearily—played upon as he played the harmonica. She remembered "The Flower of Portencross" in the mild stock-scented dusk. Surely he must have been honestly moved then; the island had reached him somehow, touching him in ways he must have tried to fend off. Then her damnably stubborn brain persisted in more pictures, beginning with the arrival of the *Conqueror* and finishing with the imagined drive in an unknown vehicle through the moonlit night, wildly happy (she was sure he wasn't afraid) in this new adventure. He was Peter Pan learning how to fly.

Would George be wildly happy too, or wildly scared to death? He was not a very bright boy—not bright about his own interests (he must have known Sky would report him). But he could be blissfully magnetized into believing that somewhere ahead of them Dream Girl was waiting, in another state where there was no winter, and the Limerock Police didn't exist. Not Dream Girl in Union or Appleton, but nonetheless a Dream Girl.

She was as revved up as if *she* could fly like Peter Pan, a feat she'd once believed possible, though only Pickie knew she believed it. She'd convinced herself that the reason why she hadn't tried it and astounded her brothers was the possibility that Pickie couldn't fly with her, and she certainly wouldn't leave him behind.

Problems, problems even then, she thought. But it's just as well the thought of Pickie abandoned kept me from taking off from the barn roof. Joanna pulled Pip up until his head was under her chin, and she stroked the warm vibrating length of him. He murmured and fell into a deeper sleep, and she began listening for the small noises of the house. The clock ticking was the loudest and most constant. Then there were the little mysterious clicks and snaps and creaks, sometimes the suggestion of a cautious footstep. Pip was not disturbed. She imagined unseen personages moving through the house, ghosts whom Pip took for granted. She remembered the jokes about Gunnar and her own charming picture of Anna telling fairy tales.

She and Helmi had even joked a little about Hal sending them a ghost. Had anyone ever felt or seen the ghost of a person still living? Or been haunted by someone he had yet to meet? If she were writing a book about it, what would be a good title?

Listen, O! Listen! Where did that come from? Then she saw the strange words on Hal's shirt. "Listen for what?" she had asked him, and he answered, "For everything." Another voice, another phrase came along, a broken one saying something about "all day," which made no sense at all. The voice became very clear, and she knew the voice.

"Are you going to sleep all day?"

The moonlit windows were now full of blue sky, and Pip was gone. She sat up straight, rumpled and constricted in her clothes, her eyes blurry, her throat dry. Nils was standing at one of the front windows, looking toward the harbor and Brigport. He was dressed to go haul. At once she had an angry reaction, familiar since childhood when she had napped too long; she'd been tricked, cheated out of *hours,* she would have to catch up on what everybody else knew, and they would laugh at her.

It was only for an instant, but she'd still slept too hard for comfort now. "I didn't mean to fall asleep," she said crossly. "Where are the boys?" He turned around, looking not in the least as if he'd been up all night and acting as if it were a perfectly ordinary morning.

"*Sea Star's* on her mooring. The boys are out to haul, and so is everybody else. And that's where I'm going."

"Did you get any sleep at all?"

"No, but I'm glad you did." He came over to the couch. "I woke you up so I could tell you what's going on before I go out." He sounded easy enough. "Come on out and have a cup of fresh coffee. Specialty of the house. Helmi sent some Finnish bread."

"I can't resist that. Just let me wash the sleep out of my eyes—oh, boy, do I feel *stupefied.*"

Even the deep sleep hadn't wiped away Hal's face. It was as if she'd just been looking at him. In the bathroom she splashed the icy cistern water over her face several times, sluicing away the grogginess; then she combed her hair, and straightened her blouse. She'd have rather gotten out of all these clothes and started fresh, but she didn't want to hold Nils up. It looked like a perfect day to haul; it was often like this following a heavy frost.

He had her coffee poured and asked if she wanted the Finnish bread toasted. "No, it's good plain, with butter. Thank you, Nils. You're such a nice man. Does anyone ever tell you that?"

"All the time." He sat down opposite her. "The news goes like this, and it's not the kind you get on television or from *Annie-Elmina.* Hugo's been notified."

She had to set down her mug. "Thank God it didn't have to be me. Who did it?"

"I did," he said tranquilly. "And it was earlier than we expected. Everybody went home as soon as the boys were in and tied up. I stayed on with Mark and Helmi because he was pacing and blowing and sweating—I haven't seen him in such a taking since the night Young Mark was born. Seems he thought the longer we waited, the more chance of *him* getting a call that the boys had gone off the road into a river somewhere or hit a tractor-trailer truck head on. It was even getting to Helmi. This is the best coffee I've had all night."

"So you called," she urged.

"Helmi and I agreed we could leave a message on his machine right then—no details, just saying that Hal had left and that we didn't know whether he was heading west or south. Hugo'd get it when he came in. So we went down to the store to do it. Hell, I wanted to get away, either to you and my bed or to my boat. If I had to I'd go through Information, call his house, and to hell with what his wife thinks." This was so mildly spoken that it was all the more impressive.

"There wasn't any machine. Hugo answered. He's not living at home; he's had a room above his office made over, and he's been there quite a while. It must have been about three out there, and when he answered he sounded either drugged or drunk, but I guess it was just hard sleep. I said, 'This is Nils. Everybody's all right on the island. We just wanted to let you know Hal's left here. He may be on his way home.' There was a long silence, and I thought he'd disappeared; then he came back and yelped, '*Nils Sorensen?* My God, how *are* you?' He said something meant to be Swedish, but he never could get his tongue around that." Nils was smiling. "He sounded so damned *natural,* even on the telephone and after all these years. 'I'm not dreaming this, am I?' he said. He was laughing. Then, as if somebody'd punched him in the gut, he asked, 'Did you say Hal's *gone?* Just up and left? What did he take?' "

The coffee surged up into her throat and went down again. "He really said that?"

"As Pete Grant used to say, I winked and blinked a bit. Hugo wasn't laughing anymore. 'He took a boat,' I told him, 'and seven crates of lobsters.' It was like talking to a dead phone. I said, 'The rest of us were up at the clubhouse giving the kids a Hallowe'en party and ourselves a dance.' Then I could hear the breathing, and I thought he was having a heart attack." Nils reached for her hand. "My God, I felt helpless, so I kept on talking. Hell of a lot of help *that* would be. 'He wasn't alone,' I told him. 'His partner is somebody's sternman. *He* was the one who knew where to meet the customer, and then they must have gone off with him.' I told him the rest of it and said that Mark wasn't bringing charges. When Hugo spoke, his voice had aged twenty years since he'd first answered the phone. He said, 'Hal probably put him up to it.' 'It's six of one, half-dozen of the other,' I said. 'The boy's on probation, went to jail for breaking and entering over on the mainland. He was in his sister's custody out here, working for his brother-in-law.'

" 'Is there anything more to it?' he asked. 'We don't know anything more yet,' I told him. 'George's probation officer's been notified; they'll be looking for him. They didn't know what the vehicle was, so they don't have that to go on. George's far from being a desperate criminal. I don't know how the process works; they're looking for some tougher customers than him, and where Mark's not bringing charges, it's only George's probation they're interested in. So even if they pick him up for that, Hal's in the clear.'

" 'Hal always manages to be,' he said and kept on talking. Jo, the boy was a thief long before he came to us." He lifted her hand to his cheek. "That's cold," he said. "And you're pale. Do you feel sick? Come on, I'll see you into bed."

"I'm not sick!" she said angrily. "Except with rage! We've been barraged with lies, and we've treated them like a flock of butterflies or migrating warblers! Oh, *damn* it all! Talk about con men!"

He squeezed her hand and put it to his lips. It was a moving and calming gesture. "Do you want me to stop here or tell you the rest?"

"Let's get it over with in one fell swoop."

"I told him he didn't have to talk anymore, but he wanted to. Who else has he got? Not his wife. He never wanted to complain of one of his kids to the others—especially when he knew they'd have plenty to say. But Nicole knows about this disappearance, because Hal robbed her for traveling money. . . . All I did was let him talk," Nils said. He sounded tired now.

"You're easy to talk to, Nils," she said, moving her fingers inside his hand until she could hold it. "Mark would have been swearing a blue streak, and some operator would have cut him off. Why did Hal leave home when he did? What happened?"

It hadn't been a scrap about his wanting to be in the yard instead of college. Hugo had bought him an apprenticeship in one of these wooden-boat institutes; he'd be learning the trade from the keel up. He'd be actually building boats, starting with small craft, and if he did get into the yard eventually, it would be on his own merits, not as the boss's son. The school was up north along the coast, and he left early one morning full of thanks and promises. That night, the institute called to say he'd never arrived. The police found the car at a motel on the way. He'd registered, told someone he was going for a walk, and didn't come back. He left the keys, but he took his billfold with him. This same person saw him take it from the car when he set out. Hugo wanted to turn the business over to the police, but Vivian stopped him by telling the police that they'd just heard from Hal, that he was all right, that he'd just gone away to think.

"So that was the end of it," Nils concluded softly. "She didn't want his disappearance in the papers. People would *talk*." He said it without expression. "Especially if he was found dead somewhere."

"That would reflect his common blood," Joanna agreed. "Getting murdered is so lower class. Vulgar. You said he's robbed his sister."

"They found that out when Nicole came home for the emergency. One Christmas when she and Hal were kids, somebody'd given them each a big piggy bank. Hal's pig never had a chance to put on weight, but Nicole's was better fed. She wanted to see what you could do with small change, how long it would take to get enough to buy this or that. She was independent and she wanted to do things for herself. Nicole did well and kept it up all this time. At the end of every week she'd put all her coins in Cupcake. Sometimes she added any one-dollar bills she had. Right then she was working on a fancy kind of trail bike. The next thing—she said she'd be through college before she had enough—was a Caribbean holiday.

"When she rushed home because Hal was missing, Cupcake was waiting, wearing a big pink smile—Hugo's words—and thoroughly empty. He must have got a supply of coin wrappers in advance; they found a couple of loose ones in the car. Nicole was pretty sick. Seems he'd done it before, but there'd never been that much money in the pig. It was when they were still kids, and she'd given him a hard time until he paid it back. She thought those days were gone forever."

Joanna's face was burning. "He's a cheap little crook!"

"What other kind be they?" he asked, amused.

And she said angrily, "You know what I mean! At least George had a vision, and he didn't steal from his family!"

"Hal might have a vision too, but I doubt it was life on Bennett's Island. 'Being a crook wasn't the way he was raised!' Hugo said, and then his voice broke. I never felt so sorry for a man in my life. It was hell, hearing him try to talk. Finally he made it clear that if Mark wasn't bringing charges— and he wished he would, it wasn't doing the boy a favor to let him off— then *he* was going to pay for the lobsters. I have to admit the sweat was running down my back by then. I kept signaling Mark like hell, and then Helmi practically shoved him at me; I jammed the telephone in his hands and got out fast."

He grinned. "Helmi came out after me, and we went out to the end of the wharf and had a nice conversation at dawn without calling anybody names or cussing them out."

"What about?" Joanna asked. "The in-laws or the outlaws?"

"For one thing, she told me the Finns are the way they are because they're really misplaced Hungarians and crave gypsy fiddlers in their lives. I told her that while the Norwegians and the Danes were sacking, raping, and burning one side of Europe, a bunch of Swedish traders sailed down the Volga and became the first Russians. Head man was named Rurik. Then Mark came out of the store and roared at us. He and Hugo'd been having a high old time, yelling across the nation at each other, Hugo wanting to pay for the lobsters and Mark shutting him up by saying he'd only accept a check if Hugo handed it to him in person. Hugo agreed. I guess if he could have flown out a window then and there, he'd be on his way now. I'm going to haul." He pushed back his chair and stood up.

"Hugo's *really* coming?"

"He wants to, and now he's been forced into it; there's no waiting for Thanksgiving. They've just laid the keel for a new vessel, but he says he's got one hell of a good superintendent, even if he's from Oregon. . . ."

"That sounds like Hugo." Her chest was loosening up; she was beginning to believe.

"He says after they get some things worked out, he'll be on his way. Mark's given him two weeks; then he's going out there, he says, and he swears the rest of the family will be with him, all wearing their rubber boots. He says he left Hugo half laughing and half snuffling, and Mark looked pretty beat up himself. I left," he said moderately. "This time I'm *really* going to haul. I don't suppose you want to come. Pretty day," he added, reluctantly, she thought.

"After that passionate invitation, I'd be a fool to refuse. Just kidding." She went to him and put her arms around him. "I know you must be panting after solitude as the hart pants after cooling streams. Have a wonderful day, my love, but for God's sake—no, *mine*—don't fall asleep and start heading for open sea. God doesn't need you, but I do."

He pulled her suddenly into his arms, and they kissed like young lovers who cannot bear to be parted.

34

All the other men were gone, and there were no children in sight for the moment, but she didn't want to chance an unexpected meeting with anyone. Pip came in when Nils went out and made his usual cheerful noises. She heated the coffee—her first cup had gotten cold—and cut off a thick slice of Helmi's Finnish bread. *Hugo was coming.* It was true, and for a few minutes he nearly eclipsed his son. Where would he stay? In this house, or would Laurie have his old room ready for him, or would it be the Homestead? Everybody would want him, and all would try to make it up to him, she thought, with a homecoming that will leave all the rest of it behind. Then Joanna saw Hal's new rubber boots standing by the door, and it was as if they had kicked her in the midriff. She made herself finish the coffee and bread, recognizing her hunger, but she moved around the table to where she couldn't see the boots. Then she grew practical, wondering if they'd fit Hugo.

She took a shower and changed into slacks, a sweater, and thick socks and shoes that could stand deep wet grass; she was taking no chance on walking where she'd meet anyone.

It would be nice to be able to turn my brain to another channel, she thought. Outside, the hens were busy in their yard; Nils had fed them. She'd look for the eggs later. If last night had brought the killing frost, it was followed by a superb funeral, bejeweled wherever one looked. The sun turned every drop into a prism, whether in the grass, hanging from twigs, or shaking free in a scintillating shower whenever a bird lighted on a shrub.

A few of the stocks survived, looking fresh in the shade, as if wet by a summer rain. They still held their spicy sweetness when she bent down to them; there were always a few that refused to die for a long time. She thought of Hal, talking about their fragrance in the dusk. "*Never mind that!*" she said aloud, but it was like defying a swarm of blackflies. She didn't feel Pip until he was there, rubbing wet whiskers against her cheek. She carried him into the house, fed him, and went out again.

It was a day to delight the senses. The phrase "glory days" best described these times before winter, which would have its own glories, days and nights too. She stood in the field, deciding where she would go. Over to Barque Cove, of course; she didn't look back at the house, where Pip was staring out, bereft, between the plants on a windowsill.

When she left the sunny field for the damp and shady path, the clubhouse door was wide open, and she heard the sound of brisk sweeping. "*Damn,*" she whispered. She'd forgotten the cleanup detail—Marjorie Percy and Maggie Dinsmore. They were remarkably quiet after such an eventful night, unless they'd seen her coming and were being considerate. She could make a wide circle around the building, hoping they weren't pitying her; that would be as bad as the swarm of blackflies.

"*Jo.*" Softly it reached her as she went around the far corner of the porch, and it was Binnie Campion in the doorway.

Joanna went up onto the low porch. "Are you cleaning up? *Alone?*"

"That's the way I wanted it." The tone was crisp, and Joanna felt herself flushing, but Binnie went on. "I went around and told both of them I'd like the job, and they didn't argue." Her lips moved in a nervous little smile. "I'm glad you came by. I've been trying to get up the courage to come to you, if I could catch you alone." She had gotten very flushed too.

"Well, here I am!" said Joanna, hearty in spite of the turmoil in her stomach. "I wanted to see you, too, but so far I haven't got myself lined up yet." She was embarrassed because she hadn't given Binnie a thought this morning. Now her neck and back were wet. "I want to apologize," she began, and at the same time Binnie was saying, "I wanted to tell you that—"

They broke into shaky laughter. Binnie wiped her eyes and said, "Oh, dear, you go first. Did you say *apologize?*"

"Yes, because George was doing fine, and if Hal hadn't come here—well, he's part of our family. So we all owe you and Sky an apology."

"No," Binnie said. "You didn't know anything about Hal, so how could you have guessed? And to tell you the truth, I was real happy to have someone close to George in age, working on his chess and all, with winter coming along. It was going to be lonely for George because he wasn't allowed to go to Limerock over the holidays unless we all went and kept him with us every minute. And we weren't planning to go. Come on in."

They sat on one of the wall benches, where they could look out at the usual spatter of chickadees in the alders. Blue jays sharply signaled each other; crows were always calling somewhere. "In a way it's a relief, because it was always in my mind that he'd up and run sometime. Not with John Haker, because John'd never take him; but if somebody else stopped in here and was leaving just before dark and thought George was just a kid looking for a free trip ashore . . . Or he might have worked it on his own, taken a boat sometime when we were all up at the clubhouse like this time, wondering what was keeping him. He couldn't have managed all those crates on his own—maybe only a couple—but he'd be just as gone." She sounded winded, now that she'd gotten it out. "Well, you see what I mean? He didn't *have* to have somebody else put the idea in his mind. Just made it easier, that's all."

"Listen, Binnie," Joanna said. "Hal was . . . You can share this with Sky, but there's some family business—apart from taking the lobsters and so forth—that we'd like to keep quiet. Nils and Mark talked with Hal's father this morning, not to tell him about the theft but just to say that Hal had gone. The first thing Hugo said was, 'What did he take?' Binnie, Hal was already a thief." Her mouth had gotten very dry. "Any cold drinking water here?"

"No, but I brought some cranberry juice." They went into the kitchen, filled two mugs, and came back to the bench.

"It's about broken his father's heart," Joanna said.

"Well, nobody will hear it from *me*," Binnie said fervently. "Except Sky. The kids are already blaming Hal for *everything*, and they hate him all the more because they've been so crazy about him. But they have to think Hal was to blame."

"That's normal," said Joanna. "Don't we all—"

"But we went through this with the first arrest," Binnie said. "They wanted to blame the other boy. We had to convince them nobody put a gun to George's head and said, 'Do it or else.' It was the same way with the other youngsters in my family, when it all came out in the papers and went to trial. They were all so loyal to good old Jockey George—they were fighting mad the whole time. It was tough convincing them that George made his own mistakes. With our kids, Sky used himself as an example, saying he can't blame anybody else for what he did to himself." She lowered her voice and leaned out to look along the path in both directions. "Personally, I think he's been too generous to his folks. He says Foss was in a hard place all those years, but I blame Foss for not speaking out. I *will* say he's tried to make up for it since Helen died. Well, that's neither here nor there!" She slapped her hands on her knees. "You talk about heartbreak! Last night I decided George wasn't ever going to break *my* heart. I've done all I could, and even now he's getting favors—Mark not bringing charges and not wanting to be paid and all. Sky and the kids are the ones *I* should be taking care of." She took a long drink. "My, that was good. Better than champagne could be. It's because *I* feel good. I'm not going to fight anymore about selling the home place. I've stood the rest of them off because I thought George might be able to have it some day. Well, he's made good use of it—that's where they tied up the boat and met their customer and their ride. . . . We've been offered a great price; there's a good bit of waterfront—deep water, too—and nice woods, and the house is in good shape. I certainly can use my share, and they can bank George's for him till he's in the clear again. I've shed my last tears for Jockey George."

"Will he have enough to buy a horse?" Joanna asked.

"More than one—if he doesn't lose it in a poker game or some crazy bet first hop out of the box. He's got plenty of money with him now, not enough yet, but a good start, if he can just *not* forget his Dream Girl. He never wanted to set up a bank account with his earnings out here; he put his dollars in a box so he could count them whenever he wanted to. Well, there wasn't anything we could do, he's of age, but he'd be safe here; there are no go-to-hell gamblers on the island, and the Poker Club's all grownups like Nils." She smiled at that. "George has his dollars, and he'll have his share of the lobster money. I can't believe it'll be anywhere near intact for long, whenever he gets picked up. I hope after he's done his time, he'll be grown-up enough to find Dream Girl and hold onto her. What about Hal?"

"All his thieving, as far as Hugo knows, has been in the family, but there still could be more that's not known. Who knows what he will try next? You know, if a Bennett's going in for a life of crime, we'd expect him to have a grand design." She laughed, and it was easy. "Up till now, nobody's ever accused a Bennett of being petty in anything he did, good or bad."

"Maybe he'll surprise you all someday," Binnie said. "One way or the other." Then suddenly she smiled with what appeared to be a complete, unblemished happiness. "One thing I'll always give Hal thanks for—and I meant to tell you this first. You all knew what I was afraid of last night; I was thinking that if anything was going to make Sky desperate for a drink, this was it. I was sicker about that than I was about George. It was no use thinking everything would be closed up by the time they got into Limerock, in the middle of the night. If you've been a drunk," she went on, "you always know where you can get a drink. You always have old drinking buddies who won't turn you down, and you can say you need it—just *one* drink, this *one* time. . . . I know all this from Sky," she said, "not from myself."

"I didn't think so," said Joanna, "but I've been pretty well acquainted with a few of these characters in my lifetime. Even if some of them are dry as a cork leg nowadays."

"Well, I was about ready to throw up when the two boats came into the harbor around three this morning. Sky came straight to the wharf and tied up, and I was there when he came up the ladder. The first thing he said was, 'I'm cold sober. And I didn't want anything while I was over there but to get home to you and the kids. And the island.' You'd think we were a courting couple for a few minutes there, until Stuart and Dorrie came pounding down the wharf. They wouldn't go to bed until they saw for themselves what they wanted to see. And know what? Right then I didn't give a damn about George. But it's too bad I can't thank Hal."

"I'm happy too," Joanna told her. "I've known Sky since he was younger than Stuart. We're all *for* him, you know that. It's a funny thing, just a few nights ago Hal was telling us so earnestly that he'd like to do something useful for somebody, and by God he's done it! He's done a good deed while he was planning a bad one." They were both laughing as if the stream had just been undammed. It was a little crazy, but it was marvelous too. "And he did something for us too. His father's coming home, and he hasn't been here since before the war. In one way it'll be awful, because he's so upset. But he'll be back here among us, where he used to be, and maybe the rest of us can make it worthwhile. Almost."

"If anybody was going by, they'd think we were drunk," said Binnie.

"Or else somebody snuck in and spiked that cranberry juice," Joanna said.

Binnie was wiping her eyes. "And the other Hugo's coming home? Charles and Mateel's son? Is that still on?"

"It was the last I knew. Look, I'll help you with the dishes," Joanna said.

"I don't mind being alone now that I've talked with you."

"And laughed and cried," said Joanna. "Ain't life grand?"

"Times when it is," Binnie said sedately. "You know, Dorrie and Stuart will be sensitive about going back to school, because of George, but I don't think it'll be anything like what it was in town."

"Losing George like this, and Hal too, will be hard for all the children," Joanna said. "They thought those two were the greatest. But if anybody wants to give yours a hard time—and I don't know who it would be— well, you heard what happened to Shannon. That's when he found out about fair play. The school's a community in itself, as much as the island is. Holding that thought, I guess I'll go and do something constructive with the day."

"Dorrie may come trailing over when she wakes up, and she'll be in a mood to talk, I hope. Kate's got Dennis. He adores her—and Johnny, because he's so BIG. . . . I think he probably slept in his pirate suit, but no one would let him take a jack-o'-lantern to bed."

Standing out in the path, thinking what she would do next, Joanna heard Binnie beginning to sweep again, singing to herself along with it.

If I was roosting on a rock in Barque Cove, she pondered, what could I do that I haven't already done this morning? I couldn't talk, or even laugh, as I have with Binnie. Looking back, she was astonished at the ease with which she'd spoken; it was perfectly timed, this meeting, and she hoped it had done as much for Binnie as for herself. Now perhaps she could spare Nils's patience.

She went back across the field, to the pleasant voices in the hen yard, the raucous cries of the blue jays, and the small busy sounds of the little birds. She stopped halfway and tilted her head back to watch the lovely skaters' rhythm of the gulls as they rode the currents of wind. Then she was surprised by the other bird tracing unhurried circles far above them, so high that her eyes had to be narrowed to keep out too much light. As the bird turned toward the sun, its head shone white. An eagle. What do we all look like to him? she wondered. Or to *her*? It could be a female. It *must* be. I've just decided to be sure of it. She remembered the comfort and satisfaction of making such decisions when she was small. Don't tell anybody who can argue about it, and it's like giving yourself a present. "Hello, girls," she said to the hens, and she went into the house to Pip.

He ran upstairs ahead of her and was on the bed before she began to strip it; he was as much help now as when she'd been making it. She folded the spread and the blankets, throwing the sheets and pillowcases downstairs. She tossed the hooked bedside mat out the window, for a good sweeping later, and left the windows open to let the gently rising breeze blow through. There were no visible traces of Hal, but she felt something like an impression of his recent presence. When she had the room ready for Ellen and Robert at Christmas, it would be as if Hal had never been there.

Supper was easy. Just heat it up. She would have a long walk this afternoon and let Pip come along; they would go down to Pickie's place.

But first she would carry pathetic Joselito out behind the barn and leave him to the curiosity of the blue jays and the crows.

Nils's skiff was picked up that day; Steve found her going to sea out around the Head at the Eastern End.

"You want to watch her, Nils," he said solemnly. "She's never going to be contented in the harbor again."

35

The next boat day was Friday, two days later. Sky had called the probation officer twice, and there was no news. Hugo had phoned Mark the night before to say he had no word about Hal, but he had his ticket for Portland and would be home in two weeks—"If all goes well and nothing breaks water by the shingle," he said. It was a saying from the family's distant past, when a pebble beach was called *shingle*. Once he reached the island he didn't intend to hurry back, he said. He didn't mention Vivian; Nicole would have come with him, but she had a heavy course load. She was already feeding Cupcake again.

There was a comforting ordinariness to this boat day, even to the typical early-November weather: open and shut, periods of watery light, vivid glimpses of sunlit blue sea, then stiff short gusts of wind and gunmetal clouds moving past the sun, silver-edged. Sometimes there was even a brief snow squall that had Peter talking about his sled and Sara Jo trying to catch snowflakes on her mittens (they were always gone in the next burst of sunshine). Most of the men were out, but Owen was letting his traps set over for a few days. Sam and Richard were going back today, to stay with Kristi for the weekend and see some local soccer games. They wouldn't show up at the wharf until the *Clarice* was ready to start back. Owen was at home in his workshop; Willy was in the wharf shed, putting new bottoms on a couple of crates. Only the women were in the store— except for Mark, who was in the post office supposedly ignoring them, though nobody ever took this for granted.

The stove felt good. Conversation was easy and ordinary. Binnie had come around with Van and Kate; she seemed comfortable, if not talkative.

Kate was suggesting a Welcome Home party for Philippa at the next Circle meeting, now that it was official that she'd keep teaching. "Who's going to write her an ode of appreciation?" Marjorie Percy was asking when the mailboat whistled outside. At the same time a snow squall had Peter shouting, "It's snowing again!" He was halfway out the door, with Sara Jo squealing behind him, before their reins were seized.

Instant sun followed the squall, and *Clarice* crossed the tide rip amid flashing spray and moved through a blue-green harbor at a decorous speed. "Ho! Hi!" Peter yelled, waving his arms, and Sara Jo imitated him. The whistle answered obligingly. The tide was quite low, so *Clarice* came in to the outer end of the wharf, where the *Conqueror* had tied up. Willy was already waiting to catch one line, and Mark had appeared to handle the other one. It looked as if today there would be just mail and freight until Willy, at the edge of the wharf and looking down, called, "I'll be right down to fetch that case up for ye, Mrs. Harmon."

Nan's voice arose from below, "Thank you, Willy." Or it was another voice, one that bore a family resemblance to Nan's as Joanna knew it. Some of the others had never heard it. Their amazement was all but vocal; they hadn't even known she'd been gone. And how—and where? Now they heard her speaking aboard the boat, and then she came up the ladder, wearing a blue suede beret, lipstick, a trench coat, and a vividly patterned scarf in a floppy bow at her neck.

Marjorie Percy, nearest the head of the ladder, automatically held out a balancing hand as Nan came over the top. "We thought there weren't any people on board, unless they were laid out sick below," Marjorie said.

Nan took the offered hand and said, "Thank you. It wasn't bad at all. Not what I'd call sick-making, and I've known a lot of that weather." She looked pleasantly around her, acknowledging the variety of greetings, which ranged from reserved to hearty. She smiled at Joanna and shaped "Hello" with her lips.

"Welcome back, Nan," Joanna said, wondering if Nan wanted to be welcomed or not. Willy came up the ladder with her bag, and the way she thanked him made him touch a finger to the visor of his baseball cap. "Any time, Mrs. Harmon," he said handsomely. Laurie winked at Joanna. From aboard the boat there came sounds of freight being moved and readied for unloading. Duke came up with the mailbags; Mark took one, and they went up to the store.

Nan moved over to one side. "I know you're busy," she said to Willy, "but when you get a chance, I've got several boxes aboard besides my groceries, and I've marked them. Would you see that they're put somewhere all together, for the children to collect?"

"Oh, yes, *Ma'am*." Willy was at full blaze as they walked toward the shed. "Everything'll be right in here, next to them piles of new buoys."

"Thank you very much."

After that, Willy was clearly refusing a tip. "Oh, no, Ma'am! Part of it's my job and part's just being neighborly."

"You've been handling things for me all summer, and it's time I showed you I appreciate it."

"Myles, he lets me know," said Willy.

"I'm glad of that. But thank you anyway." She had a good brisk gait and walked very straight. That's how she must have crossed the lobby of the courthouse to her job, Joanna thought. Happy in spirit, using that pleasant voice for all her Good Mornings. Nan passed the store without looking toward it and went out of sight around the utility shed.

There was a stirring in the bemused silence she had left behind her. "This must be the first time she's spoken to any of us," Vanessa said, "or even looked around. Unless she's talked with you, Jo."

"Not really," Joanna said. It was an answer she hated, but it came in handy now. "Just across the yard," she added vaguely.

"She looked really elegant," Carol Fennell said. "In an understated way, as they say. Who'd have believed it? Of course I've only seen her on the wing, hanging out clothes or going to the well, but you'd never guess. . . ." She let it trail off.

"Did she suffer a sea change or a mainland change?" Lisa asked. Nan had come into sight past the utility shed, and they watched her turn up past the Binnacle toward Dave's house.

"Maybe she's been worried sick about something all this time," Kate Campion said. "Maybe she finally made up her mind to go to the doctor, and she's found out it's not terminal after all."

This was considered logical and probable. "Well, if she's going to be different now," Maggie said happily, "that'll be real nice. She'll likely be a good addition to us this winter, if this morning means anything."

Joanna was suddenly tired of being here; she wanted her own company. She'd felt this way often since the day after Hallowe'en. She knew it was probably temporary, but for now she felt that her attention span had been severely overstretched. There was a general move toward getting out of the way of the freight's progress up the wharf and finding shelter from another snow squall. The conversation went back to the celebration for Philippa. As they went along talking, with the two small children lively as colts—*articulate* colts—no one seemed to notice at the time that Joanna hadn't gone into the store with them. She simply walked away.

The Harmon house looked empty as she passed it, as if the woman they had seen from the wharf had kept on past it and disappeared; Joanna wondered how she had felt when she went into that kitchen, if the aura she had brought back from the mainland had disappeared when she stepped over the threshold, to be replaced by the old miasma. She was just opening her own door when she heard Nan's voice behind her. "Joanna, can I speak to you for a minute?" She was coming off her doorstep.

"Speak to me for five minutes, even for ten!" Joanna called back. "I've got a lot of spare minutes today." Events hadn't killed her curiosity, especially about something outside the family. It could only be a relief.

Nan came across the yard and up onto the doorstep. She'd taken off the beret, and her short fair hair was fluffed out by the wind. Her color was good, and she looked into Joanna's face with a calm, almost humorous, candor.

"I want you to know this, Joanna," she said, "because you've got the right."

To know what? She didn't ask. *Listen, O! Listen!* "How about a cup of tea or coffee?" They went in, and Pip hurried to inspect a new pair of feet.

"Do you have any more of that English Breakfast tea?" This was not the same woman who had grimly accepted it a few weeks ago.

"We have. Would you like toast with it? Crackers? Spiced pumpkin cookies left over from Hallowe'en?"

"Those sound gorgeous, but I'd better stick with just the tea." She took off her trench coat, laid it over a chair, and stood in the kitchen doorway while Joanna heated the water and set out the Swedish mugs. Nan was wearing narrow-cut slacks in a muted plaid pattern, with a matching waistcoat over a long-sleeved blue shirt. Accentuated by the shirt and new life, her eyes amazed. "You listened to me," she said, "that day when I lost all my pride, or most of it." She was suffused with life, not only in her eyes, her skin, her voice. "But I found something else. I was so furious and ashamed at what I'd done, running out of the house like a maniac and coming here, I couldn't stand myself afterward. I didn't know what to do."

"Yes," Joanna said, moving about the room, making the tea, moving chairs. "In here or out in the sun parlor?"

"*Here* is fine. Maybe who I am today will wipe out that other demented creature. I have a job. I'm only out here until next boat day. They've given me a week to . . . to stabilize things."

At Joanna's sudden turn toward her, she blushed but went on. "Yes. Not my old one—no hope of that—but some people I used to do tax work with have begun their own company, and I have a chance with them. Of course there's a lot of new material to learn. . . ."

"You're *really* going to work?" Joanna's instinctive reaction delighted her; she could be happy, in her whole being, about *something*. As she put out her hand to Nan and heard herself offering congratulations, knowing Nan couldn't doubt her pleasure, she was very nearly blissful. Something positive had happened, something positively *good*. I can hardly believe it of her, she thought, but she's here, and she's new-made.

If Nan didn't know what had happened here with Hal, she'd know soon enough. But she would probably never know how perfect her timing was. "Come on, sit down," Joanna said. "We'll drink a toast to you in tea—that sounds sort of foolish, doesn't it? You don't know how pleased I am, Nan, to see you looking so . . . so . . . "

"Now when I see myself in a mirror I think, 'This be none of I.' But I don't want to look at the past any more than a recovering alcoholic wants to."

"Are you taking the children in with you?"

"*No.*" It was incisive enough to fend off questions, which Joanna wasn't going to ask anyway. "They'll have until Christmas to make up their minds. If they don't want to leave then—though I don't know what would hold them out here in winter—they needn't go. I was given an ultimatum once. Myles wouldn't put it into words and have a confrontation, but it was there, and suddenly I was *here*." She was quiet, not with the old memories; it was the quiet of a marble-hard decision. "I'm not giving ultimatums to him or the children. They can do as they please. I'll be right over there in the mainland house, anytime anyone wants me."

Peacefully she sipped her tea. "I must get some of this. My relatives are staying on in the house for the time being, and we'll share expenses. They'll be looking for a place in the spring, in case the family does move back."

"Do you think they will?"

"Not Myles, even to be with them. I don't think he's ever been happier in his life. He'd be running back and forth, I suppose." She might have been talking about anyone, not necessarily the man with whom she'd had these children. "As for *them* . . ." She shrugged. "They're all mysteries to me, even Tracy Lynn. I'm not cramming them into carefully marked boxes. I'm doing what I want. Just as Myles is happy lobstering out here, I was always happiest when I was working. And it's just as good as it ever was, maybe better—yes, I'm sure of it—because I almost lost it and myself as well."

She drank down the rest of her tea. "I'd better go across the yard and see what they've got planned for their lunch. There'll be something to heat up. Myles is good that way, and both Cluny and Shannon can cook if anybody has the patience to let them. I didn't have it all summer—I think I was like a raw sore most of the time."

"I have one comment," said Joanna. "You knew what you needed, and you went for it. You've saved yourself."

"I had to be driven to it," Nan said dryly, "like the Gadarene swine. I don't know whose devils I was carrying—maybe they were all my own—but I expect to keep them good and drowned." She stood up and reached for her coat. "Thank you for the tea and the generous ear."

"It was a pleasure, and I mean it." Joanna walked to the door with her. Wishing her luck would be extraneous; she seemed to have found her luck already.

There was no staying in the house now, and she didn't want to go back to the store. She'd taken her long walk along the shore yesterday with Pip, to Bull Cove; now she was going again, taking a woods path that would shelter her in the squalls, which were getting quite stiff as the day went on. It was all the same to Pip, wherever they went.

She followed the trail out to the open slopes of Sou'west Point, the fields where wild strawberries ripened in the tall grass, and roses grew down to the edge of the tide. Through surf and wind they bloomed so constantly that in the most dense fog the scent of unseen roses met and surrounded approaching boats.

There was no fog today, and the last rugosas had given up, but their cherry-size hips were bright through the snow squalls; the smaller wild roses, with wine-red leaves, were thickly studded with hips like berries. "Plenty of vitamin C for the birds," Joanna remarked to Pip. She decided to pick him up while he was within reach and start back with him before he disappeared down some steep rock face that called for exploration.

It was about half-past two when she came back. She was getting herself a mug-up of crackers and cheese with packaged hot chocolate on the side, when Nan came to the door. She'd have nothing to eat, but yes, a cup of hot chocolate. "I ate corned beef hash and fried eggs with the kids," she said. "Myles is bringing in some lobsters for tonight. They're happy because I'll be here for that," she said. "It's escaped them all these years that I haven't been able to look at a lobster since I had to go as my father's sternman."

Joanna looked suitably blank, as if John Haker had never told Nils about it. "Can you wing it?" she asked, and Nan laughed. "I can always say I'm too full of hash. I'll settle for hot biscuits and jam. Cluny's still practicing on them, but never mind. I wanted to tell you about the kids before they're home from school and their father's in. . . . They had their winter already planned without me; evidently they were going to live it *around* me. But now that I won't be here, they're all set."

"I don't know whether I'm shocked or not," said Joanna. "*Startled* is more like it."

"They were honest with me. They've had some conferences with their father about how to manage Life with Mother." She smiled. "Survival tactics. The main change would be that Shannon can spend more time with his father, baiting up and so forth. They're going to build him a skiff this winter. It was all a waste of effort on my part anyway—I was just trying to make somebody else miserable. But they're like me—they want what they want, and they're going for it. They'll work it sooner or later."

"And you're proud of them for it."

She nodded. "Oh, yes, as long as what they want is not criminal; that would be hard to manage with Myles, the Harmons having such a high reputation and all. Like the Bennetts," she added innocently. And Joanna thought, She doesn't know yet. "Myles is a sticker, too, in his own way. All in all, we make quite a houseful, and if one house isn't enough for all of us, so be it. . . . I'll be out for Christmas; they don't want me to miss the big tree at the clubhouse, the concert, and the carol sing. Oh yes, and Mrs. Marshall's son, who's been off in the Peace Corps, is writing a Christmas play that will use every pupil in the school, and he'll be here in time to direct it. Apparently nothing on the mainland can compete with all this. As for the winter to follow, it seems to be full of untold delights and I can't honestly see that . . ."

". . .you have to be here," said Joanna solemnly, and they both laughed.

"I suppose so. Well, as long as they stay well. . . . I can understand more about the school. Tracy Lynn won't give up being the *only* second grader; that could *never* happen on the mainland, she says. Cluny has a couple of good friends here, and that wasn't so on the mainland, she tells me now. I was too busy and she was too—I don't know what—to complain. She was called a snob not because she was a Harmon but because she was so wound up in her ballet studies and wouldn't go out for track and basketball. *Now* I hear about it, because if I'd gone to school to fight for her, that would have been even harder on her, she says. Nobody calls her a snob here."

She got up and walked around the sun parlor, looking out first one window and then the other. "What a rotten day! But I can stand it because I'm leaving on Tuesday."

"Shannon has friends too," Joanna said.

Nan turned back, her smile ironic. "Because he's fought with every blessed one of them," she said. "In a free-for-all that I never heard a word about . . . He says I don't know anything about going to a school like this one. He makes city classrooms sound like jail. And, oh yes, he's learning algebra. He was very nonchalant about it."

"What about high school?"

"Oh, he knows he has to go. We've both made that clear to him. But he's got another year here after this one—if he sticks it out. Besides, if he doesn't decide he's going to be a lobsterman"—she turned down the corners of her mouth in a mockery of herself—"he may be thinking of skippering a Harmon vessel someday. Or about twenty other things. If it's lobstering, he'll still have to go to high school somewhere, he knows that; apparently they all go from here."

"There's a very low percentage of dropouts from this school," Joanna said. "What about Cluny? She's in the eighth grade now, and she's the only eighth-grade girl, unless somebody gets a chance to skip a grade and go with her. She's going to miss this school when she leaves it." She was already sorry for Cluny, but Nan was not. She looked oddly triumphant.

"If I know my daughter," she said, "she'll be working out a deal to get herself to Portland so she can attend the Portland School of Ballet. There are some Harmon cousins up there, and her dancing teacher knows some people too. She'd be a good, conscientious baby-sitter if she can have time for lessons and practice. . . . Oh, I leave Cluny to Cluny!" It was almost a grin. "And she still may have a boat named after her, even if it'll be Delphine instead of Cluny."

Leaving to be back at the house when the children came, she said, "I'll be in touch with them. I won't keep sending groceries; Myles told me to quit—in his words it embarrasses hell out of him. They can send the washing in to me if they want to. They probably won't. Then there are special things for Cluny, now that she has her period, that'll save her going into the store to buy them. I always hated that. She doesn't have any trouble with her period though, thank goodness. I never did, either. She takes after me."

"I wish I'd met this Nan Harmon earlier," Joanna said.

"Well, you know her now," Nan said cheerfully. "You'll see me from time to time, and we'll always drink to the Big Day of the hurricane." Then she turned serious and said, "It's not that I don't love the children—and Myles. I *do*. But I love myself, too; it's in a different way, but it's just as important. *Essential*. Without it I'm nothing." She knocked on the door frame. "So here we all start out new." She went across the yard with her head up as if the sun were out, and she walked as she had walked up through the shed on the wharf this morning.

Joanna and Pip finished her mug-up; his favorite part was the cheese. Then they went into the living room—Joanna to lie down and read, and Pip to sit on a harbor-facing windowsill. As an incongruous background to her new Ngaio Marsh book, she heard boats returning to the harbor, and when Pip suddenly jumped off the windowsill and hurried out of the room with his tail erect, she got up and followed him. As Nils came in, stopping just inside the door to kick off his boots, she said, "Oh, man, do I have a story for *you!*"

36

There was very light snow on Tuesday, no wind to speak of, and the prospects of clearing by afternoon. Everybody went out to haul, but Myles came in before noon to see Nan off on the boat. Home for lunch, the children all kissed and hugged their mother at the back door; everyone seemed happy, which was promising. Joanna gave Myles and Nan a chance to walk to the wharf alone, in case they had anything more to say; then she put on her boots and raincoat, and went down by herself, with a couple of plastic bags for mail and groceries. She'd felt no urge to go over earlier for the boat's arrival; they'd all be together at the Circle tomorrow anyway, for Philippa's special occasion.

It was departure time and the school's lunch hour, so no one was there now, just Rosa and Carol with the small children. Joanna heard them in the store as she went down the wharf to say good-bye to Nan.

The two Harmons were aboard and standing in the lee of the pilothouse, talking quietly, but Nan welcomed Joanna as if she'd been waiting for her.

"I'll see you at Christmas, remember! I've got ten days. I asked for it before I even mentioned pay."

"You can see how much they want her," Myles said proudly.

"Yes, and I'm happy for her," Joanna said. "You ought to have a good chance going over, Nan. It isn't supposed to breeze up." And your house will be waiting, she added silently. And oh, yes, your car.

"We aren't taking a chance on Thanksgiving," Nan said, "with only the weekend off and always a chance of bad weather."

"They'll probably be invited out," Joanna said. "Unless Myles and Cluny want to collaborate on a turkey."

"By God, we might do that!" said Myles. He had his arm around Nan's waist and gave her a squeeze. "Think what you'll miss."

There was an outbreak of stamping and whinnying in the utility shed; it was a good day for horses. Unless there was a real snowstorm or a downpour, these two expected either to meet the boat or see her off, or both. Today it would be her leaving. The horses came first, blowing hard, their mothers in firm control of the reins. Mark and Duke came lugging the mailbags; the engineer followed, using pot holders to carry a covered dish. Apparently, Helmi had given them something special for their dinner. Matt Fennell the elder came last; he was on his way to the mainland to get his glasses changed.

"Have a high old time, Matt," Joanna said to him.

"Gorry, I've been thinking on it ever since I woke up this morning. Nora's got the sniffles, or she'd be going too."

"So I'm going to give him some good telephone numbers," the engineer said. Out on the wharf the horses jumped and neighed and shook their bells. Joanna said good-bye to Nan and left the wharf rather than take up Myles's last few minutes with his wife; she had never seen them together like this, never even seen them *together*, now that she thought of it.

Helmi was alone in the store. Young Mark and Willy were on their way up to the house to eat their lunch. Joanna accepted a mug of coffee, and Helmi told her that both Hugos' plans still held. Young Hugo could be here anytime, with anyone coming this way—maybe with the Hakers. Hugo from California would let them know when he would arrive in Portland, and he expected a station wagon full of Bennetts to be there, all wearing rubber boots.

"And they can even bring along a pair for him," Joanna said, seeing the new boots in the sun parlor. She rubbed Louis's big blunt head and concentrated on the grocery list, which she'd forgotten. From the harbor mouth the mailboat sounded her farewell, and through the quiet snowy air Peter's ritual chant could be heard. "*There she goes, there she goes!*"

Mark came in whistling, stopped short when he saw Joanna, and said, "I'll get your mail." He went directly into the post office.

"I'm in no hurry," she protested. "Or Helmi could have got it."

"You don't want to wait for this," he said in a tone she distrusted. Her stomach squirmed, or seemed to. *A postcard from Hal?* He was probably

capable of it. She went over to the window—she'd rather have gone out—
and he held up not a card, but a business envelope addressed to Haliburton
Bennett. The printed return address in the upper left corner was "Office
of Town Clerk, Cape Blue, Maine" and the zip code.

"Oh, Good Lord!" she exclaimed. For an instant Hal was before her,
earnest, appealing, and irrepressible. "Do you think he actually *meant* it
for the few minutes it took to write for his birth certificate? What's the
postmaster going to do about it? Return to sender?"

"I guess so." He tapped it on his hand. "I'd hate like hell to give it to
Hugo." He tucked it into an empty pigeon hole. "Good God, you'd think
that kid invented the word *sincere*. We've had sunshine boys around here
before, but that one beats 'em all hollow. I wonder who he's dazzling now."

"Guess what, Mark," she said. "*I don't care.*" She smiled at them both
and went out into the light, luminous noon. *Clarice* was out of sight now,
her engine unheard through the muted rote; in any case, the return of the
horses, enchanted by the way the shed multiplied their noise, would have
drowned her out.

Myles was coming up behind them, not in a hurry, his hands in his
pockets. He smiled at the children and their mothers, who—mystified by
Nan's leaving again and an apparently affectionate parting—were overquiet
in their friendliness. It was almost as if they were in awe of good-natured,
easy-going Myles, standing there looking much as usual. But still different.
Carol urged Peter toward home. Myles went into the store. Sara Jo, with
Peter's whinnies growing fainter as he galloped into the distance, tried to
keep the excitement going on her own. Joanna seized her in the middle of
a jump.

"Give Gramma a good hug, honeybunch, and then you can run and
scream some more."

"I don't scream," Sara Jo objected. "I'm a *norse*."

"So you are. How could I have missed it?" She looked past the child's
cheek into Rosa's face; snowflakes were melting on her lashes and her nose.
She was as happy as the children.

"I can't help it, the first snow always does this to me."

"Me too," Joanna said. "Know something, Rosa? We got cheated out of
our dance a week ago tonight. At least some of us were, and then it was
cut short for all the rest. So we're owed a dance, and we'd better have it
pretty soon, before we begin to feel a serious deprivation. When will you
and the fiddler be ready?"

Laughing, Rosa raised her arms in an embracing gesture toward the snow or perhaps toward the world. "Anytime!"

Sara Jo flung her arms wide in imitation. "Anytime!" she screamed joyously into her grandmother's ear.

In that deafening instant, all the successive steps of dismissal during the last week came to an end in a pair of simple facts. She would never hear "The Flower of Portencross" again; and she would never forget it.